ONCE UPON A BROKEN HEART

A #1 *New York Times* bestseller
A Goodreads Choice Award finalist
An Indie Next pick

"An explosively rich fairytale that takes place inside an intricate world that's weaved with fast-paced plot and intriguing twists."
                                                    —*BuzzFeed*

"The lush worldbuilding Garber is known for is on full display here. . . . No one will be complaining about the opportunity to revisit this intricately imagined world."
                          —*School Library Journal* (starred review)

"Garber enchants readers with exquisitely imagined worldbuilding and her trademark heady romance."
                                              —*Publishers Weekly*

"A lushly written story with an intriguing heart."
                                              —*Kirkus Reviews*

"A sparkling story filled with adventure, broken hearts, and magic as one girl learns she's capable of more than she could have imagined. . . . If I had to pick a defining heroine for 2021, it would be Evangeline Fox."   —*Miss Print*

ONCE
UPON A
BROKEN
HEART

ALSO BY
STEPHANIE GARBER

Caraval

Legendary

Finale

ONCE UPON A BROKEN HEART

STEPHANIE GARBER

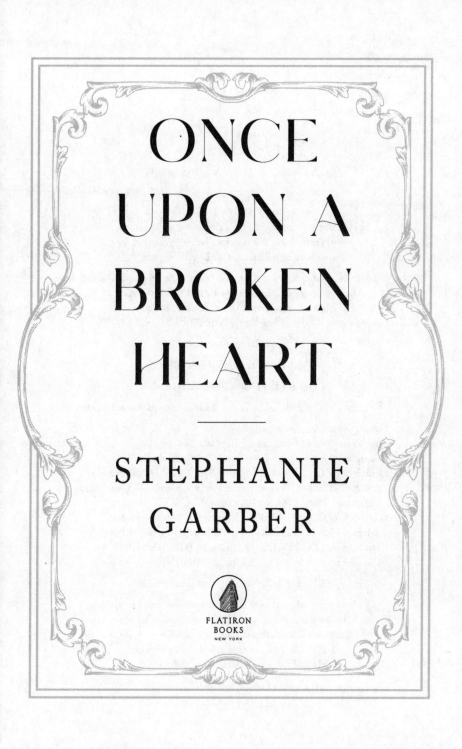

FLATIRON BOOKS
NEW YORK

ONCE UPON A BROKEN HEART. Copyright © 2021 by Stephanie Garber. All rights reserved. Printed in the United States of America. For information, address Flatiron Books, 120 Broadway, New York, NY 10271.

www.flatironbooks.com

Map illustration by Virginia Allyn

Designed by Donna Sinisgalli Noetzel

The Library of Congress has cataloged the hardcover edition as follows:

Names: Garber, Stephanie, author.
Title: Once upon a broken heart / Stephanie Garber.
Description: First edition. | New York : Flatiron Books, 2021.
Identifiers: LCCN 2021024206 | ISBN 9781250268396 (hardcover) |
    ISBN 9781250841339 (international, sold outside the U.S., subject to
    rights availability) | ISBN 9781250268389 (ebook)
Subjects: CYAC: Love—Fiction. | Blessing and cursing—Fiction. |
    Magic—Fiction. | Fantasy. | LCGFT: Novels. | Fantasy fiction.
Classification: LCC PZ7.1.G368 On 2021 | DDC [Fic]—dc23
LC record available at https://lccn.loc.gov/2021024206

ISBN 978-1-250-26840-2 (trade paperback)

Our books may be purchased in bulk for promotional, educational, or business use. Please contact your local bookseller or the Macmillan Corporate and Premium Sales Department at 1-800-221-7945, extension 5442, or by email at MacmillanSpecialMarkets@macmillan.com.

First Flatiron Books Paperback Edition: 2023

15   14   13   12   11

For anyone who has ever made a bad decision
because of a broken heart

WELCOME TO THE

STORIES

Fortuna Castle

Wolf Hall

The Docks

Warnings and Signs

The bell hanging outside the curiosity shop knew the human was trouble from the way he moved through the door. Bells have excellent hearing, but this little chime didn't need any particular skill to catch the crude jangle of the gaudy pocket-watch chain at this young man's hip, or the rough scrape of his boots as he attempted a swagger but only succeeded in scuffing the floor of Maximilian's Curiosities, Whimsies & Other Oddities.

This young man was going to ruin the girl that worked inside the shop.

The bell had tried to warn her. A full two seconds before the boy opened the door, the bell rang its clapper. Unlike most humans, this shopgirl had grown up around oddities—and the bell had long suspected she was a curiosity as well, though it couldn't figure out exactly what sort.

The girl knew that many objects were more than they

appeared and that bells possessed a sixth sense that humans lacked. Unfortunately, this girl, who believed in hope and fairytales and love at first sight, often misinterpreted the bell's chimes. Today the bell was fairly certain that she had heard its cautionary ring. But, from the way her voice affected an excited edge as she spoke to the young man, it seemed as if the girl had taken the bell's early toll as a serendipitous sign instead of as a warning.

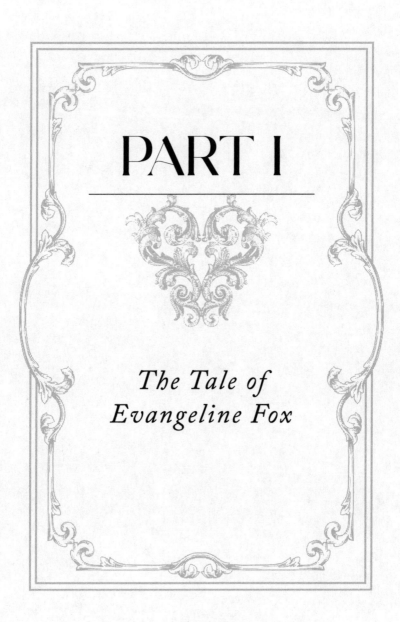

PART I

The Tale of
Evangeline Fox

1

The Whisper Gazette

WHERE WILL THE
BROKENHEARTED PRAY NOW?

By Kutlass Knightlinger

The door to the Prince of Hearts' church has disappeared. Painted the deep bloodred of broken hearts, the iconic entry simply vanished from one of the Temple District's most visited churches sometime during the night, leaving behind an impenetrable marble wall. It's now impossible for anyone to enter the church—

Evangeline shoved the two-week-old newsprint into the pocket of her flowered skirt. The door at the end of this decrepit alley was barely taller than she was, and hidden behind a rusted metal grate instead of covered in beautiful bloodred paint, but she would have bet her father's curiosity shop that this was the missing door.

Nothing in the Temple District was this unattractive. Every entry here was carved panels, decorative architraves, glass awnings, and gilded keyholes. Her father had been a man of faith, but he used to say that the churches here were like vampires— they weren't meant for worship, they were designed to entice and entrap. But this door was different. This door was just a rough block of wood with a missing handle and chipped white paint.

This door did not want to be found.

Yet it couldn't hide what it truly was from Evangeline.

The jagged shape of it was unmistakable. One side was a sloping curve, the other a serrated slash, forming one half of a broken heart—a symbol of the Fated Prince of Hearts.

Finally.

If hope were a pair of wings, Evangeline's were stretching out behind her, eager to take flight again. After two weeks of searching the city of Valenda, she'd found it.

When the gossip sheet in her pocket had first announced that the door from the Prince of Hearts' church had gone missing, few imagined it was magic. It was the scandal sheet's first article, and people said it was part of a hoax to sell subscriptions. Doors didn't simply disappear.

But Evangeline believed that they could. The story hadn't felt like a gimmick to her; it had felt like a sign, telling her where to search if she was going to save her heart and the boy that it belonged to.

She might not have seen much evidence of magic outside of the oddities in her father's curiosity shop, but she had faith it existed. Her father, Maximilian, had always spoken of magic as if it were real. And her mother had been from the Magnificent North, where there was no difference between fairytales and history. *All stories are made of both truths and lies,* she used to say. *What matters is the way that we believe in them.*

And Evangeline had a gift when it came to believing in things that others considered myths—like the immortal Fates.

She opened the metal grate. The door itself didn't have a handle, forcing her to wedge her fingers into the tiny space between its jagged edge and the dirty stone wall.

The door pinched her fingers, drawing a drop of blood, and she swore she heard its splintered voice say, *Do you know what you're about to step into? Nothing but heartbreak will come from this.*

But Evangeline's heart was already broken. And she understood the risks she was taking. She knew the rules for visiting Fated churches:

Always promise less than you can give, for Fates always take more.

Do not make bargains with more than one Fate.

And, above all, never fall in love with a Fate.

There were sixteen immortal Fates, and they were jealous and possessive beings. Before they'd vanished centuries ago, it was said they ruled over part of the world with magic that was as malevolent as it was marvelous. They never broke a bargain, although they often hurt the people they helped. Yet most people—even if they believed the Fates were merely myths—became desperate enough to pray to them at some point.

Evangeline had always been curious about their churches, but she'd known enough about the mercurial nature of Fates and Fated bargains to avoid seeking their places of worship. Until two weeks ago, when she'd become one of those desperate people the stories always cautioned about.

"Please," she whispered to the heart-shaped door, filling her voice with the wild and battered hope that had led her here. "I know you're a clever little thing. But you allowed me to find you. Let me in."

She gave the wood a final tug.

This time, the door opened.

Evangeline's heart raced as she took her first step. During her search for the missing door, she'd read that the Prince of Hearts' church held a different aroma for everyone who visited. It was supposed to smell like a person's greatest heartbreak.

But as Evangeline entered the cool cathedral, the air did not remind her of Luc—there were no hints of suede or vetiver. The dim mouth of the church was slightly sweet and metallic: apples and blood.

Gooseflesh covered her arms. This was not reminiscent of the boy she loved. The account she'd read must have been wrong. But she didn't turn around. She knew Fates weren't saints or saviors, although she hoped that the Prince of Hearts was more feeling than the others.

Her steps took her deeper inside the cathedral. Everything was shockingly white. White carpets, white candles, white prayer pews of white oak, white aspen, and flaky white birch.

Evangeline passed row after row of mismatched white benches. They might have been handsome once, but now many had missing legs, while others had mutilated cushions or benches that had been broken in half.

Broken.

Broken.

Broken.

No wonder the door hadn't wanted to let her enter. Perhaps this church wasn't sinister, it was sad—

A rough rip shattered the church's silence.

Evangeline spun around and choked back a gasp.

Several rows behind her, in a shadowed corner, a young man appeared to be in mourning or performing some act of penance. Wild locks of golden hair hung across his face as his head bowed and his fingers tore at the sleeves of his burgundy topcoat.

Her heart felt a pang as she watched him. She was tempted to ask if he needed help. But he'd probably chosen the corner to go unnoticed.

And she didn't have much time left.

There were no clocks inside the church, but Evangeline swore she heard the tick of a second hand, working at erasing the precious minutes she had until Luc's wedding.

She hurried down the nave to the apse, where the fractured rows of benches ceased and a gleaming marble dais rose before her. The platform was pristine, lit by a wall of beeswax candles and surrounded by four fluted columns, guarding a larger-than-life statue of the Fated Prince of Hearts.

The back of her neck prickled.

Evangeline knew what he was supposed to look like. Decks of Destiny, which used Fated images to tell fortunes, had recently become a popular item in her father's curiosity shop. The Prince of Hearts' card represented unrequited love, and it always depicted the Fate as tragically handsome, with vivid blue eyes crying tears that matched the blood forever staining the corner of his sulky mouth.

There were no bloody tears on this glowing statue. But its face did possess a ruthless kind of beauty, the sort Evangeline would have expected from a demigod that had the ability to kill with his kiss. The prince's marble lips twisted into a perfect smirk that should have looked cold and hard and sharp, but there was a hint of softness to his slightly fuller lower lip—it pouted out like a deadly invitation.

According to the myths, the Prince of Hearts was not capable of love because his heart had stopped beating long ago. Only one person could make it work again: his one true love.

They said his kiss was fatal to all but her—his only weakness— and as he'd sought her, he'd left a trail of corpses.

Evangeline couldn't imagine a more tragic existence. If one Fate were to have sympathy for her situation, it would be the Prince of Hearts.

Her gaze found his elegant marble fingers clasping a dagger the size of her forearm. The blade pointed down toward a stone offering basin balanced on a burner, just above a low circle of dancing white flames. The words *Blood for a Prayer* were carved into its side.

Evangeline took a deep breath.

This was what she'd come here for.

She pressed her finger to the tip of the blade. Sharp marble pierced her skin, and drop after drop of blood fell, sizzling and hissing, filling the air with more metal and sweet.

A part of her hoped this tithe might conjure up some sort of magical display. That the statue would come to life, or the Prince of Hearts' voice would fill the church. But nothing moved save for the flames on the wall of candles. She couldn't even hear the anguished young man in the back of the church. It was just her and the statue.

"Dear—Prince," she started haltingly. She'd never prayed to a Fate, and she didn't want to get it wrong. "I'm here because my parents are dead."

Evangeline cringed. That was not how she was supposed to start.

"What I meant to say was, my parents have both passed away. I lost my mother a couple of years ago. Then I lost my father last season. Now I'm about to lose the boy that I love.

"Luc Navarro—" Her throat closed as she said the name and pictured his crooked smile. Maybe if he'd been plainer, or poorer, or crueler, none of this would have happened. "We've been seeing each other in secret. I was supposed to be in mourning for my father. Then, a little over two weeks ago, on the day that Luc and I were going to tell our families we were in love, my stepsister, Marisol, announced that she and Luc were getting married."

Evangeline paused to close her eyes. This part still made her head spin. Quick engagements weren't uncommon. Marisol was pretty, and although she was reserved, she was also kind—so much kinder than Evangeline's stepmother, Agnes. But Evangeline had never even seen Luc in the same room as Marisol.

"I know how this sounds, but Luc loves me. I believe he's been cursed. He hasn't spoken to me since the engagement was announced—he won't even see me. I don't know how she did it, but I'm certain this is all my stepmother's doing." Evangeline didn't actually have any proof that Agnes was a witch and she'd cast a curse on Luc. But Evangeline was certain her stepmother had learned of Evangeline's relationship with Luc and she'd wanted Luc, and the title he'd someday inherit, for her daughter instead.

"Agnes has resented me ever since my father died. I've tried talking to Marisol about Luc. Unlike my stepmother, I don't think Marisol would ever intentionally hurt me. But every time I try to open my mouth, the words won't come out, as if they're also cursed or I'm cursed. So I'm here, begging for your help. The wedding is today, and I need you to stop it."

Evangeline opened her eyes.

The lifeless statue hadn't changed. She knew statues didn't generally move. Yet she couldn't help but think that it should have done *something*—shifted or spoken or moved its marble eyes. "Please, I know you understand heartbreak. Stop Luc from marrying Marisol. Save my heart from breaking again."

"Now, that was a pathetic speech." Two slow claps followed the indolent voice, which sounded just a few feet away.

Evangeline spun around, all the blood draining from her face. She didn't expect to see him—the young man who'd been tearing his clothes in the back of the church. Although it was difficult to believe this was the same person. She had thought that boy was in agony, but he must have ripped away his pain along with the sleeves of his jacket, which now hung in tatters over a striped black-and-white shirt that was only halfway tucked into his breeches.

He sat on the dais steps, lazily leaning against one of the pillars with his long, lean legs stretched out before him. His hair was golden and messy, his too-bright blue eyes were bloodshot, and his mouth twitched at the corner as if he didn't enjoy much, but he found pleasure in the brief bit of pain he'd just inflicted upon her. He looked bored and rich and cruel.

"Would you like me to stand up and turn around so that you can take in the rest of me?" he taunted.

The color instantly returned to Evangeline's cheeks. "We're in a church."

"What does that have to do with anything?" In one elegant move, the young man reached into the inner pocket of his ripped burgundy coat, pulled out a pure white apple, and took one bite. Dark red juice dripped from the fruit to his long, pale fingers and then onto the pristine marble steps.

"Don't do that!" Evangeline hadn't meant to yell. Although she wasn't shy with strangers, she generally avoided quarrelling with them. But she couldn't seem to help it with this crass young man. "You're being disrespectful."

"And you're praying to an immortal who kills every girl he kisses. You really think he deserves any reverence?" The awful young man punctuated his words with another wide bite of his apple.

She tried to ignore him. She really did. But it was like some terrible magic had taken hold of her. Rather than marching off, Evangeline imagined the stranger taking her lips instead of his snack and kissing her with his fruit-sweet mouth until she died in his arms.

No. It couldn't be . . .

"You're staring again," he purred.

Evangeline immediately looked away, turning back to the marble carving. Minutes ago, its lips alone had made her heart race, but now it just seemed like an ordinary statue, lifeless compared to this vicious young man.

"Personally, I think I'm far more handsome." Suddenly, the young man stood right beside her.

Butterflies fluttered to life inside Evangeline's stomach. Scared ones. All frantic wings and too-fast beats, warning her to get out of there, to run, to flee. But she couldn't look away.

This close, he was undeniably attractive, and taller than she'd realized. He gave her a real smile, revealing a pair of dimples that briefly made him look more angel than devil. But she imagined even angels would need to beware of him. She could picture him flashing those deceptive dimples as he tricked an angel into losing its wings just so he could play with the feathers.

"It's you," she whispered. "You're the Prince of Hearts."

2

The Prince of Hearts took a final bite of his apple before it dropped to the floor and spattered everything with red. "People who don't like me call me Jacks."

Evangeline wanted to say that she didn't dislike him, that he'd always been her favorite Fate. But this was not the lovesick Prince of Hearts she'd imagined. Jacks didn't look like heartbreak come to life.

Was this all a nasty joke? The Fates had supposedly disappeared from the world centuries ago. Yet everything Jacks wore—from his untied cravat to his tall leather boots—were of the latest fashion.

Her eyes darted around the white church as if Luc's friends might jump out at any moment to have a laugh. Luc was the only son of a gentleman, and though he never acted as if that mattered with Evangeline, the young men he kept company with considered her beneath them. Evangeline's father had owned several shops across Valenda, so she'd never been poor. But she wasn't from the upper tier of society like Luc.

"If you're searching for the way out because you've come to your senses, I won't stop you." Jacks folded his hands behind his golden head, leaned back against the statue of himself, and grinned.

Her stomach dipped in warning, telling her not to be deceived by his dimpled smile or the torn clothes. This was the most dangerous being she'd ever met.

Evangeline didn't imagine he would kill her—she would never be foolish enough to let the Prince of Hearts kiss her. But she knew that if she stayed and made a deal with Jacks, he would forever destroy some other part of her. And yet, if she left, there would be no saving Luc.

"What will your help cost me?"

"Did I say I would help you?" His eyes went to the cream ribbons trailing up from her shoes to wrap around her ankles until they disappeared under the hem of her eyelet dress. It was one of her mother's old gowns, covered in a stitched pattern of pale purple thistles, tiny yellow flowers, and little foxes.

The corner of Jacks's mouth twisted distastefully and stayed that way as his gaze continued up to the ringlets of hair she'd carefully curled with hot tongs that morning.

Evangeline tried not to feel insulted. From the brief experience she had with this Fate, she didn't imagine most things found his approval.

"What color is that?" He waved vaguely toward her curls.

"It's rose gold," she answered brightly. Evangeline never let anyone make her feel bad about her unusual hair. Her stepmother was always trying to get her to color it brown. But Evangeline's hair, with its waves of soft pink streaked through with pale gold, was the thing she liked best about her appearance.

Jacks cocked his head to the side, still observing her with a scowl. "Were you born in the Meridian Empire or in the North?"

"Why does that matter?"

"Call it curiosity."

Evangeline resisted the urge to return his scowl. Normally, she loved answering this question. Her father, who'd liked to make Evangeline feel as if her whole life were a fairytale, had always teased that he'd found her packed up in a crate along with other oddities that had been delivered to his shop—that's why her hair was pixie pink, he'd always said. And her mother had always nodded with a wink.

She missed the way her mother winked and her father teased. She missed everything about them, but she didn't want to share any of their pieces with Jacks.

She managed a shrug instead of a verbal reply.

Jacks's brows slashed down. "You don't know where you were born?"

"Is it a requirement to get your help?"

He looked her over again, eyes lingering on her lips this time. Yet he didn't regard her as if he wanted to kiss her. His appraisal was too clinical. He looked at her mouth the way someone might study wares in one of her father's shops, as if her lips were a thing that could be purchased—a thing that could belong to him.

"How many people have you kissed?" he asked.

A tiny bolt of heat struck Evangeline's neck. She'd worked in her father's curiosity shop since she was twelve. She hadn't exactly been raised like a proper young lady; she wasn't like her stepsister, who was taught to always keep three feet away from a gentleman and to never talk about anything more controversial than the weather. Her parents had encouraged Evangeline to be curious and adventurous and friendly, but she wasn't bold in every way. Certain things made her nervous, and the way the Prince of Hearts kept staring at her mouth was one of those things. "I've only kissed Luc."

"That is pathetic."

"Luc is the only person I want to kiss."

Jacks scratched his sharp jaw, looking doubtful. "I'm almost tempted to believe you."

"Why would I lie?"

"Everyone lies—people think I'm more likely to help if they're after something noble like true love." A hint of derision crept into his voice, chipping away a little more at the Prince of Hearts she'd imagined. "But even if you do really love this boy, you're better off without him. If he loved you back, he wouldn't be marrying someone else. End of story."

"You're wrong." Her voice held the same conviction as her

heart. Evangeline had questioned her relationship with Luc after his abrupt engagement to Marisol, but the question was always answered with months of meaningful memories. The night Evangeline's father had died—the night her heart wouldn't stop pounding or hurting—Luc had found her wandering the aisles of the curiosity shop, looking for a cure for broken hearts. Her cheeks had been tear-stained, and her eyes were red. She feared her crying would scare him away, but instead he'd pulled her into his arms and said, "*I don't know if I can fix your broken heart, but you can take mine because it's already yours.*"

She'd known she loved him for a while, but that was when she knew Luc loved her. His words might have been borrowed from a popular story, but he backed them up with heartfelt actions. He'd helped her hold her heart together that night, and so many of the nights that followed. And now she was determined to help him. Proposals and engagements didn't always mean love, but she knew that moments like the ones she'd shared with Luc did.

He had to be cursed. As extreme or as silly as it might have made her sound to others, this was the only explanation she could believe. It didn't make sense that he wouldn't at least speak to her, or that every time Evangeline tried telling Marisol the truth, she would open her mouth and the words wouldn't come out.

"Please." Begging wasn't beneath her. "Help me."

"I don't think what you want will help you. But I do

appreciate a good lost cause. I'll stop the wedding in exchange for three kisses." Jacks's eyes took on an entertained gleam as they returned to her mouth.

A fresh surge of heat rose to Evangeline's cheeks. She'd been wrong about him not wanting to kiss her. But if the stories were true, one kiss from him and she'd be dead.

Jacks laughed, harsh and short. "Relax, pet, I don't wish to kiss you. It would kill you, and then you'd be no use to me. I want you to kiss three *others*. Who I choose. When I choose."

"What sort of kisses? Little pecks . . . or more?"

"If you think that counts, maybe you haven't been kissed." Jacks shoved off the statue and stalked closer, towering over her once again. "It's not a real kiss if there isn't any tongue."

The blush she'd been fighting burned hotter until her neck and her cheeks and her lips all caught fire.

"Why the hesitation, pet? They're only kisses." Jacks sounded as if he were holding back another laugh. "Either this Luc is horrible at using his mouth, or you're afraid to say yes too quickly because you secretly like the idea."

"I do not like the idea—"

"So, your Luc is a hideous kisser?"

"Luc is an excellent kisser!"

"How do you know if you have nothing to compare it with? If you end up with Luc, you might even wish that I'd asked you to kiss more than three people."

"I don't want to kiss any strangers—the only person I want is Luc."

"Then this should be a small price to pay," Jacks said flatly.

He was right, but Evangeline couldn't simply agree. Her father had taught her that Fates didn't determine one's future as their name suggested. Instead they opened doors into new futures. But doors opened by Fates didn't always lead where people expected; instead they often led people to new desperate deals to fix their first bad bargains. It happened in countless stories, and Evangeline didn't want it to happen in hers.

"I don't want anyone to die," she said. "You can't stop the wedding by kissing anyone there."

Jacks looked disappointed. "Not even your stepsister?"

"No!"

He brought his fingers to his mouth and toyed with his lower lip, covering half of an expression that could have either been irritation or amusement. "You're not really in a position to bargain."

"I thought Fates liked bargains," she challenged.

"Only when we make the rules. Still, I'm in a good mood, so I'll grant you this request. I just want to know one more thing. How did you get the door to let you in?"

"I asked it politely."

Jacks rubbed the corner of his jaw. "That's all? You didn't find a key?"

"I didn't even see a keyhole," she answered honestly.

Something like victory glimmered in Jacks's eyes, then he captured her wrist and brought it up to his cold mouth.

"What are you doing?" she gasped.

"Don't worry, I'm still not going to kiss you." His lips

brushed over the delicate underside of her wrist. Once. Twice. Three times. It was barely a touch, and yet there was something incredibly intimate about it. It made her think of the other stories that said his kisses might have been fatal, but they were worth dying for. Jacks's cool mouth dragged intentionally back and forth over her racing pulse, velvety and gentle and—his sharp teeth dug into her skin.

She cried out, "You bit me!"

"Relax, pet, I didn't draw any blood." His eyes shone brighter as he dropped her arm.

She ran a finger over the tender skin he'd just sunk his teeth into. Three thin white scars, shaped like tiny broken hearts, lined the underside of her wrist. *One for each kiss.*

"When do—" Evangeline looked up.

But the Prince of Hearts was already gone. She didn't even see him leave; she just heard the door to the church slam shut.

She'd gotten what she wanted.

So then why didn't she feel better?

She'd done the right thing. Luc loved her. She couldn't believe he was marrying Marisol of his own free will. It wasn't that Evangeline disliked Marisol. Truthfully, she barely knew her stepsister. About a year after her mother had died, Evangeline's father had gotten it into his head that he must marry again, that he needed a wife to look after Evangeline in case anything ever happened to him. She could still remember the worry that had replaced the light in his eyes, as if he had known he didn't have much time left.

Her father had only been married to Agnes six months before he died. During that time, Marisol never stepped inside the curiosity shop where Evangeline spent most of her time. Marisol said she was allergic to the dust, but she was so skittish around anything slightly strange, Evangeline always suspected her stepsister was really afraid of curses and the uncanny. Whereas Evangeline and Luc used to joke that if they were ever cursed, it would just prove that magic existed.

It was laughably sad that Evangeline now had that proof, but she didn't have him.

Even if Jacks returned and allowed Evangeline to change her mind, she wouldn't have. Jacks had said he'd stop the wedding, and he'd promised not to kill anyone.

Yet . . . Evangeline couldn't shake the sense she'd made a mistake. She didn't think she'd agreed too quickly, but all she could see was the gleam dancing in Jacks's eyes as he'd taken her wrist.

Evangeline started running.

She didn't know what she was going to do or why she felt suddenly sick inside. She just knew she needed to talk to Jacks again before he stopped the wedding.

If she'd been in an ordinary church, she might have caught up with him quickly. But this was a Fated church, protected by a magicked door that seemed to possess a mind of its own. When she opened it, the door did not return her to the Temple District. It spat her out in a musty old apothecary full of floating dust, empty bottles, and ticking clocks.

Tick. Tock. Tick. Tock. Tick. Tock.

Seconds had never passed so fast. Between one tick and one tock, the magicked door she'd just stepped through disappeared and was replaced by a barred window that looked down on a row of streets as crooked as teeth. She was in the Spice Quarter—across the city from where Luc and Marisol were supposed to be wed.

Evangeline cursed as she fled.

By the time she crossed the city and reached her house, she feared that she was already too late.

Marisol and Luc were going to say their vows in her mother's garden, inside the gazebo that her father had built. Crickets filled it with music at night, and birds chirped during the day. Evangeline could hear all their little songs as she entered the garden now, but there weren't any voices. There were just the delicate birds, flapping merrily through the gazebo before landing on a group of granite statues.

Evangeline's knees went weak.

There had never been statues in this garden before. But there were nine of them now, all holding goblets as if they'd just finished a toast. Each face was disturbingly lifelike and terrifyingly familiar.

Evangeline watched in revulsion as a buzzing fly landed on the face of a statue that looked just like Agnes before flitting off and alighting on one of Marisol's granite eyes.

Jacks had stopped the wedding by turning everyone to stone.

3

Horror raced through Evangeline's veins.

The fly buzzed off, and a gray bird, the same dull color as the statues, found the wreath of flowers in Marisol's hair and began peck-peck-pecking.

Evangeline and Marisol might not have been close—and maybe Evangeline was more jealous of her stepsister than she'd wanted to admit—but Evangeline had only wanted to stop her wedding. She hadn't wanted to turn her to stone.

It hurt to breathe when Evangeline faced Luc's statue. Usually, he appeared so carefree, but as stone, his face was frozen in alarm, his smooth jaw was rigid, his eyes were tight, and—a crease formed between his granite brows.

He was moving.

His stone lips parted next as if he were fighting to speak, to tell her something—

"In another minute, he'll stop twitching."

Evangeline's gaze shot toward the back of the gazebo.

Jacks leaned casually against a trellis covered in cloudburst-blue flowers and bit into another brilliant white apple. He looked half–bored young noble, half–wicked demigod.

"What have you done?" Evangeline demanded.

"Exactly what you asked." Another bite of his apple. "I made sure the wedding didn't happen."

"You need to fix it."

"Can't." His tone was laconic, as if he'd already grown tired of this conversation. "A friend of mine who owed me a favor did this. The only way it can be undone is if someone takes their place." Jacks cut a look toward a patch of grass next to the gazebo, where a brass goblet rested on an aged tree stump.

Evangeline stepped closer to the drink.

"What are you doing?" Jacks shoved off the trellis, no longer indifferent as Evangeline eyed the chalice.

If she drank from it, would it fix everything?

"Don't even think about it." His voice turned sharper. "If you drink that and take their place, no one is going to save you. You'll be stone forever."

"But I can't leave them like this." Although part of Evangeline agreed with Jacks. She didn't want to become a garden statue. She couldn't even bring herself to pick up the goblet as she read the words etched onto its side.

Poison

Do Not Drink Me

The smell of sulfur wafted from it, and she wasn't even sure she could drink the foul liquid. But how could she live with herself if she let them all remain cursed?

Evangeline's eyes shot from the bird still pecking at Marisol's wedding crown, then back to Luc and his frozen plea for help. Luc's parents stood on either side of him. Then there was the unfortunate marriage minister, who'd picked the wrong union to officiate. Evangeline didn't want to feel bad about Luc's three friends or about Agnes. But even though her father had not married Agnes for love, he would have hated all of this. Both of her parents would have been so disappointed that this was where Evangeline's faith in magic had led her.

"This wasn't what I wanted," she whispered.

"You're looking at this the wrong way, pet." Jacks dropped his half-eaten apple, letting it roll across the gazebo floor until it hit Luc's stone boot. "Once this story spreads, everyone in the Meridian Empire will want to help you. You'll be the girl who lost her family to the horrible Fates. You might not get Luc, but you'll forget about him soon. With your stepmother and stepsister stone, I'm guessing you'll inherit some money. By tomorrow morning, you'll be famous, and not poor."

Jacks flashed both dimples as if he really had done her a favor.

Evangeline felt sick again.

In the stories, the Fates were wicked gods that only wanted mayhem and chaos. But *this* was what people should have been scared of. Evangeline looked at these human statues and saw it as a horror, but Jacks saw it as helpful. The Fates weren't dangerous because they were evil; the Fates were dangerous because they couldn't tell the difference between evil and good.

But Evangeline knew the difference. She also knew that sometimes there was a murky space in between good and evil. That was the space she'd thought she'd entered that morning when she'd gone into Jacks's church to pray for a favor. But she'd made a mistake, and now it was time to fix it.

Evangeline picked up the goblet.

"Put that down," Jacks warned. "You don't want to do this. You don't want to be the hero, you want the happy ending— that's why you came to me. If you do this, that will never happen. Heroes don't get happy endings. They give them to other people. Is that what you really want?"

"I want to save the boy I love. I'm just going to have to hope he'll decide to save me, too." Before Jacks could stop her, Evangeline drank.

The poison tasted worse than it smelled—like burnt bones and lost hope. Her throat closed as she struggled to breathe and then to move.

She thought she saw Jacks shake his head, but it was difficult to be sure. Her vision was breaking. Black veins were filling the garden, spreading like escaped ink. Darkness, darkness everywhere. It was night, without any moon or stars.

Evangeline tried to tell herself she'd done the right thing. She'd saved nine people. One of them would save her, too.

"I warned you," Jacks murmured. She heard him take a frustrated breath, heard him mutter the word *pity*. And then ...

She heard nothing.

4

At least Evangeline still had the ability to think. Although sometimes that ability hurt. It usually happened after days of endless nothing, when Evangeline imagined she finally felt something. But it was never what she really wanted. It was never warmth on her skin, tingling in her toes, or the touch of another person letting her know that she was not completely alone in the world. It was usually just an arrow of heartbreak, or a pinch of regret.

Regret was the worst.

Regret was sour and bitter, and it tasted so close to the truth she had to fight sinking into it. She had to battle against believing that Jacks had been right—that she should have left the goblet alone, let the others stay stone, and played the role of victim.

Jacks was wrong.

She'd done the right thing.

Someone would save her.

Sometimes, when she was feeling especially hopeful, Evangeline even thought that Jacks might come to her rescue. But as hopeful as Evangeline was, she knew the Prince of Hearts wasn't a savior. He was the one people needed saving from.

5

And then . . . Evangeline felt something that was not heartbreak or regret.

6

Something like light tickled her skin.

Her skin.

Evangeline could feel her skin.

She hadn't felt anything for—she actually didn't know how much time had passed. For so long, there had been so much nothing, but now she could feel everything. Eyelids. Ankles. Elbows. Lips. Legs. Bones. Skin. Lungs. Heart. Hair. Veins. Kneecaps. Earlobes. Neck. Chest.

She was trembling from her chin to her toes. Her skin was coated in sweat, and it felt incredible—cool and damp and alive.

She was alive again!

"Welcome back." A solid arm wrapped around Evangeline's waist as her wobbly legs adjusted to being muscle and bone.

Her vision came into focus next.

Perhaps it was just that she hadn't seen a face in a while,

but the young man who'd wrapped an arm around her was extraordinarily handsome—dark brown skin, eyes fringed in a thick rim of lashes, a smile that hinted at an arsenal of charm. His shoulders were cloaked in a dramatic green cape lined in copper leaves as dazzling as his face. "Can you speak?" he asked.

"Why—" Evangeline coughed to clear some gravel from her throat. "Why do you look like a forest mage?"

She cringed as soon as the words were out. Clearly some of her senses—like the filter on her mouth—weren't doing their job yet. This stranger had saved her. She hoped she hadn't offended him.

Thankfully, the man's brilliant smile widened. "Excellent. Sometimes the voice doesn't return immediately. Now tell me your full name, darling. I need to make sure you have your memory before I let you go."

"Go where?" Evangeline tried to take in the rest of her surroundings. She seemed to be in a laboratory. Every worktable and apothecary shelf was littered with bubbling beakers or foaming cauldrons that filled the air with something like resin. This wasn't her mother's garden. The only familiar thing in the room was the Meridian Empire's royal crest painted on one of the stone walls. "Where are we? And how long was I a statue?"

"Only about six weeks. I'm the palace potion master, and you're in my most excellent lab. But you can leave as soon as you tell me your name."

Evangeline took a moment to collect her thoughts. Six weeks meant they were in the middle of the Hot Season. Not too devastating a loss. It could have been six years, or sixty.

But if it had only been six weeks, why was no one there to greet her? She knew her stepmother didn't care for her, and she wasn't very close to her stepsister, but she had saved their lives. And Luc . . . but she didn't want to imagine why Luc wasn't there. Could it be none of them knew she had been revived? "I'm Evangeline Fox."

"You may call me Poison." The potion master's arm left her waist to make a magnanimous gesture.

And Evangeline immediately knew who this young man was. She should have realized it right away. He looked remarkably like his fortune-telling card from Decks of Destiny. He wore a long flowing cape, jeweled rings on all his fingers, and clearly worked with potions. Poison was the Poisoner. A Fate, just like Jacks.

"I thought all of the Fates had disappeared," Evangeline blurted.

"We recently made a grand return, but that's not what this story is about." Poison's face drew eerily still, warning her this was not a subject he wanted to discuss.

Evangeline might have still been groggy, but she knew better than to push, despite all the questions this revelation prompted. Poison's reputation wasn't as deadly as Jacks's. According to the myths, he didn't usually hurt anyone directly, but he created toxic tonics, peculiar potions, and strange serums for others, who sometimes put them to terrible use.

Evangeline peered at the goblet still in her hands.

Poison

Do Not Drink Me

"Mind if I take that?" With one jeweled hand, Poison extracted the cup.

Evangeline took a wary step back. "Why am I here? Did Jacks ask you to help me?"

Poison laughed, turning his expression friendly once again. "I'm sorry, darling, but Jacks has probably forgotten all about you. He found some trouble during the weeks you were stone. I can assure you he won't be returning to Valenda."

Evangeline knew she shouldn't be curious. After her last encounter with Jacks, she didn't want to ever see him again and give him a chance to collect on the debt she owed him. But Jacks didn't seem like the sort to run away. He couldn't be killed—unless that part of his history wasn't true and Fates weren't entirely immortal?

"What type of trouble did Jacks get into?" she asked.

Poison squeezed her shoulder in a way that made Evangeline think the word *trouble* was putting whatever happened with Jacks mildly. "If you have any sense of self-preservation, you'll forget about him."

"Don't worry," Evangeline said. "I have no desire to see Jacks ever again."

Poison raised a skeptical brow. "You may say that, but once you step through the door to our domain, it's nearly impossible to return to the ordinary. Most of us have fled this city, so you probably won't run into any other Fates by chance. But now that you've gotten a taste of our world, your life will start to feel bland. You'll be drawn to our kind. Even if you never want to see Jacks again, you'll gravitate toward him until you fulfill the deal you've made with him. But if you desire a chance at happiness, fight the pull—Jacks will only lead to your destruction."

Evangeline's mouth screwed into a frown. She didn't disagree, but she also couldn't understand why a Fate would give her this warning.

"I'll never comprehend humans." Poison sighed. "All of you seem to welcome our lies, but you never like it when we tell the truth."

"Maybe it's difficult to believe a Fate would want to help a human out of the goodness of their heart?"

"What if I told you I'm being self-serving?" Poison took a sip from his goblet. "Valenda is my home. I'd rather not be forced to flee to the North for misbehaving like the others—I don't like what the magic there does to my abilities, and it's too cold. So I'm trying to be helpful to the crown. Now go on, there are others waiting in the great room to see you."

Poison turned her toward a set of spiral stairs, where Evangeline got a whiff of one of the most delicious scents: pink sugarbelle cake.

Her stomach growled. She hadn't realized how famished she was.

After thanking Poison, she climbed the steps.

Within seconds, the air grew even sweeter, and the world turned bright in a way that made her feel as if her life before now had been dull. The great room appeared to be made of glimmer and light; golden chandeliers shaped like crowns reigned over gilded tables, harps, and grand pianos with golden keys. Yet it was the sight of all the people that made her forget how to breathe.

So many people. All clapping and smiling and grinning at *her*.

Evangeline was friendly with many from her father's curiosity shop, and it seemed as if every one of them was there to welcome her back. It was touching and warming, but also a little odd that so many people were present.

"Hello, lovely!" called Ms. Mallory, who collected maps of fictional places. "I have so much to tell you about my grandson."

"I can't wait to hear," Evangeline replied before accepting a handshake from a gentleman who always ordered obscure foreign cookbooks.

"I'm so proud of you!" called Lady Vane, who favored pots of disappearing ink.

After weeks of endless nothing, Evangeline was cocooned in hugs and kisses on cheeks. And yet her heart dipped as she failed to find Luc among the crowd.

Her stepsister stood somewhat to the side, and Luc wasn't with her either. But Evangeline didn't feel the relief that she would have expected at not finding them together. Did he not know about this gathering? Or was there another reason Luc had chosen not to attend?

Marisol's expression was difficult to read. She was wobbling on her feet and trying to keep a fly from landing on the sparkling pink sugarbelle cake in her hands. But as soon as Marisol spied Evangeline, her grin widened until it was as bright as the beautiful cake.

Agnes disdained her daughter's love of baking—she wanted great things for Marisol and said that cooking was too common a hobby—but Evangeline wondered if she'd let Marisol make this treat for today. There were four tiers of fluffy pink cake, alternate layers of sugarbelle cream, a frosting bow, and an oversize shortbread gift tag that read: *Welcome back, sister!*

Guilt, thick and heavy, mingled with Evangeline's unease. She would never have expected such a gesture from her stepsister, and she certainly didn't deserve it.

"Oh, there's my precious, lovely girl!" Agnes approached and threw both arms around Evangeline. "We were all desperately worried. It was such a relief to hear there was someone who could fix you." Agnes squeezed Evangeline tighter and whispered, "So many suitors have been inquiring about you. Now that you're back, I'll arrange for the richest ones to visit."

Evangeline wasn't sure how to respond—to what Agnes had just said or to this version of her stepmother who believed in hugging. Even when Agnes had first married Evangeline's father, she'd never embraced Evangeline. Agnes had married Maximilian for the same reason he'd married her—to make sure her daughter was provided for. Maximilian Fox had not been rich— his business ventures failed nearly as often as they succeeded— but he was a respectable match for a widow with a daughter.

Agnes released Evangeline from the embrace, only to turn her toward a gentleman that Evangeline hoped was not a suitor.

He wore a flowing white silk shirt with a lacy jabot that cascaded down to a pair of black leather pants so tight she was surprised he could move.

"Evangeline," said Agnes, "this is Mr. Kutlass Knightlinger of *The Whisper Gazette*."

"You write for those scandal sheets?"

"They are not scandal sheets; it's a periodical," Agnes corrected with a sniff, making Evangeline think that the fledgling paper had grown in readership and credibility since the article that had inspired her to search for the door to the Prince of Hearts' church.

"I actually don't care what you call it, Miss Fox, as long as I'm allowed to feature you in it." Kutlass Knightlinger brushed a black-feathered pen across his lips. "I've been covering everything related to the return of the Fates, and I have several questions for you."

Evangeline was suddenly unsteady on her feet. The last thing she wanted to talk about was what had happened with Jacks. No one could ever know she'd made a deal with a Fate.

If Evangeline had been fully recovered, she would have pulled away with a clever excuse. But instead, Mr. Kutlass Knightlinger, of the lacy jabot and the black leather pants, was the one who did all the pulling.

Quickly, he wrangled her away from the party, through a pair of thick gold curtains and onto a bench hidden in an alcove that smelled of mystery and musk and imitation magic. Or was that Kutlass Knightlinger's cologne?

"Mr. Knightlinger—" Evangeline pushed up from the bench, and the world began to spin. She really needed to eat. "I don't believe today is the best day for an interview."

"Don't worry, it doesn't really matter what you say. I make the people I interview look good. And everyone already loves you. After the sacrifice you made, you're one of Valenda's favorite heroes."

"But I'm really not a hero."

"You're too modest." Kutlass leaned in closer. The heavy scent around her was definitely his cologne. "During the Week of Terror—"

"What's the Week of Terror?"

"It was so exciting! It started right after you were turned to stone. The Fates returned—would you believe they were trapped inside a deck of cards? So much mischief and mayhem when they escaped and tried to take over the empire. But the story of how you took the place of that wedding party and turned yourself to stone inspired people all over during that difficult time. You're a hero."

Evangeline's throat went suddenly dry. No wonder so many people were there. "I hope that I did what anyone else would have done in my situation."

"That's perfect." Kutlass pulled out an impossibly small notebook from his leather vest and began scribbling away. "My readers are going to love this. Now—"

Her stomach cut him off with a loud grumble.

Kutlass laughed, quick and practiced as his pen strokes. "A little hungry?"

"I can't remember the last time I ate. I should probably—"

"I only have a few more questions. There are rumors that while you were still stone, your adoptive mother started receiving marriage proposals for your hand—"

"Oh, Agnes is my stepmother," Evangeline cut in quickly, "she never adopted me."

"But I think it's safe to say she will now." Kutlass winked. "Your star will only continue to rise, Miss Fox. Now, may I have a parting word of advice for all your admirers?"

The word *admirers* left a bad taste on Evangeline's teeth. She really didn't deserve any admirers. And everyone would undoubtedly feel differently if they knew what she'd truly done.

"If you're a little speechless, I'll come up with something brilliant." His feathered pen swished over his journal.

"Wait—" Evangeline still didn't know what she was going to say, but she shuddered to think what he might be writing. "I know that stories often take on lives of their own. I already feel as if the horror I went through is turning into a fairytale, but I'm nothing special, and this is not a fairytale."

"And yet it turned out well for you," Kutlass cut in.

"She was stone for six weeks," said a soft voice behind them. "I wouldn't say it turned out well."

Evangeline looked over Kutlass's shoulder to see her stepsister.

Marisol stood in between the gold curtains, holding her sugarbelle cake like a shield.

Kutlass pivoted in a swish of lace and leather. "The Cursed Bride!"

Marisol's cheeks turned a painful shade of red.

"This is excellent!" Kutlass's feathered pen began moving again. "I'd love to have a word with you."

"Actually," Evangeline interrupted, sensing that Marisol was the one who needed rescuing now. "My stepsister and I haven't had any time together, so I think I'm going to steal her away to enjoy some cake."

Evangeline finally pushed past him, linked arms with her stepsister, and departed through the curtains.

"Thank you." Marisol clung tighter to Evangeline, and though they'd never been much for linking arms before, Evangeline felt as if her stepsister had grown thinner. Marisol had always been slender like her mother, but today she felt fragile. And her skin was almost waxen in its paleness, which could have been from interacting with Kutlass. But there were also circles beneath her light brown eyes that looked as if they'd been there for days or maybe weeks.

Evangeline stopped abruptly before they rejoined the rest of the gathering. Earlier, she'd wondered why Luc wasn't there, but now she felt afraid of the answer. "Marisol, what's wrong? And . . . where is Luc?"

Marisol shook her head. "We shouldn't talk about this now. This is your happy day. I don't want to spoil it."

"You made me cake and saved me from the king of scandal sheets—I think you're actually the hero."

Marisol's eyes welled with tears, and Evangeline felt a knife twist inside her.

"What is it?" Evangeline pressed. "What's the matter?"

Marisol worried her lip between her teeth. "It happened four weeks ago, when Luc and I decided we'd try to get married again."

They tried to get married again when she was still stone? This time, the knife inside Evangeline felt as if it were drawing blood. The news shouldn't have wounded her so much. When she hadn't seen Luc waiting for her in Poison's laboratory or at the welcome party, she'd imagined that nothing had changed between them. But it still hurt to hear he hadn't even mourned her, that a mere two weeks after she'd been turned to stone, he'd planned another wedding.

"We thought we would be safe because the Week of Terror had ended. But on his way to the wedding, Luc was attacked by a wild wolf."

"Wait—wait—what?" Evangeline stammered. Valenda was a bustling port city. The largest animals it had were dogs, followed by the feral cats that prowled the docks for mice. Valenda didn't have wolves.

"No one knows where the wolf came from," Marisol said miserably. "The physician told us it's a miracle Luc survived. But I'm not sure he really did. He was badly mauled."

Evangeline's legs lost their bones. She tried to open her

mouth, to say that at least he was alive. As long as he was still alive, it would be all right. But the way Marisol spoke, it was almost as if he were dead.

"It's been weeks, he still hasn't left his house, and—" Marisol's words turned choppy, and the lovely cake in her hands quivered until a dollop of cream fell to the carpet. "He refuses to see me. I think he believes it's my fault."

"How could it be your fault?"

"You heard Mr. Knightlinger. Everyone in Valenda has been calling me the Cursed Bride. Two weddings and two terrible tragedies within a few weeks. Mother keeps saying that it's not a bad thing, that I'm special because when the Fates returned, I was the first to capture their attention. But I know I'm not. I'm cursed." Tears streamed down Marisol's pallid cheeks.

Until that moment, Evangeline had been fighting hard not to regret her choices. It might have been a coincidence that Luc had been attacked on his way to the wedding, but it seemed far more likely Luc's assault was not just the work of a wild wolf. Jacks had told her he'd stop the wedding, and he'd clearly kept his word.

Evangeline should have never made the deal with him.

She wanted to blame Jacks completely, but this was her fault as much as it was his. She knew as soon as she saw the statues in the garden that she'd made a mistake. She thought she'd fixed it with her sacrifice, but she should have never sought out the Prince of Hearts for help in the first place.

"Marisol, I have to tell you—" The words stuck to

Evangeline's tongue. She worked her jaw to get out the confession, but she knew it wasn't the sudden tightness she felt that caused the problem. She was afraid.

Evangeline was trembling, just as hard as when she'd first heard the news of Luc's engagement to Marisol. Her words had also stuck in her throat that day when she'd tried to talk to Marisol about Luc. She'd been so convinced it was some sort of curse. And she still wanted to believe that. But Evangeline could no longer ignore the possibility that maybe she'd been mistaken.

Maybe the real reason Evangeline had never been able to talk to Marisol about Luc wasn't because of a spell. Maybe it was fear that had paralyzed her tongue. Maybe, deep down, Evangeline feared that she and Luc weren't actually cursed, but he was just an unfaithful boy.

"It's all right, Evangeline. You don't have to say anything. I'm just glad you're back!" Marisol set her cake on the closest gilded table and threw her arms around Evangeline, hugging her the way Evangeline always imagined that real sisters hugged.

And she knew she couldn't tell her the truth, not today.

Evangeline had just spent the last six weeks alone as stone. She wasn't ready to be alone again, but she would be if anyone learned what she'd done.

7

If storms were made of scandal sheets, queues of gentlemen dressed with starched cravats, and notes of questionable origins, then the perfect storm was brewing in Evangeline's world the next morning. She just didn't know this yet.

All she knew about was the note of peculiar origin, which had prompted her to slip out of the house at daybreak.

> *Meet me.*
> *The curiosity shop.*
> *First thing after sunrise.*
> *—Luc*

Evangeline's heart had nearly burst after she'd discovered the message in her bedroom the night before. She didn't know if it was a new note or an old one that she was only finding now. But she'd fallen asleep reading it again and again, hoping that Luc would be waiting for her in the morning with a story that was different from the one she'd heard from Marisol.

Yesterday's conversation with Marisol had shaken Evangeline; it had almost convinced her that she'd been deluding herself about Luc. But hope is a difficult thing to kill, just a spark of it can start a fire, and this note had given Evangeline a new spark.

Her father had owned four and a half shops across Valenda. He'd been the silent half partner of a tailor that sewed weapons into clothing. He'd built a secret bookshop, only accessible via secret passage. Then there was his store in the Spice Quarter, covered in decorative Wanted posters with captions that read like short outlandish crime stories. His third shop was a secret, even from Evangeline. And his fourth store was her favorite place of all: Maximilian's Curiosities, Whimsies & Other Oddities.

This was the store where Evangeline had started working as soon as her father had allowed it. He used to tell customers that everything inside was *almost* magical. But Evangeline had always believed that some of the items that passed through his shop really were enchanted. She'd often tracked down chess pieces that had wandered from their boards, and sometimes the paintings wore different expressions from those they'd had the day before.

Evangeline's chest tightened with something like homesickness as she turned a corner onto the bricked street that Maximilian's Curiosities called home. She'd missed the store during the weeks she'd been made of stone, but she hadn't felt just how much until that moment. She missed the walls her mother had painted, the shelves packed with her father's finds, the bell—

Evangeline skidded to a halt.

Maximilian's Curiosities had closed its doors. The copper-lined windows were boarded up. The awning was ripped off, and someone had painted over the name on the door:

Under New Ownership
Closed Until Further Notice

"No!" Not the shop! Evangeline banged and banged on the door. This was the last piece of her father that she had left. How could Agnes do this?

"Excuse me, young miss." A patroller's stout shadow fell over her. "You're going to need to stop that pounding."

"You don't understand. This store was my father's—it was willed to me." Evangeline continued knocking as if the door might magically open, as if Luc were waiting on the other side, as if she hadn't just lost the last piece of her parents. "How long has it been closed?"

"I'm sorry, miss. I think it shut nearly six weeks back and—" The young patrolman's face lit up. "Fallen stars—it's you— you're Valenda's Sweetheart Savior." He paused to smooth back his hair. "If you don't mind me saying so, miss, you're even prettier than the papers say. Do you know where I can get one of those applications?"

"Applications for what?" Evangeline stopped knocking, suddenly uneasy, as the patrolman reached into his back pocket and retrieved a black-and-white sheet of newsprint.

The Whisper Gazette

FROM THE STREETS TO STONE TO STARDOM:

AN INTERVIEW WITH
VALENDA'S SWEETHEART SAVIOR

By Kutlass Knightlinger

Seventeen-year-old Evangeline Fox looks like a fairytale princess with her shimmering pink hair and her innocent smile. But weeks ago, she was a parentless orphan. When I spoke with her recently, she told me that she couldn't remember the last time she'd eaten.

She hadn't been invited to the wedding ceremony of Luc Navarro and Marisol Tourmaline, whom many of you know as the Cursed Bride. And yet, when Evangeline stumbled upon the gathering, which had been transformed to stone by one of the Fates,

Evangeline didn't hesitate to save the entire wedding party by taking their place and becoming a statue.

"I think I just did what anyone else would have hopefully done in my situation. I'm really not a hero," she told me.

Evangeline was so humble. It was difficult to get her to speak about her own heroics. But Valenda's Sweetheart Savior was eager to talk when I mentioned the Cursed Bride's mother, Agnes Tourmaline, and her magnanimous plans to adopt Evangeline.

"I already feel as if the horror

I went through is turning into a fairytale," she said.

Agnes also informed me that Evangeline is eager to move on with her life as soon as possible.

She's accepting suitors by way of applications for her hand in marriage—

(continued on page 3)

"Oh my . . ." Evangeline gave the patroller an unsteady smile. "I'm sorry, this paper is mistaken. I'm not looking for suitors." She cringed at just using the word. It didn't surprise her. She knew Agnes's hugs and smiles yesterday had been false. But Evangeline hadn't expected her stepmother to sell her off so quickly.

Other passersby on the street had already stopped to stare. A few eager gentlemen looked as if they were building up courage to approach.

If Jacks had been there, he'd probably taken it as proof that he'd done Evangeline a favor by making her so popular. But this wasn't what she wanted.

Evangeline threw the scandal sheet in the closest trash bin and looked once more at Luc's note. The message was old. She knew that now—he wouldn't have asked her to meet at the shop knowing it was shuttered.

Evangeline didn't want to cry so much as she wanted to find a way back in time, to before. To before Agnes, to before Luc, to before she'd lost both her parents. She just wanted one more hug from her father. One more moment of her mother smoothing her hair. The pain she felt at missing Luc wasn't even a scratch in comparison to the absence of her mother and father. She still wanted Luc, but what she really wanted was the life and all the love that she'd lost.

It was difficult not to feel heartsick as Evangeline trudged back to a house that hadn't been home since her father had died. Normally, she adored the city. She loved the tangle of noise, the bustling of people, and the way her street often smelled of fresh-made cakes from the bakery around the corner. But that afternoon, the street smelled of too much unfamiliar cologne.

The scent made her nauseous, but it was the sight of all the gentlemen that stopped her in her tracks. Decked out in their finest coats and capes and hats, the men lined the street to her house, where Agnes stood on the doorstep happily receiving flowers, compliments, and paper pages.

She's accepting suitors by way of applications for her hand in marriage—

Evangeline's hands curled into fists. A fraction of the men were almost attractive, but many of them were the age her father had been or older. She might have turned around if she had somewhere else to go, but thanks to Agnes, the curiosity shop was closed. And Evangeline found she was more in the mood to fight than to run.

She marched toward the house with a demure smile.

"Oh, there she is," Agnes cooed.

But Evangeline didn't give her the chance to say anything else. She quickly turned to the gentlemen, raised her voice, and said, "Thank you all for coming, but I wish to turn everyone away." She paused and theatrically pressed the back of her left hand to her forehead and closed her eyes, mimicking a move she'd once seen in a tragic street play with her father. "I'm not a statue anymore, but I'm still cursed, and anyone I kiss will turn to stone."

Murmurs erupted everywhere. "Stone . . ."

"Cursed!"

"I'm getting out of here."

The gentlemen quickly dispersed, and with them went her doting stepmother's façade.

Agnes grabbed Evangeline's shoulders and dug her slender fingers in. "What have you done, you wretched girl? Those suitors weren't just for you. This was Marisol's chance at getting noticed again."

Evangeline winced and pulled away. She felt a stitch of guilt for her stepsister, but as of yesterday, Marisol wasn't over Luc either.

"Don't pretend I'm the villain," Evangeline said. "You shouldn't have done this, and you shouldn't have sold my father's shop. That store was willed to me."

"You were considered dead." Agnes took a menacing step.

Evangeline blanched. Her stepmother had never hit her, but she'd also never grabbed her before today. And Evangeline hated to consider what else Agnes might do. If her stepmother tossed her out onto the streets, Evangeline had nowhere to go.

Evangeline probably should have thought about that before she turned away the suitors, but it was too late to take it back, and she wasn't sure that she would have.

"I hope that's not a threat, Agnes." Evangeline spoke with all the bravado she could muster. "You never know who might still be listening, and it'd be a shame if word of your true nature made it to someone like Kutlass Knightlinger."

Agnes's nostrils flared. "Kutlass can't protect you forever. I would think you'd know how quickly a young man's attention can shift. Kutlass Knightlinger will either turn on you or soon forget you like your beloved Luc did."

The barb hit Evangeline straight in her chest.

Agnes smiled as if she'd been itching to say those words. "I was going to wait and share this with you after Marisol saw it, but I've changed my mind." Agnes reached toward her table of applications, retrieved a folded page, and held it out for Evangeline.

Cautiously, she unfolded the note.

> Marisol, my most precious treasure,
>
> I wish I didn't have to say goodbye this way. But I'm hoping this will not be a true farewell. I'm leaving Valenda in hopes of finding a healer. The next time I see your beautiful face, I will be the Luc you first fell in love with, and we can be together again.
>
> With every heartbeat from my heart—

Evangeline couldn't read any more. She didn't need to reach the end to know the handwriting belonged to Luc.

Luc had written her letters, but they were usually brief, like the note she'd found last night. He'd never called her his most precious treasure or mentioned his heart beating.

"This can't be real," Evangeline breathed. "What have you done to him?"

Agnes laughed. "You really are a stupid child. Your father used to say you believed in things you couldn't see as if it were a gift. But you should start believing in the things that you do see."

Luc Navarro's family lived on the fashionable far edge of town, where the houses were larger and farther apart. The type of neighborhood that always made Evangeline feel the need to take a deep breath as she approached.

On the day that Marisol had announced her engagement to Luc, Evangeline had run all the way here. She'd knocked on Luc's door, sure that when it opened, Luc would tell her it was all a great misunderstanding.

Luc was her first love, her first kiss, her heart when hers had stopped working. It was unimaginable that he didn't love her, as impossible as traveling through time. A part of her had known there was a chance it could be true, but her soul had told her that it wasn't. She had expected Luc to confirm it. But Luc never told her anything. The servants sent her away and slammed the door. They did the same the next day and every day that followed.

But today was finally different.

Today, no one answered the door when she knocked.

Evangeline heard no footsteps in the house, no voices. When she found a crack in the drawn curtains, all she saw on the other side were sheets covering the furniture.

Luc and his family had left, just as Luc's note had said.

Evangeline didn't know how long she stood there. But eventually, she recalled Jacks's words, and she wondered if he'd been right when he'd said, *If he loved you back, he wouldn't be marrying someone else. End of story.*

8

Time passed.

Days cooled.

Leaves changed.

Apple stands popped up on street corners, selling tarts and pies and harvest treats. Every time Evangeline walked by a stand and caught a hint of its fruit-sweet scent, she'd think of Jacks and the debt she owed, and her heart would race like a horse hoping to escape her chest. But it seemed Jacks had forgotten about her, just as Poison had said.

Luc never returned either, and the curiosity shop did not reopen.

Evangeline convinced Agnes to let her work in her father's hidden bookstore. It wasn't as magical as the curiosity shop, but it gave her something to look forward to. Although some days she felt like one of the dusty used books on the store's back shelves. The volumes that had been popular once, but no one picked up anymore.

She was still too well known for her stepmother to toss onto the streets, but Evangeline feared it would happen one day. The scandal sheets had printed the rumor about her kiss turning gentlemen to stone. Since then, her name only made brief, infrequent appearances. Kutlass was starting to forget her, too, just as Agnes had said.

But Evangeline refused to give up hope.

Her mother, Liana, had grown up in the Magnificent North, and she had raised Evangeline on their fairytales.

In the North, fairytales and history were treated as one and the same because their stories and histories were all cursed. Some tales couldn't be written down without bursting into flames, others couldn't leave the North, and many changed every time they were shared, becoming less and less real with every retelling. It was said that every Northern tale had started as true history, but over time, the Northern story curse had twisted all the tales until only bits of truth remained.

One of the stories Liana used to tell Evangeline was *The Ballad of the Archer and the Fox,* a romantic tale about a crafty peasant girl who could transform into a fox and the young archer who loved her, but was cursed with the need to hunt her down and kill her.

Evangeline loved the story because she, too, was a Fox, even if she wasn't the sort who could turn into an animal. She might have also had a tiny crush on the archer. Evangeline made her mother tell her the tale over and over. But since this story was cursed, every time her mother neared the end, she would suddenly forget what she'd been saying. She could never tell Evangeline if the archer kissed his fox-girl and they lived happily together forever, or if he killed the fox-girl, ending their story in death.

Evangeline would always ask her mother to just tell her how she thought the story ended. But her mother always refused.

"I believe there are far more possibilities than happily ever after or tragedy. Every story has the potential for infinite endings."

Evangeline's mother repeated this sentiment so often that it grew inside Evangeline, rooting itself into the heart of her beliefs. This was one of the reasons she'd drunk the poison that had turned her to stone. It wasn't because she was fearless or terribly heroic; it was because Evangeline simply had more hope than most. Jacks had told her that her only option for a happy ending was to walk away; that if she drank the poison, she'd be stone forever. But Evangeline couldn't believe that. She knew her story had the potential for infinite endings—and that belief hadn't changed.

There was a happy ending waiting for her.

The bell attached to the door of the bookstore chimed. The door hadn't even opened yet, but the bell must have sensed someone special was entering, for it rang a touch early.

Evangeline found herself holding her breath, hoping Luc would walk through. She wished she could break the habit. But that same hope that led Evangeline to believe there was still a happy ending waiting for her also made her think that one day Luc would return. It didn't seem to matter how many weeks or months passed. Whenever the bell to the bookshop rang, she couldn't help but hope.

She knew some people would think this made her foolish, but it was tremendously hard to fully fall out of love with someone when you had no one else to love instead.

Evangeline quickly barreled down the ladder she'd been standing on and hurried past several patrons exploring the aisles. The last person who'd walked through the door was not Luc, but she was also unexpected.

Marisol had never visited Evangeline at the bookshop. Marisol never really left the house, she barely left her room, and she looked visibly uncomfortable at having done both today. She wrung her gloved hands with every step.

Given that the bookstore was a bit of a secret, it didn't look like much from the outside. Just a door with a knob that always seemed on the verge of falling off. And yet there was a certain sort of magic once you stepped inside. It was the feel of candlelight at twilight, paper dust caught in the air, and rows and rows of unusual books on crooked shelves. Evangeline treasured it, but Marisol moved through the stacks as if they all might fall on her.

Over the last few months, the Cursed Bride had become part of local lore. Weddings were no longer held in gardens, and if a wedding was canceled, it was now bad luck to reschedule. Since she rarely went out, Marisol wasn't widely recognizable as the actual Cursed Bride, but Evangeline could already see her stepsister's skittishness making the other customers feel as if there were something to fear. Conversations had grown hushed, and patrons made a point of avoiding Marisol.

Evangeline continued toward her with a smile, hoping Marisol wouldn't notice the less-than-friendly glances. "What brings you here? Did you want a book? We just got in a shipment of cooking books."

Marisol shook her head, almost violently. "It's probably best I don't touch anything. People might think I've cursed the books." She shot a furtive look toward the door, where a couple happened to be quickly exiting.

"They're not leaving because of you," Evangeline assured her.

Marisol frowned, unconvinced. "I won't stay long. I only came in to give you this." She held out an elaborate piece of expensive red paper accented with whirls of gold leaf and sealed with a red wax symbol.

"When I saw it delivered, I thought it looked important, and I wanted to make sure Mother didn't hide it from you." Marisol finally managed a smile, one that looked a little sly around the corners. "I know I'll never make up for the weeks that you were stone, but it's something."

"I've already told you, you don't owe me anything." Evangeline felt a familiar stab of guilt. Every day, she was tempted to tell Marisol the truth, but every day, she wasn't quite brave enough. Between Evangeline working at the shop and Marisol hiding in her room, the girls hadn't grown much closer. But Marisol was still the nearest thing Evangeline had to family.

Someday, Evangeline would tell her stepsister the truth, but she still couldn't do it yet.

And Marisol didn't even give her the chance. As soon as she handed Evangeline the red page, Marisol disappeared the way she came, leaving Evangeline to open the mysterious note alone.

Dear Miss Fox,

My sister and I would love to have the pleasure of your company tomorrow for afternoon tea in the Royal Hummingbird Court at two o'clock. We've admired you from afar, and we have an exciting opportunity we'd like to discuss.

Warmest regards,
Scarlett Marie Dragna
Empress of the Meridian Empire

9

Evangeline read the empress's invitation one more time as her sky carriage landed on the pristine palace grounds. She had spent the last day trying to imagine what sort of opportunity the empress might want to discuss, but she still had no idea what it was. Marisol had no clue either. When Evangeline had returned to the house and told Marisol what the red note contained, her stepsister had repeatedly said she was happy for Evangeline, but she'd also looked nervous.

If Evangeline's invitation was mysterious, the new empress was even more so.

Before Evangeline had been turned to stone, there had been a different heir to the throne: a young man nicknamed His Handsomeness. Unfortunately, she'd learned that during the Week of Terror, the Fates had made their reappearance known to the public by murdering this unlucky royal. The new empress, and her younger sister—whom people called the Fate

Slayer—had battled the Fates to get the empire back, killing one, and proving that Evangeline's theory had been correct—the Fates weren't true immortals. They didn't age, but they could die.

Most of the city adored the sisters for their victory over the Fates, but some believed the new empress was actually a Fate. The scandal sheets claimed that she could read minds and her fiancé was a pirate covered in a web of scars.

Evangeline knew better than to believe all the rumors. Yet she was still anxious about the mind reading. She didn't want the empress seeing her thoughts and learning that Evangeline was not the savior everyone believed.

Evangeline toyed with the buttons of her cream capelet, suddenly hot as she left her carriage and followed a palace servant down a flower-covered path to a door with a golden handle shaped like a hummingbird.

After opening the door, the servant bowed. "Your Majesty, Miss Evangeline Fox has arrived." He stepped aside, welcoming her into a garden full of fairy-green trees dripping coral, pink, and peach-colored flowers that made Evangeline think of soft kisses on cheeks.

"Welcome!"

"It's so lovely to finally meet you, Evangeline!"

"Your hair really is divine!"

The empress and her sister, Princess Donatella, spoke at once as hummingbirds zipped above their heads.

"We weren't sure what you liked, so we ordered a bit of

everything," announced the princess. With cloudburst-blue ribbons in her blond curls and a playful expression on her pretty face, she was not at all how Evangeline had imagined the brazen, Fate-slaying hellion from the scandal sheets.

"We have blackberry creams, harvest terrines, pumpkin pudding, walnut tarts, and every type of tea." The princess waved a hand toward a tiered tower of colorful teapots piping pretty pink steam. If the royal sisters were trying to dazzle her, they were doing an excellent job.

Evangeline felt like a princess herself as she finally removed her capelet and took a seat at the generous table. "This is wonderful. Thank you for inviting me."

"We're so pleased you could join us," said the empress. She was young—probably around Evangeline's age—although it was difficult to be sure, as she had a thick gray streak cutting through her dark hair. She wore an off-the-shoulder ruby gown, pretty lace gloves, and a smile so sweet Evangeline found it hard to believe she'd been anxious about meeting her. "We've wished to meet you ever since hearing about your heroism during the Week of Terror."

"But we also want to ask for a favor," the princess chimed in.

The empress eyed her sister, who was apparently going off script.

"What? I'm sure she's dying with curiosity. I'm just trying to save her life." The princess reached across her sister's plate and picked up a square of cream paper covered in copper print.

*In Honor of
His Highness Crown Prince
Apollo Titus Acadian
You Have Been Summoned to
the Magnificent North
to Attend Nocte Neverending
Festivities Begin on
the First Winter's Day
and They Will Not End
Until Prince Apollo Has
Found His Bride*

The metallic ink shimmered as if it were still wet—*or touched with Northern magic.* Evangeline tried not to leap to any conclusions and failed almost immediately. She'd been hoping there was another happy ending waiting for her, and as she looked at this invitation, it was practically impossible not to imagine that this could be her way to find it.

"The North has different customs from ours," the empress said softly. "The crown prince can't fully ascend to the throne until he's wed, and hosting a ball to choose a bride is one of their oldest traditions."

It was also a tradition that Evangeline was familiar with, which felt like another sign. Her mother had told her all about Nocte Neverending. As a little girl, Evangeline thought it was the most romantic thing she'd ever heard. Secret ballrooms were built for it in forests where fallen stars had once landed, leaving everything laced with bits of enchantment. Liana Fox used to say that there were special kinds of magic that only existed in the North, and not even memories of this magic could pass to the south. Then she would tell Evangeline how every night during Nocte Neverending, the current crown prince would watch from a hidden location until he picked five ladies to dance with. Night after night, he'd follow the same routine, watching and then asking ladies to dance until he found the perfect bride.

"I'd always hoped Nocte Neverending was real," Evangeline said. "But I was never quite sure."

"Well, it is, and we want you to go." The empress took a sip of tea as a hummingbird dropped peach flower petals into her cup. "We would attend, but I don't believe it's wise to leave the empire so soon after being crowned and—"

"There's someone in the North that I'm avoiding," inserted the princess.

"Tella," the empress scolded.

"What? It's the truth." The princess turned back to Evangeline. "I love balls and parties that have a high probability of ending dramatically. But I could cause an international incident—possibly a war—if I attend this celebration."

The empress's forehead creased with mortified lines.

"We can't ignore the invitation," the empress went on more diplomatically. "And I'd rather not begin my reign by neglecting one of the North's most treasured celebrations. So my counsel and I have given a great deal of thought as to who should represent the Meridian Empire." Her hazel eyes met Evangeline's. "What you did during the Week of Terror was brave and selfless, and it made us think you're exactly the type of person whom we'd like as an ambassador." Her royal smile widened as her sister nodded.

Evangeline finally shoved a blackberry cream in her mouth to hide the sudden strain on her own smile.

She wanted to say yes. She'd always wished to go north, to explore the world where her mother had grown up and find out which of her mother's tales were true. She was desperate to know if there really were pastry goblins that dropped off sweets on holidays and pet-size dragons that turned to smoke if they tried to fly south. And she wanted to go to this ball. She wanted to meet the prince and dance all night and finally let go of Luc.

If there was anything on earth that could make her forget about him, Nocte Neverending was it.

But could Evangeline say yes? The empress and her sister wanted a hero as their ambassador, they wanted the orphan savior from the scandal sheets, and Evangeline was not that girl. She was the opposite. These sisters had fought against the Fates, and Evangeline had made a deal with one.

Her throat went suddenly dry. No matter how much Evangeline tried not to think about Jacks, he was always tucked away in the back of her thoughts, a secret she feared would escape one day.

She still didn't know where Jacks had disappeared. Poison had said that most of the Fates had ventured to the North, where they'd been given asylum, and every rumor she'd heard since confirmed it. None of these rumors had specifically mentioned the Prince of Hearts. But hadn't Poison warned her that she'd be drawn to Jacks, whether she wanted to be or not? What if that was what this was really about? What if this wasn't Evangeline's chance at a happy ending but fate manipulating her path?

After Evangeline's last encounter with the Prince of Hearts—when he was actually trying to help her—she'd been turned to stone. She didn't want to imagine what might happen if she saw Jacks again and he decided to collect on the three kisses she owed him.

The best way to protect herself from the Prince of Hearts was to turn down the offer to go to the North.

But then what? At best, Evangeline would continue working at the bookstore and holding her breath every time the bell rang. Which suddenly felt a little pathetic rather than hopeful.

"If you're worried about that nasty rumor, we've already had it fixed," said the empress.

"Oh yes, that was so fun!" Princess Donatella held out her hand, and a pair of spirited hummingbirds delivered a sheet of black-and-white newsprint to Evangeline.

The Whisper Gazette

SPECIAL EDITION ANNOUNCEMENT

By Kutlass Knightlinger

Just in from a reliable source, Valenda's Sweetheart Savior has been cured. Her touch no longer turns men to stone.

Evangeline hadn't even thought to worry about this rumor, but she was impressed the sisters had already taken care of it.

"It just went out. By tonight, no one will think you're cursed anymore," confirmed the princess. "Though I think most people should know by now they can't believe everything they read. You should have seen some of the things said about me after the Week of Terror."

"I might have read a few of them," Evangeline admitted. "The bookshop where I work keeps all the old papers."

"And what did you think?" the princess pressed, appearing excited rather than embarrassed as she plopped a small tart into her heart-shaped mouth.

Evangeline couldn't help but laugh. She liked these sisters.

"I think Mr. Knightlinger got it all wrong. You're far fiercer in person than the gossip sheets made you out to be."

"I told you she'd be perfect." The princess clapped. "Tell us you're going to say yes! You don't have to do anything but go."

The sisters gave her a pair of matching grins as flower petals rained down and more hummingbirds buzzed around.

If they knew the truth about the day she'd turned to stone, they never would have asked her to do this. But maybe Evangeline could use this ball to become more of the person they thought she was. The invitation could be fate manipulating her path and bringing her back to Jacks, but that didn't mean it wasn't also her chance at finding a happier end to her own story. She knew it was wishful thinking to imagine that if she went north she'd meet Prince Apollo and he'd fall in love and choose her. But she'd been raised to believe in wishes and fairytales and things that seemed impossible.

And what if this wasn't just her chance at a happy ending but Marisol's opportunity as well? Evangeline had wanted to find a way to make things better for her stepsister. Maybe this was the way.

If Marisol went north with Evangeline, no one would know her as the Cursed Bride. She'd just be a girl at a ball, and Evangeline would make sure it was the best ball of her life. By the time they returned to Valenda, Luc would be a forgotten memory for both of them.

Evangeline returned the royal sisters' smiles. "If I said yes, would it be possible for me to take my stepsister?"

"That's a lovely idea," said the empress.

"I should have thought of that," muttered her sister. "But don't worry, we've thought of everything else. You might have noticed the North's seasons are different from ours. Their first day of winter is only three weeks from now, so we might have already started preparations."

There was a great deal of talk after that about lodging, then dresses. Fashion in the North was quite different. Gentlemen wore doublets and lots of leather. Ladies wore gowns with double skirts and ornamental belts. And then the princess was oohing and aahing about jewels and pearls, and Evangeline's insides were like curling ribbons, all giddy and excited.

Finally, she asked the last question she was curious about. "Do either of you know anything about the prince?"

"Yes!" both sisters answered enthusiastically.

"He's—" Princess Donatella's eyes went foggy. "Actually, I can't remember what I've heard."

"I've—" The empress broke off in a similar manner as she tried to recall what she had heard as well.

Evangeline wondered if information about the prince was cursed in the same way that many Northern tales were. Neither sister could remember a thing about Prince Apollo Acadian or his family.

If Evangeline wasn't quite so familiar with the North, this might have unnerved her. But she was far more uneasy about the three broken heart scars on her wrist that had suddenly started to burn.

10

When Evangeline Fox had lived as a stone statue, her life had become stagnant. As still as a forgotten pond, untouched by rain or pebbles or time. She did not move. She did not change. But she felt. She felt so very much. Loneliness touched with hints of regret, or hope colored by impatience. It was never just one pure emotion. It was always one thing plus another. Exactly like today.

The scars on Evangeline's wrist had stopped burning. They no longer felt as if Jacks had just bitten into them. But her insides were still a riot of butterflies as she reached the pretty door to Marisol's room. White with a transom window, the door had once been Evangeline's.

Evangeline knew Marisol hadn't stolen the room; she'd moved in at her stepmother's urging when Evangeline had been stone. As soon as Evangeline had returned, Marisol had tried to give it back. But Evangeline had felt guilty then, and she'd let her stepsister keep the room. Evangeline still felt guilty. But right now, it was a different sort of guilt, a guilt that came because she couldn't bring herself to knock on the door that had once been hers and invite Marisol to the North.

Evangeline just kept thinking that Luc had also once been hers. And though Evangeline was more determined than ever to let go of Luc, perhaps she hadn't completely let go of the idea of Marisol and Luc. It was one of those things she tried not to consider. She didn't believe that Marisol had known Evangeline loved Luc—Marisol had always been so kind and timid. She didn't seem capable of stealing a book, let alone a boy. But it was hard not to wonder.

What if Marisol had known Evangeline loved Luc? What if she'd knowingly stolen him, and what if Evangeline found love again in the North and Marisol took it once more?

Evangeline's hand hovered in between knocking and lowering. When . . .

"Mother, please—" Marisol's words weren't particularly loud, but the narrow hall was so quiet, Evangeline could hear them through the door. "Don't say that."

"It's true, my little girl." Agnes's voice was like treacle. Too sweet to actually be palatable. "You have let yourself go these past few months. Look at you. Your complexion. Your hair. Your posture is like a damp ribbon, and those circles beneath your eyes are hideous. A man might be able to overlook your little cursed reputation if you were something to look at, but I can barely tolerate the sight—"

Evangeline opened the door, unable to hear another cruel word.

Poor Marisol was sitting on her pale pink bed, and she did look like a wilted ribbon, though it was probably because Agnes had trampled all over her. Whatever Marisol was or wasn't, she was also a victim of Agnes. But unlike Evangeline, Marisol had been living with this awful woman her entire life.

"Do you have any manners?" Agnes shrieked.

Evangeline desperately wanted to say that Agnes was the one lacking in manners and kindness, as well as a few other things. But angering her further was probably not the wisest idea right now.

Evangeline forced herself to say, "I'm sorry," instead. "I have news I thought you'd both like to hear right away."

Agnes immediately narrowed her eyes.

Marisol covertly wiped at hers.

And Evangeline felt further convinced that going north for Nocte Neverending was exactly what she and Marisol both needed. Marisol might have needed it even more. Evangeline couldn't believe she'd considered not asking her. Looking at her now, Evangeline couldn't imagine her stepsister even thinking about stealing Luc from her, and even if she had, wasn't Luc the one Evangeline should have really been blaming?

"Well?" Agnes said. "What is it, girl?"

"Today I met with the empress," Evangeline announced. "The crown prince of the Magnificent North is having a ball, and the empress has asked me to be the Meridian Empire's ambassador. Transportation, lodging, and clothing have all been taken care of. I'll leave one week from today, and I want to bring Marisol with me."

Marisol glowed as if Evangeline had given her a bouquet of wishing stars.

But Agnes didn't say a word. She looked vaguely haunted as if she'd seen a ghost or a glimpse of her own wicked heart. Evangeline was almost certain she'd say no when she opened her pinched mouth. But instead, Agnes's voice was far too sweet again as she clapped and said, "What wonderful news! Of course you can go and take Marisol with you."

PART II

The Magnificent
North

11

For fourteen days, there had been only dark waves and gray sea foam and biting salt spray. And then, as if it had been plucked from one of her mother's bedtime tales, Evangeline saw the snow-covered curves of the Great Gateway Arch to the Magnificent North.

Made of granite with marbled blue veins and as tall as a castle's keep, the arch's weathered columns were carved to look like mermaids holding tridents that pierced through carvings of men, the way a sailor might spear a fish. The men's backs were bowed, and their hands stretched to hold out the sign forming the top of the enormous arch.

WELCOME TO THE MAGNIFICENT NORTH

STORIES BE HERE

"It's even larger than I imagined," said Marisol. Her light brown hair was shining, and her delicate face was full of healthy color. The weeks at sea had done her good. The first couple of days aboard the ship, she'd been too nervous to leave her cabin. But each day, she'd ventured out a little more, and today she huddled beside Evangeline at the railing.

"Is this where we need to be quiet?" she whispered.

Evangeline nodded with a smile, glad her stepsister was starting to believe in her Northern stories the same way Evangeline did. During their journey, Evangeline had not been surprised to learn that Agnes never told Marisol any stories growing up. So Evangeline had shared some of her mother's tales, including her warnings about entering the North:

Never speak a word as you go through the Gateway Arch. The ancient magic of the North cannot pass the borders, but it always tries. It collects around the Gateway Arch, and if you speak as you travel through, the magic will steal your voice and use your words to lure unsuspecting travelers into helping it escape to other parts of the world.

It must have been a common myth, or everyone felt the same sense of gravitas that Evangeline did, for the whole of the ship sailed under the arch in silence.

On the other side, the air was cool as ice and full of clouds so low that Evangeline could taste them.

"I wish we could sail faster," a sailor grumbled. "This part always gives me the collywobbles."

The waves stopped lapping, and the nearby clouds drifted over the sun, shadowing their ship as it silently cut through the stretch of sea known as Valor Row, graveyard for the first royal family of the North.

The Valors' ancient monuments were exactly as her mother had described them. Standing knee-deep in the blue-gray waters, the statues were nearly as tall as the arch, every inch of them carved to appear as if they wore armor or finery—except for their heads, which were all missing. And yet, as her ship sailed past, Evangeline could still hear their voices, or perhaps they were the voices stolen from those who had traveled through the arch before.

Free us, they rasped.

Restore us.

Help us.

We can . . .

Evangeline didn't hear the rest of the plea as the ship reached the docks of Valorfell and everyone became busy disembarking.

"Miss Fox? Miss Tourmaline?" asked a silver-haired woman in a sea-salt-blue gown with a silver underskirt and a belt that held a number of tied-up scrolls in it. "I'm Frangelica. I'll be escorting you to your lodgings and ensuring Miss Fox makes it to her dinner this evening."

Frangelica's smile was warm and her wave brisk as she urged the girls from the ship. But Evangeline could not bring herself to rush as she stepped onto the drizzly dock full of fishmongers, trading stalls, and knobby barrels of oysters.

She'd always loved living in the south. She loved the heat of the sun and the overbright colors everyone wore. But now the brilliant streets of Valenda seemed too lurid. Here, everything was mist-touched. It was all foggy grays, rainy blues, and deep purples the exact color of fresh plums.

The burly men at the docks all looked as if they could step into a forest and fell a tree with one swing of an ax. They wore leather boots covered in heavy buckles, while the women wore thick woolen gowns with belts like Frangelica's, which held everything from bottles of tonics to palm-size crossbows.

Just taking in the cool, crisp air made Evangeline stand a little straighter and breathe a little deeper. And—

"Marisol, look, tiny dragons!"

"Oh my—" Marisol went pale as a robust pop sounded and a tiny pepper-black dragon about the size of a chipmunk shot out streams of red fire to sear a fish stick at a nearby stall.

On the docks, the adorable little beasts appeared to be as common as squirrels. Almost every vendor had one. Marisol was clearly not fond of the small winged creatures but Evangeline was delighted to spy tiny blue dragons sitting on shoulders and leathery brown ones perched on carts. The miniature beasts roasted apples and meats, blew glass baubles, and heated earthen mugs of drinking chocolate.

It all was as charming as her mother had said.

Evangeline had to look down at the damp cobbles to make

sure her feet were still on the ground and that she hadn't taken flight, for parts of her were soaring. Stepping into the North didn't just feel like the start of something, it felt like the start of everything.

Beyond the docks, spires of hearty wooden shops grew upward instead of outward. Each glorious level had storybook-quaint storefronts, all connected by fog-laced footbridges that crisscrossed above Evangeline's head in a maze of wonderful patterns. The North made her think of her mother of course, but with a pang, she realized it was also somewhere she would have loved to have explored with her father. The few shops she could see inside looked exactly like the sorts of places he might have found all kinds of new oddities for his shop.

"Get your *Daily Rumor!*" cried a girl with a satchel full of rolled-up papers. "Perfect if you're placing bets on who the prince will propose to—or if you want to know who your competition is!"

"We should buy one," Marisol said, eyeing the papers with curiosity. Given Marisol's dislike of scandal sheets, her interest was not what Evangeline would have expected. But it was just the kind of adventurous spirit that she'd hoped the North would bring out in her stepsister.

Evangeline reached into her coin purse. Their currency was different, but the empress had generously supplied her with Northern pocket money. "How much?"

"Just half a marque," said the paper girl. "Wait—" The girl's brows jumped as she took a real look at Evangeline. "It's you!

And you really do have pink hair." The girl shoved a mist-damp paper in Evangeline's hands and winked. "It's on me. I placed a bet that Prince Apollo chooses you over the others."

Evangeline didn't know how to respond other than insisting on paying the girl twice as much as the paper cost.

The Daily Rumor

LET THE BETTiNG BEGIN

By Kristof Knightlinger

Tomorrow is the first night of Nocte Neverending. The chancery is now accepting wagers on everything from dancing partners to proposals and, as promised, I have my predictions!

We all know that Prince Apollo has said he might not choose any bride, and once Nocte Neverending begins, it may never come to an end. But I would not place bets on that happening. I have it upon good authority that Apollo has his eyes on several ladies, and I have a few excellent theories as to whom these young women might be.

My first favorite is Thessaly Fortuna, who I'm sure needs little introduction. Given that she's from one of the Great Houses, I wouldn't be surprised if Thessaly was Prince Apollo's first choice for a dancing partner tomorrow night.

However, if our crown prince is hoping to garner favor with those of us who aren't from prominent bloodlines, he might ask the recently popular Ariel "LaLa" Lagrimas to dance first. LaLa's family is shrouded in mystery, which is often code for being common. But her beauty is almost mythical. And we all know how much Prince Apollo values beauty.

Unfortunately, I'm not sure I'd place any marriage bets on LaLa. I've heard repeatedly that Prince Apollo might already be taken with famed foreign princess Serendipity Skystead of the Icehaven Isles. The pair has known each other since childhood.

"She used to send weekly letters to the palace," a secret source revealed.

If you're wagering on whom the prince might propose to, Princess Serendipity may be the safest bet.

Although, if you're fond of taking risks, like I am, you may want to put your money on another foreigner—Evangeline Fox of the Meridian Empire. Orphaned, cursed by the Fates, and now a darling of the new Meridian empress, the stories that swirl around Evangeline sound a bit like one of our own cursed tales—it's hard to believe they could be entirely true.

My cousin from the south tells me that Evangeline has shimmering pink-and-gold hair and a bold adventurous streak to match. She once turned down a string of suitors as long as a city street so that her hand would be available if Prince Apollo wished to take it—and I might place a bet that he does.

Evangeline found herself grinning at the page and forgetting Luc just a little more. She had been trying not to let her hopes fly too high. Even when she and Marisol spoke of Nocte Neverending, it was never just about the prince. They talked of dancing and fashion and what sorts of people they might meet. But Evangeline had to confess that she really did want to believe she had a chance at Prince Apollo's affections. She knew it wasn't the most practical thing to imagine marrying someone she hadn't met yet, but she also didn't believe it was entirely unpractical.

Her parents had a fairytale romance that had taught Evangeline to believe in things like *love at first*.

Every time they told the story, it was a little different, as if it were another one of her mother's Northern tales. It always began when her father was searching for curiosities in the North, and he happened upon a well with the most hypnotic song floating out. He'd thought the well enchanted, so of course he'd tried to talk to it. The well had answered back. Or rather her mother had replied. She'd heard his voice come out of her family well, and she'd liked the idea of convincing this southern stranger that she was a magic water sprite. She'd toyed with him for weeks in some versions of the story. In others, Evangeline's father had known early on that it was really a young woman playing games. But in every telling of the tale, they fell in love.

"Love at first sound," her father would say. Then her mother would always kiss him on the cheek and say, "For me, it was just love at first."

Then her parents would both be sure to tell Evangeline that not all loves happened at first; some took time to grow like seeds, or they might be like bulbs, dormant until the right season approached. But Evangeline had always wanted love at first—she wanted love like her parents, love like a story. And looking at this paper convinced her just a little more that she could find it here, at Nocte Neverending.

"This is all so very exciting," Marisol squealed. It was a perky, purely happy sound. But a second later, Evangeline saw an unsettling shadow cross her stepsister's petite face. "Even though it says you're a risky choice, you're going to need to be careful tonight with the other girls. They'll definitely be all claws and teeth now."

Evangeline knew this reaction was undoubtedly Agnes's poison influence. But Evangeline did feel a sting. Right as

Marisol had said the word *teeth*, the heart-shaped scars on Evangeline's wrist had started to burn. She'd felt them more and more since she'd decided to go north. Usually, she ignored the stinging pain and the thoughts of Jacks that came with it. But just then, Evangeline couldn't shake the unnerving idea that it wasn't other girls she'd need to worry about tonight, but the blue-eyed Fate who'd left his marks on her.

Nocte Neverending didn't officially begin until tomorrow, but this evening, there was a private dinner to welcome all the foreign ambassadors. Unlike the official ball where the prince only danced with five girls, this evening, he would privately meet with everyone, including Evangeline.

"Ladies!" Frangelica clapped. "None of this will matter if Miss Fox doesn't make it to her dinner." She waved them into a waiting coach.

The burning sensation at Evangeline's wrist grew fainter but didn't completely disappear as they rumbled down a bumpy gray lane lined with inns and taverns named after various Northern tales and historical figures. They passed a fortune-telling den called Vesper's Whispers, and a clanging forge named Wolfric's Weapons. The Eternal Prince appeared to be a popular pub, though Evangeline was more curious about the serpentine line of people leading to Fortuna's Fantastically Flavored Waters. She didn't recognize the name from her mother's stories, but she wondered if the establishment was connected to the Fortuna girl who'd been mentioned in the local gossip sheet as a potential favorite.

They finally stopped near the end of the merry road at the Mermaid and the Pearls: Inn for Adventurous Travelers. Rumored to have been built out of the wreckage of a sunken ship, the inn was full of creaking floorboards and roaring warmth that immediately thawed Evangeline's chilled skin.

The walls were papered in sepia-tinted pages covered in drawings of dazed sailors and wicked mer-girls. The theme continued in Evangeline and Marisol's suite. The frames of their beds mimicked open wooden treasure chests with posters formed of the largest white pearls she'd ever seen.

According to her mother, *The Mermaid and the Pearls* was the story of a mermaid who tricked sailors into letting her turn them into giant pearls. It was one of the myths that always seemed more fairytale than history. But just in case it was more true than false, Evangeline avoided all the pearly bedposts as she dressed for the evening. She'd tried to get an invitation for Marisol, but tonight's dinner was extremely exclusive.

Everyone in attendance was supposed to wear fashions that represented something about them or the kingdom they were from, and Evangeline's dress from the empress clearly represented her. Instead of sleeves, there were merely thin lines of silver that wrapped around her arms and décolletage and then continued down, flowing over her snow-white bodice and fitted white skirt like veins of marbled stone.

She looked like a statue come to life.

Marisol went pale.

"I suppose it's a good thing I wasn't invited to this dinner. If

I'd been given a gown to symbolize my life, it would have probably had a skull and crossbones embroidered over the chest." Marisol said this as if it were a jest, but her voice was a little too high and a little too raw.

And just like that, the familiar wedge of guilt was back.

"It's going to be different here." Evangeline took her stepsister's hand and squeezed. Once again, she was tempted to confess the truth and tell Marisol that her supposed curse was all Evangeline's fault.

"Miss Fox!" Frangelica called through the door. "It's time to depart, my dear."

Evangeline closed her mouth and swallowed down her secrets. Confessing might ease her guilt, but it would ruin so many other things, and not just for her. If she told Marisol the truth, she might not feel cursed anymore, but she would feel betrayed.

For now, Evangeline would just have to hope that things really would be different here—and that the North had enough magic to create happier endings for both of them.

12

Evangeline didn't know if it was the light of the moon or the North's unusual magic, but the fog had turned to iridescent mist that set the streets aglow and made the tips of the needle-trees shimmer with hints of gold blue and fairy green as her carriage rumbled forward, over dips and divots and uneven roads that made her insides twist and churn. Or perhaps she was just nervous.

She told herself there was no reason to be anxious. Earlier, when the scars on her wrist had burned, she had feared seeing Jacks tonight. But given how exclusive the dinner was, any chance of the Fate attending seemed narrow. If Jacks was in this part of the North, Evangeline wasn't even sure he'd want to attend. Most of the ladies would be there for a chance to meet Prince Apollo, and if Fates were as jealous as the stories said, she couldn't imagine that Jacks would like that.

No, she reassured herself. Jacks would not be there. The only prince she'd see tonight would be Prince Apollo.

Her stomach tumbled once again when the carriage finally halted. Frangelica didn't move to leave, but she cheerily said, "Good luck! And don't pluck any of the leaves."

"I wouldn't dream of it," Evangeline said, mostly because it seemed like the correct reply as she stepped into the frost-touched night.

She'd expected to arrive at a snow-tipped castle or a story-book château, but there was only a forest of spindly trees dripping ice and an arch made of the same marbled blue granite that formed the Gateway Arch to the North.

This arch was not nearly as large as that one had been, but the torches on either side of it illuminated carvings that were equally intricate and far more inviting. Evangeline saw symbols from countless Northern tales and ballads: star-shaped keys and broken books, knights in armor, a crowned wolf's head, winged horses, bits of castles, arrows and foxes, and twining vines of harlequin lilies.

It reminded her a bit of her mother's embroidery. She was always stitching curious images like foxes and keyholes into dresses. Evangeline wished her mother were there right now and that whatever happened next would have made her proud.

"Are you going to stand here until you freeze, or step through?" said a smoky voice.

At first, Evangeline thought the voice came from the arch. Then she saw him.

The young man stood beside the arch the way a tree stood in a forest, as if he'd always been there. He wore no cloak or cape, just sinuous leather armor and an unusual bronze helm. The top portion almost looked like a crown, thick and decorated with unfamiliar symbols that wrapped around the young man's forehead. The helm left most of his wavy brown hair uncovered but concealed much of his face with a wide curve of harsh, spiked metal that bracketed the sides of his head and covered his jaw all the way to the bridge of his nose, leaving only a pair of eyes and slashing cheekbones exposed.

Instinctively, she took a step back.

The soldier laughed, unexpectedly soft. "You're not in any danger from me, princess."

"I'm not a princess," she corrected.

"But maybe you will be." He winked, and then he disappeared from view as she stepped through the arch and heard a voice rasp, *We're so pleased you found us.*

Another step, and the world transformed around her.

Warmth coated her skin like afternoon sun. Evangeline remained outside, but the fog and the mist and the cold were gone. Everything here was burnished bronze and red and orange—the colors of leaves on the verge of change.

She was in another forest clearing, but this one was set for a party with lively musicians playing lutes and harps, and trees dangling celebratory ribbons. In the center of it all, a royal phoenix tree reigned, and Frangelica's cryptic warning suddenly made sense. It was the first time Evangeline had ever seen such a tree, but she knew about them from her mother. A phoenix tree took over a thousand years to mature, branches stretching, trunks thickening, and leaves turning to *real* gold. They shone like dragon treasure in the candlelight, tempting people to pluck them. Although, according to myth, if one gold leaf was taken before all of them turned, then the entire tree would burst into flames.

Milling around the tree were all sorts of important-looking people. If the men at the docks had looked as if they could fell a tree with one strike of an ax, these people looked as if they could end lives with a few choice words or the stroke of a pen. Most men were in fine velvet doublets that matched the warm décor, while the ladies wore a variety of gowns. The majority were dressed in the fashion of the North with overskirts of heavy brocade, belts covered in jewels, and dramatic slashed sleeves that hung past their fingertips.

Thankfully, Evangeline didn't see the Prince of Hearts among them. There were no young men with apples, cruel faces, and torn clothes.

She breathed a little easier and shifted her attention to searching for Prince Apollo among guests who casually sipped from crystal goblets as if attending events where princes chose their brides were as common as family bruncheon. Disappointingly, no one wore a crown, leading Evangeline to assume the prince had yet to arrive.

She might have asked someone at the party about him, but despite the ease everyone else seemed to feel, none of them included a stranger in their conversations. Circles closed and mouths snapped silent every time she moved near.

It made her feel unusually shy, and grateful that Marisol hadn't been invited. She would have probably imagined that people were excluding her because of her *curse*.

A few people glanced Evangeline's way, probably wondering if her rose-gold hair meant she was the girl from the scandal sheets. But clearly it wasn't enough to enter any circles.

The only other girl who appeared to be intentionally ignored was another young lady around Evangeline's age, dressed in an arresting dragon-scale gown the color of burning rubies. No one spoke to her, but they had to notice her. She was probably the prettiest girl there, and her dress was by far the boldest. It lacked Northern-style long sleeves in favor of having no sleeves at all—better to reveal swaths of smooth brown skin and shoulders with paintings of dragon flames that covered her arms in vibrant inked gloves.

Evangeline picked up two crystal goblets and headed toward the girl, who now swayed a little as if dancing with herself.

"Do you want one?" Evangeline held out one of her drinks.

The girl appraised the goblet, and then Evangeline with narrowed eyes.

"Don't worry, it's not poisoned." Evangeline took sips from both of her goblets before offering one to the girl again. "See?"

"Unless one is poisoned and the other has the antidote. That's what I would do." The girl flashed a surprisingly diabolical grin, and Evangeline had the sudden impression that there was a reason she was being excluded. Perhaps she was not a very harmless girl. Or perhaps Evangeline was just haunted by Marisol's earlier warning about all the claws and teeth that would come out.

"I'm Evangeline, by the way."

"I know," hummed the girl.

Evangeline expected she'd introduce herself then, but the other girl only said, "I recognized the pinkish hair. I also noticed you looking for the prince when you walked in. But your gaze wasn't high enough." The girl finally accepted a goblet and used it to point toward the royal phoenix tree.

Evangeline didn't know how she hadn't seen him there before. Now that she knew what to look for, Apollo and his unexpected pose were impossible to miss. He was high up in the tree, in a wooded balcony, lounging daringly sideways across the rail.

The picture of a dashing princeling, dressed in shades of wine and wood, and wearing a golden crown shaped like a tangle of antlers. From so far away, she couldn't clearly make out all his features, but as he lay draped across the railing, Apollo peered down on the party with utter concentration as if desperately searching for the love of his life. He almost looked as if he was posing for a portrait. No—

He *was* posing for a portrait!

Evangeline spied another balcony hidden in the trees on the other side of the clearing. There, a painter appeared to be capturing the prince's dramatic arrangement with fevered brush strokes.

"You should see Apollo when it's warmer out," the girl beside her murmured. "He always does these poses with his shirt off."

"He does this often?"

The other girl nodded vigorously. "It was rather exciting when his younger brother, Tiberius, used to taunt him by shooting arrows, or releasing herds of kittens upon him."

"I think I might have liked to have seen that."

"It was fantastic. Alas, Tiberius doesn't appear to be here." The other girl sighed. "The princes had a temporary falling-out some months ago. Tiberius disappeared for weeks, no one knows where he went, and ever since he returned, he's avoided most functions."

"What—" A bolt of cold shot up the back of Evangeline's neck, making her completely forget whatever she was going to say next and think of one name instead. *Jacks.*

She didn't know how she knew that's what the spike of cold meant, but she would have bet her life that the Prince of Hearts had just entered the party.

13

Don't turn around.

    Don't turn around.

    Don't—

Evangeline only meant to look for a second. Just to make sure he was really there, that the phantom cold covering her skin was not from some unseen ghost or breeze.

Her eyes went toward the arch first. Jacks was just beyond it, fog from the other side still clinging to the buckles on his boots as he cut across the clearing.

The ice at the back of Evangeline's neck traveled around her throat and across her décolletage. *What was he doing there?*

Since the last time she'd seen him, Jacks had changed his hair to a striking shade of dark blue. If his sharp face weren't so unmistakable, Evangeline might not have recognized him so quickly. But even his face looked colder than before. His lips were two wicked slashes, his eyes ice, and his perfect skin more marble than she remembered, pale and smooth and impenetrable.

In his church, there'd been a hint of twisted playfulness that softened some of his merciless edges. But all of that was gone. He'd lost something since she'd last seen him as if he'd been a touch human before but now he was not. Now he was all Fate, and she needed to make sure he didn't discover her.

"Ah, you've spotted Lord Jacks."

Evangeline quickly spun back to her new friend.

"He's a close confidant of Apollo's," the girl said. "But he won't help you win the prince."

"I—I just thought he looked familiar," Evangeline babbled. And she tried, she really tried, not to look at him again.

The last time she'd seen Jacks, he'd walked away as she'd turned to stone. She didn't want to know what else he might condemn her to if he spotted her. But she was like the tide drawn by the tremendous force of the moon. It was no wonder waves were always crashing; they must have hated the pull as much as she did.

When she turned, Jacks was still cutting through the party, all cold-blooded grace and disinterest. Instead of a traditional doublet, he wore a loose shirt of gray linen, raven-black pants, and rugged leather boots, the same dark color as the fur-lined half cape casually slung over one of his straight shoulders. He didn't appear to be dressed for a party—the buttons on his shirt weren't even all done—but he captured more than just Evangeline's attention. People looked away from Apollo, lounging across his balcony rail, simply to watch Jacks rudely ignore everyone who attempted to engage him.

No one appeared afraid of him the way they should have been. No one flinched or paled or ran. Evangeline had never found out exactly what sort of trouble Jacks had gotten into during the Week of Terror, but since then, he must have decided to conceal his true identity. Here he was just an insolent young aristocrat with a ruthless face and the ear of the prince.

Jacks walked straight toward the phoenix tree and was immediately given permission by the guards to climb the stairs winding around it. Not once did his gaze drift from his path or venture anywhere near her. Which was good. She didn't want Jacks to notice her.

"Lord Jacks doesn't really speak to anyone," said Evangeline's new friend. "There are rumors he's recovering from a great heartbreak."

Evangeline stifled a humorless laugh. Jacks didn't look heartbroken to her. If anything, he looked even more unfeeling than the last time she'd seen him.

The safest bet for her would have been to run. To escape back through the arch while Jacks was out of sight. But if she left now, she'd also disappoint the empress and abandon her best chance at meeting Prince Apollo.

Evangeline looked back up at the balcony where the prince still lounged across the rail. His pose was outlandish, but it was also interesting and a little like something Luc might have done if he were a prince. Not because Luc was vain. Luc merely enjoyed attention. He was always teasing and entertaining, and Evangeline wondered if Apollo was like that, too. What if Apollo really was her chance at a happily ever after, and she ran away because of a different what-if named Jacks?

Just thinking about him made the scars on her wrist pulse. But Jacks hadn't even noticed her.

"What else have you heard about Lord Jacks?" Evangeline asked. "Do you know why he's here? Is he some sort of ambassador?"

"Oh no." The other girl laughed. "I'm fairly certain Jacks would be an abominable ambassador. I've actually heard he ended up exiled here after getting into some nasty business with a princess from the south."

It was said the way most people relayed common gossip, light and dry like sparkling wine. But the words gave Evangeline a feeling that was far from bubbly. She recalled how the empress's sister, Donatella, had said something about causing a war if she ran into someone in the North. Could she have been referring to Jacks? Was this why Jacks had left the south, because he'd done something terrible to Princess Donatella? "Do you know exactly what happened?"

"It's hard to really know with the way that stories get twisted around here, but I think the southern princess was the person who broke his heart."

Evangeline tried to hide her skepticism. Princess Donatella was lovely and lively—Evangeline had liked her a great deal.

But it was difficult to imagine any human girl breaking any part of Jacks.

"LaLa! Evangeline!" a voice interrupted from behind. "I've been wanting to talk to you two."

Evangeline shot a glance over her shoulder.

A man who looked almost exactly like Kutlass Knightlinger, dressed in the same black leather and lace-lined shirt, was striding toward them.

"Kristof Knightlinger," provided the other girl—who must have been the same LaLa that had been mentioned in *The Daily Rumor*. And it seemed they were both about to be mentioned again.

Evangeline's stomach turned. Though Kristof had been kind to her in his writings today, she didn't want to do another interview where all her words were twisted until she sounded like a penniless orphan scheming for a prince, or worse. "Is it too late to run?" she whispered.

"Probably, but I could always say I scared you away by threatening to chop off all your pretty pink hair if you talked to Apollo tonight."

At first, Evangeline thought the other girl was joking, but that fiendish smile was back.

"Don't look so horrified. I merely like being in the papers." LaLa lifted her glass as if toasting herself. "Despite what *The Daily Rumor* says, I already know I have no real chance of marrying the prince, but I enjoy being a part of the fun. Now scamper off before I can't save you."

"I'll owe you," Evangeline promised before hurrying away.

Her skirt was too fitted to go very fast, and she wasn't really paying attention to where she was going. She was so caught up in the threat that was Kristof that she'd forgotten about her other threat until she nearly smacked into his solid chest.

Evangeline tried to infuse her spine with mettle as her heart raced with panic.

She'd seen Jacks from far away, but this close was different. He was a thousand cuts happening all at once. Devastation made of hair as blue as dark ocean waves, and lips sharp as cracked glass that would delightedly cut her.

How could no one else here know that he was a Fate?

Evangeline could feel his inhuman gaze gliding over her skin, making her blood rush as his eyes raked over every silver line wrapping tightly around her hips, her waist, her chest. He stopped—gaze drifting off before meeting her eyes as if she wasn't worth the effort to continue.

"What are you doing here?" He tossed a burnished gold apple with one hand. "I thought you'd already be married to that boy you *loved* by now." His voice was even more pitiless than the last time she'd heard it, when he'd left her in the garden as she'd turned to stone.

Evangeline tried to stop herself from lashing out. She needed to get away from Jacks, not fight with him. But something about his lack of care made her care even more.

"You ruined any chances I might have had with Luc when you had him mauled by a wolf!"

Jacks stopped tossing his apple. "I've never had anyone mauled by a wolf. That's incredibly messy." He studied her for a beat, eyes finally meeting hers.

Before, she'd sworn his eyes were bright, arresting blue, but tonight they were pale blue ice and utterly soulless. One look and Evangeline felt cold all over. She thought about LaLa's claim that he'd had his heart broken by Princess Donatella. But Jacks's next words destroyed any sympathy Evangeline might have had for him.

"So you didn't really love him in the end. Were the scars all over, or did you just take a look at his mutilated face and run the other direction?"

Evangeline scowled. Jacks would think the worst of her, because that's probably what he would have done. But she didn't correct him. She'd rather have the Fate think badly of her than know that he'd been right and the real reason she wasn't with Luc was because he had chosen Marisol, and then he'd disappeared. But Evangeline wasn't going to dwell on that. She'd come here to forget about Luc, to find a new happy ending, and she planned to do just that, hopefully with a very different prince from the one standing before her. "I'd rather not discuss this with you, and I think they're calling everyone for dinner—"

"Oh no, Little Fox. We have unfinished business." Jacks dropped his apple and took her neck, cupping her pulse with his cold palm.

"Jacks—" Evangeline gasped. "What are you doing?" And what had he just called her?

His other hand slid into her hair, mussing her curls. The touch was inappropriate and intimate as the too-familiar nickname he'd just given her. She could feel her chances at happily ever after slipping further away as she heard the party chatter shifting to whispers. A hundred tongues all suddenly talking about the scandalous way Jacks was holding her right under the prince's balcony. "Jacks, I told you I'd kiss three other people, not you."

"Then why aren't you pulling away?" he taunted.

"I can't fight you—you're a Fate."

"Liar. I'm not hurting you or kissing you." He moved the hand at her neck to toy with her racing pulse, softly dragging his fingers up and down over the frantic *beat-beat-beat*, making her heart pound even faster. "I think this excites you."

"You're delusional!" Evangeline finally pulled away. Her heart was racing, but it wasn't from excitement, she was sure. Although, maybe, there was just a tiny hint of it, but she couldn't fathom why.

Jacks laughed under his breath. "Relax, Little Fox. I'm not trying to ruin you." He stole her wrist and tugged her closer in a mockery of a dance.

She stepped back, and he stalked forward until her thighs met the hard table. "What are you doing, Jacks?"

"I'm trying to make you more interesting." He leaned in closer. He didn't touch her anywhere other than her wrist, but someone watching from afar might have thought they were on the verge of kissing from the intentional way he angled his body and canted his head. Only Evangeline could see that his eyes were dead. "Earlier, you were just a minor threat, one that people imagined might disappear if they chose not to look your way. But now that I've noticed you, there will be no disappearing."

"You think too highly of yourself," Evangeline hissed.

But people were definitely watching. At least half the eyes of the party were on them. From her peripheral vision, she could see that Kristof Knightlinger had taken out a pen and started jotting things in a notebook.

"If you're lucky," Jacks murmured, "Apollo is watching, too, and he's already jealous."

"I don't want to make him jealous."

"You should. It will make your job so much easier, since Apollo is the first person I want you to kiss."

In one of his preternaturally quick moves, Jacks dropped her wrist, pulled a jeweled dagger from his boot, and pricked the tip of his ring finger. Dark red blood glittered with impossible flecks of gold.

Evangeline tried to lean away, but he moved faster. He brought his hand up to her mouth and marked the seam of her lips with the blood. Metallic and sweet. Incredibly sweet. She wanted to hate the taste, but it was more like a feeling than a flavor. It was the last perfect moment before a dream ends, drops of sunshine falling like rain, lost wishes that had been found. Evangeline wanted to lick—

"No." Jacks lifted his hand quickly, closing her lips with his fingers. "Don't lick it, you need to let the blood sink into your lips or the magic won't work."

Evangeline's euphoria turned to cold, slick dread. When she'd made the deal with Jacks, she'd been nervous about kissing strangers—it had never occurred to her that her kiss could actually hurt them, that Jacks might paint her lips with blood and infect her with his magic.

"What did you do?" she asked. "What will happen if I kiss Prince Apollo?"

"When," Jacks corrected flatly. "If you don't kiss Prince Apollo before tonight's party is over, you'll die. Which would be a shame, since there are much better ways to go." Jacks's unfeeling eyes dropped to the mouth he'd just painted with his blood.

Then he strolled back toward the rest of the party.

14

Evangeline didn't know if time was like magic and worked differently in the North. But she would have bet her life that it started moving faster the instant Jacks strode away.

Dinner took place at an elaborate table encircling the phoenix tree. It was set with pewter goblets and honeycomb candles shaped like castles, and beside each plate were wooden figurines of tiny dragons all displaying names. Jacks's name had been placed beside hers. He didn't show up, but his chair was perpetually full of curious nobles—the Prince of Hearts had apparently been correct about his attention doing wonders for her popularity.

Everyone was friendly in an I'm-only-talking-to-you-because-someone-else-made-you-look-important sort of way. Evangeline heard a lot of *what a pretty color of hair, it was just like that princess*—of course no one could remember *that princess's* name or which prince she'd been married to, but almost everyone remarked on it. Evangeline tried her best to be attentive and polite, but all she could think about was kissing Prince Apollo. A part of her was slightly intrigued by the idea—who wouldn't want to kiss a prince?—but she didn't want it like this. She didn't want to force herself on him, and she didn't know why Jacks would want her to do this either. What did Jacks have to gain by this?

She wanted to hope that Jacks had been joking earlier when he'd said she would die if she didn't kiss Apollo tonight. But Jacks seemed like the sort who was probably deadly serious even when he sounded as if he were joking. And given the way he'd left her when she'd turned to stone, Evangeline couldn't imagine he'd care if she also turned into a corpse. Or—

"Excuse me, Miss Fox." A palace servant tapped her on the shoulder. "It's your time to die."

Evangeline startled but quickly realized that wasn't what the servant said. He'd actually said, *It's your time to meet the prince.* But in that moment, it felt like the same thing. She'd come up with only one theory why Jacks would want her to kiss Prince Apollo—Jacks wanted to kill him. Jacks had painted her lips with his blood, giving her some of his magic, and his magic was in his fatal kiss—which possibly meant her kiss was now deadly.

Her breathing quickened as she approached the steps circling the phoenix tree.

Jacks inclined against the stair rail at the base, head tipped back, blue hair tumbling over one eye, and giving the impression he'd been waiting for her half the night. "Ready, pet?"

He held out his arm like a gentleman.

Evangeline ignored his offer, but leaned closely enough to whisper as they started up the winding steps. "Why do you want me to kiss Prince Apollo? Is this going to kill him?"

Jacks side-eyed her. "I appreciate a good imagination, but use it when you kiss the prince, not when you think about what the consequences might be."

"I'm not going to kiss him unless you tell me why you want this."

"If I wanted you to kill the prince, I wouldn't be climbing these stairs with you." Jacks wrapped the arm she'd just refused around hers. His gray shirtsleeves were rolled up, so she could feel his skin, cool and rock solid. The contact covered Evangeline's flesh with tiny unwanted bumps as he brought her closer to his side. "There's no point in having another person commit murder if you're going to be in the room with them."

Evangeline wanted to keep arguing, but Jacks made a convincing point, which was a small relief. Evangeline really didn't want to die, but she also knew that she couldn't kiss the prince if she thought that it would hurt him. "If that's not your plan, what will happen when I kiss him?"

"Depends on how good at it you are." Jacks's chilling gaze went to her lips. "You do know how to kiss, right?"

"Of course I know how to kiss!" She yanked her arm free.

Jacks frowned. "Why are you so angry? Do you think the prince is ugly?"

"This is not about how he looks. I don't want to hurt him."

"I'm not going to tell you to trust me, because that's a terrible idea. But you can believe that if I were going to have you harm Apollo, I wouldn't be around when it happened."

The air turned redolent with the thick scents of balsam and wood as they reached the top of the steps. Above them, tawny and gold leaves rustled, and Evangeline spied at least half a dozen guards in matching tawny-and-gold tunics sitting on the branches that formed the roof of Prince Apollo's balcony suite.

She darted Jacks a panicked look.

"Don't worry," he whispered. "No one is going to shoot you with an arrow for kissing the prince."

But *something* would happen when she kissed the prince. Evangeline should have tried harder to get out of this. She thought about trying now.

Prince Apollo was standing at his balcony rail, his back to Evangeline as he looked out on the scene below. But then he had to go and turn around.

He was tall, but not as impossibly attractive as Jacks.

Apollo's face was more interesting than classically handsome. He possessed a slightly crooked aquiline nose, which might have overwhelmed another person's face, but all his features were a bit intense, from his thick dark brows to his deep-set eyes. His skin was olive. His hair was heavy and dark and cropped closer to better show off his strong features. He'd forsaken the antler crown, but he was still obviously a prince. Utterly commanding as he leaned one elbow against his balcony rail and gave her a smile that said, *I might not be the most handsome person in the room, but you know that you're intrigued.*

Evangeline couldn't deny that she was. Though she wasn't sure if it was because he was simply a prince or if it was the way he managed to smolder at her. Luc had tried to smolder, but he'd never quite mastered it like Apollo—his eyes were deep brown and amber with tiny flecks of glowing bronze.

"You're drooling a little," said Jacks, and he didn't even have the decency to be quiet about it.

Apollo laughed, darkly musical and absolutely mortifying.

Evangeline considered hiding, but the balcony's lounge was too low to the ground to duck under, and the prince was already striding closer.

"Don't feel bad, Miss Fox." Apollo finished closing the short distance between them. She was surprised that despite the intensity of his face, he appeared to be only a couple of years older than she was. Nineteen or twenty-one at the most. "I think our mutual friend is jealous. He's been telling me for weeks how gorgeous you are, but until now, I thought he was exaggerating."

"Jacks told you about me?" Evangeline didn't even try to hide her shock as her gaze shot to Jacks.

He'd already left her side to wander the small suite, and he met her stare with the same taciturn disinterest he'd shown everyone else when he'd first entered the party. If looks could speak, this one would have told her, *Just because I said it doesn't mean I believe it.*

But he had said it. She didn't care if he'd meant it or not. Jacks had acted as if her appearance that night was a surprise and all of this was unplanned, yet he'd known she was coming for weeks. He'd been setting up this kiss. Why? What did Jacks want? What would happen when she kissed the prince?

Evangeline couldn't come up with a single new theory. She tried, but it was growing difficult to focus. Something felt very wrong with her heart. It had beat faster when she'd first met with Jacks, but now it was almost as if she had two hearts—her pulse was going wild, pounding painfully in her chest as if it might soon run out of beats.

When she looked back at Apollo, her heart began pounding, *Kiss him. Kiss him. Kiss him.*

It didn't feel like a desire so much as a need.

Apollo was close enough that she could just take one step, tilt her head, and then press her lips to his. And yet, Evangeline couldn't, not until she'd at least tried to learn why Jacks had set this up.

Instead, she managed to say, "How well do you know Jacks?"

The prince's bold smile faltered. "I'm not accustomed to ladies coming up here and asking about other young men."

"Please don't mistake my question as interest in Jacks. I'm not interested in Jacks—"

"And yet you keep saying his name." Apollo's words came

out as teasing, but his gaze was not. He looked at her the way that Evangeline imagined portraits stared at people when their backs were turned. No more magnetic smiles. No smoldering brown eyes. It was the gazing equivalent to pulling out a knife and tilting it so it caught the light.

It seemed Prince Apollo's confidence had its limits, or maybe he wasn't that confident after all. Perhaps he and Jacks were more rivals than friends? Maybe that's what this was somehow about? Evangeline still didn't understand what Jacks was really after or what this kiss would do, but she didn't have time to figure it out.

Her heart wasn't just pounding now, it was hurting, straining. Jacks said she'd die if she didn't kiss the prince by the end of the party, and although it wasn't quite over, Evangeline knew this meeting was. Apollo's posture was shifting; he was about to dismiss her. Soon he would turn and walk away without another word. If she was going to kiss him, this was her final chance.

Evangeline lifted her eyes, seeking his lips, but somehow her gaze drifted over Apollo's broad shoulder to Jacks. He leaned against the balcony rail flicking a silver coin with his long fingers.

The corner of his lips twitched ever so slightly, and he continued flipping the coin as he silently mouthed: *Will she kiss him? Will she die? Will she kiss him? Will she die?*

Evangeline would die eventually, but it would not be tonight.

She focused her gaze on Apollo. Spots danced around the

edges of her vision, turning the prince into a blur of dread. "I'm sorry."

She reached up to cup his cheek, rose on the tips of her toes, and brought her lips to his.

Apollo didn't move.

Evangeline's heart skipped. This wasn't working. Apollo was going to pull away and call down the guards, who would surely shoot her or arrest her or drag her from the party by her hair. But instead of shoving her off, Apollo's lips pressed against hers, as if this were how he frequently finished conversations with his female guests, and it wasn't surprising in the least that Evangeline had wanted a goodbye kiss.

His warm hand went to her hip, pulling her close as his tongue slid inside her mouth, stroking hers as if giving her a goodbye gift.

Her cheeks heated at the thought that Jacks was watching the embrace, but she didn't pull away. Apollo's technique was better than Luc's, who was always a little too eager. And yet everything about the way Apollo touched her felt more practiced than passionate.

Fleetingly, she wondered if he'd had painters capture the way he kissed, if that's why everything felt a little like a performance.

His fingers gently squeezed her backside, digging in just enough to make her feel a jolt of surprise. "Goodbye, Miss Fox," he murmured against her mouth. "I liked this more than

I expected." He started to pull away, but then his grip around her hip tightened.

And he was kissing her again. His lips greedily slanted over hers as his other hand slid into her hair, destroying the curls Jacks had already mussed as Apollo plundered her mouth. He tasted like lust, and night, and something lost that should have stayed that way.

Evangeline's heart became a drum, beating harder and faster as he pressed in closer. There were layers of clothing between them, but she could feel the heat coming off him. More heat than she'd ever felt with Luc. It was almost too hot, too hungry. Apollo burned like a fire that consumed instead of warmed. And yet there must have been a part of her that wanted to be scorched, or at the very least singed.

She wrapped both hands around his neck.

Apollo's mouth left her lips and dropped to her throat, trailing kiss after kiss down to her—

A cold hand clamped on her shoulder and wrenched her free of the prince's grasp. "I think it's time we go."

Jacks pulled her toward the balcony stairs with supernatural swiftness. One moment, Apollo was all Evangeline could feel, and then she was tucked underneath Jacks's hard arm, pressed close to his cool side as he ushered her toward the steps.

"Keep moving," he commanded. His eyes had changed from soulless ice to the sharpest blue. "Don't look back."

But of course she had to look back. She had to see what she'd done.

Apollo remained rooted in place—thankfully, he was still very much alive—but he didn't look quite right. He stood in the middle of the suite, intently tracing his lips with his finger. Tracing and tracing as if the act could reveal to him what had just happened, why his control had slipped with a girl whom he'd thought to turn away.

Evangeline wondered the same thing.

Apollo caught her eyes. There were still embers of heat in his gaze, but she couldn't tell if it looked like passion or anger.

"Jacks, what did you do?" she whispered.

"It's not what I did, Little Fox. It's what you've done. And tomorrow night, you get to do even more."

15

The Daily Rumor

(continued from page 1)

Evangeline Fox has lived up to her reputation as a wild card!

While most of the ladies present at last night's dinner were preening for Prince Apollo, Evangeline Fox was seen wrapped in a wicked embrace with one of the prince's close friends.

I'm not sure if Evangeline heard the rumors that Apollo might not choose a bride and therefore set her sights on someone else, or if she merely hopes to make Apollo jealous. But it seems I was right when I called her a risky bet.

16

Evangeline tried to ignore the nearby whispers and the ever-present pit in her stomach. She was in the Magnificent North, home to her mother's fairytales, surrounded by fantastic sights, and about to enjoy a dragon-roasted apple. But the murmurs were like villains at the end of a story. They just wouldn't die.

"It's her, I'd bet a dragon on it."

"I read she kissed one of Prince Apollo's friends last night—"

"Ignore them," Marisol said, shooting an impressively scathing look over her shoulder toward the line of muttering people behind them. "They should know better to believe everything they read in the scandal sheets," she added loudly.

And Evangeline loved her just a little then. Although much of what Kristof had written about her in that morning's paper was accurate. She had been seen in a scandalous position with

Jacks, he'd held her as if he'd wanted to kiss her, backed her up to a table, and then he'd painted her lips with his blood. Her stomach tumbled just at the thought.

Marisol had believed it all a lie as soon as she'd seen the paper, and Evangeline hadn't corrected her. She'd simply tried to forget about it as she and Marisol had set off that morning to make the most of their time in the North by exploring a variety of spire shops. Her stepsister had sought Northern recipes and rare ingredients, while Evangeline had wanted to find the impossible things mentioned in her mother's stories—like the dragon-roasted sticky apples they were waiting for now.

Her mother used to say that dragon fire made everything sweeter. Dragon-roasted apples were supposed to taste like true love. The queue for the treats was so intense, Evangeline and Marisol had been waiting nearly half an hour. All the while locals still chattered about Evangeline and her rumored kiss with Apollo's friend.

A part of Evangeline was relieved that this was today's gossip. It could have been so much worse. She'd left the party last night fearing her real kiss with Apollo had placed him under a spell. She'd been half-terrified she'd open the scandal sheets this morning and learn that something terrible had befallen the prince. But the only thing that had changed was her reputation, and the things people were saying weren't even terrible. Still, they unnerved her.

She wondered again what Jacks was really after. She'd sensed a rivalry between Jacks and Apollo. But she didn't understand why she would fit into that. Jacks had to want something from her kiss. But what?

Evangeline rubbed her wrist. Only two broken heart scars remained. The third had disappeared after last night's kiss. Jacks had hinted he'd collect on another kiss tonight. But first he'd have to catch her, and this evening, she did not plan on being caught by him.

Avoiding the first night of Nocte Neverending was not an option. This morning's rumors might have diminished her chances with Apollo, but Evangeline couldn't bring herself to believe they'd ruined them. Something had happened between them when they'd kissed. The only question was, had the heat in Evangeline's kiss with Apollo been a part of Jacks's plan, or something he hadn't expected? Evangeline didn't know the answer, but she hoped to find Apollo again tonight and figure it out before Jacks found her.

"Salt! Get your salts and seasonings!" cried a vendor, pushing a heavy cart across the cobbled street. "Imported from the mines of the Glacial North. I've got sweet, I've got savory—"

"Evangeline, would you hate me if I left you alone?" Marisol gave the salt cart a longing look. "I'd love to take home some Glacial spices."

"Go ahead," Evangeline said. "I'll grab you an apple."

"That's all right. I don't actually want one." Marisol was already backing away.

Evangeline sensed that although her stepsister was enjoying the North, she hadn't quite gotten over her discomfort with all the little dragons.

"I'm still full from the goblin tarts we bought earlier," said Marisol. "But you enjoy one! I'll meet you back at the inn."

Before Evangeline could argue, she was at the front of the line and Marisol was on her way to making her dreams of imported salts come true.

"Here ya go, miss." The vendor handed Evangeline a smoldering apple on a stick, still sparking with dragon fire.

The outside of the apple was the caramelized color of gold, and when it finally cooled enough for Evangeline to bite, it tasted like hot, searing sweetness and Jacks—

Evangeline closed her eyes and cursed.

Suddenly, she didn't want an apple anymore.

A pair of stray speckled blue dragons flew about her hands, and she gave them her treat as she started toward the climbing spire shops.

It was growing close to sunset. The sky was a haze of violet light and gray clouds that told her it was probably time to head back to her room at the Mermaid and the Pearls and dress for Nocte Neverending. But Evangeline wasn't quite ready.

She and Marisol must have visited at least fifty stores that day, and there was one shop she was keen to revisit. Lost and Found Stories & Other Distinguishables. The storefront was tired and covered in faded paint, but when Evangeline had peered in the dusty window, she'd spied a book that had never found its way to a shelf outside of the North. *The Ballad of the Archer and the Fox.*

The story her mother used to tell her, the story that she'd never heard the true ending of. It had been such a thrill to spy the book until she'd also noticed the sign:

Gone for Lunching
Should Return Eventually

Unfortunately, it seemed *eventually* hadn't happened yet. Evangeline now found the sign still nestled against the scuffed door. She knocked, in case the proprietor had returned and had just forgotten to remove the sign, unlock the door, and light any of the lamps. "Hello?"

"The door's not going to answer back."

Evangeline startled as she turned, noticing how dark the spires had grown, how night had overtaken twilight quicker than it should have. The soldier looming before her looked more shadow than man. She might have run if she'd not recognized the punishing bronze helm concealing all but his eyes, his waves of hair, and his striking cheekbones. He was the soldier who'd been guarding the arch last night. He'd jokingly called her a princess and charmed her just a bit. But tonight he didn't seem so charming.

"Are you following me?" she asked.

"Why would I be following you? You planning on stealing

the fairytales?" He said it as if it were a joke. But there was a predatory spark lighting his eyes, as if he wished that she were there to steal something so that she'd give chase and then he'd be able to hunt her down.

Covertly, Evangeline cast a look behind him, to see if anyone else was nearby.

The soldier made a soft *tut tut tut*. "If you're searching for someone to help you, you won't find it here. And you shouldn't be here either." His tone was unexpectedly concerned. But his presence continued to unsettle her as he lifted his head toward all the steps that now ended in errant banks of fog and the narrow bridges that disappeared into dark instead of storefronts. "The spires are not safe at night. Most of the people who get lost here don't ever get found." He nodded toward the door behind Evangeline.

On instinct, she turned. It was almost too dark to read the sign now, but she could see that it was weathered and worn, and from that moment on, she'd always wonder if it had been sitting on that door longer than just a day.

When she turned back around, the mysterious soldier was gone. And she did not wait to see if he would return. She hurried back along the closest set of downward steps, tripping on her skirts more than once.

She'd have sworn she'd been in the spire for less than an hour, but more time must have passed. The gas lamps had come alive, and the streets were thick with coaches, all carrying people to Nocte Neverending.

Marisol was already dressed when Evangeline finally reached their room at the inn.

Since Marisol loved baking, the empress had sent her a frothy gown with a scalloped, off-the-shoulder neckline and a double skirt that looked as if it were made of one layer of honey and one of pink sugar.

"You look as if you were born to attend balls," Evangeline said.

Marisol beamed, appearing more radiant than she ever did in the south. "I've already set your gown out on the bed."

"Thank you." Evangeline would have hugged her stepsister, but she didn't want to wrinkle her. "I'll only be a minute."

Evangeline tried to hurry. There wasn't time to curl her hair with hot tongs, but she managed a quick waterfall braid, which she decorated with the silken flowers she'd purchased earlier that day.

Tonight, her dress was designed to mimic the flower trellis in her mother's garden, where she'd saved Marisol's wedding. But no one looking at her would think about that. The base of Evangeline's bodice was nude silk, making her look as if she were wrapped in nothing but the crisscrossing cream-velvet ribbons that went to her hips. There, pastel flowers began to appear, growing denser until every inch of her lower skirts were covered in a brilliant clash of silk violets, jeweled peonies, tulle lilies, curling vines, and sprays of gold crawling paisleys.

"I'm ready—" Evangeline froze as she reached the sitting

room, where Marisol stood statue-still as she clutched a sheet of black-and-white newsprint.

"Someone shoved it under the door," Marisol squeaked, her white-knuckled fingers crinkling the edge of the page before Evangeline managed to extract it.

17

The Daily Rumor

BEWARE THE CURSED BRIDE

By Kristof Knightlinger

I heard a rumor that Valenda's famous Sweetheart Savior, Evangeline Fox, isn't the only well-known lady in attendance from the south. It seems that Valenda's infamous Cursed Bride, Marisol Tourmaline, is here to ruin Nocte Neverending.

Evangeline's chance at winning the prince might currently be on rocky ground after last night's display. But it seems the Cursed Bride is so jealous of her, she's determined to crush any chance Miss Fox has of marrying the prince and becoming our next queen. My sources spotted Miss Tourmaline in several high-tiered spell shops and witcheries today searching for ways to turn Evangeline back into stone.

The Cursed Bride will no doubt be at tonight's festivities. If you see her, beware—

(continued on page 3 ¾)

Evangeline crumpled the sheet.

Why would someone give them this? She couldn't believe a person had been cruel enough to shove this under the door, and she was disappointed that the lies about Marisol had followed her here.

Marisol had gone off alone earlier that day. But even if she had wandered into a spell shop, as Kristof had claimed, it must have been purely accidental; she'd probably thought it was a store for exotic recipes. Marisol had been too terrified of magic to even step inside the curiosity shop back home.

"I can't go now." Marisol wilted onto a clamshell chair and started tugging at the buttons of her long silk gloves.

"Stop." Evangeline grabbed one of her stepsister's hands before she destroyed the sheathes entirely. "Everyone knows the scandal sheets aren't true. You said as much earlier today. People read them for entertainment, not reality."

"But people still believe them," Marisol moaned. "There's always a piece of truth in those pages, enough to make the lies seem real. If I show up tonight, like the paper says, people will take it as evidence that everything else printed about me is correct."

"Then prove them wrong. *When* you show up tonight and I'm not turned to stone, people will know you're not out to curse me."

"What if something else terrible happens, and I get blamed for it?"

Evangeline wanted to tell her stepsister that she didn't have to worry about disasters befalling Nocte Neverending. But it wasn't a promise within her power to make, especially since Jacks would be there tonight.

"In the off chance a catastrophe does strike this evening, you're more likely to get blamed for it if you don't make an appearance. It's easy to villainize a shadow, but anyone who meets you will see how thoughtful and kind and gentle you are."

"I think you have too much faith in me." Marisol sniffled. "Just let me stay here. You look as if you should be a princess in that gown, and if you take me with you, I really will ruin your remaining chances of becoming one. No one wants a cursed sister-in-law."

"You are not cursed. And I'm not concerned about what happens with the prince." Evangeline was tempted to say that after what had been printed about her in the scandal sheets that morning, her chances with Apollo were slim. But Evangeline didn't actually believe that. She believed that she still had a chance with Apollo, or another wonderful happily ever after, and she believed the same for Marisol. Marisol was not the rumors and the lies that had been printed about her. And if she and Marisol showed up tonight together, smiling and happy and untouched by fear, people would be able to see the truth and stop believing all the lies.

"One of the reasons I agreed to this trip was because I wanted to bring you. I thought if you came here with me, you might find your confidence again and possibly a fresh start.

Nocte Neverending isn't just a ball, it's a chance at stepping into a fairytale, at changing the course of your life and finding opportunities that some people search their whole lives for. This is a night to reinvent who you are, to dazzle everyone you see, and prove to anyone foolish enough to believe the gossip pages that you're not so jealous of me you've set up a magical plan to turn me back to stone."

"When you say it like that, I sound rather powerful." Marisol sniffled again, but it inched closer to a laugh this time.

She was starting to change her mind. Her voice was lighter, and the right sort of pink was coloring her cheeks. "I'll go with you to the ball, but only because it's really silly of me to think I could ruin your chances when you look so beautiful. I bet you'll receive five proposals before the prince picks his first dance partner tonight." Marisol reached out with a gloved finger to touch one of the hundreds of silk flowers clinging to Evangeline's skirts.

"Oh no!" The cloth violet in Marisol's fingers tore free of the dress. "I'm so sorry—"

"It's all right," Evangeline said. "You don't notice it." There were so many flowers on the gown, a person would have to look very close to see one missing violet. And yet, Evangeline's eyes went back to the damaged bit of skirt where the flower had been. There were five purple threads poking out. Thick threads that should not have broken easily.

Could Marisol have torn the flower on purpose?

Evangeline tried to ignore the wretched thought as soon

as she had it. This doubt was just Kristof's article getting to her, resurfacing some of the suspicions that Evangeline had tried to leave behind in the south. Marisol wasn't her enemy. Marisol would never intentionally hurt Evangeline or damage her gown.

But Evangeline's doubt was like salt. There wasn't much of it, yet it seemed to alter the taste of her thoughts. She recalled the way Marisol's face had shadowed yesterday after reading the scandal sheet that declared Evangeline one of the favorites. And Marisol had gone off alone earlier that day. Evangeline still wanted to believe that if she'd stepped into a spell shop it had been an accident, but what if Marisol was a little jealous? What if that jealousy had tempted her into a store despite her fears of magic?

"Ladies, I hope you're both ready. It's time to go!" Frangelica's friendly voice accompanied two cheery knocks on their door.

A minute later, they were all heading out of the inn, walking toward a carriage pulled by four black horses as shadowy as the bits of doubt still clinging to Evangeline. She really didn't want to think the worst of her stepsister, but the truth was, Kristof's observations of Evangeline last night had been mostly accurate, so it was possible he'd written the truth about Marisol as well.

"I'm so sorry." Evangeline stopped before stepping inside the coach. If Kristof was right about Marisol, Evangeline needed to know before reaching the ball. "I seem to have left my gloves in the room. I'll be right back."

Evangeline raced back into the inn and up the stairs in a blur of flowered skirts that weren't meant for running. She needed to be quick, and she needed to make sure that her stepsister didn't come after her. If she was wrong about Marisol—and Evangeline was almost certain she was wrong—she didn't want Marisol to catch her searching her room for spell books. If her stepsister knew that even Evangeline had been tempted to believe what Kristof Knightlinger had written, she'd be crushed.

Once back in the suite, Evangeline walked past the sitting room table where she'd intentionally left her gloves and marched directly into Marisol's room. The hearth fire was still burning, casting warm light over a bedroom exactly like Evangeline's, save for the scents of vanilla and cream that always clung to her stepsister.

There were books, but they didn't appear to be of a magical nature. The only tomes Evangeline found were in a pile of pretty pink cooking volumes on the nightstand.

Recipes of the Ancient North: Translated for the First Time
 in Five Hundred Years
How to Bake Like a Pastry Goblin
Sweet Salt: The Secret Ingredient to Everything

"Evangeline—"

Time stopped at the sound of Marisol's voice.

Evangeline spun around to find her stepsister standing in the rounded doorway.

It seemed everyone was sneaking up on her today. No—Evangeline quickly corrected herself. Marisol hadn't been sneaking. Evangeline had just been too busy suspecting her of witchcraft to hear her walk inside.

"What are you doing in my room?" A tiny, confused line curled like a comma between Marisol's petite brows.

"I'm sorry—I—" Evangeline cast a frantic look about the room as she searched for something to say. "Did you happen to see my gloves?"

"Are these the ones you're looking for?" Marisol held up a pair of cream gloves. "They were on the table in the sitting room."

"Silly me." Evangeline laughed, but the sound must have been as unconvincing as Marisol's earlier smile.

The comma between Marisol's brows turned into something like a question mark. Now she was the one experiencing doubts. The look didn't last long, but it was enough to remind Evangeline that she was concealing more than just her reasons for entering this room. Unlike her stepsister, Evangeline did have secrets to hide. And if Marisol ever found out what they were, they'd hurt her far more than any of Evangeline's fleeting doubts—and they would absolutely ruin Evangeline.

18

Last night, when Evangeline had exited her coach, there'd only been clouds of fog and the arch. But now, as she and Marisol arrived at the first night of Nocte Never-ending, Evangeline barely saw tonight's new arch in between all the brawny ax jugglers and the acrobats doing flips on the backs of armored horses.

Music from minstrels in puffed sleeves floated around white-haired men dressed as sorcerers with long silver robes and large cauldrons full of everything from sparkling cranberry cider to foaming luck punch. Although more people appeared to be drawn to the woman beside them who sold gem-bright bottles of Fortuna's Fantastically Flavored Water.

Evangeline wasn't even inside the official ball, and already it felt like the start of a Northern fairytale, when everything was just a little more than it should have been. The happiness felt touchable, the magic in the air was tasteable, and the sky seemed a little closer to earth. If Evangeline had a dagger, she imagined she could have sliced into that night as if it were a cake and stolen a piece of it to take a bite of all the wondrous dark.

Despite some flinching at a few of the slightly magical things, Marisol appeared to be enjoying herself as well. All the earlier awkwardness and doubt was gone, and Evangeline hoped that nothing would happen tonight that might bring any of it back.

Evangeline cast a quick look about for Jacks, relieved that he wasn't in the throng of people waiting to enter tonight's arch. Not that she could picture the Fate lining up for anything. If Jacks was there, he was probably already inside the actual ball, leaning indolently against a tree and dropping apple cores on the dance floor.

The dormant butterflies inside Evangeline began to stir. She really hoped to see Apollo tonight before Jacks spotted her.

There were only two more people ahead of her and Marisol now. Both were girls, dressed in gowns with bodices formed of leather book spines and skirts made of love story pages.

Evangeline heard the first bookish girl giggle as she approached the entry. It was a different arch from last night. The words *May You Find Your Ever After* were boldly emblazoned across the top, and instead of a variety of symbols, there were two figures carved on either side—a groom and a bride. The groom's strong face was that of Prince Apollo, but the bride carving shifted so that she looked like whichever girl was about to step through next.

Evangeline could see pure delight on the faces of the girls who entered just ahead. Hope spilled through them, clear as light filtering through glass, as they no doubt imagined that Prince Apollo might choose one of them.

Perhaps that was the true magic of Nocte Neverending—not the minstrels or magicians, but the incredible hope that everyone found. There was something fantastically bewitching about the idea that a person's destiny could change in one single, wondrous night. And Evangeline felt that power as she stepped underneath the arch.

Warm, curling wind brushed her skin, and she heard a rasping whisper: *We've been waiting for you . . .*

Another step and the air turned spicy with the scent of mulled cider and possibilities. Evangeline tensed as she caught a whiff of apples. But the remaining two scars on her wrist weren't burning, and she didn't see any painfully handsome young men with waves of dark blue hair.

This evening, she was in the ballroom of an aged stone castle, and Evangeline had never seen so much wonder on so many faces. Most of the ladies—and several of the gentlemen—appeared to be looking upward toward the tapestries and decorative balconies in search of Crown Prince Apollo, but just as many seemed to be losing themselves in the party, literally.

All around the great room were tall doors with words like

chance, mystery, or *adventure* burned into the center of them. Evangeline watched as a pair of young men holding hands slid through the door labeled *love.* Just beyond them, a girl with straw-gold hair topped off with a paper crown took a shuddering breath as she stepped onto an enormous black-and-white checkered board. There were other players on the board as well, all either wearing bishops' cloaks over their colorful doublets, gloves of pawns, or other identifying markers as they played a type of chess where the human pieces kissed one another instead of kicking each other from the board.

Evangeline felt a curious blush as she watched a pawn lock lips with a knight dressed in black leather.

"The game is really rather fun," said LaLa, appearing by her side in a spark of shimmering gold and orange. Her strapless gown matched the dragon fire tattoos on her brown arms, and the slit of her skirt flickered around her exposed leg as if it were aflame.

"You look marvelous!" Evangeline said. "Candles all over the world must be jealous of you tonight."

"Thank you! I've always wanted to make fire envious." LaLa executed a little bow. "Now back to the game," she continued, nodding toward the chessboard where the young woman in the paper crown was now standing on her tiptoes to kiss a tall young man in a black bishop's cape. The girl's hands were trembling, but her cheeks were flushed with excitement, and the boy appeared almost as nervous. He stood completely still.

Evangeline couldn't tell if he was afraid of the kiss or afraid that the girl might change her mind.

Evangeline wondered if the game might be good for her stepsister, if it might improve her confidence, but it seemed Marisol hadn't come through the arch yet.

"Are you going to give it a go?" LaLa asked.

"I'm not sure I even understand how it works," Evangeline said.

"There aren't many rules to kissing chess. Each side has one player who moves their human pieces about, coupling them up with opposing pieces until a pair decides that they'd rather kiss each other than anyone else."

"Is there a winner to the game, or is it just an excuse to make people kiss?" asked Evangeline.

"Does it matter? It's kissing . . ." LaLa finished on a sigh.

"Why don't you play?" Evangeline asked.

"I would, but I can't help but try for a chance with Prince Apollo." She made a show of lifting her face toward an empty inner balcony and affecting a longing stare.

Evangeline stole a moment to look about the ball, scanning for a different prince. It would have been easy to get swept up in the gala, but she needed to stay vigilant. The scars on her wrist still weren't burning, but she found it hard to believe Jacks wasn't there yet. Everyone else seemed to be. The castle was filling with people faster than water could pour into a sinking ship.

Maybe she just had to search harder. Her eyes darted from gentleman to gentleman, cutting across the bustling ballroom until—Jacks.

Her heart leaped over a beat.

He was near the edge of the dance floor, lounging on a winged chaise and tossing a black apple with one hand.

He looked like a bad decision some unfortunate person was about to make. His midnight-blue hair was unruly, and his sable half cape was rakishly crooked, hanging over one shoulder to reveal a partially buttoned, smoke-gray doublet.

He dropped his apple, shoved off the lounge, and approached a nearby girl in a frothy pink sugar gown. A girl that bore an unnerving resemblance to Marisol.

Evangeline blinked as if the vision before her might shift and she'd see Jacks conversing with the pink fountain of punch instead. But the girl was definitely Marisol, and she was beaming so brightly, Evangeline could see her glow from across the ballroom.

When had she even entered the party?

Evangeline assumed that the arch would have deposited her stepsister the exact same place it had brought her, but either it hadn't, or Marisol had crossed the ball after failing to see Evangeline and then walked straight over to Jacks like an innocent bunny hopping into the path of a hunter.

Evangeline watched in horror as Marisol smiled coyly. Jacks turned his mouth into a tempting twist, and he gave her a gentlemanly bow. Last night, Jacks had ignored everyone except for Evangeline and Apollo, but now it appeared he was asking Marisol to dance.

Something uncomfortable tightened around Evangeline's rib cage. Of all the young men that her stepsister could have met at Nocte Neverending, why did it have to be Jacks? Evangeline doubted it was purely a coincidence. She still had no idea of what sort of game Jacks was really playing, but she couldn't let him drag poor Marisol into it as well. She'd already been through enough.

Evangeline needed to stay far away from Jacks, but she couldn't let him hurt her stepsister.

She turned to LaLa, about to excuse herself from their conversation, when the entire castle began to rumble and quake. The stone balconies filled with trumpeters in crisp copper coats.

Every head looked up. Then every head turned as a door labeled *Majesty* flew open, and Crown Prince Apollo Acadian rode into the ballroom on a thundering golden horse.

"Your Highness!"

"Prince Apollo!"

"I love you!" people shouted as if they couldn't help themselves.

Apollo looked less refined than he had last night. He'd forsaken his crown, and he didn't even wear a doublet. Tonight, he was dressed like a hunter in rugged boots, wood-brown breeches, an open-collared shirt, and a fur vest decorated with crisscrossing leather straps, which held a golden bow and a quiver of arrows against his straight back.

He could have been the Archer from Evangeline's favorite Northern tale, *The Ballad of the Archer and the Fox*. As he searched the ballroom, his eyes burned with the same level of intensity they'd had when he'd watched her leave the balcony last night.

"I think he wants to find you!" LaLa threaded her arm through Evangeline's, tugging her close as she squealed, "You must be his Fox."

"Is that a good thing or a bad thing?" Evangeline murmured. "I still don't know how that story ends."

"No one can remember how that story ends, but it doesn't matter. He's not trying to re-create the tale. He's making a romantic gesture!"

Evangeline was at a loss for words. Apollo must have been truly affected by last night's kiss.

She was tempted to look for the Prince of Hearts again, to see what he was thinking of this. But she couldn't take her eyes off the prince of the Magnificent North as his golden steed slowed its steps and stopped in the center of the ballroom.

"Good evening," Apollo announced, his deep voice quieting the sound of his subjects. "I know I'm supposed to ask five ladies to dance, but I can't hold up this full tradition tonight." He paused, looking briefly torn. "This evening, I only wish to dance with one girl." His dark eyes finally locked onto Evangeline's. And they were ravenous.

Her legs turned to custard.

Ladies all over the ballroom swooned.

"I knew it," LaLa crowed.

"You're right beside me. He could be looking at you," Evangeline whispered.

"We both know he's not."

More swooning followed.

Apollo dismounted his horse, and then he was striding her way with unabashed confidence, the way only someone who'd never been rejected could move.

Evangeline unlinked her arm from LaLa's and stepped forward to curtsy.

But Apollo stopped a few feet away and reached his arm out for another girl, a very pretty girl in a champagne gown with a shining curtain of straight black hair, topped off with a slender golden circlet.

Evangeline could have turned back into stone.

LaLa quickly took her arm once again and drew Evangeline back into the crowd, but it wasn't before several laughs and snickers reached her ears.

"Did you see her?"

"She thought the prince was coming for her."

"Ignore them," LaLa said. "I thought he was going to ask you, too."

"I suppose I've learned my lesson about listening to what they say in the gossip pages," Evangeline tried to joke, hoping to staunch any embarrassed tears.

LaLa was kind enough to laugh, but the sound of it was quickly drowned out by all the other voices. The pretty girl

Apollo had chosen was the favored Princess Serendipity Skystead, and it seemed everyone else had expected it.

"I knew it."

"She's so sophisticated—and she speaks twenty-seven languages."

"Her family has such good blood. There really was no other choice."

With every comment, Evangeline felt herself grow smaller, shrinking inside the crowd as she tried to drown the voices and quell her growing humiliation.

It was silly. She didn't even know him. She shouldn't have felt so rejected, but it was hard to believe that this was how her adventure in the North would end, before it had even truly begun. And a part of her really had thought that their kiss had left an impression, but maybe it had just left an imprint on her.

Evangeline extracted herself from LaLa's arm. "I think I'm going to go get some punch." Maybe enough to drown in.

Self-pity doesn't look good on you, Little Fox.

Evangeline froze.

The low voice in her head sounded a lot like Jacks's. She had never heard his voice like this. She wasn't even certain it was really Jacks—it could have been her imagination—but it did remind her of Marisol and that Evangeline still needed to rescue her.

Evangeline scanned the ball for her stepsister and Jacks. But she didn't find them. The crowd had grown too dense.

"Excuse me," a deep voice said from right behind her. It

sounded a lot like Prince Apollo. But Evangeline knew better than to give into another mortifying delusion and imagine he'd find her hiding by the punch fountain.

"Evangeline . . ." The voice was a little louder and followed by a brush of soft leather gloves touching her bare shoulder. "Would you mind turning around? Lovely as your back is, I'd much rather see your face."

Evangeline hazarded a cautious look over her shoulder.

Prince Apollo stood right behind her. She swore he was taller than she remembered as he looked down on her with a smile that was a little shier than the one he'd flashed the ballroom. Just a subtle tilt of lips.

"Hello again." His voice went hoarse and soft. "You look like a dream come true."

Something inside Evangeline melted. But after her earlier assumption, she was afraid to imagine why he might be standing there, staring at her as if he really meant what he'd just said.

A small crowd started to form around them, and no one even pretended that they weren't watching.

Attempting to ignore them, Evangeline finished turning and managed to give the prince a steady curtsy. "It's a pleasure to see you again, Your Highness."

"I'd hoped that after last night, you'd just call me Apollo." He took her hand to his lips and gave her knuckles a careful, almost reverent kiss.

The touch sent soft shivers across Evangeline's skin, but it was the look in his burning bronze eyes that stole her breath.

She could feel her legs going boneless again, and her hope imagining things it shouldn't.

She waited for him to say more, but the prince only swallowed. Several times. His Adam's apple bobbed up and down. He appeared to be at a loss for words. Nervous. She was making the prince who'd draped himself across a balcony last night nervous.

It gave her the burst of courage to say, "I thought you were only asking one lady to dance tonight."

"I wouldn't have even done that, but there's an unfortunate law that says I had to ask at least one girl." Another swallow, and then his voice went a little deeper. "I would have asked you, but I knew that if you were in my arms, I wouldn't get through an entire dance before doing this."

Apollo went down on one knee.

Evangeline abruptly forgot how to breathe.

He could not be doing what she thought he was doing. She didn't even want to think about what she thought he was doing—not after how she'd made such a fool of herself earlier.

But all the people she was trying to ignore must have been thinking the thing that she was trying not to think. The whispers were starting up again, and the crowd around them was increasing, caging Evangeline and Apollo in a circle of ball gowns, silk doublets, and shocked faces. She could see Marisol among them, grinning widely. Evangeline didn't spy Jacks, but she wondered what he was thinking of this. She still didn't know what he wanted. But if Jacks was Apollo's rival, she couldn't have imagined Jacks had planned for this turn.

Apollo took both of her hands in his warm grip. "I want you, Evangeline Fox. I want to write ballads for you on the walls of Wolf Hall and carve your name on my heart with swords. I want you to be my wife and my princess and my queen. Marry me, Evangeline, and let me give you everything."

He brought her hand to his lips again, and this time, when he looked down at Evangeline, it was as if the rest of the celebration didn't exist. His eyes said a thousand exquisite words. But the word she felt most was *wanted*. Apollo wanted her more than anyone else in the ballroom.

No one had ever looked at Evangeline like this before—not even Luc. In fact, she couldn't even picture Luc anymore. All she could see was the longing and the hope and the hint of fear swirling in Apollo's expression, as if she might say *no*. But how could she?

For the first time in months, her heart felt full to bursting.

And so when Evangeline opened her mouth, she said exactly what most girls would say if a royal prince were to propose to them in the middle of an enchanted ballroom. "Yes."

19

As soon as Evangeline squeaked out her yes, the trumpeters above released a brassy cheer, the entire ballroom exploded in clapping, and Apollo gallantly scooped her up into his arms.

His grin was pure joy. He might have kissed her then. His eyelids were lowering, and his mouth was descending. And—

Evangeline tried to lean into it.

She was in the midst of a fairytale, floating in the middle of an enchanted castle, held by a prince who'd just chosen her over every other girl there.

But the way he was leaning in to kiss her made her think of another kiss. Of their last kiss, a kiss Jacks had orchestrated for reasons she still didn't understand. But what if *this* was why he'd wanted it? Evangeline didn't want to think this proposal was Jacks's doing. He couldn't have known one kiss would do this—and she didn't understand why he'd even want this engagement. It was much easier and more pleasant to imagine this wasn't what Jacks wanted at all.

Weren't Fates supposed to be jealous?

"Are you all right?" Apollo's warm hand climbed her spine, rubbing softly as if coaxing her back from a bad dream. "You haven't changed your mind, have you?"

Evangeline took a timorous breath.

She still didn't see Jacks among the crowd, but it felt as if the entire kingdom were watching. The whole ballroom had gathered, surrounding them with looks that ranged from awe to envy.

"You're overwhelmed." Apollo's fingers found her chin and tilted her face toward his. "I'm sorry, my heart. I wish I could have made this private for us. But there will be plenty of secluded moments for us in the future." He dipped his head, preparing once more to lean in for his kiss.

Evangeline just needed to close her eyes and kiss him back. This was her chance at a happy ending. And when she pushed aside her doubts, Evangeline did feel happy. This was what she'd been hoping for, the entire reason that she'd come to the North. She'd wanted a love story like her parents'. She'd wished for love at first, and a chance with the prince, and now it was hers.

She lifted her head toward his.

Apollo's mouth met hers before she could close her eyes. Last night, he'd hesitated at first, but tonight, he took with the confidence of a prince who'd never been denied. His lips were soft, but the kiss was flowers falling off her gown and shocked sighs from the crowd as he picked her up and spun her around and kissed and kissed and kissed her. It was the sort of kiss fever dreams were made of, a blur of dizzying heat and touch, and this time Jacks didn't end it. Evangeline didn't feel his cold hand on her shoulder or hear his voice in her head, telling her she'd made a mistake. All she heard were Apollo's murmurs promising her everything she could ever want was about to be hers.

20

After Evangeline's father died, she would have dreams where both her parents were still alive. In her dreams, Evangeline would be in the curiosity shop, standing by the door, looking out the window and waiting for them to arrive. She'd see them coming down the street, walking hand in hand, and just as they would reach the door—right as she was about to hear their voices and feel their arms wrap her in a hug—Evangeline would wake. She'd always try desperately to fall back to sleep, to just have one more dreaming minute.

Those dreams had been the best part of her day. But now, waking up felt like dreaming. A little unreal and a little wonderful. Evangeline didn't dare open her eyes at first. For so long, her hope had been as fragile as a soap bubble, and she was still afraid that hope might burst. She was nervous she might find herself all alone inside her cramped room in Valenda.

But Valenda was half a world away, and soon she would never be alone again.

When Evangeline opened her eyes, she was still in Valorfell in her treasure chest bed at the Mermaid and the Pearls, and she was engaged to a prince!

Evangeline couldn't stop the smile that spread across her face or the giggle that erupted from her chest.

"Oh, good! You're finally awake." Marisol popped her head through the door, bringing a rush of warmth from the fire in the neighboring room. She must have been up for some time. She was already dressed in a gown the color of peaches and cream, her light brown hair was neatly plaited, and she held two cups of steaming tea that filled Evangeline's chilly suite with the scent of winterberries and white mint. Both girls had been so exhausted by the time they'd finally left the ball, they'd practically collapsed inside of their carriage and then slept the entire way back to the inn.

"You are an angel." Evangeline sat up and gratefully accepted the hot cup of tea.

"I can't believe you managed to sleep in with all that happened last night," Marisol gushed, but her voice was unnaturally high, and her fingers wobbled as she held her tea.

Evangeline imagined that although her stepsister appeared excited, this couldn't have been easy for Marisol—watching Evangeline find her happy ending while people still called her the Cursed Bride.

All because of Evangeline.

And now Evangeline had even more to lose if she told Marisol the truth about her dealings with Jacks.

The tea suddenly tasted like tears and salt as Marisol continued, "Prince Apollo's proposal was the most romantic thing I've ever seen—it might actually be the most romantic thing that has ever happened. You're going to be such a beautiful bride!"

"Thank you," Evangeline said softly. "But we don't have to keep talking about this."

Marisol frowned. "Evangeline, you don't have to hide your happiness to make me feel better. You're going to be a princess. No one deserves it more than you. And you were right about last night. Not a single person recognized me as the Cursed Bride. Someone even asked me to dance. Did you see him?" Marisol bit down on her lip and smiled. "I think he was the handsomest person there—next to Prince Apollo, of course. He had dark blue hair, and bright blue eyes, and the most mysterious smile. His name is Jacks, and I'm already hoping—"

"No!"

Marisol reared back as if she'd been slapped.

Evangeline cringed. She hadn't meant for that to come out so harshly, but she had to protect her stepsister from Jacks. "Sorry, I've just heard dangerous things about him."

Marisol's lips pinched tight. "I know the gossip sheets have been kind to you, but I would think that you'd still know better than to listen to the nasty words whispered behind other people's backs."

"You're right, I shouldn't listen to gossip, but it's not just the rumors." Evangeline tried to say it softer this time. "I've met Jacks. He was at the party that first night, and . . . I don't think he's good for you."

Marisol snorted. "We can't all marry a prince, Evangeline. Some of us are lucky to get any attention at all."

"Marisol, I—"

"No, I'm sorry," Marisol rushed out, color draining from her face. "I shouldn't have said that. That's my mother—not me."

"It's all right," Evangeline said.

"No, it's not." Marisol looked down at the splash of tea she'd just spilled on her skirts, and her eyes turned watery. But Evangeline knew she wasn't really crying about the skirts. It was never about the skirts.

Marisol perched on the edge of the bed, still staring at the stain on her gown, her voice far away. "Did you ever play that game as a child—the one where there's a circle of chairs, and when the music stops playing you have to find a chair to sit in? But there's never enough chairs for everyone, so one person is always left without a seat in the circle and then tossed out of the game. That's how I feel, as if I missed my chance at a chair and now I've been tossed out of the game."

Marisol took a shuddering breath, and Evangeline felt it in her own chest.

It had always been a challenge for her to connect with Marisol. They'd never seemed to have much in common, except for Luc, which was a terrible thing to share. But that was starting to feel like the least of what they'd shared.

Looking at Marisol now reminded Evangeline of those months when she had worked in the bookshop and started to feel like one of the forgotten novels on the used shelves in the back, overlooked and alone. But Evangeline always had hope that things would change. She might have lost her parents, but she'd had their memories to hold on to, their stories and their words of encouragement. But all Marisol had was her mother, who had torn her down instead of building her up.

Evangeline set aside her tea, slid across her bed, and hugged Marisol tightly. She wasn't sure if she'd ever be brave enough to talk to her about Luc or confess what had really happened the day of Marisol's wedding. But she would keep trying to find ways to make it up to Marisol, especially now that Apollo was putting Evangeline in an ideal position to do so.

Her stepsister leaned in with a sniff. "I'm sorry for spoiling your happiness."

"You didn't ruin anything, and you haven't been thrown out of any game. In the North, they don't even play that musical chair game. I've heard it was outlawed and replaced with kissing chess." As she said it, Evangeline could already imagine setting up a match for her stepsister with every eligible young man in the land. Maybe she'd ask Apollo for help?

It might not remedy everything, but it was a start. Evangeline was about to suggest the idea when the pounding on the door began.

Both girls quickly leaped from the bed, spilling more tea, on the carpet this time. The only person who'd ever knocked on their door was Frangelica, but her taps were gentle. These sounded almost angry.

Evangeline only spared a second to throw on a wool robe before rushing to the door. The wood shook as she approached.

"Evangeline!" Apollo's voice cried from the other side. "Evangeline, are you there?"

"Open it!" Marisol urged her. *It's the prince,* she mouthed, as if his title meant his actions weren't at all alarming.

"Evangeline, if you're there, please let me in," Apollo begged. His voice held shades of fear and desperation.

She undid the latch. "Apollo, what's—" Evangeline was cut off as the door opened and Apollo poured into the girls' suite, along with a dozen royal soldiers.

"My heart, you're safe!" He took her in his arms. His chest was heaving. His eyes were shadowed in circles. "I was so worried. I should never have let you leave last night."

"What's wrong?" she asked.

The closest soldier held out a damp gossip sheet for Evangeline to read as Apollo loosened his hold on her.

The Daily Rumor

ENGAGED!

By Kristof Knightlinger

In the past, Nocte Neverending has gone on for weeks, sometimes months. But last night, mere minutes after arriving at the ball, Crown Prince Apollo Acadian proposed to everyone's favorite southern wild card, Evangeline Fox.

Apollo sealed his engagement with a kiss that left half the ladies weeping. Although a number of girls appeared more angry than sad. After the prince abandoned Princess Serendipity Skystead in the middle of the dance floor to propose to his new bride, the princess looked practically murderous. The Cursed Bride didn't succeed in harming Evangeline, but as she watched Apollo's declaration of love, it looked as if she wanted to turn the couple to stone. And one of my keen-eared sources also heard the matriarch of House Fortuna mutter to her granddaughter, Thessaly, how the prince should have chosen her, but that it wasn't too late to change that.

Prince Apollo and Miss Evangeline Fox are to wed in one week's time—that is, if no one harms her first.

Evangeline stopped reading.

"What does it say?" Marisol asked.

"Just another twist on the truth," Evangeline hedged. She took the paper from the guard and tossed it into the fire before Marisol could see any of the words about her. "Kristof is just trying to sell papers by saying I'm in danger.

"No one has tried to harm me," she assured Apollo. "After

you and I parted last night, Marisol and I returned here, and I slept until a bit ago."

Apollo cracked his jaw and turned to Marisol as if just now noticing her presence.

Marisol tensed. She had stopped her tears, but she still looked small and fragile. And Evangeline knew she needed to jump in before more mistakes could be made. "My stepsister would never hurt me. In fact, is it possible to stop Mr. Knightlinger and *The Daily Rumor* from printing more nasty lies about her?"

Apollo looked as if he wanted to object; clearly, he believed the gossip. But the longer Evangeline looked up at him, the more he seemed to soften. The lines around his eyes disappeared, and the hard set of his broad shoulders relaxed. "Would that make you happy?"

"It would."

"Then I'll make sure it's done. But I need a favor from you." Apollo cupped Evangeline's cheek.

She still wasn't used to the feel of him. His hand was larger than Luc's, but his touch was more tender. And yet the look in his deep-set eyes was entirely haunted. "I want you to move into Wolf Hall with me, where you'll be safe from any type of threat."

21

The Daily Rumor

SIX DAYS LEFT!

By Kristof Knightlinger

No one knows exactly how old Wolf Hall is, but legend says Wolfric Valor built every spiraling tower, every vaulted great room, every torturous dungeon, every romantic courtyard, and every secret passage of the castle as a wedding gift to his bride, Honora.

I don't know what Apollo plans to give Miss Evangeline Fox as a wedding gift, but I've heard a rumor that he's already moved her into Wolf Hall, along with her stepsister, Marisol Tourmaline, who my sources have assured me is not cursed, nor does she have plans to curse her stepsister. In fact, it has been confirmed that Miss Tourmaline will remain here as part of the Northern royal court after the wedding.

(continued on page 7)

22

The following day, the wedding dress arrived. Evangeline found it spread across her princess bed inside of Wolf Hall. The gown was white and gold, and it came with a pair of feathered wings that touched the ground.

My dearest Evangeline,
 I saw this gown and thought of you, because you are an angel.
 Forever your truest love,
 Apollo

23

The day after that, Evangeline woke to find her bathtub full of what looked like glittering pirate treasure.

My dearest Evangeline,
  You deserve to be bathed in jewels.

        Forever your truest love,
        Apollo

24

Then it was an entire stable of horses. The steeds were gleaming white and adorned with rose-gold saddles, the same color as Evangeline's hair.

"So that we can ride off into the sunset together," Apollo said. His eyes were full of adoration as his hands reached for hers.

Her fingers felt small in his warm grip, but they were starting to fit. "You don't have to give me so many gifts," she said.

"I'd give you the world if I could. The moon, the stars, and all the suns in the universe. Anything for you, my heart."

25

It was all more than Evangeline could have dreamed of or wished for. The last few days had been a whirlwind of wonderful. Her royal suite was covered in colorful gowns and flowers and gifts. Even Empress Scarlett had sent her something, though how the small package had been delivered so quickly, Evangeline had no clue.

Evangeline should have felt flutters. She should have felt excited and romanced and loved. Apollo was generous and attentive and terribly kind to her. And she definitely felt something whenever she thought about him, but it was sadly not butterflies. It was closer to the unsettled feeling she'd had after making a deal with Jacks, or the wrongness she'd felt when she'd learned that Luc had proposed to Marisol.

Something was not as it should have been.

Evangeline sat on the wide hearth in front of her fire, set

down the little red box that Empress Scarlett had sent, and then picked up that morning's gossip sheet.

The Daily Rumor

THREE DAYS LEFT!

By Kristof Knightlinger

Evangeline Fox and Prince Apollo Acadian have been engaged less than one week, and already people are writing songs about them and saying that theirs is the greatest love story the Magnificent North has ever seen. The rumors floating around are extravagant—especially for a prince who once said he wouldn't choose a bride at all—and I'm thrilled to report that I was able to acquire a rare interview with the crown prince to find out which tales about him are true.

Kristof: Everyone has been talking about you and Evangeline Fox. People say you're entirely bewitched. I've heard you stand in the courtyard outside her window each night to serenade her, you've declared her birthday a holiday, and you're having all one hundred and twenty-two of your

portraits redone so they include her likeness as well. Is there any truth to these stories?

Prince Apollo: I've done much more than that, Mr. Knightlinger. (With a proud smile, the prince unbuttoned half his shirt and spread it apart to reveal a vibrant tattoo of a pair of swords curved to form a heart that contained one name: Evangeline.)

Kristof: That's quite impressive, Your Highness.

Prince Apollo: I know.

Kristof: No one who sees the two of you together could doubt that you're in love. But I've heard whispers that the Council of Great Houses is unhappy you chose not only a foreign bride but one without a prominent family. People are saying they wish to have the wedding called off and that's why you've set such a quick date for it.

Prince Apollo: That is a complete lie. Even if there were truth to it, nothing could keep me from the love of my life.

Kristof: What about your brother, Prince Tiberius? There are rumors that you two had another falling-out this week. They say he's backed the Great Houses' objection to your choice of bride because he wants to stop your marriage and keep you from becoming king.

Prince Apollo: That's absolutely false. My brother couldn't be happier for me.

Kristof: Then why are people saying he's disappeared again?

Prince Apollo: Some people forget Tiberius is also a prince and has royal duties of his own.

Prince Apollo wouldn't tell me if Prince Tiberius will be at the wedding, but our interview did confirm the rumors that the crown prince has been completely bewitched by his bride-to-be. I've never seen anyone as in love as Prince Apollo.

If only Evangeline could believe that Apollo was truly in love. But sadly, she feared that Kristof was right when he called her betrothed *bewitched*.

Evangeline believed in love at first sight, she believed in love like her parents', love like a story. It was the love she'd come to the North hoping to find. But Apollo's actions and feelings were so extreme, they didn't feel like love. They felt more like an obsession—hungry and outrageous, and if she were being entirely honest, a little unsettling. Like the work of a spell or a curse—or a Fate.

Like Jacks.

When Apollo had proposed, Evangeline had been so quick to think that Jacks wouldn't want this marriage. But now she couldn't help but wonder: Was Jacks the reason for this engagement? What if the blood Jacks had painted on her lips had infused her kiss with magic that made Apollo fall in *love* with her?

She didn't want to think it. She didn't want to think about Jacks at all. But if Jacks had done something to Apollo, it would explain Apollo's over-the-top behavior.

Why, though?

Evangeline couldn't figure out any reason why Jacks would want her and Apollo to wed, which gave her hope that her theory was wrong and that Apollo really was experiencing a dramatic love at first sight.

She wanted so badly to believe that they were going to have a fairytale love story. She wanted it all to be real. She didn't want to go back to Agnes's house or return to Valenda, where the best part of her day was when a bell rang outside of a bookstore door.

And then there was Marisol. Her stepsister might have started here on rocky footing, but Apollo had made it so the papers wouldn't say another bad word about her, and if Evangeline married Apollo, she'd be able to do even more for Marisol.

But if Apollo was under a spell from Jacks, none of that mattered, and none of this was real.

Evangeline slowly rolled up the gossip sheet, knowing what she had to do, but dreading it all the same.

She didn't want to see Jacks again. But if he had done this to Apollo, then she needed to convince him to undo it.

Evangeline doubted that the Prince of Hearts would lift a

curse from Apollo out of the goodness of his heart, since all the stories said Jacks's heart didn't even beat. But Evangeline didn't need to rely on Jacks's goodness. If Jacks wanted her to marry the prince, that gave her leverage, and she planned to use it to get Jacks to fix Prince Apollo, and then to find out exactly what Jacks wanted.

Dear Jacks,

I was hoping you and I might have a chance to speak about an important matter that requires your immediate assistance. If you are not otherwise engaged, I would be very happy to run into you while I take my morning walk in the wood just outside Wolf Hall tomorrow.

Sincerely,

Evangeline Fox

26

Little Fox,

If you were attempting to write a
threatening or persuasive letter, your skills
need work. I don't have time to tromp
through the woods with you, but you can
meet me at noon tomorrow in Capricorn
Alley.

—J

Dear Jacks,

I was only trying to be polite. It's a shame you're so used to conniving and deception that you cannot even recognize courtesy. Not all of us rely on manipulation to get what we want.

Sincerely,

Evangeline Fox

Of course Evangeline couldn't send that message, but it had felt good to write it before sneaking out to meet Jacks on the following day.

She'd been a little worried as to how she'd manage it. After the incendiary scandal sheet article about her safety, Apollo had given her a pair of guards to make sure no one hurt her. But he also gave her absolute freedom to do as she wished, and she used that freedom to gain information about Wolf Hall's secret passages. There was one conveniently located in her room that she'd used to make her escape.

Evangeline didn't know if anyone would notice she was gone. But she hoped they wouldn't track her down to the narrow strip of fog and dark that was Capricorn Alley.

She huddled deeper into her fur-lined cape and rubbed her hands together, wishing she'd worn thicker gloves. Away from all the docks and shops, this alley felt like the sort of place a person would only find if they were lost. Snow had fallen across all of Valorfell overnight, but it seemed to have missed this uninviting spot, leaving its grim gray stones untouched. The only door had a ring of skulls emblazed upon it, which made her think the business done here was not the savory sort.

An unmarked black lacquered coach pulled up.

Her heart kicked out several extra beats. She wasn't doing anything illicit or wrong. She was trying to do something right, something noble. But her heart must have felt a threat, for it continued to race as the door swung open and she slipped inside the carriage.

Jacks looked like a debauched stable boy who'd stolen his master's coach. He lounged across one side of the carriage, one scuffed leather boot propped carelessly up on the cushions. A smoke-gray doublet was crumpled on the soft leather seat beside him, leaving him in a linen shirt with rolled-up sleeves and half-done buttons. Evangeline caught a hint of a rough scar on his chest, right as he set his jeweled dagger to a silver apple and began to slice.

"Do you stare at everyone like that, or just me?" Jacks looked up. Vivid blue eyes met hers.

It shouldn't have made her blood rush the way that it did. It wasn't even that much of a gaze, more of an idle glance before he went back to slicing the metallic peel off his apple, filling the air with crisp sweetness.

Evangeline decided to get straight to the point. "I need you to undo whatever you've done to Prince Apollo."

"What's the matter?" *Slice.* "Has he hurt you?"

"No, I don't think Apollo would harm me. He practically worships me—that's the problem. I'm all he thinks about. He gives me bathtubs of jewels and tells me that I'm the only thing he needs."

"I fail to see how that's an issue." Jacks's sullen mouth settled somewhere between a frown and a laugh. "When you first came to my church, you'd lost your love. Now I've given you a new one."

"So this is your doing?"

Jacks's eyes met hers, returning to ice. "Leave, Little Fox. Go back to your prince and your happily ever after, and don't ask me that question again."

In other words: *yes.*

One by one, the tiny bubbles of hope inside of Evangeline broke. *Pop. Pop. Pop.*

She had known it was all too much to be true. She sensed that she was living in an illusion and if she looked closely, she'd see that everything she'd thought was stardust was really just the burning embers of a wicked spell. Apollo didn't love her; for all she knew, he didn't even like her. He'd once said she was his dream come true, but she was really his curse.

"I'm not leaving this carriage until you fix Apollo."

"You want him to fall out of love with you?"

"Apollo doesn't actually love me. What he's feeling isn't real."

"It feels real to him," Jacks drawled. "He's probably happier than he's ever been in his life."

"But life is about more than happiness, Jacks!" She hadn't meant to yell, but the Fate was absolutely maddening. "Don't pretend you've done nothing wrong."

"Wrong and right are so subjective." Jacks sighed. "You say what I've done to Apollo is wrong. I say I've done him a favor, and I'm doing one for you as well. I suggest you take it—marry the prince and let him make you a princess, and then a queen."

"No," Evangeline said. This was not as bad as when Jacks had turned an entire wedding party to stone, but Apollo's condition wasn't something she could live with. She wanted to be someone's love, not their curse. And if Apollo knew what had been done to him, she imagined he wouldn't want to live with it either.

She also didn't believe for a second that this was some sort of favor. Jacks wanted this wedding to happen. She still didn't know why, but he'd gone to a lot of trouble for it.

"Fix Apollo, or I'll call off the wedding."

Jacks smirked. "You're not going to break an engagement with a prince."

"Try me. You didn't believe I'd drink from Poison's goblet either, but I did it."

Jacks clenched his jaw.

She smiled, triumphant.

Then the coach started rumbling ahead.

Evangeline clutched the cushions to keep from falling forward into Jacks's lap. "Wait—where are we going?"

"Your next assignment." Jacks's gaze landed on her wrist, and the two remaining broken heart scars started to burn. *Prick. Prick.* It was like hot teeth digging into her skin.

Evangeline gripped the cushions tighter, suddenly feeling queasy. She was still dealing with the consequences of her last kiss. She wasn't ready for another one. And she was engaged, at least for now.

Jacks's blue eyes twinkled as if he found her worry amusing. "Don't fret, Little Fox. This will be a different sort of kiss. I'm not about to ask you to do something that could put this wedding in jeopardy."

"I already told you. There's not going to be a wedding if you don't fix Apollo."

"If I fix Apollo, there also won't be a wedding."

"Then I guess I'm canceling my engagement."

"Do that, and you'll be the one destroying him, not me." Jacks stabbed his apple with the knife. "If you don't marry Apollo, he'll be more heartbroken than you can imagine. And it will never heal with time, it will only grow and fester. Unless I will it, Apollo will never get over his unrequited love for you. He will spend the rest of his life consumed by it until it eventually destroys him."

Jacks finished with a smile that bordered on downright

cheerful, as if the idea of leaving someone forever broken-hearted put him in a better mood.

He was terrible. There was no other word to describe him—except maybe *heartless* or *depraved* or *rotten*. The way Jacks seemed to enjoy pain was absolutely staggering. The apple in his hand probably possessed more sympathy than he did. This was not the same young man who'd practically bled heartbreak all over the knave of his church. Something inside of him was broken.

LaLa had said there was a rumor that Jacks had been heart-broken by the empress's younger sister. Evangeline hadn't be-lieved it initially. Jacks hadn't appeared sad her first night in Valorfell, just crueler and colder. But maybe that's what heart-break did to Fates? Maybe it didn't leave them hurt and lonely and horribly unhappy. Maybe broken hearts just made Fates even more inhuman. Was that what had happened to Jacks?

"Are you feeling sorry for me?" Jacks laughed, harsh and mocking. "Don't, Little Fox. It would be a mistake for you to tell yourself that I'm not a monster. I'm a Fate, and you are nothing but a tool to me." He brought the tip of his dagger to his mouth and toyed with his lips until he drew several drops of blood.

"If you're trying to scare me—"

"Careful with your threats." Jacks shot across the carriage and pressed the bloody tip of the dagger to the center of her mouth.

Evangeline might have gasped if she'd not feared he'd slip the blade between her lips. His blue eyes were back to bright as he taunted her with the blade, pressing it to her closed mouth until she could taste the disturbing sweetness of his blood.

"The only reason I'm entertaining this conversation is because, as you've realized, I need you to marry Apollo. So, I will give you a wedding gift. I promise to restore the prince and erase all his artificial feelings for you after you marry him."

The coach rocked to a sudden halt. But Jacks didn't move, and neither did Evangeline. She didn't even look out the window to see where they'd stopped. She just kept her gaze on him.

Jacks had backed her into a corner. She had to marry Apollo to save him. And if she saved him—if Jacks erased Apollo's feelings for her *after* they were married—Apollo would surely hate her almost as deeply as he thought he loved her right now.

The only person who'd truly win would be Jacks.

Cautiously, she leaned back until Jacks's knife was no longer at her lips. But she could still taste the sharp of his blade, the cold of the metal, and the sweet of his blood still staining her lips. She felt as if she'd taste it forever. "At least tell me why you want this wedding."

"Just accept the gift. What I want isn't going to hurt anyone."

She eyed the jeweled dagger he'd just pressed to her lips. "I don't think you and I have the same definition of hurt."

"Be thankful for that, Little Fox." Jacks gave her a smile that was all sharp edges. A drop of blood fell from the corner of his mouth, and something godforsaken washed over his expression. "Hurt is what made me."

27

Evangeline's mother once told her that there were five different types of castles in the North. The fortress castle, the enchanted castle, the haunted castle, the ruined castle, and the storybook castle. Evangeline had yet to see all the different types of castles. But she immediately thought the words *storybook castle* as she stepped out of Jacks's carriage and took in the lovely structure before her.

Made of sparkling purple bricks, gabled blue roofs, and pink-lined windows with golden light blazing through, Evangeline imagined this was the place where fairytales were formed. Then she immediately hoped she was wrong, given that Jacks would only ruin whatever was inside.

"Did you bring me here to destroy someone's happily ever after?" she asked.

Jacks glared at the castle, eyes like daggers, as he started down the cobbled path. "You will not find any happy endings here. The matriarch of House Fortuna lives inside these ridiculous walls. She likes to pretend she's a loving storybook grandmother, but she's about as sweet as poison. If you want to get through this visit alive, when you meet the matriarch, you'll kiss her cheek or hand as quickly as possible."

"Why?" Evangeline asked. "What do you want from her?"

Jacks gave her a look that said he couldn't believe she actually thought he would answer.

She didn't, of course, but she had to try. "Will this hurt her?" she pressed.

A frustrated sigh. "Once you've met the matriarch, you won't worry about hurting her."

"But—"

"Little Fox." Jacks brought a cool finger to her mouth, quieting her protests with more gentleness than he'd used in the carriage. As if she could have been tricked by it. "Let's skip the part where we argue about this. I know you don't want to do this. I know you don't want to hurt anyone and that your sensitive human heart is trying to make you feel guilty. But you will follow through with this to fulfill your debt to me, and if you don't, you'll die."

"If I die, I can't marry Prince Apollo."

"Then I'll find another person to do the job. Everyone is replaceable." He stroked her lower lip once before pulling away and striding carelessly down the cobbled path to the house.

She would have loved to have turned and gone the opposite

way. She didn't completely believe she was expendable. But she also couldn't forget the way Jacks had walked away when she'd turned to stone. She might not have fully believed she was replaceable, but she did believe Jacks would allow her to get hurt or worse if it got him what he wanted.

"I now understand why you ignore everyone at parties," Evangeline huffed, practically jogging to catch up with him. "If anyone actually spoke with you, they'd stop whispering about how mysterious you are and talk about how much they can't stand you."

Jacks speared her with a sideways glance. "Meanness doesn't suit you, Little Fox. And I don't ignore everyone. The other night, I had a lovely conversation with your stepsister."

"Stay away from her," Evangeline warned.

"That's funny. I was about to tell you the same thing." Jacks's lips curved like a crescent blade, waiting for her to take the bait. To ask why he'd warned her away. The question was on the tip of her tongue. But Evangeline didn't want to doubt her stepsister again. Marisol was not the one who'd turned a wedding party to stone or bewitched a prince so he would love her. She was a cursed reputation she didn't deserve, and exactly what Evangeline might have been if she'd been raised by Agnes instead of her parents.

"I'm guessing you're ignoring me because you already know she's jealous of you."

"Stop it," Evangeline said. "I will not let you drive a wedge between us."

"The wedge is already there. That girl is not your friend. She might tell herself she wants to be, but she wants what you have even more."

"That's not true!" Evangeline snapped. And she could have kept arguing. She could have continued fighting with Jacks until the end of Time. Luckily for Time, the path to the Fortuna cottage was short, and they'd already reached the door. It was the soft purple of frosted plums, with a cherub-shaped knocker buried in its center.

Jacks took the cherub's ring and gave it two quick raps.

Evangeline swore the knocker frowned, and she understood how it felt.

She wouldn't want to be touched by Jacks either. Not again. Her lips still tingled from where he'd touched her, and if she licked them, she knew she'd taste his blood again. He'd marked her. Now he planned to use her.

Nerves writhed inside her as the door before her opened. She wondered once more at what Jacks really wanted and what her kiss would do to the Fortuna matriarch.

As a servant led her and Jacks inside, she tried to figure out what he could possibly be after. It became immediately clear that the Fortunas were very wealthy. Everything in their storybook castle was twice as large as the items inside of the house where Evangeline had grown up. Even the carpets were thicker, swallowing the heels of her boots with every step. But Evangeline doubted Jacks was simply after wealth.

She watched him closely, specifically his eyes to see if they landed on any particular objects. The servant led them past a line of portraits of people with white-blond hair and painted smiles before finally settling them into a warm sitting room with two crackling marble fireplaces, a polished quartz piano, and a large bay window. There was a charming view of a snow-covered garden, where a fluffy snow cat pounced after a merry blue dragon laughing sparks.

Jacks didn't even glance at the scene or any of the lovely things in the room. He stopped at one of the fireplaces, leaned an elbow against the mantel, and watched her with shameless intent.

Don't worry, Little Fox. You might even enjoy this.

Before she could think too much about how Jacks's lazy voice had made it into her head again, the door to the study swung open.

"I'll give you one minute to get out of here before I let Jupiter and Hadez attack." The older woman, who must have been the Fortuna matriarch, stormed into the room, flanked by a pair of steel-gray dogs that came up to her waist. "It's not their dinner yet, but they're always hungry for the meat of my enemies."

"Tabitha," Jacks sighed, dramatic as his pose. "There's no need for over-the-top threats."

"I assure you, my threats are genuine." One wrinkled hand brushed over the dog to her left, and it bared a set of gleaming teeth. "You now have forty-two seconds. I meant it when I told you that I'd kill this little upstart if I ever crossed her path."

The matriarch's gaze swung over to Evangeline. With two circles of rouge painted on her cheeks and her dusky-lavender dress belted with a hanging gold chain, the older woman looked like a very expensive doll. The type that people had nightmares about coming to life and killing them in their sleep.

"Clearly, the papers have exaggerated your looks," she said. "I can't believe Apollo chose you over my Thessaly. Although after you're out of the picture, I'll make sure he fixes that."

Evangeline wanted to hope the woman was joking. She had to be joking. People who lived in sparkly purple castles didn't threaten to feed guests to their dogs.

Evangeline shot an uneasy look toward Jacks. He glared at the standing clock in the corner, tick-tick-ticking away.

Not joking, then.

"You have eight seconds," said the matriarch.

The dogs both snarled, gray lips pulled back over canine teeth, as their owner toyed with the short fur on their heads.

Evangeline's breathing turned shallow.

She told herself they were only dogs, and it wasn't as if she needed to kiss their muzzles. She just needed to kiss the woman who was petting them.

"What pretty animals you have," chattered Evangeline, heart racing with every word. She moved as if to pet the beasts, but she grabbed the woman's shoulders instead and pressed a kiss to her papery cheek.

The Fortuna matriarch stiffened and squawked, "How dare—"

Her words were cut off by the yip and the bark of the dogs as they both jumped. Strong paws hit Evangeline's torso. She tried to step back, but the hounds—

—were licking her?

One wet tongue smacked a sloppy dog kiss to Evangeline's cheek, while the other lapped her neck affectionately.

Across from her, the Fortuna matriarch now wore a soft smile on her gently lined face, suddenly looking as sweet as her pretty purple castle.

"Jupiter! Hadez!" she commanded. "Stand down, my loves. Leave our precious guest alone."

The dogs obeyed immediately, returning to all four legs.

Then the matriarch was giving Evangeline a hug as warm as fresh-baked cookies and knitted blankets. And for the first time, Evangeline was actually thankful for Jacks's magic, because this was clearly his doing. The kiss had turned the matriarch from Killer Doll into Doting Grandmother.

"Forgive Jupiter and Hadez. They only act naughty like that when they're exceptionally excited to see someone. You'll have to pardon my deplorable behavior as well. I wish I would have known you were visiting today. I'd have had Cook make you some hobgoblin fudge."

Jacks laughed and covered it up with a cough that sounded a lot like *hobgoblin fudge*.

"The fudge is my Thessaly's favorite," the matriarch prattled on. "Have you met her yet? We thought Prince Apollo might actually propose to her, and even though she was rather upset he didn't, I think the two of you would be dear friends. I could send a carriage to have her brought here right now."

"That won't be necessary, Tabitha." Jacks shoved off from the fireplace and sauntered to Evangeline's side with insouciant grace. "I believe what Miss Fox would really love is to see the Fortuna vault."

"No." The older woman's silver head shook, wooden but insistent, as if she didn't want to say no, but something stronger than Jacks's magic compelled her. "I don't let anyone in the vaults. I'm—I'm sorry." Her shoulders sagged, and the lines in her face stood out more starkly as she turned back to Evangeline.

The expression was uncomfortably reminiscent of Apollo. Whenever he thought Evangeline unhappy, it was as if his heart forgot how to beat and the rest of him began to fail along with it.

"I don't like this," Evangeline muttered to Jacks.

"Then help me end it," he whispered. "The sooner I get what I want, the sooner she gets her nasty temperament back."

"There are other places I could take you," the matriarch went on. "What if I give you a tour of the house and show you portraits of all my favorite grandchildren?"

"As interesting as that sounds, Jacks is right." Evangeline felt a pang of guilt for willingly aiding Jacks, but this wouldn't end until he achieved his goal. This was also her chance to figure out what he was after, and why he wanted her to marry Apollo. "I would like to see the vaults."

The Fortuna matriarch gnawed on her lip and squeezed the broken skeleton key dangling around her neck. She didn't want to do this, not even a little. There must have been something very precious—or dangerous—in her vaults. But since this request came directly from Evangeline, the enchanted woman seemed unable to fight it. She was doll-like again, lips forming a jolly smile that was completely at odds with her shaking limbs as she turned and led them toward the vaults.

28

A twist of narrowing halls.

A handful of locked doors.

A passage hidden in a vanity.

A long flight of iron stairs.

A thousand too-quick heartbeats.

And they were almost there. Deep underground, in the bowels of the storybook castle.

It was the sort of place that made Evangeline want to hug her arms to her chest. The damp granite walls were covered in soot-stained sconces, but only a few were lit, and all their flames were too weak to chase the shadows from the corners. It was merely enough light to reveal the lonely arch in the center of the chamber.

Evangeline hugged her arms to her chest.

Since coming to the North, she had seen three other arches.

The enormous Gateway Arch to the North, the symbol-covered arch at Apollo's first party, and the ever-changing arch of brides that had led to Nocte Neverending.

This arch was much plainer, yet it thrummed with a similar power to the others. Covered in dried moss and sepia cobwebs, it looked more gray than blue and it made her think of something that had gone to sleep a long time ago and been intentionally left alone.

"Looks as if I'm not the only one who's been misbehaving." Jacks raised an imperious brow as his gaze swung from the mossy arch to the trembling Fortuna matriarch.

"You can't tell anyone!" the older woman cried, arms flapping at her sides before her hands went to pat the dogs that had stopped following her at some point in their quest. "Evangeline, please don't think poorly of me for having this here."

"Why would I think less of you?"

"Because this arch was supposed to be destroyed." Jacks stopped right in front of the structure and went absolutely still. Evangeline doubted he was even aware of it. No—he most certainly wasn't aware. If he had been, he would have shuttered his features much sooner than he did. Locks of blue hair fell across his forehead, but they didn't hide his eyes. They were wide, broken star-bright, and full of something that looked a lot like hope.

Evangeline felt as if she shouldn't stare so blatantly, but she couldn't turn away. The look in his eyes had softened some of his sharp edges, making Jacks appear more like the Prince of

Hearts she'd imagined before meeting him, all tragically hand-some and heartsick.

They were getting closer to what he wanted. Evangeline only wished she knew what that was.

She scrutinized the sleeping arch again, wondering what made this one different from the others. It took several moments and some squinting to see through the grime, but she found a set of foreign words etched in small letters across the top. A jolt of excitement raced down her spine. Evangeline couldn't read the words, yet somehow she recognized the language.

"Is this the ancient tongue of the Valors?" she asked, flashing back to the beheaded statues that had whispered to her across the sea when she'd first entered this part of the world.

Jacks cocked his head, surprised. "What do you know about the Valors?"

"My mother used to tell me about them." Of course, as Evangeline worked to recall what her mother had said, she couldn't seem to remember much. All she had were hazy images of an ancient royal family who'd had their heads removed. "They're like the Northern equivalent to Fates."

"No—"

"Not at all—"

Both Tabitha and Jacks answered at once.

"The Valors were merely humans," Jacks corrected.

"There was nothing *mere* about them," the matriarch bit back. Her spine straightened, making her look more like the formidable woman Evangeline had first met. "Honora and

Wolfric Valor were the first king and queen of the North, and they were extraordinary rulers."

The matriarch's eyes took on a faraway, glassy look, and Evangeline feared she might not say more, that as with so many other Northern tales, this story was cursed in a way that made people forget. But then the woman went on. "Wolfric Valor was a warrior who could not be bested in battle, and Honora Valor was a gifted healer who could mend or cure almost anyone with life left in them. All their children possessed abilities as well. Their daughter, Vesper, had foresight, their second-eldest son could shift form, and when multiple Valors combined their powers, it was said they could infuse magic into inanimate objects and places."

"Of course," Jacks cut in smoothly, "like all gifted rulers, the Valors became too powerful, and their subjects turned on them. They cut off their heads, and then they went to war against what remained of their magic."

"That wasn't how it happened," the matriarch volleyed back. The words were quick and sure, but then her jaw hung wide as if the next words she wanted to say would not come out. It seemed the story was cursed after all.

Jacks's mouth curved as the matriarch struggled, until she finally looked at Evangeline and found her words again. But she was telling a different part of the story now. "The arches were one of the most incredible things that the Valors created. They can serve as portals to faraway and unreachable places, and as doors they are impenetrable. Once locked, an arch can only be opened with the proper type of key. If a sealed arch is destroyed, there's no finding what's on the other side."

"However," Jacks added, "the main reason the Valors built the arches was so that they could use them to travel anywhere in the North. Some, like this one, may have been given as gifts. But even those have secret back doors built inside them that only the Valors could use, allowing them access to anywhere in possession of an arch."

"Those are lies." The matriarch snorted. "People made up those stories to take away power from the Great Houses. They condemned the arches, requiring they be destroyed, except for the royal ones, because the Valors are gone and they are not returning. You'll see, Evangeline, it's completely harmless." The matriarch stepped closer to the arch and held an upturned palm toward Jacks. "If you wouldn't mind, young man."

"Not at all." Jacks retrieved the jeweled knife he'd used in the carriage and flicked it across the woman's palm.

"By my gifted blood, I seek entry for my friends and myself." The matriarch pressed her bleeding hand to the stone, and it pulsed like a heartbeat. *Throb, throb, throb.* The stones came alive before Evangeline's eyes, turning a shimmering blue touched with green as the dried moss refreshed and dripped with dew.

"See, dear?" The matriarch dropped her bleeding hand, and the arch's empty center filled in with a shining oak door that smelled of fresh-cut wood and ancient magic. "This can only be opened by freely given blood, straight from the hand of the head of House Fortuna."

"Making it impossible to break into," mocked Jacks, right as he opened the newly appeared door.

Evangeline approached, and just like with all the other arches, another rasping whisper came from the stones: *You could have unlocked me as well.*

Evangeline jumped at the words. Then she went corpse-still, surprised and unnerved to see that Jacks was watching her instead of the vault he'd so desperately wanted to enter.

"What is it, Little Fox?" His voice was friendly. She didn't like it, didn't trust it. Jacks was many things, but he was not friendly.

"Nothing." She wasn't even sure it was a lie. The arches probably whispered different things to everyone, and if they didn't, she was not about to let Jacks know they had been talking to her.

Silently, they continued into the vault. She'd expected it to be hiding something illicit or awful, but at first, it looked like a rather strange kitchen. Lots of cauldrons, and bottles and dangling wooden spoons labeled with things like *Only Stir Clockwise* and *Never Use After Dark.*

"Here is my family collection of recipes for our Fantastically Flavored Waters," the matriarch announced, pointing to a wall of thick tomes bound with a variety of ribbons and ropes and a few chains.

Evangeline vigilantly watched Jacks, noting if anything caught his attention. She expected him to be at least mildly intrigued by the shackled volumes. But he didn't spare them more than a cursory glance. Not that she thought he was after a recipe book.

She continued to scrutinize his every move, but he remained unimpressed with all that they passed. His hands stayed in his pockets, and if he stared at anything, it was always fleeting.

When they reached a cupboard of jeweled goblets, Evangeline thought she felt his eyes on her, watching her with more concentration than he'd looked at anything else. But when she turned to check, Jacks was already stalking ahead.

The Prince of Hearts' mouth became more sullen as the matriarch pointed Evangeline toward a shelf of ancient dragon eggs. Then there was the cabinet of pulsing hobgoblin hearts, which made her very grateful the cook hadn't made any fudge.

The items grew more haphazard after that. There were some possibly magic mirrors, ornamental robes, and a series of eerie but appealing framed pictures. But like the rest of the items, none held any interest for Jacks.

"Not having fun?" Evangeline needled.

"I feel as if I'm backstage at a bad magic show," Jacks grumbled.

Evangeline probably should have been pleased Jacks wasn't finding what he wanted. But that also meant that she wasn't finding out what he wanted either.

"Let me help you," Evangeline whispered, hoping to finally coax an answer out of him. "If you tell me what you're looking for, I can try to find it."

Jacks didn't even acknowledge her offer. Completely ignoring Evangeline, he picked up a skull made of emerald and tossed it up and down like an apple, graceful and quick, and a little violently, as if he wanted something to hurt.

Jacks was either too proud to accept her help, or he didn't want her to know what he was after. Regardless, he was clearly becoming tired of the vault. And it could have just been her imagination, but it appeared the magic from her kiss was flagging as well. The matriarch's smile sagged, her shoulders slumped, and she'd stopped bragging about her favorite things. She hadn't even bothered to scold Jacks for tossing around the skull.

If Evangeline wanted to know what Jacks was looking for, she needed to do something.

"Coward," she coughed.

Two sharp eyes slid her way. "What was that?"

"Nothing," Evangeline murmured. "Although . . . now that I think about it, it's rather disappointing that your sinister plan is so weak that telling me one tiny piece could thwart it all."

"Very well, Little Fox." Jacks continued tossing his skull with the ruthless elegance of a young man who'd catch it just as easily as he would let it fall. "If you want to help me, ask your friend the matriarch if you can see her collection of stones."

"You're looking for *stones*?" Evangeline asked.

Jacks gave her one silent shake of his head as if he'd already said too much.

She felt as if he was toying with her. But she'd also come

to believe that even when Jacks played with her, he was being serious.

"Lady Fortuna," Evangeline called. The woman was now a few steps ahead, far enough that Evangeline had to cry out a second time. "Mistress Fortuna!"

"Yes, my dear." She finally turned around. "Is there something you wanted me to show you?"

"I heard you had a collection of stones, and I would love to see it."

"Oh no, my dear, I'm afraid I don't have any . . . *stones.*" The woman's entire countenance shifted as she said the last word. Her mouth started twitch-twitch-twitching, cracking what remained of her adoring expression, until the grandmother façade was gone and the murderous doll was back. "You—it's you—"

"Little Fox." Jacks's voice turned eerily soft. "I think it's time for you to run."

"How did I not see it?" The older woman gasped, staring at Evangeline as if she were the most dangerous one in that vault. "You're the one who will open the Valory Arch."

"Jacks," Evangeline hissed. For all the matriarch's talk about how glorious the arches were, she suddenly looked horrified. "What is she talking about? What is the Valory Arch?"

"Why are you still here?" Jacks took Evangeline's arm and fluidly shoved her behind him.

But he wasn't leaving, and neither was she.

"*You will know her because she will be crowned in rose gold,*" the woman chanted. "*She will be both peasant and princess.*"

"She's mad," Jacks growled. "You need to get out of here now."

Evangeline's heart pounded, urging her to do the same exact thing. *Get out. Get out. Get out.* But she stayed rooted to the spot, listening to the matriarch chant:

"You will know her because she will be crowned in rose gold. She will be both peasant and princess."

Evangeline didn't believe the woman was mad. The words sounded almost prophetic.

"You cannot marry the prince! The Valory Arch can never be opened!" the matriarch cried. Something metallic flashed in her hands. And then she surged forward with an item that looked like a knife.

Evangeline grabbed for the closest object—a framed painting of a cat.

"What are you going to do with that?" Jacks muttered a curse, and then he took the emerald skull and cracked it over the matriarch's head.

She crumpled to the ground in a heap of rumpled lavender.

Evangeline's mouth fell open, though it took her several seconds to form words. "Did you—did you know this was going to happen?"

"You think I wanted her to try to kill you?" Jacks sounded more offended than she would have expected. He dropped the skull, letting it fall to the ground, where it landed beside the matriarch with a loud thud. The woman's chest moved up and down with a slow, unsteady rhythm. She was still breathing, but barely.

"She's not going to tell us anything now." Jacks lowered onto his haunches and leaned closer, lips pressing together.

Something sick twisted in Evangeline's stomach. He was going to kiss the woman—*and kill her.*

"Jacks, stop!" Evangeline grabbed his shoulders. Somehow, she managed to wrench him back, probably due to the livid tone of her voice rather than the force of her trembling hands. She didn't fully understand what had just happened, but she wasn't going to let Jacks make this worse.

"If you kiss her, we are done," Evangeline said. "I'm not going to be involved in any murders."

"We can't leave her like this." His voice was perfectly reasonable and completely unemotional. Killing this woman wouldn't bother him at all. "As soon as she wakes, she'll come after you."

"Why is that, Jacks? What's the Valory Arch? And who does she think I am?"

Jacks pressed his mouth shut and rocked back on his heels, which felt like answer enough. He believed this chant was about her. The room started to spin, all the baubles and uncanny items blurring around her as Evangeline tried to make sense of this latest turn.

You will know her because she will be crowned in rose gold.

She will be both peasant and princess.

Evangeline had the rose-gold hair, she was currently a

peasant, and she would be a princess in two days if she married Prince Apollo.

This must have been why Jacks wanted her and Apollo to marry. Jacks had arranged all of this so she could become the girl in the Fortuna matriarch's chant, who, according to the matriarch, would open up this Valory Arch.

"What's the Valory Arch?" she asked again. "And why was she so afraid that I'll open it? What's inside?"

Jacks slowly brought himself back up to his full towering height, as he looked down on her and drawled, "You don't need to worry about the Valory Arch. All you need to do is marry Prince Apollo."

"I—"

Jacks cupped her cheek, silencing her with one icy touch. "If you wish to break the spell on Apollo, your only option is to marry him. Or do I need to remind you how desperate a broken heart makes you? How it hurts so much that it compelled you to make a deal with a devil like me? Do you really want to call off your wedding and leave Apollo like that—forever in love with someone who will never feel the same way?"

Jacks's eyes took on the same disturbing, godforsaken look from the coach.

"It wasn't that long ago that I saw you in my church, willing to promise me almost anything to make the pain stop. Was that a lie? Or have you already forgotten the way heartbreak rips apart the soul piece by piece, how it turns you into a masochist, making you long for the thing that just eviscerated you until there's nothing left of you to be destroyed?"

His cold fingers dug into her cheek.

She squared her shoulders and pulled away. "Are you still talking about my heartbreak, or about yours?"

Jacks laughed and gave her a smile so sharp it could have sliced a diamond. "You're getting better at the meanness, Little Fox. But you have to have a working heart for it to break. I do not. I can keep Apollo under this spell for eternity. So you can either marry him and save him from a life of misery, or you can try to prevent a dusty prophecy that you don't even understand."

29

Evangeline kept her head turned toward the window, watching the icy glass as the carriage rambled back to Wolf Hall. She acted as if Jacks weren't there, even as she kept replaying his last words. *A dusty prophecy you don't understand.*

Now Evangeline could think of nothing else. She knew most Northern stories were not entirely reliable, but was a prophecy considered a story?

Her mother had never spoken of prophecies. Were they one of those pieces of magic that couldn't leave the North? A prophecy seemed more like its own type of magic than a story. Anything could be turned into a story, but by definition, every part of a prophecy had to be something that would come to pass or it wasn't a true prophecy.

Evangeline would have asked Jacks more about it, but she

didn't want to engage with him anymore. She didn't expect he'd give her any answers anyway.

Jacks had acted as if Evangeline didn't have much of a choice, that her only option was to marry Apollo. But Evangeline rarely believed there was only one option. She believed what her mother had taught her, that every story has the potential for infinite endings.

Although Evangeline couldn't imagine leaving Apollo forever brokenhearted by calling off the engagement now.

But what if Evangeline really was the girl with the rose-gold hair mentioned in this prophecy? And what if marrying Apollo set off a chain of events that would open up this Valory Arch and release something horrific into the world? She didn't know what the arch actually contained, but the Fortuna matriarch left her with the impression it was nothing good.

Evangeline hugged her arms to her chest and continued to stare out the window at the frosty Northern streets.

When the empress had first invited Evangeline here, she had thought this was her chance at stepping into a fairytale, at finding new love and a happily ever after. But now she wondered if it was actually fate manipulating her path. She wished she could talk to Marisol, but that was out of the question.

If either of her parents were still alive, Evangeline tried to imagine what they'd say. They'd probably gently reassure her that her future was determined by her choices, not her destiny. They'd say she was not part of any calamitous prophecy. But since they were the sort of people who would have believed in things like prophecies, they'd have also gone behind her back and looked into it in secret. Which was exactly what Evangeline planned to do.

Wolf Hall was more fortress than storybook castle, with sturdy slate-gray stones, tall towers, and crenelated parapet walls.

Evangeline took an airy breath and pretended that she wasn't sneaking about as she reentered via the same secret passage she'd used earlier. Someone had probably noticed her absence by now, but Evangeline planned to say she'd gotten lost in the vastness of the castle. It was easy enough to do.

Wolf Hall was enormous, filled with stretching corridors and high-ceilinged chambers that fires were always working hard to keep heated. The rooms had all looked similar when Apollo had first given her a tour. Lots of wood and pewter and tufted carpets in rich earthy shades that made her think of damp forests and enchanted Northern gardens.

Thankfully, the castle was also full of helpful little signs with cheery pointing arrows that showed where everything could be found.

Evangeline followed one sign to the Scholar's Wing and the royal library. It was cooler here than everywhere else, void of windows that might let in book-damaging light.

Evangeline softened her steps as she entered, hoping to

go unnoticed as she passed librarians in long white robes and scholars penning on parchments.

Apollo had told her she could visit any part of Wolf Hall, but she didn't want a soul to know what she was looking for, in case it triggered a reaction like the one by the Fortuna matriarch.

You cannot marry the prince! The Valory Arch can never be opened . . .

Evangeline took a shaky breath as she scanned the shelves for any books on arches, the Valors, or prophecies. She didn't really expect to find volumes full of prophecies, and given what the matriarch had said about arches being destroyed, Evangeline was unsurprised there didn't appear to be any books on *Arches of the North,* or *An Arch with a Deadly Secret.* But it did seem peculiar that she couldn't find a single book on the Valors, who had created all the arches.

Evangeline found volumes on botany, puppetry, auctioneering, blacksmithing, and nearly everything else. But not one spine mentioned the Valors.

It made no sense. The Valors were the famed first royal family. There were enormous statues of them just outside the harbor. The capital city, Valorfell, was named after them. There should have been at least one book mentioning them.

The light became fainter and the air thickened with the scent of dust as she ventured deeper into the library, where the shelves grew closer together and the volumes looked more impacted by age.

"Is there something I can help you with, Miss Fox?"

Evangeline startled at the scratchy voice, and she turned to find a diminutive librarian who looked as old as Time.

"Forgive me for frightening you. My name is Nicodemus, and I could not help but notice that you seem to be searching for something." The smile he gave her was framed by a long silver beard with threads of gold that matched the trim on his white robes.

"Thank you, I'm just a little lost," Evangeline hedged, and she almost left it at that. But if she walked out of the library now, she'd be leaving with more questions than she'd come in with. She still didn't think it was wise to ask about the Valory Arch, but maybe she could dance close enough to the subject without raising alarms that might lead to another attack on her life. "I was actually looking for books on your Valors, but I haven't been able to find any."

"I'm afraid that's because you've been looking in the wrong place."

For someone so old, Nicodemus moved swiftly, rapidly disappearing down a nearby hall, giving her only a moment to decide and follow.

She had no reason to hesitate, but clearly she wasn't past her recent experience with the matriarch. No one had ever tried to kill Evangeline before, and it left her feeling as if death was a little too close.

She had to stop herself from turning around several times as Nicodemus guided her deeper into the library, past more bookshelves, broken up by the occasional striking portrait of Apollo. A few steps later, the tiled floors shifted to aged green stones, and the walls changed from shelves of books to a series of curious doors labeled with symbols of weapons and stars and a few other figures she couldn't quite make out.

Finally, Nicodemus stopped in an alcove harboring a rounded door that was branded with the head of a wolf wearing a crown.

"It is believed that every story about the Valors is on the other side of this door," he said. "Unfortunately, no one has been able to open this door since the Age of the Valors."

30

The handbell choir had arrived in the grand courtyard of Wolf Hall the day after Apollo's proposal to Evangeline. They had appeared precisely at noon, clad in heavy red capes to better contrast with the snow that would surely fall soon. There had been 144 members of the choir, one for every hour until the wedding. And every hour, one silently departed.

Tonight there were only twelve ringers left—twelve hours until tomorrow morning's wedding—and then there was the cursed prince who'd joined them.

With a deep breath, Evangeline cracked open a pair of twin doors. Cold brushed against her as she stepped onto her balcony, letting the sweet hum of the bells and the deep sound of Apollo's serenade surround her.

"My love!" he shouted. "What should I sing for you tonight?"

"It's too cold out there for you," she called. "You're going to freeze if you keep this up."

"I would happily freeze for you, my heart."

Evangeline closed her eyes. It was the same thing he said every night, and then every night she stood there watching and listening until the tips of her hair were turned to frost and her breath became ice. Freezing along with Apollo felt like penance for what she'd helped Jacks do to him. It was tempting to do the same thing tonight, to simply stand there and disregard everything that had happened in the Fortuna Vaults, marry Apollo, break the spell, and hope that they could start over. Just because he was cursed didn't mean their story had to be cursed.

But, no matter how much Evangeline wanted to, she couldn't forget about the prophecy, and she couldn't marry Apollo without knowing more about the Valory Arch and what would happen if it opened.

She took another deep breath, and before she could change her mind, she cried, "Apollo, I don't want you to catch cold before our wedding. Why don't you come up here instead?"

It was dark, but Evangeline swore his face lit up. Then he was climbing the wall.

"Apollo! Stop—what are you doing?"

He paused, already quite a few feet off the ground, hands grasping thick stones that must have been slick with ice, to say, "You told me to come up."

"I thought you'd use the stairs. You'll fall to your death."

"Have a little faith in your prince, my bride." He continued to scale the wall, only pausing when his personal guard attempted to follow. "I'll be fine on my own, Havelock."

Apollo reached the balcony a few agile moves later and deftly hopped over the railing.

"I'm almost saddened that after tonight there will be no need to show you how far I'd go just to be with you, my heart." His eyes flared with heat as he took her in.

Evangeline hadn't changed into a nightgown. Having planned on inviting him up, she was still bundled in a long-sleeved wool dress and a fur-trimmed robe. But from the ravenous way Apollo looked her over, she could have been merely wrapped in a spool of ribbon.

In one dashing move, he lifted Evangeline into his arms and carried her inside.

The room was built for a princess. The pink-and-cream carpets were plush as pillows, the glowing fireplace was crystalline rock, and the floral bed was elegant white oak with floor-to-ceiling posts and a carved headboard the length of an entire wall.

Evangeline briefly forgot how to breathe as Apollo took her straight to that enormous bed and set her down in the middle of its satiny quilts, laying her out like a sacrifice. "I feel as if I've been waiting for this forever."

"Apollo—wait!" She thrust out a hand before he could join her.

"What's wrong, my heart?" A wrinkle formed between his brows, but his dark eyes were still on fire. "Isn't this why you wanted me up here?"

Evangeline took a deep breath. She hadn't anticipated this response from him. All she'd wanted was to talk.

Yesterday, she had tried her hand at opening the library door that led to the books about the Valors, but like every person who'd tried before her, she'd failed. The door was locked by the same curse that warped so many Northern histories and turned them into fairytales. She'd gone back early today to search the library again, but she'd found nothing even remotely related to the Valory Arch, and she'd been too nervous to ask anyone.

Evangeline was also nervous to ask Apollo about the Valory Arch or the prophecy connected to it. She shouldn't have been. If her questions did break Jacks's spell, as they had with the Fortuna matriarch, it would be a good thing for Apollo—he would be free of the curse and she would no longer have to worry about fulfilling a dangerous prophecy by marrying him.

But if she was being honest, a part of her did want to marry him. She wanted the chance at the fairytale—another chance at love.

But she knew this wasn't really love. As soon as she married Apollo, he wouldn't be *this* prince anymore. He'd be the prince she'd met her first night in Valorfell, far more likely to dismiss her than to scale a wall to see her.

She sat up and placed her legs over the side of the enormous bed, facing her betrothed like an equal rather than lying down like an offering. "I'm sorry for the confusion. I do want you here, but it's because I need to ask you about something private."

"You can say anything to me." Apollo dropped to his knees, shook the damp from his hair, and looked up at her with utter adoration, eyes smoldering flecks of brown and bronze.

"If this is about tomorrow," he said, "if you're nervous about our wedding night, I promise I'll be gentle."

"No, it's not that." Although now that he mentioned it, Evangeline was suddenly anxious about that, too. But now wasn't the time for it, since she still hadn't decided if she was actually going to marry him tomorrow.

"I've been trying to learn more about your country, to prepare to be your bride—"

"That's a wonderful idea, my heart! You're going to be such an excellent queen," Apollo crooned, practically breaking into song again.

Evangeline was tempted to end the conversation there. It would be a crime to leave him forever trapped like this. But she couldn't ignore the prophecy.

She took a deep breath and braced herself, gripping the plush edge of the bed as she asked, "Have you ever heard of the Valory Arch?"

Apollo's grin turned boyish. "I thought you were going to ask me something frightening."

She thought she had.

"The Valory Arch is what you would call a fairytale."

Evangeline wrinkled her brow. "Where I'm from, we call all of your history fairytales."

"I know." His dark eyes twinkled with mischief, and for a moment, he didn't look quite so enchanted. He just looked like a boy, trying to tease a girl.

"Our history was cursed, but there are some tales we believe in more than others. Everyone believes certain things to be real history, like the existence of the Valors. But some of the stories about them have become so twisted over time they're considered to be what you would call fairytales. Among these is the myth of the Valory Arch." His voice deepened, turning more dramatic as he slid onto the bed beside her, close, but not quite near enough to touch.

"The stories about the Valory Arch are among our cursed tales. Stories on the Valors can only be passed down via word of mouth, and in the case of the Valory Arch, there are two different versions of the tale. Lucky for you, I know them both."

He graced her with a proud grin, and Evangeline felt more of the tension uncoil inside of her.

"The Valory Arch is believed to be the gateway to the Valory. In one version of the story, the Valory was a magical prison built by the Valors. Magic cannot be destroyed, so the Valors said they created the Valory to lock away any dangerous magical objects of power, or foreign captives with magical abilities. They said the Valory was built to protect the North from forces who would wish to destroy it, but . . ."

Apollo paused, looking as if he were searching for his next word as he slyly slid closer until their legs touched.

Evangeline's heart skipped over a beat.

"Is this all right?" he asked, deep voice suddenly soft and

utterly sincere. He would move away if Evangeline wanted, but it would crush the fragile hope that he was trying to hide behind his shy smile.

"This is nice," she said, and she was surprised to realize how much she meant it. Ever since first suspecting Apollo was under Jacks's spell, everything Apollo did felt like a little too much and a lot too unreal. But this—having him tell her a story as he timidly tried for the smallest touch—felt as if it could be real, as if this was how things might have been if Apollo actually cared for her. And it felt good to feel cared for.

She reminded herself it wasn't genuine, this was just Jacks's spell making Apollo act this way, but it had been so long since she'd felt so important to anyone. And Apollo didn't know he was under a spell; all he knew was how he felt for her.

Evangeline gently put a hand on his knee, and Apollo smiled as if she'd just given him the sun.

"Unfortunately," he went on, "the Valors lied. They didn't build the Valory to protect the North from its enemies. They built it to lock up an abomination that they'd created. No one knows exactly what the Valors made, but it was so terrible that all the Great Houses turned on the Valors and chopped off all their heads. Alas, they did this before the Valors had locked away their horrible creation, so it was left to the Great Houses to imprison this abomination in the Valory and seal the arch that led to it. Normally, arches are locked with blood, but no one wanted to risk this arch being opened, so a special sort of lock was created. A prophecy."

Evangeline fought the temptation to panic. This was only one version of a story that was cursed, and therefore unreliable. But she still asked, "How do you lock something with a prophecy?"

"The way I always heard it told is that the lines of a prophecy work like the ridges and the notches of a key. A number of prophetic lines are strung together by a diviner, and then they are carved into a door—or, in this case, an arch. Once this is done, the arch will remain locked until each line of the prophecy has been fulfilled to create the key that will allow the arch to be opened again. It's rather ingenious. If done well, a prophecy can ensure something stays unopened for centuries."

"Do you know what this prophecy supposedly said?"

Apollo looked amused, as if he wanted to say the prophecy wasn't real. But he continued to humor her. "This version of the story says that the arch containing the prophecy was broken into pieces and they were parceled out to the Protectorate—a secret society that vowed to never let the arch reopen. But no one has ever found the missing arch pieces. And most everyone in the North has searched at some point."

At her surprised expression, he explained, "The second version of the story is entirely different. This one claims that the Valory wasn't a prison for a terrible magic but a treasure chest holding the Valors' most powerful magical objects. Some believe this was really why the Valors were killed, because the Great Houses wanted to steal their magic and treasure. In this account of the story, the Wardens, those who had remained loyal to the Valors even after their death, locked the arch with the prophecy so that the Valors' powers and treasures would be prevented from falling into the wrong hands."

Hands like Jacks's.

Evangeline could definitely see Jacks being interested in magical treasure. Unfortunately, she could also picture him being interested in the magical terror from the first version of the story.

She tried to remember what Jacks had said about the Valors to see if she could figure out which version of the tale he believed in. But all she knew for certain was that whatever it was that was locked away, Jacks wanted it desperately. The look on his face when they'd reached the Fortunas' arch had been one of utter hope. But why? Why did he believe in a story that Apollo clearly thought of as a fairytale?

Was Jacks hoping to find the Valors' greatest treasure, or free their greatest terror?

"When I was younger," Apollo went on, "my brother, Tiberius, and I would go on quests to search for the Valory. It was one of our favorite games . . ." Apollo's voice turned wistful as he trailed off, lost in the memory of a brother he rarely mentioned.

When Evangeline had first moved into Wolf Hall, a chatty servant had told her that Tiberius's room was right next to hers. But when Evangeline had tried to ask more questions, the servant's lips had sealed shut. Apollo kept denying the rumor that he and his brother had had another falling-out after Apollo's engagement to Evangeline. But Evangeline had yet to see Tiberius inside the castle, and whenever she'd asked Apollo where his brother had gone or why he'd left, Apollo just told her she'd love Tiberius when they finally met. Then he would abruptly change the subject.

Evangeline was tempted to ask Apollo about his brother again, before tomorrow happened and everything changed. For by this time tomorrow, nothing between them would be the same. Because she was going to marry Apollo. Jacks was going to lift Apollo's curse, and then Apollo might never again look at her the way he looked at her tonight.

She didn't know if it was the right thing to do or the wrong thing. She only knew that after tonight, it was the thing she wanted to do.

Keeping Apollo under this curse felt a lot like letting Marisol and Luc remain stone statues; it would be less painful for Evangeline, but she couldn't do it. She couldn't doom Apollo to living life under a spell.

The prophecy still made her nervous, but with so much unknown about the Valory Arch, Evangeline decided that she had to do the best with what was known. And she knew the only way to save Apollo from his curse was to marry him, regardless of the consequences.

"Evangeline, my love, are you all right? Why are you trembling?"

She looked down at her hands. When had they started shaking? "I'm—I'm—" She didn't know what to say. "Cold—aren't you cold?"

Apollo frowned, clearly not believing she was cold in her heavy cloak, while a fire roared behind them. "This is sudden, and I know I've rushed you, but I swear, I will take good care of you."

She started to shake harder.

Apollo's face completely fell. "Just give us time. I know you don't feel quite the same—"

"It's not that—" She broke off, unsure of what to say, wishing there were some magic words that would spare his feelings now and still keep him at an arm's distance. He'd do anything for her in this state, and she didn't want to take advantage. She didn't want to hurt him, or herself by growing closer, or buying into the delusion that this was real. "You've been so sweet to me."

The lines bracketing his mouth grew deeper. "You say that as if tomorrow will change things."

"Of course it will change things," she said. "Isn't that why we're doing it?" And for a moment, she was so tempted to lean into him. The leg pressing against hers was warm even through all the layers of clothing, and she imagined his arms would be warm as well. Warm and soothing and solid. Apollo had embraced and kissed her, but no one had simply held her since Luc. She missed it, not just being held by him but being held by anyone. Since losing both her parents, all those soothing, loving little touches had become far more precious to her. She missed the way her father hugged her, the way her mother used to comfort her, and—

Apollo's arm slid around her shoulder, tender and warmer

than she'd imagined, and there was nothing that could have stopped her from leaning into him. Just for a few heartbeats, then she'd pull away.

"If you want, I could stay . . ." He said each word as if he were holding his breath. "We don't have to do anything. I could sleep in my clothes and just hold you."

Evangeline didn't trust herself to speak.

She should have said no. She really should have said it.

Apollo wasn't himself; if he had been, he'd not be offering this. He wouldn't even be in her room. But he was in her room, and he was looking at her as if all he wanted in the world was for her to say yes to him.

"Please, Evangeline, let me stay." He wrapped his other arm around her and held on to her like a promise he intended to keep. The way he touched her was soft and reverent and full of all the comfort she'd missed so much.

She still should have said no. But something had changed between them since he'd climbed up into her room. She knew that it would shift again tomorrow, but maybe it wouldn't be so bad to take advantage of it for one night. "That would be nice."

And it was. It was very nice.

Possibly the last nice thing between them.

31

The Daily Rumor

THE DAY WE'VE ALL BEEN WAITING FOR

By Kristof Knightlinger

I'm almost saddened that today Prince Apollo and soon-to-be Princess Evangeline Fox will wed. There's been so much excitement I'm loath for it to end. Although if half the rumors I've heard about the wedding are true, it should be a spectacular day.

Unfortunately, it seems that there will be at least one notable person missing from the royal celebration. Tabitha Fortuna of House Fortuna had a terrible fall several days ago. It's hard to believe that someone so formidable could be bested by a set of stairs, but apparently, the fall was so bad it's done some damage to her mind. I've heard people mutter the words *sedated*, *mad*, and *magic curses*, making it sound as if it could have been more than just a fall. Or could it be that someone is trying to steal the sunlight from our fair Evangeline Fox?

32

onths ago, on a damp, blustery day, when rain clouds did battle with the sun and the clouds came out victorious, Evangeline Fox planned her wedding to Luc Navarro.

She hadn't meant to plan a wedding. Before that stormy afternoon, she hadn't even thought about marrying Luc. She was only sixteen then; she wasn't ready to be a wife. She just wanted to be a girl. But the mighty rain had kept everyone from the shop that day, leaving her alone with a new shipment of oddities that included a fountain pen with a curious label: *For finding dreams that don't exist yet.*

Evangeline had been unable to resist trying the pen, and as soon as she did, a fledgling dream had taken form. She didn't know how long she'd spent drawing, only that when her piece was done, it felt like a picture of a promise. Evangeline and her love were at the end of a dock covered in candles, which made the ocean glow so that it looked like a sea of fallen stars. Only night and her moon watched. No one else was there, just Evangeline and her groom. Their foreheads were pressed together— and she might not have known exactly what they were doing, if not for the words her pen had etched into the sky: *And then they will write their vows on their hands and place them over each other's chests, so they may sink into their hearts, where they will be kept safe forever and always.*

It would have been a ceremony her parents would have approved of. It would have been a simple wedding made of oaths and love, and promises of an ever after spent together. It was the opposite of what would happen today.

The enormous wings attached to Evangeline's bridal gown dragged across her suite as she looked out a window edged in webs of frost.

In the towers at every corner of Wolf Hall, caged doves waited, ready to be released after Apollo and Evangeline exchanged their vows underneath an arch of gold-flecked ice that sparkled in the morning sun. Night and her moon wouldn't even glimpse this ceremony. But what felt like a kingdom of people would be there. They were already waiting, decked out in their finest furs and jewels. They'd be there when Apollo kissed his bride and then promptly fell out of love with her.

Evangeline's stomach fell.

There would be no happily ever afters following this wedding.

Last night, she'd felt good about her choice, but today, it

broke her heart just a little. She shouldn't have let Apollo spend the night with her. She shouldn't have let him hold her. She shouldn't have let him remind her of everything she didn't have and might not have again after today.

She didn't want Apollo to fall out of love with her.

Since he'd proposed, Apollo had been sweet and kind and thoughtful, if a little extreme in his declarations. But who would he be when Jacks's spell was broken? Would he still be the tender Apollo who had held her all night long? Would he be the vain prince who'd been ready to dismiss her almost as soon as he'd met her? Or would something else happen, something even worse?

Evangeline tried not to think about the Valory Arch prophecy. She'd already decided that she couldn't trust anything she'd heard about the arch. Yet she couldn't seem to fully erase her worries. If she was part of this prophecy, what would happen when it was fulfilled?

"Why do you look so nervous?" asked Marisol, coming up beside her. She wore a candied apricot dress with a sugary cream underskirt and a thick pearl belt, and she looked beautiful. No longer dubbed the Cursed Bride, Marisol had spent the last few days enjoying teas and dress fittings and all the delights of Wolf Hall. She looked happy and refreshed, but her eyes were all awe as she took in the extravagance that was Evangeline's wedding gown.

The gold-tipped wings were outrageous, but Evangeline rather liked the dress. Its heart-shaped neckline was flattering to her smallish chest, while its ball gown skirt was terribly fun, made of endless layers of impossibly delicate white fabric, except for the wide train of golden feathers that flowed from her waist down the back of the dress.

"There's nothing to be scared of," Marisol said. "You're about to marry a prince who adores you."

He wouldn't for much longer.

Ding.

Ding.

Ding.

For one moment, the distant bell felt like a warning, until Evangeline remembered. One bell ringer from the choir remained in the courtyard. Not a warning, just the sound of her soft music coming to an end.

"What if he falls out of love with me?" Evangeline blurted. "What if we get married, he decides it was a mistake, and then he tosses you and me out of the North?"

"I don't think you have to worry about that," Marisol said. "Most girls would have to employ magic to make someone love them the way that Apollo loves you."

Evangeline stiffened.

"I didn't mean to imply that you put a spell on him," Marisol amended, cheeks flushing in a way that made Evangeline more inclined to think it had been an accident and not a barbed insinuation.

"It's not a surprise that he loves you so much," Marisol went on determinedly. "You're Evangeline Fox. You haven't even married the prince yet, and there are already fairytales about you. You're the girl who defied the Fates and turned herself to stone, the girl who wasn't afraid to reject a street of suitors or to bring her cursed stepsister with her to a royal ball, where she then captured the heart of a prince. Just love him the same way you live your life—love him without holding back, love him as if every day with him will be more magical than the last, love him as if he's your destiny and the world will be better if you two are together, and he won't be able to ever stop loving you."

Marisol finished her speech with a hug so warm and earnest it was easy to believe she was right. Evangeline had been so consumed with what Apollo's feelings for her might be that she hadn't thought much about her feelings for *him*. She knew that she didn't love him now, but she could love him easily. She'd felt glimmers of affection last night, and she felt even more this morning after spending the night in his arms.

They might not have had love at first, but her parents had said that some loves took time. All she needed was for him to give her time, to give her a chance. Maybe it would be rough when Jacks lifted the curse, but if Apollo let her, Evangeline's love could be strong enough to give them both a happy ending.

Hope was not lost.

In the back of her head, a tiny voice reminded her that she was ignoring the prophecy again, but she chose not to listen. She would worry about that tomorrow.

Evangeline left her wedding suite determined to fall in love with her prince. But the day must have been cursed, or the story curse was affecting it, for she couldn't seem to hold on to any of the memories of her wedding, even as they happened.

One moment she was stepping into Wolf Hall's snowy yard, cool air biting her cheeks as a court of scrutinizing faces looked her way. Then she was holding Apollo's hands as the wedding master tied her wrist to Apollo's with silken cords. Evangeline felt her blood rushing through her veins. Her skin was on fire, and so was the prince's, as if they were bound together by more than just a gilded rope.

"And now," the wedding master said, loudly enough for everyone present to hear, "by my words, I join these two together. I tie not only their wrists but also their hearts. May they beat as one from this moment on. If one is pierced with an arrow, may the other bleed for them."

"I would gladly bleed for you," Apollo whispered. He held her hands tighter as his eyes latched on to hers with even more burning intensity, as if the flames she'd lit the first night she'd kissed him had multiplied tenfold.

She just hoped that Apollo's spark still remained after Jacks broke his spell.

33

Now that they were wed, Evangeline kept bracing for Apollo to drop her hand, to spear her with an angry glare, to shake his head as if waking from a dream. But if anything, he held her tighter. He looked at her more reverently—as if there really had been magic in their vows and they were truly joined together.

Moments after the ceremony, they were poured into a silver sled pulled by a pack of snow-white wolves. Apollo kept her warm, holding her close as they glided to a castle of ice, built only to last for this one single night. Glowing blue and ephemeral and transcendently lovely, the sight made it easier to hope and believe that their story was just beginning.

Oh, how she wanted to believe.

Inside the gleaming glass-like walls, guests were given shining silver goblets of mulled wine and individual forest-green cakes that tasted like luck and love. Instead of musicians, a grand music box opened and life-size clockwork players stepped out to perform an endless stream of ethereal sounds. The notes were like threads of gossamer and tails on kites, springy and enchanting in a way that made Evangeline think of warning fables of boys and girls so bewitched with magic songs that they danced until they died.

Apollo downed the contents of a goblet in one draft before turning his attention to the chattering crowd of courtiers and Northern nobles. "Thank you all for being here to celebrate the greatest day of my life. I didn't actually have a wish to be married until meeting my beloved Evangeline Fox. In honor of my bride, you'll notice there are ghost foxes here." He waved his empty goblet toward a merry fox made of smoke perched atop an ice sculpture of a stag. "These are special creatures. Charm one and you'll receive a gift, so that you may find love, too."

"To love and to foxes!" cheered the crowd, voices echoing against the sparkling ice.

Evangeline took a drink from her goblet, but she could barely swallow. Her throat was too tight with so many fears lodged in it as she waited for Apollo to fall out of love with her.

Why wasn't he falling out of love?

She didn't want him to stop loving her, but this waiting felt like torture as well.

Apollo graced her with a dreamy smile as a slower song drifted from the clockwork players and floated across the glistening ice. "Are you ready to finally have our first dance?"

Evangeline managed to nod as her eyes darted over his

broad shoulders to search for Jacks's face among the crowd. What was he waiting for?

Was Jacks's magic broken? Had he forgotten? Was he even at the wedding?

Evangeline forced herself to keep dancing, to keep smiling. But the wings at her back grew heavier with every twist and twirl. Jacks didn't appear to be in the crowd. He wasn't there to fix Apollo. Unless . . .

What if Jacks wasn't there because the spell had already broken? And maybe it didn't feel as if it had broken because Apollo had actually come to love her. It was probably too much to hope for, but Evangeline had always had a weakness for hoping in things others thought impossible.

She dared to meet her husband's eyes. In the past few days, she'd seen stars shine in his gaze and infatuation cloud his vision. But right now, Apollo's eyes were just eyes. Brown and warm and steady.

"How do you feel?" she asked. "Do you feel any differently from this morning?"

"Of course, my heart. I'm married to you." He pulled her closer, the hand at her waist sliding under her wings as it traveled up her spine, sending fresh shivers over her skin. "I feel the confidence of a hundred kings and the passion of a thousand princes. I could do battle with Wolfric Valor tonight and come out victorious."

His gaze might have smoldered then.

Undoubtedly still enchanted.

But, like last night, it didn't feel quite so terrible. Wasn't this the way that a groom was supposed to look at his bride right after their wedding? She knew Apollo was still under a curse, but Evangeline hoped that he was also starting to fall a little in love with her.

He twirled her around the floor once more, and Evangeline didn't look for Jacks. She would look for him again, but not yet. Not now. Not during her first dance. She would just enjoy this one moment. Then she'd find Jacks and get him to break the spell.

Apollo brushed his lips to Evangeline's temple.

Excited murmurs ebbed their way through the crowd. It sounded like a moving smile, like joy and bubbles. And then. *Hush.*

A wave of quiet moved across the glittering ice castle.

Evangeline looked away from her groom, expecting that Jacks had finally arrived. But everyone was staring at another young man dressed in a striped green doublet.

He wasn't particularly tall, and his build was rather slight, but he glided through the crush like a person in possession of power, shoulders straight, head tipped high, eyes daring anyone to tell him not to interrupt the bride and groom's first dance.

Evangeline watched whispers die on lips and jaws of shocked faces hang open. By the time this young man reached Evangeline and Apollo, the entire ballroom was silent, save for the odd chime of music box instruments and the soft pitter-patter of ghostly fox feet.

"Hello, brother," the stranger said, his voice soft and a little damaged as if it had been recently lost and only just recovered.

So this was the mysterious Tiberius. They didn't look like brothers. Although Evangeline didn't get much of a chance to examine him before Apollo stopped dancing and quickly hid her behind his back.

Tiberius laughed.

"I don't want any trouble," Apollo said.

"Then why is your hand on the hilt of your sword? Do you think I'm going to tell her—"

Apollo pulled the blade from his sash.

Half the wedding guests gasped, and a few might have clapped, eager for a royal brawl.

Evangeline needed to do something now. She'd suspected there was bad blood between Apollo and Tiberius, but she didn't think Apollo would be so prone to violence if he hadn't still been enchanted to be so obsessed with her.

She stepped between her groom and his brother. "My dearest." Evangeline pressed a hand to Apollo's chest. But the action no longer appeared to be necessary.

As soon as she called him *dearest,* Apollo's entire demeanor changed. She'd never used an endearment with him before, and now that she had, he looked as if he could have dropped the sword and kissed her in the middle of the dance floor.

Tiberius choked back another laugh. "I can't believe the rumors are true—you love her. Or you've been bewitched."

Evangeline turned brittle. She hoped he was kidding, but

maybe he wasn't. Maybe he suspected the truth, and this was why the brothers had their most recent falling-out.

Apollo shook her off and lifted his sword, rage flashing in his eyes once more. "Insult my wife again, and I'll cut your tongue from your mouth."

"My dearest," Evangeline tried again. But the words didn't have the same effect.

Ignoring her, Apollo took a step toward his brother. Hairline cracks formed in the ice beneath his boots.

Tiberius lifted his hands in surrender. "I didn't come here to fight." He pivoted and gave Evangeline a deep bow. "My apologies, princess. I'd love to make up any offense to you with a dance."

Apollo looked as if he wanted to object with his sword, but Evangeline spoke first. "Thank you. I'd be honored." Then to Apollo, "Maybe for my wedding gift, the two of you can make amends?"

Apollo worked his jaw.

Evangeline held her breath. She hoped she hadn't pushed him too far. It would be terrible timing for Jacks's spell to break now.

After a painful beat, Apollo sheathed his sword. "Whatever you wish, my bride."

The clockwork performers plucked an unfamiliar tune as Tiberius took her hand. He held her much closer than he should have. It might have been to spite his brother, though she also suspected Tiberius was a poor dancer. He seemed the type who wouldn't have the patience for lessons.

This close, the brothers' differences in appearance were even more obvious. If Apollo's face was more roughly carved than chiseled, Tiberius's face wasn't sculpted at all. It was soft, decorated with a dusting of freckles that gave him an impish appearance. He couldn't have been much older than Evangeline, if he were older at all. His hair was copper and longish, but tied back just enough to reveal a hint of a tattoo at the base of his neck, which made him look the part of rebel younger brother even more.

"You're not what I expected." Tiberius narrowed one eye and raised a brow.

Evangeline might have been offended by his scrutiny had she married Apollo through traditional means, but given the circumstances, the younger prince's inquiry was understandable.

"If you're thrown off by the wings you're currently crushing," she said, hoping to get him to loosen his grip, "they are sadly just part of my gown. I'm far from being an angel."

Tiberius's mouth twitched, but Evangeline couldn't tell if it was the start of a smile or smirk, if he was trying to make a good impression or if he wanted her to know he didn't trust her. And that wasn't the only thing she was curious about.

"Why did you disappear after I became engaged to Apollo?"

Tiberius's eyes flickered with surprise. "You're bold."

"What were you expecting?"

"Not much, if I'm being honest. Apollo used to say if—" Tiberius broke off with a wince. "Sorry, I shouldn't be saying that at his wedding. It's just habit for me to be mean to him. It's how I show my love." Another smile that was possibly a smirk as Tiberius increased the speed of his steps, spinning her in a rapid circle across the icy floor. "Do you love my brother, Evangeline?"

Her breathing quickened. *Yes* was clearly the right answer, but she had a feeling Tiberius already knew that was a lie. He looked at her like a puzzle he wanted to take apart instead of put together. Clearly, Tiberius and Apollo fought, but Evangeline got the impression that Tiberius really did care for his older brother and was unsure of her because of it.

"I loved someone before," she admitted. "When I lost him, I thought I'd never love anyone else the way that I loved him. But I have hope that I'll love Apollo even more." As long as they could just get through whatever happened when Jacks lifted the spell. "I'd like to be friends with you as well. I've never had a brother."

She gave Tiberius a timid smile. If she and Marisol could mend things, there was hope for Apollo and Tiberius, as well. Perhaps in time they could all be a family, to make up for the people they'd lost—or in Marisol's case, the family member she was better off without.

Tiberius's expression was inscrutable, making it unclear if Evangeline had passed his test. But she noticed he no longer crushed her wings as took her on a final turn about the icy floor.

"Thank you for the dance, Evangeline. The next time I see you, I'll tell you why I disappeared. I don't want to spoil anything else for you tonight." Tiberius released her with a formal bow as the music stopped.

Then he was striding away, twirling a feather that he'd stolen from her wings.

34

Northern wedding receptions were supposed to last until dawn. People were meant to eat and drink until every cask was dry and every crumb of cake was gobbled up. But shortly after twilight, when there were still towers of cakes and an empire of more goblets waiting to be passed out for yet another toast, Prince Apollo leaned close to Evangeline and whispered in her ear, "I love my kingdom, but I'd rather not spend my entire wedding night with them." He pressed a lingering kiss to her lobe. "Sneak away with me, my heart. Let's go to the wedding suite."

Evangeline's insides coiled up in anxious spirals. This had gone too far. She needed to find Jacks. Enjoying part of a reception wasn't bad, but things weren't supposed to reach this point, not while Apollo was still under a spell.

It was time to end this curse and find out how the prince she'd married really felt.

It took her multiple promises of meeting Apollo in the wedding suite shortly before he finally let her go. Even then, she felt his eyes on her, watching as she wove through the guests, the clockwork musicians, and the towers of cakes, on a mission to track down Jacks.

After dancing with Apollo, Evangeline had finally glimpsed the Prince of Hearts heading out of the main hall and into one of the icy corridors. At the time, she and Apollo had been introducing Marisol to the group of noble bachelors who'd be participating in the kissing chess game that Evangeline had set up for her stepsister. Evangeline hadn't wanted to sneak after Jacks then. But she'd seen others scurry off in that direction. Most returned later, with pale or alarmed faces, making Evangeline suspect that Jacks was holding some sort of terror-inducing clandestine court.

And it seemed she was right. She was shivering, ready to be done with the cold of this glacial castle by the time she finally found him in a commandeered throne room. The ceiling was all thick, vaulted beams of ice. The walls were shimmering frost etched with images of stars and trees and one smirking crescent moon.

Jacks reclined in a throne of ice as he glared down at a fox that looked more corporeal than ghost—all fluffy white fur, save for a circle of tawny surrounding one of its coal-dark eyes.

He appeared horrified by the animal, as if its adorableness might somehow soften some of his nasty edges. Evangeline wished it would as she stood back a little to watch, enjoying that, for once, Jacks was the one in the uncomfortable position.

He flinched when the creature nuzzled his scuffed boots.

She laughed, finally drawing his attention. "I think it likes you."

"I don't know why." Jacks scowled at the beast.

It responded by affectionately licking the buckle at his ankle.

Evangeline continued to smile. "You should name it."

"If I do that, it will think it's a pet." Jacks's words dripped with disgust, which only further convinced Evangeline this fox might be the best thing that had ever happened to this Fate.

"How about I name her for you? What do you think of Princess of the Fluffikins?"

"Don't ever say that again."

She smiled softly. "Next time I make a deal with a Fate, it will be with one who has a sense of humor, like Poison."

Jacks slowly dragged his eyes up to Evangeline. They were pale blue, like the ice of his throne, and surrounded by a crown of dark blue hair that curled around his face from the cold. He wore a half-undone doublet of smoky blue gray, raven-black pants, and a low-slung belt that rested just above his hips, giving him the appearance of a tousled winter king. An angry one, from the way he glared at Evangeline. "I would have thought you'd have learned your lesson about making deals with our kind."

"I have, which is why next time I need something, if I make a deal, it won't be with you."

"This isn't something to joke about," Jacks growled.

"I didn't think you cared."

"I don't. But you still owe me one more kiss, and until I collect it, you're mine, and I do not like to share."

"If I didn't know you better, I'd say you sounded jealous."

"Of course I'm jealous. I'm a Fate."

"If you're so envious, then why haven't you undone the spell that's on Apollo?"

"I couldn't care less about what happens between humans."

"Then undo it, because Apollo and I are married," she said firmly. "I kept up my half of our bargain. It's time for you to keep your promise to me."

"Very well," Jacks drawled, shocking her with his easy acquiescence. "I still think this is a shortsighted choice, but if you really want Apollo to no longer feel for you, I'll give you the means to do it." Jacks pulled out his jeweled dagger and pricked the tip of his finger, drawing a drop of familiar gold-flecked blood.

The fox sniffed the drop once and reared back with a whimper.

"See?" Jacks said blandly. "Even the creature knows this is a bad idea."

"No, it knows you're bad. There's a considerable difference." Although Jacks's blood made Evangeline uncomfortable as well. "What's the catch?"

"Is it that difficult to believe that I'm willing to keep my word?"

Fates were actually known for keeping their word when it came to bargains. It was why, despite all the warnings, people were willing to make deals with them. But something kept her from moving forward.

"Having second thoughts? I'll be the last being to judge you if you want to keep him under your thrall."

"It's not my thrall, it's yours." Evangeline took a step toward the throne.

Jacks's brows jumped up, betraying his surprise.

It should have made her feel triumphant. But instead it made her think of the last time she'd shocked him. When she'd drunk from Poison's cup and turned herself to stone.

She swallowed thickly.

Jacks leaned forward with indolent grace and lightly pressed his bleeding finger to her lips.

Gooseflesh pebbled across her skin. His touch wasn't colder than the castle, but it was always unnerving to be caressed by Jacks.

"Once you kiss him, any false feelings that Apollo has for you will disappear." Jacks dragged his icy finger more firmly across her mouth, rough and a little punishing. Today, his blood tasted bitter instead of sweet. The taste of a mistake. "You must kiss him before sunrise for the magic to work. But I warn you, if you do this, your prince won't think that you've done him a favor. Heroes don't get happy endings."

35

Evangeline had not thought this through quite enough. If she had, she would have asked Apollo exactly where the wedding suite was. Upon learning that it was at the top of one of Wolf Hall's spiraling towers, she then might have suggested they meet somewhere else—somewhere closer to the ground, preferably with multiple exits.

She didn't actually believe that Apollo would throw her from the tower window once she'd rid him of Jacks's magic. But Evangeline still didn't know who Apollo would be after she broke this spell. Would he be the sweet prince who had told her fairytales, or would he become the angry prince who'd nearly attacked his brother tonight?

Would this be the true beginning of their love story or the end of it?

Evangeline was committed to the idea of loving Apollo and making this marriage work after the spell was broken. But all she could hear were Jacks's words. *Your prince won't think that you've done him a favor.*

There were six soldiers guarding the wedding suite she was about to enter.

It was suddenly very tempting to turn around, to leave things as they were.

Or she could go in and avoid kissing Apollo. She had until sunrise to break the spell. What if she went in but didn't kiss him right away? They could stay up talking. How long was it until dawn?

Evangeline tried to take a deep breath, but it became lodged somewhere in her throat as she approached the wedding suite door. She didn't turn around. But she wished she had once she stepped inside and the door snapped shut behind her.

The room was too hot from the fire of a hundred blazing candles and too sweet with the heady scent of a thousand white flower petals. They covered almost every surface, from the floor to the lounges, to the giant four-poster bed.

"Hello, my heart," purred Apollo, who stretched across that same bed in a come-hither pose. His shirt was already gone. All he wore was a large amber stone over his bare chest, which glistened with something that looked a lot like oil.

Evangeline's stomach roiled. Any doubts she had about kissing him tonight disappeared. She had to end this spell, no matter how hard it might be for her afterward.

"You've kept me waiting, wife." He dragged a flower petal up and down his oiled chest.

Dread joined the breath still trapped inside her throat. She hoped he wouldn't hate her when she undid this, but in that moment, it felt unlikely.

"I just need a moment," she stalled. Evangeline was not particularly fond of wine, but there was a carved table with a pretty plum-colored bottle on of it. She poured herself a generous glass.

The drink sparkled but tasted of rotten blackberries and salt. She almost spit it out, but she wasn't ready to approach him yet. She took another long sip, finishing half the glass. She would have probably kept going, but she didn't want to be intoxicated for this.

She set the wine down and stepped boldly toward the bed.

Apollo licked his lips.

Before she lost her nerve, Evangeline closed her eyes and kissed him.

His arms snaked around her, slick and hot. He pulled her up onto the bed with him, and she didn't try to resist. This would all be over soon. It would all be over soon. Even as she thought it, she felt Apollo's tongue retreating, and his grip loosening.

Evangeline slid out from his arms.

Apollo didn't try to hold on as he normally would have. In fact, he gave her a little push as he sat up on the bed.

His hands fisted, and his shoulders tensed. His strong mouth opened and snapped tightly closed as his gaze darted from the flower petals, to the candles, to his oiled chest.

He scowled, ran a hand across his abdomen, and wiped the oil on the bed.

The room became smaller and the air turned hotter and far too sweet from the scent of all the flowers, but it was Apollo's silence that was smothering.

Evangeline had never understood why it had taken her so long to stop loving Luc. Even when she didn't want to love him, the feeling had lingered. People called it falling out of love, but falling was easy. Letting go of Luc had been more like climbing the face of a rock. She'd clawed her way out, fighting to shake it off, to let it go, to find something else to hold on to.

She'd wanted to just forget him, to close her eyes and have it all go away. But there were reasons powerful emotions didn't vanish in a blink, reasons why a person had to become stronger than her feelings to let them go.

Apollo gripped the sheets of the bed tightly. Then he scrubbed a hand down his face and all the anger vanished, replaced with naked hurt. His eyes were red, his mouth twisted, and his jaw clenched so tightly she thought it might crack.

"What have you done, Evangeline?" His harsh words weren't quite a yell, but they were certainly loud enough that the guards on the other side of the door probably heard. "Why do I feel as if you've stabbed me in the heart?"

He grimaced in pain as his eyes closed.

Her throat went tight with remorse. She tried to swallow down what felt like a sob. She'd expected him to be angry. But she hadn't expected him to look so wounded.

She wanted to reach out to him, to offer him comfort, but it was probably better to give him space.

"I'm sorry—I didn't want to hurt you." She slid off the bed.

"Don't—" Apollo grabbed her hand. "I—we—this—"

She thought he was trying to decide what to say.

Then all at once, he dropped her hand, his skin went gray, his shoulders slumped, his eyes rolled back, and he collapsed onto the bed.

His head lolled horribly to the side.

"Apollo!" Evangeline shot forward and pressed a hand to his chest. It felt slick and warm, but it wasn't moving.

"Apollo—Apollo—" She repeated his name as her hand went to his neck, searching for a pulse that she couldn't find. Her hands moved back to his chest, where he'd tattooed her name inside a heart made of swords. There was no beat there either, but the skin around the ink had gone an odd shade of blue. *No. No. No. No. No.*

She tried to shake him.

Nothing happened.

"Apollo, get up!" Evangeline cried, panicked tears coming fast and hard.

She shook him again. He needed to move. He needed to breathe. He needed to be alive. He couldn't be dead. He couldn't be dead. He couldn't be dead. If he was dead—

Another sob choked her throat as the worst thought of all occurred. If Apollo was dead, it meant that not only had her kiss broken the spell, it had killed him. She had killed him, and Jacks had tricked her into doing it.

36

Jacks had once told Evangeline, "There's no point in having another person commit murder if you're in the room with them." And Evangeline's last kiss with Apollo was the first enchanted kiss where Jacks hadn't been in the room.

"Help!" Evangeline cried as more ragged sobs racked her chest.

The door flew open, and a suite that had been filled with fire and flower petals moments ago turned into a rush of heavy boots, flashing weapons, and unbridled curses.

"We need a doctor," Evangeline sobbed. It felt too soon to cry, but she couldn't stop the tears.

"What did you do to him?"

"I think he's dead!"

"She killed him!"

The soldiers' words flew like arrows, quick and sharp, as two men yanked her off the bed by her wings, sending feathers flying everywhere.

"Get out of here," someone ordered.

"Wait—" Evangeline protested between tears. She knew this was partly her fault, but she wasn't the only one to blame. "I—I didn't—I didn't—"

"We heard him yelling at you. And now—" The soldier didn't even finish. He let the words hang there as two other guards hauled her toward the door. "Tie her up in an empty room. And you"—he pointed to another pair of soldiers—"find Prince Tiberius, and be discreet. We need to keep this quiet for now."

Evangeline tried to protest, but her words were strangled by more sobs. Horrible racking sobs, so intense she barely felt the chill of the tower or the soldiers' punishing grip as they dragged her down the stairs, shredding her wings with every flight and leaving a trail of feathers and tears.

"You—you need to find Lord Jacks—" she finally managed. "He did this—he's the Prince of Hearts."

"Grab a gag for her," the shorter soldier grunted as they jostled her into a dim room that smelled of damp and dust. Together, they ripped off the rest of her wings. Ruthlessly cold air hit her back as they shoved her in a lone wood chair. Her wrists were promptly tied to the arms, and her ankles to the chair's legs, before the shorter soldier stuck a fetid cloth inside her mouth.

It cut off her pleas, and its foulness briefly stopped her tears. But it didn't last long. In the silence that followed, all she could hear were the words *murderer* and *fool*, and all she could see were Apollo's desolate eyes, until a flood of tears blurred even that memory.

"Why hasn't that gag shut her up?" said the shorter soldier.

"Just let her cry," the other muttered. He was broader, and his head was shaved. He'd gone to build a fire in the empty hearth. She recognized him as Apollo's personal guard—Havelock. She couldn't imagine he cared if she was cold, but the abandoned room was like ice, and she doubted they'd leave her there alone. As if she could escape. Even if they untied her, she wouldn't get far in her current state. She sobbed harder.

She'd killed Apollo.

Apollo was dead.

Apollo was dead, and she'd killed him.

"You need to shut it now." The shorter soldier lifted up one hand to strike—

"Is that how a royal guard treats his next queen?" drawled Jacks, appearing at the half-open door. It was difficult to see him through the dark and the tears, but she'd always recognize the cruelty in his voice.

It's the Prince of Hearts! He's the murderer! Evangeline tried to yell, but the awful gag still filled her mouth. And now there was something wrong with the guards. Neither of them moved.

Evangeline rocked her chair in a feeble attempt to break free.

"Stop her from hurting herself," Jacks said flatly.

The shorter soldier who'd been about to strike her immediately put a firm hand on the back of her seat to keep all four legs on the ground.

What was going on?

It was as if the soldiers were possessed. Havelock stared at Jacks the way one might regard a shadow holding a knife, yet he didn't move until Jacks strode into the room and softly said, "Get out."

Wordlessly, both soldiers marched out, leaving Evangeline tied up and alone with the Prince of Hearts.

Get away from me! she tried to scream, shaking the chair again as Jacks stalked closer.

In the dim, he should have been difficult to see, but his eyes faintly glowed, burning blue as he raked her over. He took in the broken gold wings at her feet, the torn hem of her full white skirts, and the tracks of tears coating her cheeks.

Stop crying. Jacks's voice was low and even and invading her thoughts once again. *You're not sad. You're calm and happy to see me.*

Evangeline glared at him, wishing she could tell him just how unhappy his presence made her. She really didn't want to cry in front of him, but the sight of him standing there so cold and callous only reminded her of the way Apollo had died.

More tears splashed down her cheeks.

Jacks's gaze narrowed and dropped toward a wet puddle at her feet. "Are those *all* tears?" Something like alarm flickered in his eyes. Not that she could believe for a second that he cared about her. He was going to kill her, just as he'd killed Apollo, so that she could never tell anyone what he'd done.

She braced herself as Jacks reached for the gag at her mouth, and then she screamed as soon as it was off. "Murderer! Get a—"

Jacks's hand flew over her lips. "Do you really want me to put that nasty cloth back in your mouth?"

Evangeline stiffened.

He gave her a sliver of a grin. "I'm going to ask you a question now, and you're going to answer without screaming. How long have you been crying like this?"

His hand slowly slid away.

To Evangeline's horror, more tears leaked out before she managed to speak. "Don't pretend as if you care about my sorrow—you're going to kill me just as you killed Apollo."

"I didn't murder Apollo, and I have no intention of harming you. I still need you for that prophecy, remember?"

"I'll never help you with anything ever again," Evangeline seethed, or she tried to. The words came out with an embarrassing sniffle, but she soldiered on. "I'd rather stay tied up here forever than help you."

"You should not be so reckless with your words." Jacks pulled out his jeweled dagger, but instead of reaching for her throat or her heart, he dropped to a crouch and cut the rope binding her right ankle to the chair.

Evangeline kicked out with her free leg.

But of course Jacks was quicker. His cold hand wrapped around her calf, lifting it high enough to make her dress slide up precariously and putting her completely off balance as he rose from his crouch. "If you want to live, you need to stop fighting me."

"I'll never stop fighting you. You tricked me into murdering Apollo! I thought I was helping him, but he died as soon as I kissed him."

Jacks worked his jaw. "Apollo didn't die because of your kiss. There was no magic in that kiss."

"But—"

"There was never any magic in your kisses," Jacks interrupted. "When Apollo fell in love with you, it wasn't because you kissed him, it was because I willed it."

"How is that possible?"

"I'm a Fate. You really think my only power is in my kiss?" Jacks sounded more than a little insulted. "I wouldn't be very terrifying if that were all I could do. And before you argue and waste more time by saying you don't believe me, you just saw me use this ability on the soldiers I ordered to leave this room. I didn't even have to touch them. I only had you kiss Apollo and Lady Fortuna because it was entertaining, and when the magic wore off, it would lead back to you instead of me. People tend to avoid and distrust you when they know you can control how they feel. I have manipulated you, but I didn't murder your prince."

Evangeline tried to glare at Jacks through her tears. She really didn't want to believe him or concede that he made sense. She wanted to blame him for killing Apollo. She wanted to kick him and scream. But when she tried to scream, it turned into a frustrated sob.

"If you're telling the truth—then use your magic on me." Evangeline hiccupped. "Use it to stop my tears."

"I tried, and it didn't work." Jacks grimaced as another waterfall poured from her eyes. "Your tears aren't normal. I think you've been poisoned."

"It's grief, Jacks, not poison! Apollo just died in front of me."

"I'm not criticizing you for being emotional." Jacks ground his jaw. "But if this were purely your feelings, I should be able to take them away."

Evangeline flashed back to the words he'd spoken silently, shortly after he'd first stepped into the room. "You—tried to tell me that I was happy to see you."

Jacks didn't answer, but the brutal way he looked down at her made her suspect that she should not have been able to hear his words.

"Something unnatural is amplifying your feelings," he said gruffly. "There's another Fate who cries poisoned tears with the power to kill someone by breaking her heart. I think someone has poisoned you with those tears, and if we don't get you the cure soon, you'll cry yourself to death."

Evangeline wanted to keep arguing. Just because his powers didn't work on her didn't mean she was poisoned. She was hurting—her husband had died before her eyes. But before she could speak, she was hit by a new wave of uncontrollable sobs, and they did feel like poison. She'd never cried so hard in her life.

Her body felt as if it were being weighed down with every

sorrow she'd ever had. Each tear burned as it streaked her cheeks. And she remembered the taste of the salty wine she'd almost spit out. Was that how she'd been poisoned? Could the wine be what had killed Apollo as well? He hadn't cried, but the last look on his face had been one of utter heartbreak.

Jacks finally dropped Evangeline's ankle. Then he finished slicing off the other ropes before he slid an arm under her shoulder to help her to her feet.

"Let me go!" She tried to pull away. Even if Jacks hadn't killed Apollo, Evangeline wanted nothing to do with Jacks's cold hands, or his cold arms, or the rock-solid ice that was his chest. But her legs were about as strong as limp thread, and she found herself leaning into him instead of fighting.

He went rigid as if she'd pressed a knife to his side rather than her body. And then he picked her up and slung her over his shoulder.

"What are you doing?" she squeaked between sobs. Even as a savior, he was still wretched.

"You can barely stand, and we need to move quickly if we want to get out of here."

"Can't you"—she tried to wriggle free, but his arm was like iron as it kept her bent over his shoulder—"just magic everyone we pass?"

"My magic doesn't work the same in the North as it would elsewhere," he gritted out.

In other words, *no*. His power to control people's emotions had a limit. She combed her frantic thoughts, recalling the moment his magic had ceased working on the Fortuna matriarch. Evangeline thought she'd broken the spell with her question about the stones. But it must have been Jacks's control that had slipped. He'd probably needed a great deal of power to make Apollo love her so intensely, and there hadn't been enough magic left to manage the matriarch for long.

Perhaps Jacks could only control a few people at once. Otherwise, she imagined he'd have been using his magic on everyone. Tonight, he'd manipulated two guards, and then he'd been upset when he couldn't control her. So he could at least command three, but perhaps not more.

Jacks ripped the cape from his shoulders and covered Evangeline with it. She didn't see anything as he carried her out of Wolf Hall or set her in a waiting sled that felt like the coldest part of the night.

"We're almost there" were the only words he said during the journey, unless she didn't hear his other words between her unending sobs. They left icicle trails down her cheeks until they started to freeze her eyelids shut.

The sled came to a halt, and Jacks scooped her up into his arms again.

She couldn't see where they went. Jacks kept her covered with his cloak and pressed her tight against his chest. It was the first time his body had ever felt warm. Evangeline shuddered to think what that said about her.

Months ago, she'd turned to stone, but now she felt as if she were turning to ice as Jacks trudged across what sounded like snow and then began to ascend what felt like an endless flight of stairs. She hoped that he was taking her somewhere warm. Warm would be very good. Although even if Jacks managed to thaw her eyes open and free her of the poison breaking her apart, it wouldn't be enough to erase the fact that she was now a fugitive and a widow and an orphan. All she had was a Fate who she didn't even trust or like—

"Do not start giving up," Jacks growled. "Giving in to the poison makes it work faster." His words were followed by a swift knock on a door. Then another and another and another—

The door finally groaned open.

"Jacks?" The voice was feminine and slightly familiar. "What in Fate's name—"

The girl went silent as Jacks pulled the cloak from Evangeline's face.

"She needs you to save her now," Jacks ground out.

"What have you done?" the girl demanded, and Evangeline liked her just a little then.

"I think we both know this isn't my doing."

"Are you—never mind, bring her inside. And do not let go of her," warned the girl. "If you stop holding her, she might slip away. Try to comfort her while I put together an antidote. Pretend she's someone you care for."

Jacks's arms tensed around Evangeline.

But then the world became warmer, crackling and fiery, and

she didn't care how Jacks held her as long as he kept heading toward the warmth. She couldn't open her eyes, but after a few rough adjustments, he lowered her onto his lap.

She imagined they were in front of a fire, and he was sitting on the hearth, holding her with about as much affection as he might handle a log he was about to toss into the blaze. "There are much better ways to die than this, Little Fox."

"Your attempts at comfort are tr-tragic," Evangeline stuttered.

"You're still alive," he grumbled. His fingers found her eyelids then, and with feather-soft touches, he brushed away the melting ice.

Maybe he wasn't entirely hopeless. She wondered if he just hadn't had much practice at this. Comforting someone was an intimate thing, and according to the stories, intimacy didn't end well with Jacks. But he clearly knew how to be gentle. She felt herself thaw in increments as his fingers went to her cheeks, sweeping away the frozen tears.

"Here." It was the other girl's voice. "Feed her this."

Jacks's hand left Evangeline's cheek. Then his fingers were back, tentatively touching her lips. He painted them slowly, carefully, much as he had in the past with his blood. But unlike his blood, this didn't taste sweet or bitter. It didn't really taste at all; it was more like that bubbly feeling that accompanied the moment right before a kiss.

"The antidote's working," said the girl.

"Does that mean I can let her go?"

"Yes," Evangeline managed at the same moment that the

girl said, "No, not unless you want her to die. She'll need close physical contact for at least a full day for the cure to take."

Evangeline had a feeling that the girl was toying with Jacks—*she had to be toying with him.* And even if she weren't, Evangeline couldn't imagine that Jacks would hold on to her, or anyone else, for that length of time. And yet, he made no move to release her.

He held on to her as if she were a grudge, his body rigid and tense, as if he really didn't want her there, and yet his arms were tight around her waist as though he had no intention of ever letting her go.

PART III

Chaos

37

Evangeline woke up in a pair of unyielding arms. She tried to wiggle free, but Jacks held her tightly as her eyes opened and slowly adjusted to the warm light of day.

She hadn't even been aware that she'd fallen asleep, but she must have dozed off in Jacks's lap. Heat curled in her stomach and rose to her cheeks. It was a silly thing to be embarrassed about. She'd almost died, and Jacks had saved her life. Had it been anyone else who'd gone to so much trouble—rescuing her from soldiers, carrying her through the midnight snow, finding her a cure—she'd have thought it might have meant something. But even though Jacks had held her all through the night, his arms were wooden in their grip, his chest was a flat rock against her head. They hadn't curved into each other as she'd slept. Jacks had only saved her because he needed her alive for the prophecy.

She'd known he was lying when he'd called the prophecy dusty and said she didn't need to worry about the Valory Arch. Without the prophecy, Jacks would never have saved her, nor would he have put her in so many terrible positions.

Evangeline tried to move, but her limbs were like lead. All she could do was blink the remaining sleep from her eyes as she finally took in the rest of her surroundings.

Butter-soft light streamed through the rounded windows, gilding every surface of the unexpectedly bright flat that Evangeline found herself in. The walls were covered in bold yellow and orange flowers, the shelves were speckled with glitter, and the books on them were arranged by the color of the spine. And yet none of it was nearly as bright as the girl dressed in a sequined robe, lounging on the striped ginger chaise directly across from Evangeline and Jacks.

"LaLa?"

"Hello, friend." LaLa's grin was nearly incandescent.

Evangeline couldn't decide if it was terribly out of place or perfectly fitting for this strange tableau.

She opened her mouth to do the polite thing and thank her. Evangeline was fairly certain LaLa was the one who'd given Jacks the cure to save her life. She probably owed Jacks a thank-you as well for bringing her here. And yet somehow nothing even remotely close to words of gratitude came out. "I'm so confused. How do the two of you even know each other?"

"She's the Fate that poisoned you," Jacks said.

LaLa gave Jacks an impressive glare. "This is why everyone hates you."

He laughed in response as if they were *flirting*. Was this how Fates flirted—with accusations of murder? Still imprisoned on Jacks's lap, Evangeline couldn't quite see his face. But from the casual way he'd made his claim about LaLa, Evangeline had the impression that he didn't really believe LaLa had tried to kill her and succeeded in killing Apollo.

Unfortunately, it was difficult to be sure about anything with Jacks. Evangeline had the impression that LaLa didn't like Jacks, but perhaps she was attracted to him, or they had some sort of secret liaison. LaLa's cheeks suffused with a pretty blush as they sparred.

LaLa then explained to Evangeline that she was indeed a Fate—the Unwed Bride—though she wasn't inclined to elaborate on that much. Evangeline didn't blame her. In Decks of Destiny, the Unwed Bride was always pictured in a veil of tears. She represented rejection, loss, and unhappily ever afters. It seemed that, unlike Jacks, LaLa could easily find someone to love her whenever she wanted, but the love was doomed to never last. Every girl feared becoming the Unwed Bride, and Evangeline had pitied the idea of her, but the reality of LaLa almost made Evangeline envious.

LaLa was not a wilting maid pining away for lost love. She was the boldest girl at the party, the girl who was unafraid to dance by herself or let a pair of fugitives into her home when they knocked on her door in the dead of night. She had magic and confidence, and she was not afraid of fighting with Jacks. She didn't make being alone seem lonely as Evangeline had always feared. She made it seem like an adventure, as if every moment were the start of a story with endless possibilities.

"They were my tears that poisoned you," LaLa said, "but I didn't try to kill you or Prince Apollo. I sold off some vials of tears ages ago, and I suspect someone must have used one of those. I would tell you who, but it's been so long since I've sold tears, I couldn't even guess where they are now. I swear it. I haven't hurt anyone since coming north. Like most of the other Fates, I fled here to start afresh—after Jacks got us all exiled."

"I'm not the one who got us all exiled," Jacks interrupted.

LaLa gave him a tart look. "You might not have single-handedly gotten us all kicked out of the south, but I heard about some of the things that you did to the empress's younger sister. People said you were obsessed with her."

"This is getting tedious." Jacks suddenly sounded bored. But Evangeline felt every inch of his body flinch at the mention of the empress's sister, the girl that LaLa once said had broken Jacks's heart.

Was this the root of whatever was going on between LaLa and Jacks—was she jealous of this other girl?

"I don't even remember her," Jacks drawled. "And right now, I really think we should focus on the human's past, not mine."

One of his hands left Evangeline's waist so that he could toss a paper onto her lap.

The Daily Rumor

MURDER!

By Kristof Knightlinger

Our beloved Prince Apollo is dead. As I write this, tears keep smearing my ink, because—sadly—this is not a rumor. Every report I've received from Wolf Hall, where the prince was married only yesterday, has said the same thing. His Highness was murdered in his wedding suite.

The news spread quickly after wails from Princess Evangeline were heard from every guard and servant. "I didn't know a human could cry like that," a source close to the princess told me.

However, not everyone under royal employ is convinced that Princess Evangeline's grief was real—especially now that the princess has gone missing.

Some whispers out of Wolf Hall have said that she is a murderess seductress and that she fled with her accomplice, the Fated Prince of Hearts!

I cannot imagine it, and I know there are others who agree. Our new crown prince, Tiberius, is very concerned for his sister-in-law. He believes she may have been kidnapped by Prince Apollo's real killer. Soldiers have been sent across Valorfell and the neighboring provinces to search for Evangeline and bring her safely back to the royal grounds.

Evangeline dropped the paper.

It was tempting to close her eyes and curl into a ball as soon as she finished reading. The words about Apollo looked so cold in print, and they made all of it seem even more final. Apollo was dead, and she was never going to see him again. She was never going to have a chance to make things right or start over as she'd planned. Yesterday around this time, they'd exchanged their wedding vows. Apollo had said he'd happily bleed for her, and now she couldn't help but fear that he'd actually died for her.

She knew his death wasn't her fault, but she felt responsible, as if Apollo might have been strong enough to fight the poison in him if she hadn't just shattered his heart by breaking Jacks's spell on him.

I'm so sorry, Apollo.

Her chest tightened and her eyes burned, but it seemed that she'd shed all her tears last night or she might have started crying again.

With a dry sniffle, she looked back at the cold black-and-white paper that she'd dropped. This time, the words *murderess* and *seductress* were the ones that jumped out.

She hoped that people didn't believe it. But if she continued to stay with Jacks, they most likely would.

"Thank you both for saving me, but I need to return to Wolf Hall and tell Tiberius what really happened. As long as there's a chance that people think I did this, they may never find who actually poisoned Apollo."

"Are you mad?" Jacks twisted her around on his lap and glared. "You cannot go back to Wolf Hall. I guarantee you, Tiberius Acadian is not searching for you because he's worried about you. He wants to find you so that he can blame the murder on you, which shouldn't be difficult. I doubt Apollo's body was even cold before I first heard that you'd been arguing in the wedding suite right before he was found dead."

"I hate to say it, but he's right," LaLa chimed, picking up a cup of tea from a low table laden with a great deal of food and several empty bottles of Fortuna's Fantastically Flavored Water. "You make an excellent murder suspect. Orphan, turned savior, turned bride, turned killer—I'm actually surprised that wasn't Kristof's headline today."

"It will probably be tomorrow," said Jacks.

"But I didn't kill him. There should be proof that someone else did—maybe it was one of the other girls who'd wished to marry him." Evangeline started to stand.

Jacks's arms tightened around her waist, keeping her captive on his lap. "Tiberius and his guards won't care about proof once they have you. For all you know, Tiberius poisoned you and his brother so he could take the throne. All he needs is a wife, and then he's king."

"I don't think he did this," Evangeline argued. She knew the brothers had their differences, and now that Apollo was dead, Tiberius was heir to the throne. But yesterday, she'd really had the impression that Tiberius truly cared about Apollo. And the alternative to trusting Tiberius was trusting Jacks.

"You'd be a fool to put your life in Tiberius's hands," said Jacks. "The only way to clear your name is to find who really did this. I'm your best option for that."

"You expect me to believe that you care about who the real killer is?"

Jacks's mouth turned sullen. "I'm being accused of this crime as well."

"I'm fully aware of that, Jacks, but I also know that the Prince of Hearts has been associated with murders long before Apollo died last night."

Jacks didn't immediately reply, but Evangeline felt his hand against her back, fisting the fabric of her ruined wedding gown and betraying more of his growing frustration. "What other choice do you have but to trust me?"

"I can search on my own!" But even as she said it, Evangeline knew she wouldn't get far without help.

Yet trusting Jacks was a horrid idea. Jacks kept his word, but he also did terrible things like having people turned into stone statues. And Evangeline knew Jacks had only offered to help her because he believed she was the peasant turned princess in the Valory Arch prophecy, which would surely lead her into more trouble. She wondered if this prophecy also might have had something to do with Apollo's death. Was it just a coincidence that her prince died on the night she became the prophecy's princess? She wanted to ask Jacks more about it. But Evangeline didn't feel it was wise to bring up anything related to the Valory Arch in front of LaLa in case it incited a violent reaction.

Evangeline didn't believe that would happen. But she also didn't imagine that LaLa—or any other Fate—would dismiss the Valory Arch as a mere fairytale the same way that Apollo had.

A tremor cut through Evangeline at that particular memory of him. He'd been so playful and sweet and so very much alive as he'd told her about the arch. And he should have still been alive. Evangeline had to find out who'd killed him, and as reluctant as she was to admit it, Jacks was probably the best—and possibly the only—one who could help her.

"If I stay with you, I have a few rules." She finally pulled away from Jacks and stood up to face him. Even though he sat, he was so tall that she did not manage to tower over him. The two of them would never be equal—he would always have more power than she did. But that didn't mean she was powerless. "From now on, this will be a true partnership. You will not leave me behind or keep things that you learn secret. We work together to find Apollo's killer and clear our names. And that is our only goal. If I suspect you have another goal or that you're lying to me, I will walk away and tell Prince Tiberius exactly where to find you."

"Excellent speech!" LaLa cheered with her teacup. "You're making a terrible choice to work with Jacks, but it's a very noble one."

"LaLa," Jacks growled, "I think your services are no longer necessary."

"You're in my flat!"

"Not for much longer. The sun has almost set, and—"

His voice was cut off by a heavy knock. It wasn't on LaLa's door, but it was close enough to rattle the bones of the bright room.

Until that moment, Evangeline hadn't given much thought as to exactly where they all were, but one glance out the window revealed they were at the top of a spire, packed close to other residences. She could see several soldiers in copper tunics and white fur-trimmed cloaks pounding on neighboring doors.

"Are they searching for—"

"Shh—"Jacks put a finger to his mouth. He didn't say another word, and Evangeline didn't see him so much as wrinkle his brow, but a heartbeat later, the soldiers started clearing out of the spire.

Evangeline only counted three of them, and their controlled movements were jerkier than the two soldiers who'd been guarding her yesterday, making her wonder again what the limits of Jacks's powers were. She may have been right when she'd suspected controlling three people at a time was his maximum, at least in the North. But it was still unsettling that he had the power to manipulate her emotions at all.

Evangeline turned her gaze back to Jacks. "I think I need to amend the speech I just gave."

"Don't worry, Little Fox, you'd be far too much trouble for me to want to control. And we're partners," he said pleasantly. "So I know you won't argue with me when I say we need to get out of here now."

"Since it seems you're embracing our new partnership, you'll have no problem telling me where you want to go and why."

To Evangeline's surprise, Jacks answered without hesitation, "We're going to pay a visit to Chaos."

LaLa choked on her tea. "Chaos is a monster!"

"I thought Chaos was another Fate?" Evangeline hazarded.

"Chaos isn't like the rest of us." LaLa set her teacup down with so much force the porcelain cracked and tea spilled through.

Jacks slid her a taunting look. "Still not over things, after all this time?"

"I'll never be over what he did."

"What did he do?" Evangeline asked.

"Chaos is a murderer," LaLa spat.

"He's also extremely useful," Jacks said, kicking his boots up onto the low table. "Chaos is as old as the North, and unlike the rest of us, he was never trapped in a deck of cards. He's been here all this time, collecting favors and people and information. If anyone knows who wanted you and Apollo dead, it will be Chaos. He's the Lord of Spies and Assassins."

"He's also a vampire," LaLa supplied dryly.

38

Evangeline should not have been curious. LaLa clearly thought Chaos was a devil. Jacks didn't appear to feel the same way, but his expression had instantly soured when she'd said the word *vampire*.

Evangeline still wanted to know more. She wanted to know if vampires really slept in coffins, if they could turn into bats—or maybe dragons! But Jacks refused to answer any more questions about Chaos and vampires in general.

"These aren't things to be curious about," Jacks warned. "All you need to know is that vampires lock themselves away at dawn. So unless we want to be imprisoned with the creatures, we need to get in and out of Chaos's lair while it's still dark."

He probably would have dragged Evangeline out of the flat directly after that, if Evangeline and LaLa hadn't both insisted that Evangeline couldn't keep running around without eating or while still wearing her battered wedding dress.

A few breakfast cakes later, LaLa opened up a secret door in the floor. "Let's get you cleaned up and find the perfect outfit for meeting a vampire!" She stole Evangeline away from Jacks with a surprising amount of enthusiasm. LaLa clearly hated Chaos, but she seemed quite eager to prepare Evangeline for this meeting, which made Evangeline mildly nervous as to what LaLa had in mind.

Their journey down a flight of creaky steps was brief and ended in darkness that smelled of tears and tulle.

"Stay right there while I light some lanterns," LaLa trilled.

The snick of the match cut through the quiet, and light tripped across the room, flickering from lantern to lantern. They hung from the exposed ceiling beams, swinging blithely back and forth as they cast a warm umber glow on a jungle of dresses.

The gowns came in shades of frost white, pearl pink, romantic blue, and fresh cream. Some were simple sheaths. Others had elaborate trains or hems covered in everything from silken flowers to seashells. None of them looked as if they'd ever been worn.

"Are these all from your weddings?" Evangeline asked.

LaLa shook her head and looked unusually shy as she ran a hand over an off-white gown with a mermaid skirt. "I make the gowns and sell them. It's a good living, and it helps with the urges."

"The urges?"

"Fates aren't like humans, you know. We don't share all the

same emotions, and some humans think we are entirely un-feeling. But it's the opposite." LaLa's face turned sharp as she gave Evangeline a smile reminiscent of one of Jacks's deviant grins. "When we feel, it's intense and consuming. It devours us and drives us. And the strongest of our feelings is always the urge to be that which we were made to be. I want to feel loved. I want it so badly that I cry poison tears, even though I know every time I find someone to love me, it never lasts—it always ends with me alone at an altar, bawling out even more damned tears. So I sew."

LaLa released the off-white gown to run her fingers over a petal-pink dress with a sweetheart neckline trimmed in spar-kling bows. "I've found that if I can help a bride with her wed-ding, it feeds some of the urge to have a marriage of my own. But the desire is always there. The same is true for Jacks."

LaLa looked so pointedly at Evangeline, the hairs on her arms stood up. Evangeline only knew pieces of Jacks's history, but she knew what he was made to be: a Fate who killed any potential love with his kiss.

"Unlike me," said LaLa, "Jacks actually has hope of finding his true love someday. His story promises there's one girl who's immune to his kiss. So, I imagine the urges he experiences are even stronger than mine."

"If you're trying to warn me away, you don't have to worry," Evangeline said. "Jacks and I don't even like each other."

"I know. But that doesn't matter. Jacks doesn't really like anyone." LaLa ripped off one of the bows she'd been toying with, ruining the gown with one swift tug. "His curse is his kiss, and if there's even a hint of attraction to someone, he'll be drawn to that person in the hope that she's the girl his kiss won't kill. But he always kills them, Evangeline."

"LaLa, I promise, Jacks doesn't feel any attraction toward me. I'm not a threat to the two of you."

"What?" LaLa laughed, so light and luminescent, a few unlit candles burst into flames. "Humans are so funny. I'd never be foolish enough to develop feelings for Jacks. Jacks's idea of love is . . . well, rather terrifying."

"So you don't fancy him?"

"Not at all." She looked genuinely horrified.

"Then why—why are you warning me about him? And why did you save my life for him?"

Something like hurt danced across LaLa's pretty face, and the candles that had just burst to life died out.

"I did it because you and I are friends." Her voice was almost childlike in its sincerity, and Evangeline felt a pang of guilt and sheer stupidity for having so badly misjudged her. LaLa had just been saying that Fates emotions weren't like humans'. Evangeline needed to get better at understanding them if she was going to try to read them. But one thing she could read was LaLa's actions, and they had been one of a friend.

"I understand if you feel differently, now that you know I'm . . ." LaLa trailed off to pick up a jeweled veil as if the object could complete the sentence she seemed scared to finish. "I won't curse you or anything if you don't want to be friends with a Fate. Curses aren't really my bit anyway—I just have the toxic tears and the excessive engagements."

"And you have a friend as well," Evangeline said. "As long as you don't mind that I'm a fugitive who has a habit of making terrible deals with Jacks."

"Everyone makes terrible deals with Jacks!" LaLa squealed, and suddenly Evangeline found herself tangled up in a hug that she hadn't realized she'd needed. Without any shoes on, LaLa was more than several inches shorter than Evangeline, but her hug could not have been mightier. "You won't regret being my friend. We make excellent allies, you'll see!"

LaLa started pulling clothing out of trunks and wardrobes. Most of the items were covered in dragon scales, sequins, or other pieces of ornamentation. But she didn't choose any of those for Evangeline. "We need a different sort of dramatic," she said.

When LaLa finally finished with Evangeline, she stood before a tall mirror and stared at a reflection that seemed as if it should not belong to her.

LaLa had disguised Evangeline's hair with shimmering golden powder and dressed her in a ruffled cape that, instead of fastening around her neck, attached to the thin straps of her shapely black-lace corset, which fed into a tiered midnight-blue skirt made of tulle that only went to her knees, making it easier to move and giving a clear view of the daring black leather boots that went up to her thighs. LaLa had also given her a knife that she could place in the sheath attached to the skirt.

Evangeline looked like a fugitive princess. And even though that was exactly what she was, it was not what she'd been yesterday, and she felt a strange pit in her stomach as she realized that she would never be that girl again. She wasn't the person she had been before. Maybe she hadn't been that girl for a while. She'd known the day she'd entered Jacks's church that whatever she did would change her, and now she was seeing the effect of that choice.

She still believed in love at first sight, but she no longer believed it meant forever love—if it had, she would still be with Luc, living out her happily ever after. But now it was tempting to wonder if there really was a happy ending waiting for her.

Months ago, Poison had warned: *Even if you never want to see Jacks again, you'll gravitate toward him until you fulfill the deal you've made with him.*

And now, here she was. She'd come to the North because she'd thought this was her chance at finding love and happiness, but she wondered if she'd really just been drawn toward Jacks.

"A dark wig would probably be a better disguise, but your hair is too pretty to completely cover up." LaLa added another dusting of gold powder to Evangeline's cheeks and then to her hair, concealing any last remaining hints of pink and completing her transformation.

Her friend had done a wonderful job, but Evangeline felt

a slight stab of worry as she took in the way her cape fastened to leave her neck and décolletage intentionally exposed. She might not have received answers from Jacks about vampires, and her mother had never talked about them. But Evangeline had read a few stories, and they all said that vampires liked blood and biting, and they usually preferred to drink straight from their victims' throats.

"All this skin will drive Chaos mad," said LaLa. "But trust me, he deserves far worse than being a little tortured." With that, LaLa trotted up the stairs as if turning Evangeline into vampire bait was a perfectly reasonable thing to do.

Jacks had also cleaned up while Evangeline had dressed. Once she was upstairs again, she found him in the leather chair beside the crackling fire. He'd changed into a steel-gray doublet with silver matte buttons, which he'd acquired from some unknown source. His sharp face was freshly shaved, and his hair was damp. Blue locks curled haphazardly across his forehead while he idly tossed a pale pink apple, the same soft color as the book in in his hand. He looked up, and then directly at her, as soon as she entered the room.

Evangeline's stomach tumbled. She told herself it was because she was starting to feel hungry, not because of the way Jacks slowly took in every inch of her black thigh-high boots, her shortened skirt, and the form-fitting lace corset cinching her waist and—

He abruptly stopped when he reached all the skin that went from her chest to her neck.

A muscle jumped in his jaw. The color deepened in his eyes. For a fraction of a second, he looked murderous.

Then suddenly, without warning, Jacks tossed her his apple and his expression cleared. "You should bring a snack, it's going to be a long night."

The pink fruit landed gently in Evangeline's hands. It was heavier than an apple should have been. But before she could puzzle that out or consider what had just happened with Jacks, her thoughts shifted their course as she noticed the title of the pink book in his hands. *Recipes of the Ancient North: Translated for the First Time in Five Hundred Years.*

It was the same volume that had been on Marisol's nightstand. Evangeline didn't know how she managed to recall the title. She'd only seen the book once, and it had been over a week ago. She shouldn't have remembered it so well. But she should have remembered her stepsister before now.

"I forgot about Marisol!"

"Who's Marisol?" asked LaLa.

"Her stepsister, but I don't understand why we're talking about her now," Jacks said.

Evangeline nodded to the book in his hands. "That volume was on Marisol's nightstand, and it made me realize how defenseless she is. She's at Wolf Hall, unless the royal soldiers have taken her somewhere else for questioning about me."

Jacks laughed. Because, of course, the idea of someone in danger was amusing to him. "I don't think you need to worry about your stepsister."

"She doesn't have anyone here besides me. If the soldiers have taken her—"

"Your stepsister can take care of herself," Jacks said, "especially if she was reading this book."

"Are you certain she had *that* book?" LaLa worried her lip between her teeth as her eyes darted to the volume in question.

Nothing could have looked more innocuous. The fabric on the cover was pretty pink with lovely foil titling. It looked like the sort of tome one would wrap in a bow and give as a gift, but LaLa eyed it as if it would jump from Jacks's hands and cross the room to attack her.

"Why are you looking at that book as if it's dangerous?"

"Because it is," Jacks said.

"It's a very nasty spell book," LaLa explained. "After the Valors were killed, most magic was banned in the North. So those who still wanted to traffic in it changed the names of their spell books. It's much easier to get away with buying or possessing books of forbidden arts when no one knows what they are."

"Marisol must have bought it by mistake. She's terrified of magic, and she loves baking."

"You don't pick that book up by mistake," Jacks said. "No reputable bookshop would carry it."

"Then Marisol stumbled into another kind of store accidentally," Evangeline argued. She'd doubted her stepsister before, and she was determined not to do it again.

Evangeline knew that Kristof Knightlinger had accused

Marisol of visiting several high-tiered spell shops to turn Evangeline back to stone. But Evangeline wasn't stone. And she wasn't dead. Someone might have tried to poison her last night, but she couldn't believe it was Marisol. Marisol wasn't a killer, and if Marisol had really wanted to murder her, she'd had plenty of opportunities.

Evangeline looked at LaLa, who tugged at the sequins on her sleeve, a little embarrassed at having the book in her possession. "What types of spells are in there? Does it have a recipe for the poison I consumed?"

"No. There are no spells that can mimic my tears."

Evangeline felt a bright surge of relief. It couldn't have been Marisol, then.

"However," LaLa added, "if your stepsister is reading that book, I would agree with Jacks. She is far from helpless, and she's probably up to something."

"But you own it, too, and, Jacks—you were reading it!"

"Which proves her point." Jacks shrugged.

"We're not saying your stepsister killed Apollo and poisoned you," LaLa said, "but she might not be who you think she is."

"She's definitely not who you think she is," Jacks muttered. "But if you want to really find out if she's involved in this murder or if it's someone else, we need to leave now and talk to Chaos."

39

It looked like the sort of night that one would plan on meeting a vampire. Everything was damp mist and white snow and wan light from a moon lost somewhere in the silver fog. Luckier people were probably telling stories before warm fires or tucked away in blanketed beds, not freezing as they crossed a rickety bridge and reached an isolated cemetery where dogs howled like wolves and a vampire lord hid his underground court.

Evangeline shivered, and Jacks watched her, but he offered absolutely no comfort as a gust of wind tore through the fog and posters with her likeness flapped against gnarled gates and trees.

MISSING: Princess Evangeline
Help us find her!

Evangeline wanted to ask how the signs had been made and put up so quickly, but now that she and Jacks were on the outskirts of the city, where it felt safer to finally speak, she wanted to use her questions wisely.

"Tell me about the vampires."

Jacks's mouth twisted distastefully. "Don't let them bite you."

"I already know that. What else can you share? Maybe something helpful."

"There's nothing helpful about vampires," Jacks grunted. "I know the stories make them sound brooding and beautiful, but they're parasitic bloodsuckers."

Evangeline side-eyed Jacks, wishing the night weren't as dark or that he weren't walking so far from her so that she could have a clearer view of his face. Earlier, she'd sensed he wasn't overly fond of vampires, but he'd not been this annoyed, and he'd defended Chaos to LaLa.

"Are you jealous?" Evangeline asked.

"Why would I be jealous?"

"Because I'm so curious."

Jacks answered with an acerbic laugh.

Evangeline felt her cheeks go hot, but she wasn't sure she believed his dismissal. Jacks was used to being the most interesting wherever he went. He was the most powerful, the most unpredictable, and until now, he'd always made Evangeline the most curious. "If you're not jealous, then what do you have against them? This was your idea, and it's not as if you don't have a thing for blood."

"I also like the sun and being in control of my own life. But vampires will always be ruled by their hunger for blood. Their every desire is dominated by bloodlust. So try not to cut yourself while we're inside. And don't look in their eyes."

"What will happen if I look in their eyes?"

"Just don't do it."

"Why not? Does the mighty Prince of Hearts know so little about vampires that all he can do is warn me not to—"

Jacks moved before she could finish. He suddenly stood so close that for a pounding heartbeat she could only see his cruel face. His brilliant eyes shone in the dark, and his predatory smile could have belonged to a vampire had his teeth been just a little sharper. "There's a reason no one ever talks about them." His voice became low and lethal. "I can tell you that they're soulless monsters. I can warn you that if you look into a vampire's eyes, they'll take it as an invitation to rip into your throat faster than you can scream the word *no*. But none of this will scare you away. Their stories are cursed, but instead of warping the truth, they manipulate the way people feel. No matter what I tell you about vampires, you're going to be intrigued instead of horrified. Your kind always wants to be bitten or changed."

"Not me," Evangeline argued.

"But you're curious," Jacks challenged.

"I'm curious about a lot of things. I'm curious about you, but I don't want you to bite me!"

The corner of Jacks's mouth twitched. "I've already done that, Little Fox."

His cold fingers found her wrist and slipped underneath the edge of her glove to stroke the last remaining broken heart scar.

"Lucky for you, no matter how many times I bite you, you'll never turn into what I am. But sometimes all it takes from a vampire is one look, and you're theirs."

Jacks eyed the bare stretch of skin that went from her chest to her neck. And before she could read the look on his face, he dropped her wrist and stalked off into a dark kingdom of crypts and tombstones.

They walked in near silence until Jacks found a broad mausoleum covered in vines of demon's bittercress and guarded by two sad stone angels. One angel mourned over a pair of broken wings while the other played a harp with broken strings.

Jacks idly plucked at one of the damaged strings. After strumming several soundless notes, the door to the mausoleum slid open.

There normally might have been a gate to separate visitors from the coffins, but instead there was another door. Old and wooden with a touch of iron scrollwork, it resembled a number of the doors she'd seen at Wolf Hall—except for the glowing keyhole. Honey-thick light poured through the little curving shape, gleaming brighter the closer they drew to the door, flickering and promising, and far more inviting than the door to Jacks's church had been. That door didn't want to be opened, but this one did.

Come in from out of the cold, it whispered. *I'll keep you warm.*

Jacks speared her with a quicksilver glare. "Don't be dazzled. You're useless to me as a vampire."

"Well, let's hope I don't decide I'd rather be a vampire than be useful to you."

Jacks's eyes turned into daggers.

Evangeline fought the urge to flash him a gloating smile, but a corner of it snuck out. She knew she couldn't become too comfortable with taunting Jacks, but just because she liked a door didn't mean she was going to step through and bare her throat for a vampire. She was also feeling emboldened by the knowledge that she was not as replaceable as he'd tried to make her believe. He needed her for his precious Valory Arch, which wasn't entirely reassuring, but she'd worry about that later, after she found Apollo's real killer and cleared her name of suspicion. "Instead of telling me what I shouldn't do, you should make more of an effort to do things that make me want to continue working with you."

"Such as saving your life?"

"You did that for yourself."

"But I still did it. If it weren't for me, your story would be over." Jacks ended the conversation by hitting his knuckles against the door and saying, "We're here to see Chaos."

"The master is not accepting visitors tonight," said a voice like a heavy rain, musical and enthralling.

Jacks rolled his eyes. "Tell your master that the Prince of Hearts is here, and he owes me an unforgiven debt."

The door opened immediately.

Jacks clenched his jaw, almost as if he wished his words hadn't worked.

It would have been easy for Evangeline to anger Jacks further by making a show of being bewitched. The vampire who opened the door was exactly what she'd expected. He looked like the son of a warrior demigod—or someone who just had really excellent bone structure. Dressed like an elegant assassin in a fitted black leather tunic and a high-collared coat that had thick cuffs that folded up to his muscled forearms and revealed skin so flawless it glowed.

She remembered not to look in the vampire's eyes. But she could feel the heat pouring off him. His gaze hungrily raked over her form-fitting corset with a smile that was all sharp fangs.

Her heart raced.

His fangs grew longer.

Relax. Jacks's voice in Evangeline's head. *Fear only excites them, Little Fox.*

Her blood continued to rush. *You still can't control me,* she thought back. *And you told me you wouldn't try.*

I was only trying to warn you, Jacks silently replied.

And then, as if he weren't a monster as well, Jacks slid an arm underneath her cape and wrapped it around Evangeline's waist, holding her possessively tight as he drawled, "Stop flashing your fangs. I'm the only one who gets to bite her."

Jacks nipped at Evangeline's ear, cold and sharp. She felt the sting of it everywhere, covering her with gooseflesh, which somehow turned to blush when it reached her cheeks.

No matter how many times I bite you, you'll never turn into what I am, he'd said. And now he was doing it, just to prove that he could.

Evangeline started to pull away.

Don't. Jacks spread his fingers and tightened his grip on her waist. *Humans don't have power here. If he thinks I can't control you, he'll do it, and I guarantee you'll enjoy that even less.*

You still didn't have to bite me, Evangeline thought. And she would have shaken him off, but she wasn't there to fight with Jacks. She was there because Apollo was dead and she needed to find out who'd killed him.

So instead of battling Jacks, she gritted her teeth as he released her waist and took hold of her hand.

Without another word, their vampire guide led them forward.

At first the wide hallways and the dramatic stone staircases were not so different from the oldest parts of Wolf Hall. The walls were covered with works of art, ancient shields, and steel blades that took on a bronze tint beneath the heavy rings of candle-covered chandeliers.

The stairs took them deeper and deeper underground, where the air once again turned to frost, and Evangeline found herself fighting the urge to lean into Jacks. So far, there were no coffins or corpses, but she heard several rattling noises that sounded like chains. A few steps later, she might have caught the coppery scent of blood. And were those shackles hanging between a pair of portraits?

After another flight of stairs, their guide directed them into an indoor courtyard full of limestone columns and night-blooming flowers, where it was impossible to miss all the shackles. They gleamed against the walls and columns, polished and ready to use. Manacles for wrists and ankles and necks were proudly displayed above game tables set with black-and-white chessboards.

The seats were all empty, but Evangeline had horrible flashes of vampires lounging in leather chairs and playing with pawns and rooks while their bleeding human captives writhed against their restraints.

Her discomfort increased as she and Jacks were led from the indoor courtyard into a banquet room. It was also similar to the ones in Wolf Hall, with rich wine-red rugs and an enormous table. But here, there were human-size cages dangling in between the chandeliers, and instead of silver plates and cloth napkins, the tables were set with more chains and shackles that attached to the wood.

Evangeline felt sick.

Thankfully, all the constraints were unoccupied. But the emptiness of everything unsettled her as well. Where was everyone? And where exactly was their guide taking them?

"Still curious about vampires?" Jacks murmured.

"Why is this place so vacant?" Evangeline said under her breath. "Where—"

She froze as their guide disappeared. He moved quicker than an arrow being shot from a bow. One moment he was a few feet in front of them, and then he was gone. He darted through a door at the end of the room with preternatural speed, leaving them alone. "Where did he just go?"

"This is why I hate vampires." Jacks worked his jaw as his eyes darted from the door their guide had just gone through to the cages hanging above. "I think we might need to get out of here."

"I'm disappointed, my friend," said a voice like smoke and velvet, gritty and slightly hypnotic. "You're the one who taught me how useful cages can be."

Evangeline didn't even see this vampire enter. He was just there, slowly walking toward them. He wore no coat or cloak, just sinuous leather armor and a vicious bronze helm that concealed his face, save his eyes and the slash of his cheekbones.

"It's you," Evangeline breathed. "You're the soldier from the party, and the spires."

"Not actually a soldier, princess." His voice was softer when he spoke to her, pure velvet without the smoke. "I'm Chaos. Welcome to my home."

40

Chaos was suddenly before her, taking her gloved hand in his and bringing it to where his lips would have been had he not worn the bronze helm.

Jacks might have tried to tug her away, but she was only half paying attention to him. She'd made the mistake of looking into Chaos's eyes—although, as soon as she had done it, it didn't feel like a mistake. How could eyes so magnificent be a mistake? They were bottle green and brilliant, with slivers of gold that made it look as if they'd been shot through with broken pieces of stars. Or he was a star, fallen to the earth, and if she made a wish, he could grant it with one—

"Evangeline," Jacks growled. His cold fingers gripped her cheek and wrenched her back until her eyes met his. She wanted to return to the other, beautiful bottle-green eyes. But Jacks's harsh gaze worked like an antidote to the vampire's wonder, reminding her that looking into Chaos's eyes would not lead to wishes come true but to shackles and cages and sharp teeth tearing into her skin.

Don't do that again, Little Fox.

He dropped his hand from her face.

Evangeline felt her cheeks go red. It was just what he'd warned her about. *Sometimes all it takes from a vampire is one look, and you're theirs.* The first vampire had been attractive in an expected way, but it was as if something extra poured off Chaos, something that hadn't been there the other times they'd met. Even now she could feel it, tempting her to take another look, to forget the way that LaLa had called him a monster.

Chaos laughed, loud and easy. "You should have prepared her better, my friend. She seems particularly sensitive to allure. Or maybe she just likes me more than she likes you."

"She hates me," Jacks said pleasantly. "So even if she likes you more, that's not saying very much."

"Are you certain about that?" Chaos slid another gaze Evangeline's way.

Fresh heat prickled her skin.

There were different types of vampire gazes. Evangeline was not yet familiar with them all. She couldn't completely tell the difference between a hungry gaze and a seductive gaze, or the gaze of a vampire right before he gives chase. The gazes she'd felt so far just felt like heat, as if parts of her were too close to a fire. She could feel that burn coming off Chaos now as he offered her his arm.

"Don't worry, princess, the only people who are put in those cages are ones who wish to be there."

Evangeline still weighed her options. Earlier, it would have been appealing to take Chaos's arm just to irritate Jacks. Now that choice wasn't as inviting. But considering that they were there to acquire information from him, she wasn't sure it was wise to dismiss his offer either. In fact, it probably wouldn't have been wise to reject it even if they didn't want something from Chaos.

Evangeline accepted his arm. Despite the layer of leather, he felt much warmer than Jacks.

Don't get too cozy, Little Fox. Jacks's expression was a mask of disinterest, but the voice in her head was distinctly irritated. *There's a reason why he wears the helm.*

Why is that? Evangeline asked.

But Jacks didn't answer her question.

After a moment, she cast a quick look up toward Chaos's cruel helm. She caught a glimpse of flawless olive skin, but she didn't dare look past his cheekbones, and even they were obscured by spikes jutting out of the headpiece. It couldn't have been comfortable. The entire lower half of Chaos's face was completely covered, including his mouth, which, now that she thought about it, was peculiar for a being supposedly controlled by its lust for blood.

He turned his head, gaze scorching her as he caught her staring.

Quickly, she tore her attention away.

"You don't have to avoid my eyes." His velvet voice moved to her ear, the warm metal of his helm intentionally brushing her temple. "The helm you were staring at is cursed, and it prevents me from biting anyone. You're perfectly safe from me. Isn't that right, Jacks?"

"He's been trapped in that thing for centuries," Jacks confirmed. *But you will never be safe with him.*

They traveled through another series of hostile halls before Chaos finally released Evangeline's arm to open a heavy iron door with a mere tug of gloved fingers.

At a glance, the room they entered could have belonged to a scholar. There were bins of papyrus scrolls and shelves and tables laden with leather-bound books, pens, and parchments, all drenched in warm candlelight bright enough to read by. Even the air smelled of paper, mixed with redolent hints of mahogany.

It wasn't until Evangeline went to take a seat in one of the chairs that she noticed all the thick shackles on the arms and legs, some of which had nasty barbs that would pierce a person's skin when the manacle was put on. She went for another seat, but all the chairs contained the same ominous restraints.

"Really?" Jacks took one of the shackles and twirled it in his fingers as if it were a cheap piece of jewelry. "These are getting to be a bit much. You might want to reconsider how you entertain your guests if you have to chain them all up."

"I'm surprised you're so judgmental," said Chaos. "I heard

about what you did with that princess. What was her name—
Diana?"

"I have no idea who you're talking about," Jacks said
smoothly, though Evangeline noticed him tense just as he had
when LaLa had said that Jacks had been obsessed with Princess *Donatella.*

Unfortunately, Evangeline didn't get further answers. Chaos
didn't say more on the subject as he crossed over to a pair of burgundy curtains and parted the drapes halfway. Not quite enough
for Evangeline to see what they'd been concealing, although she
heard chatter from the other side; it sounded like a number of
people all trying not to talk too loudly as their voices echoed
upward.

Giving into her curiosity, Evangeline moved closer to the
parted curtains.

It seemed they were actually on a balcony overlooking a
small amphitheater. The railing on the other side of the drapes
was all marbled stone, as was the floor far below, where a gathering of vampires and humans stood on a massive black-and-
white checkered board.

She hoped they were playing kissing chess. She couldn't
bring herself to imagine other more likely reasons as to why all
the vampires were dressed in bloodred and the humans were
clad in white, and standing on opposite sides of the board.

Many of the humans might have appeared attractive or
strong under other circumstances, but in comparison to the
row of vampires, they looked tired and worn. Their shoulders

weren't as straight and their hair was duller; their various shades of skin did not gleam like polished stone.

"I hope you all know," Chaos called down, "I've come to think of many of you as my family, and I hope your fate turns out better than theirs did. Good luck."

The amphitheater erupted in movement.

"What are they doing?" Evangeline's hands clutched the marble rail as she watched the vampires cross the checkered floor in blurs of speed. Bloodred collided with white as each vampire found a human, and Evangeline could already tell none of them were going to be kissing.

"Isn't this practice rather archaic?" Jacks asked. He'd dropped the chair's fetter to join them at the balcony rail. But he appeared far from entertained by the scene below. If Evangeline hadn't known better, she might have thought Jacks was concerned. He gripped the railing almost as tightly as she did while the vampires bared their fangs and bit into the necks of every human on the floor.

41

Gasps and wails and a few harsh grunts consumed the amphitheater.

"Stop them!" Evangeline cried.

"None of them would be pleased if I did that," Chaos said. "All the humans have been waiting for this night."

"Why would anyone want this?" Evangeline watched helplessly as chains rattled and a number of human-size cages were lowered to the checked ground.

A girl about her age, with long spirals of red and copper hair, fought against the vampire who'd bit her as he shoved her in one of the cages and closed it with a heavy lock.

Everything was clattering metal and pained pleas as some people were dragged out of the amphitheater. Other humans filled the rest of the cages, which were then raised back toward the ceiling. And any lingering romantic notions of vampires that Evangeline had completely disappeared.

"Let them out," she demanded. She might have done something terribly reckless then, like grab for anything with weapon potential and toss it toward the cages, but Jacks's hand slid across the rail and twined his cold fingers with hers. He didn't hold her back, he just held her hand, stunning her into silence.

"You don't want any of them out of their cages," Chaos said. He sounded faintly amused, but it was difficult to be sure when his bronze helm concealed most of his expression.

"This is the final phase of our initiation process to join the Order of Spies and Assassins. There are two different types of vampire bites. We can bite a human merely to feed from them. Or we can infect our bites with vampire venom to turn a human into a vampire. Every human on that floor received a bite infected with venom."

"So they're all turning into vampires now?" Evangeline hazarded a look toward the cages. The captives were rattling the bars and ripping at the locks, looking close to feral. Yet they also appeared more attractive than before. Their skin glowed. Their movements were knife-quick, and even matted with blood, their hair shone like curtains of silk.

"The venom has fixed their human imperfections, but they won't become vampires unless they drink human blood before dawn," Chaos said. "At sunrise, the vampire venom will dissipate. Until that happens, the changelings will fight with all their power to get out of their prisons and feed. The ones that succeed in breaking free of their cages and drinking human blood will become full-fledged vampires and members of our order."

"What happens to the others?" Evangeline asked.

"You should be more concerned that you two are the closest things to humans here. So you might want to make the rest of this meeting quick. The urge to take that first bite is overwhelming. We call it *hunger*, but it's really pain." Chaos paused long enough for Evangeline to hear nothing, save for the rattle of cages.

Then she felt the surge of heart at her neck and chest, letting her know that Chaos's gaze was on her. Hot and hungry and—

Jacks cleared his throat.

Chaos averted his eyes.

Evangeline breathed, but not too deeply.

"The changelings might not be at full vampire strength," Chaos continued smoothly, "but the intense desire to feed and survive can sometimes make up for it. One or two of them always manage to escape."

A spark of crimson flashed in Evangeline's peripheral vision. The girl with the red and copper curls was in a cage not too far from the balcony, only now her hair looked like pure flames, and she appeared far from helpless as her fingers curled around the bars and her tongue darted out to lick her lips.

Evangeline found herself squeezing Jacks's hand harder, feeling thankful he'd not let her go.

Chaos tilted his head, eyes landing on their intertwined hands. "Interesting."

"This is getting tedious." Jacks dropped Evangeline's hand and sauntered back into the scholarly suite, where the rasp of vampire changelings and the rattle of cages weren't so all consuming.

Chaos and Evangeline followed. The vampire took a seat in a large leather chair, the only one without shackles. He motioned toward the other seats, but Evangeline chose to stand. Knowing how quickly vampires could move, she didn't want to sit in a chair where her wrists and ankles could be so easily imprisoned.

"We want to know who killed Apollo," Jacks said.

Chaos looked up at Evangeline. "I heard you did it, while in bed, on your—"

"It wasn't me," she interrupted.

"That's disappointing. I was going to offer you a job."

"I'm not a killer," Evangeline said. "Someone else poisoned my husband."

"We wanted to know if any of your people were hired for the job," Jacks added.

Chaos leaned back in his leather chair and steepled his fingers with the slow ease of someone who didn't have to worry about the rabid changelings fighting to escape their cages. Or he really just wanted to waste their time on purpose.

"You owe me a debt," Jacks reminded him.

"Relax, old friend, I was just going to say that no one came to us for this job," Chaos said eventually. "But I remember . . . about a week ago, I think it was the evening after Nocte

Neverending, my potions master received a rare request for a bottle of malefic oil."

"What's malefic oil?" Evangeline asked.

"It's a very effective method of murder," Chaos replied. "It's not typically popular, since it takes a particular skill to work with. Most toxins have the same type of effect on every human, making them easily detectable and sloppy instruments of death. But if you have the spell and the preternatural skills to combine malefic oil with the blood, the tears, or the hair of a person you wish to kill, it is only toxic to that person."

Evangeline tensed, thinking of the last time she'd seen Apollo, his chest covered in a glistening substance that looked like oil.

"Who asked for the poison?" Jacks said.

"I wasn't there when the request was made," Chaos said. "I only know it came from a female, and I'd wager she's a witch. It takes a fair amount of power and a spell to properly combine the ingredients."

Evangeline instantly thought of Marisol and her cooking spell books. But why would Marisol want to kill Apollo? Apollo had given her a new home and restored her reputation. It also didn't make sense for Marisol to go to the trouble of securing a rare toxin that would only work on the prince, and then also poison a bottle of wine with something that could kill anyone who drank from it. Unless two different people had been trying to commit murder?

But that still didn't mean Marisol was involved.

The Fortuna matriarch had already tried to kill Evangeline once. Although Kristof had written that the matriarch had suffered from a *fall* that had stolen some of her memories, making her an unlikely suspect.

"Is there anything else you can tell us about the woman who bought the oil?" Evangeline asked.

Chaos toyed with a chain hanging from his neck and shook his head.

"If that's all you have, this doesn't clear your debt," Jacks said. "We should leave."

"Wait." Evangeline's eyes were still on the chain around Chaos's neck. She hadn't noticed it before. When it had been flat against his leather armor, the chain and the medallion at the end of it had blended in. But now that the chain was in Chaos's hands, Evangeline could see the aged medallion clearly enough to make out the symbol on it—the head of a wolf wearing a crown. The same symbol that had been burned into the door in the library, the door that all the books on the Valors were locked behind.

Maybe it was just a coincidence. But it felt like a clue. Chaos might not have been able to identify Apollo's killer, but what if he knew something about the Valory Arch and what really had been locked behind it? She knew that wasn't why they were visiting the vampire, but it was the reason Jacks had sabotaged the course of her life.

"Where did you get that medallion?" she asked.

Chaos looked down as if he weren't even aware of the object he'd been toying with. "I took this from Wolfric Valor."

"We don't have time for this," Jacks groaned.

An impressive crash came from the amphitheater. A cage had fallen to the floor.

The vampires inside the other room all clapped.

Evangeline looked out to the balcony. The vampire changeling inside the fallen cage had yet to break the lock, but given the way he fought with it, all tearing fingers and fearless growls, Evangeline doubted this young man would stay imprisoned much longer. They needed to leave soon, but Chaos had just said that he'd taken the medallion around his neck from Wolfric Valor.

Chaos had been alive at the same time as the Valors. Jacks had told Evangeline that Chaos was as old as the North, but she hadn't realized the implication of that information until now.

The excitement must have shown on her face.

Beside her, Jacks went as taut as a bowstring.

Then Chaos was saying, "If you're curious about the Valors, I can tell you whatever you want to know. I was there, and I remember the truth."

No. Jacks's voice seethed inside her head, and for once, his ruthless expression matched his words. *Don't even think about it.*

More cages rattled in the background.

"It won't cost you much," Chaos said. "I'll answer any questions you have in exchange for one bite."

"I thought you couldn't take off your helm."

"He's trying to get us to stay so that his changelings will have prey to chase," Jacks said.

But Evangeline didn't need a warning from Jacks to know this was an ill-advised bargain. She might have joked with Jacks once about making a deal with another Fate, but she wouldn't do it ever again. It was bad enough she still owed Jacks a kiss; she didn't want to owe this vampire anything. "Thank you for the offer, but I think I'd rather leave before your changelings break free."

Chaos dropped the medallion and leaned back in the chair. "If you make it out and change your mind, return any time, princess."

"I—"

Jacks didn't give her the chance to finish replying before he ushered her out the door.

The halls of Chaos's underground kingdom were darker than she'd remembered. Half the candles had burned out, covering her and Jacks in shadows and smoke as they hurried down the first corridor.

"Promise me you'll never let him bite you," Jacks said.

"I won't ever need to if you tell me what you want inside the Valory Arch."

"I thought you wanted this partnership to be about finding Apollo's killer, not my other goals." Jacks's tone hardened as he reached the dining room with all the cages.

Evangeline heard the riot of chains before they stepped inside. She hadn't forgotten about the cages there, but she hadn't expected them all to be full of desperate changelings.

Dread clutched at her chest like a hand with claws every time one of them called out.

"I'll make you immortal if you unlock my cage!"

"I'll just take one tiny bite," another promised.

"Some humans like being bitten."

"Eva . . . is that you?" The voice had a more soothing timbre than the others, and the familiar sound of it lodged Evangeline's heart into her throat.

Luc.

She hadn't heard Luc's voice in months, but it sounded just like him, if not a little lovelier.

It had to be some sort of vampire trick.

"Don't stop moving." Jacks tugged on her hand. But he should have yanked harder. He should have used his Fated strength because although Evangeline's head agreed with Jacks, her human heart made her stop, pull her hand free of Jacks's hand, look up at the cage above, and lock eyes with her first love.

42

Something wet dripped down Evangeline's cheek. She was crying, but she couldn't have said why. She didn't know if her emotions were broken and leaking out all over from everything that had happened, or if it was the sight of her once beloved Luc locked in a cage, eyes staring down at her with something like adoration and terror.

"It's really you," Luc said. He gripped the bars with two beautiful brown hands, but he didn't take his eyes off hers. And no power in the world could have forced her to look away from him. It wasn't vampire allure or the shimmering gold flecks in his irises that she didn't remember from before. His eyes weren't exactly the same eyes she knew, but they weren't entirely different either. They were still the impossibly warm brown that lived in all the memories she'd tried to shove away but had been unable to forget.

"There are so many things I have to tell you, Eva. But I need you to help me out of this cage—if I don't escape by dawn, they'll kill me."

"Why are you even here?" she breathed, heart pounding so fast it was hard to form words. It felt like a twisted answer to a wish. *Here's the boy you've spent months pining for, but now he might die, and if you try to help him, you might die.*

"Little Fox," Jacks said. "We need to keep moving. He'll tell you whatever he needs to get out of that cage and take a bite out of you."

"No! I would never hurt you." Luc's voice was harsher than she remembered, desperate. "Eva, please don't leave. I know you must be terrified, but I won't bite you if you let me out—I don't want to be a vampire. I only came here because I was told that vampire venom was the most powerful healer in the world and it could erase my scars and wounds."

Every inch of his skin was flawless, more perfect than in all her memories. Too perfect. It was hard to believe there'd ever been any scars. And Evangeline wanted to tell him that she would not have cared if he had scars all over his person—in fact, she'd have preferred them to this overly polished version of him. But Luc went on before she could. "That's all I wanted, to be healed. I—" His eyes shot around the violent room of cages.

The other changelings had gone briefly still. They watched the exchange with rapt, inhuman attention. Evangeline didn't want to believe Luc was like them. His voice was pure human emotion. But when she searched beyond his eyes, he looked like the others, dried blood marring the warm brown of his throat and staining the white of his shirt. "I don't want this, I swear."

"He's lying." Jacks grabbed for Evangeline's wrist and pulled.

She couldn't blame him. This wasn't the only room full of almost-vampires. But Luc wasn't a vampire yet.

"Eva," Luc pleaded. "I know you have every reason to hate me. I know I broke your heart. But I was under a curse."

Jacks's grip on Evangeline's wrist slipped.

"Did you say curse?" she asked. And suddenly Luc no longer felt like the warped product of a wish. He felt like a truth that she was afraid to touch. Evangeline had felt half-mad for the last couple of months, wondering if Luc really was cursed or if she'd just conjured the idea of a curse as a way to survive his rejection.

Jacks's cold hand tugged again on hers, another warning that it was time to go, but Evangeline ignored it.

"What kind of curse were you under?" she asked.

Luc let go of a bar to run a hand through his hair, a familiar and terribly human gesture that brought another pang to her heart. "I didn't realize it until tonight, until the vampire venom was in me and suddenly my head cleared. I can't describe what it was like before. All I know was that your stepsister was all that I could think about. She was the reason I came here—I needed to be perfect for her. After I got mauled by the wolf, my scars weren't sexy scars—"

"He just said sexy scars," Jacks drawled. "Are you really listening to this?"

"Shh," Evangeline hissed.

"After I was attacked," Luc said, "your stepsister took one look at me and ran from the house. I tried visiting her when my injuries had improved, but she wouldn't even answer the door. I tried writing, but she wouldn't reply to my letters."

"She told me it was the other way around."

A resentful shake of his head. "She's a liar. If Marisol had written me, I couldn't have ignored her letters even if I'd wanted to. She made me desperate to do anything to have her. I was obsessed. It started the same day that I proposed to her. I'd come to the house to see you, but Marisol was the one to greet me. She took my coat, and I remember her fingers brushing my neck. After that, she was all I could think of." His tone turned disgusted.

It was just as Evangeline had believed. She hadn't been delusional or desperate. Luc had only abandoned her and asked Marisol to marry him because he'd been cursed. The only thing she'd been wrong about was who had cast the spell. It wasn't her stepmother, it was Marisol.

Evangeline felt as if she'd been punched in her stomach. She'd thought Marisol was another victim, an innocent, the one she'd needed to make amends to. All this time, Evangeline had been feeling so guilty over ruining Marisol's life, but if this was true, then Marisol had upended Evangeline's life first.

She didn't want to jump too quickly to conclusions. But she'd seen her stepsister's spell books, she'd been warned by Jacks, the papers, and now by Luc, who never even knew that Evangeline thought he was cursed.

"When I was bitten tonight, it felt like the first time in months I could freely think." Luc's eyes shone as he looked down on her. "I finally felt like myself again. But then I was being dragged into this cage, and now I'll never leave it alive unless you help me. If you're scared, you don't have to unlock it. Just hand me one of the weapons from the wall and I can break the lock myself. Then I'll prove to you that I don't want to be a vampire. All I want is you, Eva."

"Don't even consider it," Jacks said.

"But—" She stared at Luc once more through the bars. "I can't leave him like this."

"Evangeline, look at me." Jacks cupped her cheeks with his cold hands and met her eyes with a brutal stare as if he could break the spell that Luc had put her under.

But she wasn't under any vampire allure. She wasn't sure if a part of her still loved Luc. Her feelings were such a jumbled and chaotic mess. Right now, she primarily felt the need to survive. Love felt like a distant luxury. But she couldn't walk away from Luc and leave him here to die. He was a victim in all of this. He was the one put under a spell, then turned to stone, attacked by a wolf, and now put in a cage.

"This is partly my fault," she whispered to Jacks.

"No, it's not. I already told you, I had nothing to do with the wolf." Jacks spoke quietly yet firmly.

But even if Jacks was telling the truth, that didn't change what she needed to do.

She pulled free of his hand.

What happened next was a strange blur. Evangeline still wanted to think she wasn't under a spell, but maybe she was a little entranced, and not by vampire allure. She was feeling the return of her hope.

Evangeline knew that Luc could never go back to being the boy he was, and she'd stopped being the girl she was. That girl would have believed that seeing Luc again meant that something wonderful would happen, that they'd receive a happy ending after all. But all this meeting guaranteed was that they would have a different ending. What sort of ending still had to be determined, but it would certainly be better than this. Even if Luc wasn't her happily ever after, she couldn't let their story finish here, with him in this cage and her running away.

Evangeline found a blue shortsword on the wall with a heavy hilt and a polished blade; it looked strong enough to break a lock, but it wasn't too heavy for her to lift.

Other changelings cried out, asking for weapons and promising all sorts of things in exchange. They'd started battling with their cages again, filling the dining room with a cacophony of violent sounds as Evangeline climbed up onto a chair and used both hands to lift the sword above her head.

Luc grabbed the blade, not caring that it sliced into his hands. "Thank you, Eva." He smiled, but it wasn't the crooked boyish grin that she'd fallen in love with. It was lips pulling back over sharp white fangs that were growing longer.

"We're leaving now." Jacks took her hand, urging her down from the chair and propelling her into motion.

A crash sounded, making her trip over her feet as she started to run.

Luc had already broken the lock with the hilt of the weapon. The door to his cage dangled open. He was loose and feral and the worst mistake she had ever made.

"Sorry, Eva." Luc leaped to the ground in a graceful arch, bared his fangs, and lunged for her.

Jacks shoved her out of the way before she could move. Lightning fast, he darted in front of her like a shield.

Luc didn't have time to switch course, and his teeth clamped onto Jacks's neck with a sickening tear.

"No!" Evangeline screamed and scrambled for the dropped sword she'd given Luc. The weapon felt heavier than it had been moments ago. But it didn't seem necessary.

In the time it took her to grab the sword, Jacks had taken Luc's head between his hands—and with one sharp twist he broke Luc's neck.

The captives above all booed and hissed as Evangeline's first love fell to the ground.

"You—you—you killed him," she stammered.

"He bit me—" Jacks snarled, gold-flecked blood dripping

from the wound at his throat. "I wish I'd killed him. But I didn't. He's a full-fledged vampire now. The only way to permanently kill one of them is to cut off its head or shove a wooden stake through its heart."

Jacks reached for the sword in Evangeline's hands.

She clutched the weapon tighter. A part of her knew she should have let it go. Luc was not her Luc anymore. He'd bitten Jacks, and he would have bitten her. But Luc hadn't killed Jacks.

"I won't let you end his life," Evangeline said. "Luc is the first boy I loved, and I'm not responsible for his choices, but this wouldn't have happened if it weren't for me. Let him live, and I'll leave without any more stops or arguments."

She dropped the sword and reached for Jacks's hand.

He recoiled, not letting her touch him, but he didn't argue. He didn't say anything at all.

Evangeline and Jacks silently left the way they came. She struggled to keep up with Jacks's long strides as the rattle of chains and cages continued to chase them, yet it was his silence that was starting to make her uncomfortable.

Jacks wasn't the sort who'd talk simply to fill the quiet, but Evangeline couldn't shake the feeling that there was more than quiet between them. Minutes ago, he'd saved her life. He had jumped in between her and Luc without even thinking. She knew Jacks needed her alive because of the Valory Arch prophecy, but he'd acted out of pure instinct. He'd been scared for her when she'd been threatened.

But now he wouldn't even look at her. His teeth ground together as he took the stairs, jaw tight, eyes focused, knuckles starkly white.

Was he in pain from the bite? There was a smear of blood on his pale neck, but it wasn't that much. Luc hadn't wounded Jacks too deeply. But Luc had bitten him. Jacks was probably still testy about that.

But that didn't seem quite right. Evangeline remembered the way Jacks had nearly dropped her wrist earlier, when Luc had said that he'd been cursed. Jacks had been thrown off-kilter then. Had he been surprised to learn that Luc had truly been under a spell? Or . . . had it been something else? Had Jacks been unsettled that Evangeline had finally learned the truth about Luc? Luc had said Marisol cursed him, but what if she hadn't achieved it on her own?

Evangeline felt a sudden wave of sick on top of everything else.

"Did you curse him?" Evangeline asked. "Did you make a deal with Marisol and put a spell on Luc so that—"

"You can stop right there," Jacks cut in. "I already told you what I think about your stepsister. I did not make a deal with her, and I never will."

"Then why were you so alarmed when Luc revealed he'd been under a spell?"

"It was terrible timing—and you have absolutely no sense

when it comes to him," Jacks all but growled, jaw clenching in between his words. "For most people, I'm the worst thing that can happen to them. But not you. It's as if you want that boy to destroy you, and he's only human—or he was until you helped him change."

Evangeline wanted to argue. She didn't care that Jacks was clearly right about Luc and that she actually believed him about not having made a deal with Marisol—which gave her an unexpected feeling of relief. But Jacks still didn't have to be so cruel about it just because she couldn't shut off her feelings the way he did. She knew there were downsides to feeling deeply; it could get in the way of logic and reason. But shutting off emotions was just as treacherous.

Evangeline took her frustration out on the stairs, quickening her pace to pass Jacks as they took another flight. They'd finally reached the levels where shackles no longer clung to the walls and Evangeline could no longer hear the desperate sounds of vampire changelings.

And yet, she still felt the occasional bite of heat at her throat. Usually, it hovered right over her pulse. But just then, she felt it on the back of her neck.

She quickly took another set of steps and reached a well-lit landing, where at last she saw the glowing doorway that would take them outside. But the burn at the back of her neck was becoming impossible to ignore.

And why couldn't she hear Jacks anymore?

"Jacks—" Evangeline broke off as she turned.

Jacks was so close. Too close. Whisper close. She should have heard him right behind her, but he was eerily silent. And his appearance, it had changed. "Your hair—"

The blue was gone. It was gold once more, shimmering and brilliant and absolutely magnificent. She shouldn't have stared—staring at Jacks was never a good idea. But it was impossible to pull her gaze away. His skin was flushed with color, and his eyes were brighter as well, a radiant sapphire blue. He looked part angel, part fallen star, and completely devastating.

"Evangeline—stop looking at me like that. You're making this much more difficult." Jacks spoke between clenched teeth, but she still caught a glimpse of his sharpened incisors, which now looked startlingly like fangs.

There are two different types of vampire bites, Chaos had said. *We can bite a human merely to feed from them. Or we can infect our bites with vampire venom to turn a human into a vampire.*

She sucked in a sharp breath. Luc hadn't just bitten Jacks to feed. "He infected you with venom."

43

J acks took an eerily silent step back, leather boots soundless against the stone floors.

"You should go," he edged out, fangs lengthening as he spoke.

Evangeline became very aware of the blood rushing through her veins and the pounding of her heart. If she ever saw Luc again, she would use a sword. She might not be able to cut off his head, but she would definitely be able to cut him.

"Why aren't you leaving?" Jacks's nostrils flared, and Evangeline felt another bolt of heat over her pulse, further dimming the brief thrall she'd been under. Jacks was not part fallen angel; he was on the verge of becoming something so much worse.

She curled her toes inside of her boots, fighting the urge to slowly back away or burst into a run. If Jacks bit her, he would change into a vampire. He hated vampires, and she didn't like them much either. But if she left him now and he found another human before dawn, she didn't know if he'd be able to exert the same level of control he seemed to possess with her.

Jacks had gone very still. The only parts of him that moved were his pupils, dilating until his eyes were nearly full black. Luc's eyes hadn't done that. Then again, Luc hadn't been a Fate when he'd been infected.

"Do you want to be a vampire?" Evangeline asked.

"No," Jacks spat. "I don't want to be a vampire, but I do want to bite you."

Evangeline's skin went hot all over.

Jacks ground his teeth, looking furious at her for still being there. "You should go," he repeated.

"I'm not leaving you like this." Evangeline searched the entryway for shackles.

"You are not pinning me to a wall." Jacks glared.

"Do you have a better suggestion?"

An unsettling victory cry echoed below. Another changeling was probably free. The noise sounded as if it was a decent way underground, but Evangeline wondered if the changeling might sense where she was, if it was somehow aware there was a human nearby.

"How good is your sense of smell?" she asked.

Jacks's nostrils flared again. "You smell like fear and—" Something unreadable flickered across his face. But whatever he was going to say next became cut off by another sound from below—like thunder racing up the stairs.

Without another word, both of them darted for the exit.

Outside, the chilly winter night was almost too bright. The moon had come out from hiding behind the clouds to pay particular attention to Jacks, illuminating his perfect jaw, his long lashes, and the twist of his petulant mouth. He looked like ethereal heartbreak. She kept feeling the urge to turn her head and take just one more glimpse, and she knew it was vampire allure. The inescapable draw of dangerous beauty and power.

"Why aren't you running away?" he asked.

"Given the way you keep looking at me, I imagine you'll give chase, or you'll find another human who you wouldn't feel guilty about biting."

I wouldn't feel guilty about biting you.

Evangeline didn't know if the voice in her head was a threat, a lapse in Jacks's control, or just a warning that she was running out of time.

"You should go," he repeated.

She ignored him and scoured the darkened graveyard once more. A desperate but possibly inspired idea occurred as Evangeline caught sight of a mausoleum covered in flowering vines of angels' tears that glowed milky white beneath the moon.

"There." She pointed toward the structure. "We'll go inside. Families plant angels' tears when they want to protect the bodies of loved ones from demonic spirits." She knew because she'd done it for both her parents. "This mausoleum is covered in the plant, which means there are probably other protections inside—like a gate with a lock to keep the coffins safe."

A muscle in Jacks's neck throbbed. "You wish to lock me in a coffin?"

"Not a coffin, just on the other side of the gate, and only until dawn."

"I don't need to be locked up. I can control myself."

"Then why do you keep telling me to run?" She lifted her eyes to meet Jacks's stare.

A split second later, Jacks had her pinned against the closest tree. Her back hit the wood, his fevered chest pressed to hers, and his hands went for her throat, burning fire hot against her skin.

"Jacks," Evangeline gasped. "Let me go."

He moved away as quickly as he'd grabbed her.

She slumped against the tree from the force of his release. When she righted herself, he was stalking toward the crypt.

Evangeline rubbed her neck as she followed. He hadn't held her that tightly, but her skin still felt scorched from the touch of his hands. "I thought vampires were supposed to be cold." And Jacks was always cold.

"Vampire venom is hot, especially when they're hungry," Jacks rasped as he yanked open the door to the mausoleum.

As she'd suspected, this chamber had been built by the superstitious. Ever-lit torches clung to the walls, providing some warmth and casting a glow on an excellent floor-to-ceiling iron gate that separated any would-be visitors from the four stone coffins on the opposite side of it.

"What now?" Jacks said roughly.

Evangeline quickly approached the gate. She didn't recognize all the protective iron symbols that had been worked into the design, but the bars looked thick enough to hold Jacks, at least for several more hours until the sun decided to rise. She wished the lock on the gate was stronger, but it would have to do.

"Do you see a key hanging from the wall?" she asked.

"No." Jacks's voice was tight. Then, barely audibly, "Try your hands. Stab one of your fingers to draw blood, and ask the door to open."

Evangeline spun around.

Jacks was pressed against the farthest wall, skin a painful shade of pale white.

She didn't make the mistake of meeting his eyes again, but one glance at his face and it was clear he was barely holding himself back.

She'd been planning to ask if he was just trying to get her to spill blood, but she thought better of wasting more time. Pricking her finger on one of the iron gate's sharper designs, she drew a drop of blood and quickly pressed it to the lock. "Open, please."

It worked magic-fast. The lock split, the door swung wide, and Evangeline's jaw dropped. "How did you know that would work?" she asked.

Jacks moved too quickly for Evangeline to see. "This isn't the time or place to talk about it," he said from the other side of the gate, and then he slammed it shut.

The lock she'd just opened closed with a tiny *click*, making her painfully aware of how little stood between her and Jacks. He seemed mindful of it as well. He'd willingly entered the cage, but now he regarded the lock like a thief, contemplating all the ways he could break it.

44

If Jacks decided he wanted to break free of his prison, Evangeline doubted it would take much effort.

She needed to find a way to distract him.

She could question him about something he found interesting. She wanted to ask him more about the lock and why her blood had opened it. But he'd already shot that subject down. She also wondered if she already knew the answer—if her ability to magically open the lock had something to do with the Valory Arch. When Apollo had told her about the prophecy that had locked the arch, he'd said that once every line of it was fulfilled, it would create a key that would open the arch. What if she was that key?

Could it be possible? Or was it just that all the wild events of tonight were finally getting to Evangeline and giving her delusions of magical wonder? Only it didn't feel like a delusion as she thought back to every time she'd stepped through an arch. All of them had whispered to her—words that made much more sense if she was this prophesized key.

We're so pleased you found us.

We've been waiting for you.

You could have unlocked me as well.

An uncomfortable thrill kicked through her. She didn't want anything to do with the Valory Arch. She definitely didn't want to be its key, even if this ability had helped save her life just now. Although, if she wanted to stay alive, she had to keep Jacks occupied.

Fortunately, Evangeline was not at a loss for questions. There was one in particular that had been gnawing at her for a while.

"Tell me what happened between you and the princess from the Meridian Empire, the one Chaos and LaLa mentioned earlier. Donatella."

"No." Jacks's voice was pure vitriol. "I don't want to talk about her. Ever."

This subject would be perfect.

Earlier, Jacks had merely flinched and then quickly masked his expression whenever the princess was mentioned. But either he was having issues with control or the vampire venom was making his emotions even stronger. Evangeline could once again feel the pressure of Jacks's glare, but it was no longer on her neck or her pulse. It was dancing heat all over her.

"Tough luck, Jacks." Evangeline folded her arms across her chest as he prowled back and forth inside his cage. "You need something to distract you, so you're going to talk about Princess Donatella. I don't care if you tell me how much you hate her or how much you love her. You can sing verses about how pretty she is or the color of her hair."

Jacks made a strangled sound that might have been some estranged cousin of a laugh. "She's not the kind of girl you sing about." And yet something in his voice shifted, softened, and Evangeline had an oddly uncomfortable sensation that he actually would have sung songs about this girl.

"The first time I met her, she threatened to throw me from a sky carriage."

"And you liked her for that?" Evangeline asked.

"I'd just threatened to kill her." He said it as if they'd been flirting.

"This is a terrible love story, Jacks."

"Who said it was a love story?" His tone turned back to acid. Evangeline thought he might even stop talking. To her surprise, he continued. "When we met again, I kissed her."

The way he said *I kissed her* was like the way someone else might have said they'd stabbed a person in the back. There was nothing longing or romantic about it, confirming Jacks had a misshapen definition of love. And yet somehow the thought of Jacks kissing the princess made something painful wrench inside of Evangeline. "Did you kiss her because you thought she was your true love?"

"No. I needed something from her, and I told her that my kiss would kill her unless she got me what I wanted."

"Wait—are you saying that your kiss isn't deadly if you don't want it to be?"

"Careful, Little Fox, you sound curious. But you shouldn't be." Jacks stopped pacing and drummed his long fingers against the iron gate, tapping a staccato sound. "I lied to Donatella. My kiss is always deadly. I slowed her heart so that it didn't kill her immediately, but it should have ended her life in a matter of days, whether or not she did what I wanted."

"Then why didn't she die?"

"Probably because my heart started beating," Jacks said flippantly, as if it were a small detail that could have easily been left out of the story, when there were entire stories dedicated to Jacks's unbeating heart and the mythical girl that would finally make it beat again—his one true love.

Evangeline felt that terribly painful something churning inside her once again. Not that the idea of this girl being Jacks's true love should have pained her. She didn't even like Jacks. She shouldn't have been bothered that another girl had made Jacks's heart beat. She should have been happy the princess hadn't died. Maybe Evangeline was just feeling sorry for Jacks because she already knew that this story didn't end well.

"What happened then?"

"According to the stories, she was supposed to be my *one true love*," Jacks confirmed. His voice was mocking, but it didn't hide the pain clipping his words or hardening the edges of his features. "Of course, as you've probably guessed, that didn't work out. She never forgave me for that first kiss. She fell in love with someone else, and then she stabbed me in the heart with my own knife."

Evangeline took a shuddering breath, unable to imagine how such a thing would feel, especially for Jacks, whose entire driving force as a Fate was to find his one true love.

Evangeline could understand that drive. In fact, she understood it far better than she wanted to admit. She wanted to say she'd never risked killing someone for love. But she had made a deal with Jacks that had turned a wedding party to stone, cursed a prince, and ultimately led her here. She kept thinking it was fate or Jacks that was toying with her life. But it had been her own questionable choices that had started her on this path.

With Luc, she'd told herself that she was acting out of love. But she wasn't, not really. She wasn't making loving choices, she was making compromising choices because she wanted love. Luc wasn't her weakness—love was. Not even just love but the idea of it.

This was why parts of Jacks's story had twisted so painfully inside her. It wasn't because she wanted Jacks. She didn't want Jacks. She just wanted someone to want her the way Jacks had wanted this girl. And she didn't want it to be because of a spell or a curse. Evangeline wanted a real love powerful enough to break a spell, which was exactly what Jacks wanted, too.

He leaned his head against the dark iron gate, and Evangeline would forever remember the way he looked just then.

He was still indescribably breathtaking, but it was all the

tragic beauty of a sky where every single star was falling. His hair was a storm of broken gold. His eyes were a mess of silver and blue. The deadness she'd seen her first night in Valorfell was gone, but now she understood why it had been there, why he seemed so unable to give comfort or kindness. The girl who was supposed to be his one true love had literally stabbed him in the heart.

"I'm sorry Donatella wounded you so badly," Evangeline said. And she meant it. She imagined Jacks was probably leaving a few things out, but she believed his hurt was genuine. "Maybe the stories have it wrong and there's another true love waiting for you."

Jacks laughed derisively. "Are you saying this because you think you can be her?" He eyed Evangeline through the bars, gaze bordering on indecent. "Do you want to kiss me, Little Fox?"

Something new and terrible knotted up inside her. "No, that's not what I'm saying."

"You don't sound too sure about that. You might not like me, but I bet you'd like it if I kissed you." His eyes went to her lips, and the heat that swept across her mouth felt like the beginning of a kiss.

"Jacks, stop it," she demanded. He didn't really want to kiss her. He was just teasing her to deflect the pain. "I know what you're doing."

"I doubt it." He smiled, flashing his dimples as he ran his tongue over the tip of a very sharp and long incisor, looking suddenly thoughtful. "Maybe it wouldn't be so bad to stay like this. I rather like these."

"You also like daylight," Evangeline reminded him.

"I could probably live without the sun if I could trade it for other things." He cocked his head. "I wonder . . . if I were to become a true vampire, perhaps my kiss wouldn't be fatal anymore." His fangs lengthened. "You could let me bite you and we could try it out."

Another piercing lick of heat, this time right beneath her jaw, then her wrist, and a few other intimate places she'd have never thought anyone would bite.

Evangeline blushed from her neck down to her collarbone. "We're not talking about biting," she said hotly.

"Then what should we talk about?" Jacks's eyes returned to her lips, and more heat slipped between them as they parted.

Evangeline sucked in a sharp breath. Maybe she'd been wrong earlier. Maybe he did want to kiss her. But it didn't mean anything. He was clearly still fixated on Princess Donatella. And LaLa had said that Jacks's curse was his kiss—if there was even a sliver of attraction, he'd be tempted to kiss. But it didn't mean he possessed any real feelings for the person.

"I'm curious," she asked. "If you have the ability to control people, why didn't you just use it to make the princess love you?"

Jacks's taunting smile vanished. "I did."

"What happened?"

"I think my turn is over," he said sharply. "Your turn now. And I want you to tell me about Luc."

Evangeline winced. She really didn't want to discuss Luc now, not after what had just happened, and not with Jacks, who had teased her about him since the moment she'd met him. "I'd like another question, please."

"No. I answered your questions. You're answering mine."

"Why do you want to know about Luc? You just saw how the story ends."

"Tell me how it started." Jacks gave her one corner of a falsely cheerful smile. "Your tale clearly began on better footing than mine. What made you fall so madly in love with him that you were willing to pray to me?"

Evangeline took a deep breath.

"Stop stalling, Little Fox, or I might remember how much pain I'm in because all I can think about is tasting your blood." Jacks's eyes lowered.

The wave of heat attacked her chest, directly over her heart, and this time it felt like a bite, not a kiss.

"Fine—Luc was there for me when my father died."

"This was why you fell in love with him?"

"No . . . I think I loved him before that." She was tempted to say that she loved him the first time she saw him, but Jacks would definitely mock her for that. "At first, I thought he was handsome. I still remember, the bell outside the shop door rang a full two seconds before the first time he walked inside, as if it, too, thought he was special."

"Or it was trying to warn you away from him," Jacks groaned.

"Do you want me to keep going or not?"

Jacks mimed sealing his lips shut.

Evangeline doubted it would last. But he surprised her by making a genuine effort to listen politely.

She noticed that Jacks's knuckles were white from clenching his fists, and his jaw appeared uncomfortably tight—he was struggling more now that he wasn't talking—but he hopped atop one of the stone coffins and sat cross-legged like a child being told a story.

Evangeline wondered if she should stay standing in case she needed to run. But maybe it would put him at more ease if she mirrored his lead. Carefully, she sat down on the cold damp ground, giving her tired legs a rest.

"I grew up working in my father's curiosity shop. I loved it—it felt more like my home than any other place in the world. But I spent so much time there that I didn't really have close friends outside of it until I met Luc. At first I thought he just liked oddities. Then one day, he came in and he didn't buy anything. He said he just wanted to see me and he wasn't too proud or afraid to admit it."

"And . . . ," Jacks prompted.

"That was when I knew I loved him."

"All he did was tell you he liked you?" Jacks sounded disappointed. "That was his grand gesture? Haven't any other boys been nice to you?"

"Plenty of young men have been nice to me, and Luc made other grand gestures."

Jacks scowled. "Tell me about these grand gestures."

Evangeline squirmed against the cold ground and tried to tuck her legs more comfortably beneath her. Jacks would think that every relationship needed some magnificent gesture to validate it. "Not every love needs to make a great story, Jacks. The start of my romance with Apollo had the makings of an epic love tale, but you saw how badly that ended."

"So you're saying you'd settle for a boring romance if it ends well?"

"Yes. I would gladly take an uneventful happily ever after."

Jacks smirked. "No, you wouldn't. You wouldn't have been happy with Luc, and definitely not forever. The two of you aren't well suited. He's not half as strong as you—he didn't even hesitate before he tried to bite you. And he wouldn't have turned himself to stone to save you."

"You don't know that."

"Yes, I do. There's always a way to break a curse. As soon as you drank from Poison's goblet, it refilled. I didn't stay to explain the rules, but they would have appeared on the side of the cup. Luc could have saved you if he wanted."

Evangeline's hands started trembling. No one had told her this. "That doesn't mean anything. Luc was under a love spell from Marisol."

"He could have broken it," Jacks said bluntly. "If he had really loved you, the spell could have been broken. I've seen it happen."

"Stop it, Jacks!" Evangeline shoved up to her feet. It was bad enough to know that she'd done so much for love; she didn't want to hear that Luc had never really loved her.

"I'm not trying to be cruel, Little Fox, I—"

"No, Jacks, that's exactly what you're doing. It's what you always do." It was also what she'd expected, but she was too tired to take it anymore. She might have made questionable choices for love, but Jacks hurt people on purpose, for fun. "You know, maybe the real reason Donatella stabbed you in the heart and chose to love someone else wasn't just because of that almost-fatal first kiss you gave her. Maybe it was your inability to understand any emotions that are remotely human."

Jacks flinched. He was quick to cover it up, and it was hard to fully see, even with all the torches, but Evangeline would have sworn his cheeks had filled with streaks of color.

She felt a stitch of guilt, but she couldn't bring herself to stop. "I bet you never even apologized for kissing her. And that's probably not even the worst thing you did. I mean, isn't your idea of romance kissing a girl and then waiting to see whether or not she dies? I know the stories say that your kisses are worth dying for, but how can they say that if everyone dies? Who wrote those stories? Did you write them to make yourself feel better?"

Jacks wiped his face of all emotion, slid off the coffin, and stalked up to the bars. "You sound jealous."

"If you think I'm jealous because someone else got to stab you, then you're right."

"Prove it."

She heard the thump of his dagger as it fell at her feet. It was the jeweled one he carried everywhere. So many of the gems were missing, but the knife's hilt still glittered in the torchlight, pulsing blue and purple, the color of blood before it was spilled.

"What am I supposed to do with this?"

"You might want to use it, Little Fox." The corner of his mouth twitched as he slowly slid his pale hands through the bars of the gate and broke the lock in half. It could have been a twig, a piece of paper, or *her*.

45

Before Evangeline could suck in a breath, Jacks was directly in front of her. His lips curved into a devastating smile that on anyone else might have looked inviting or flirtatious, as if throwing a knife at her feet and daring her to stab him was the equivalent of asking her to dance.

"Jacks—" Evangeline tried not to sound as if her heart was racing.

"Don't you want to hurt me anymore, Little Fox?" His finger reached out and lightly traced her exposed collarbone, setting every inch of her skin on fire. "You can pick up the dagger any time now."

But Evangeline couldn't pick up the dagger. She could barely manage to keep breathing. His hand was now at the hollow of her throat, careful and caressing. Jacks had touched her before—last night he'd held her while she'd slept, but he'd acted as if that had been torture. His touch hadn't been warm or curious.

Or maybe she was the one who was curious. She knew she shouldn't be. But hadn't she wondered what it would be like to be wanted with the intensity that Jacks seemed to want things?

His mouth curved wider as his hands moved from her throat to her shoulders and slowly slid the cape away, leaving more of her skin exposed.

"You should go back on the other side of the gate." Her voice was hoarse.

"You're the one who said I needed a distraction." His fingers drifted lower, trailing down her chest to the sensitive stretch of skin right above the lacy line of her corset. "Isn't this better than talking?" One finger dipped all the way into the corset.

Her breathing hitched. "I don't think this is a good idea."

"That's what makes it interesting." His other hand found her jaw, while the finger in her corset gently stroked just above her heart, coaxing it to beat even faster.

"You can always pick up the blade," he taunted. "You wouldn't like me as a vampire, Little Fox."

The warm hand at her jaw tilted her head back until she met his eyes. They were dilated to nearly full black and somehow still as bright as broken stars.

She needed to back away. This was wrong for so many reasons, and worse than that, it was incredibly stupid to let him keep touching her, to *like* the way he kept touching her.

He wouldn't even be doing this if it weren't for the vampire venom.

It didn't matter that he was being gentle, that his knuckles were barely brushing her skin as they skimmed their way from her chest to the back of her neck, while his other hand traveled to her hip, slowly gliding over her skirts as he eased her closer. The crypt was freezing, but Jacks was warm enough to heat every inch of Evangeline as the hand at her neck slid into her hair, twisting his fingers around the strands before shoving them away from her neck and—

His teeth grazed her pulse.

"Jacks—" It was suddenly impossible to form words. His hot mouth was against her throat, and his teeth were on her skin. His *teeth*! Evangeline finally pressed against his chest. But it was as useless as trying to battle a block of marble. Hot, sculpted marble. She wanted to tell him not to bite her, but saying the word *bite* didn't seem like the wisest idea just then. "You won't want this later . . ."

"Not really thinking about later." He licked her, one languorous stroke up the column of her neck.

She gasped, "You don't even like me."

"I like you right now. I like you a lot." He gently sucked her skin. "In fact, I can't think of anything I like more."

"Jacks—this is all from the vampire venom." She pressed harder against his chest, frantic, but he didn't seem to notice. His tongue was on her neck, toying with her pulse. "You—"

Her words faltered as his teeth grazed her again, raking over all her sensitized skin in a way that should not have felt so incredibly good.

She had to stop this. One bite. One spilled drop of blood and they'd both be in trouble. "If you do this . . . you'll never see the sun again. Won't you miss the sun?"

His only response was another tortuous lick, and then his other hand was tightening around her hips, pulling her closer as if preparing to—

"You need me to open the Valory Arch!"

Jacks stilled at her words.

His breath went jagged as his lips hovered over her pulse. He didn't bite her. But he didn't release her. If anything, he held her tighter. He was burning up against her. She tried to calm her breathing, certain he could feel her racing heartbeat and hear the blood rushing in her veins beneath his parted mouth. But he didn't lower his lips.

He didn't move except to breathe in and out.

She didn't know how long they stood there, wrapped in an embrace that she couldn't fight and that Jacks couldn't seem to let go of. There were moments he struggled. He tangled her hair in his fingers, their cold tips brushing her scalp—

Cold. His palm was cold.

Evangeline dared to look up as morning sunlight crept through the mausoleum window. They'd survived the night.

Jacks's arms tensed as if he'd just had the same realization.

Everything that had burned suddenly felt like ice. His chest, his arms, his breath upon her neck.

He extricated himself from her slowly with stiff, ungraceful movements. He was once again the Jacks who'd carried her to LaLa's flat. The heat, the want, the hunger, all of it had vanished with the night. His hands were awkward as he untangled his fingers from her hair. It was eerily reminiscent of when Apollo had been freed from Jacks's magic. Only Jacks wasn't angry, just exquisitely uncomfortable.

At least he wasn't laughing. Evangeline didn't think she could have borne it if he'd teased her for letting him get so close or for gasping as he'd licked her neck.

Her cheeks were suddenly burning, and she was grateful he didn't look at her when he bent down to grab his dagger.

She took a moment to turn, smooth her hair, and take a deep breath, inhaling the cool, crisp morning instead of him.

"Here." Jacks's voice was right behind her. And then she felt her ruffled cloak. He placed it across her shoulders and quickly secured the straps to her corset. "If you freeze to death, the trouble I've gone to keeping you alive will be wasted." His mocking tone was back, clipped and cutting, and yet she felt the soft brush of his fingertips lingering against her neck before he pulled away.

Evangeline tried not to react. She wasn't even sure he realized he'd done it. When she spun to face him again, he was back to being indifferent as he strode toward the mausoleum exit.

She started to follow, when she saw it, glittering against the ground. The dagger he'd tossed at her last night. The one with all the broken gems. He'd picked up her cloak, but he'd left the little knife. "Wait—"

Jacks looked at her over his shoulder.

She picked up the blade and held it out.

A ghost of a frown turned down his mouth. She couldn't read the look in his eyes, but his tone was brusque. "Leave it."

He disappeared through the door without another glance.

Evangeline closed her hand around the dagger's jeweled hilt.

She was going to keep it, but she didn't let herself wonder why.

A layer of icy dew covered the cemetery grounds, and an army of tiny dragons covered the tops of the tombstones, snoring little sparks that tempered the air from frosty to chilled.

Jacks scrubbed a hand over his face. There were bruising circles beneath his eyes that hadn't been there before. "We need to get somewhere safe," he said.

"What if we went back to Wolf Hall?" she suggested.

He gave her a look that could have withered a forest. "Do you want to be locked up in a dungeon?"

"You didn't let me finish. I've been thinking about what Chaos told us. If Apollo was actually killed by this malefic oil and not LaLa's tears, then the witch who bought the oil from Chaos and poisoned Apollo with it might have been my stepsister."

Jacks narrowed his eyes—or were they drooping? He really

did look exhausted. She was weary, too, but it was piled deep beneath a number of far more urgent feelings and needs like figuring out who had killed Apollo.

After Luc's revelation, Evangeline was becoming more inclined to think that the murderer was her stepsister. But did she only think this because Luc had said that Marisol had cursed him, or was it because Marisol was actually guilty?

"I'm not entirely sure why Marisol would have wanted to poison Apollo," Evangeline admitted, "but I keep wondering about that spell book she bought. I was thinking we could sneak back into Wolf Hall, and you could use your powers on her to compel her to tell us the truth."

"Even if I thought this was a good idea, which I don't, I couldn't help youuu . . ." Jacks trailed off, slurring his words at the end.

"Are you all right?" Evangeline asked.

He met her gaze and yawned. "I—I—" He struggled briefly before pausing to rub his eyes. "I'm fine. Just tired from—" He swayed on his feet.

"Jacks." She reached out a hand to steady him.

He flinched away. "I'm fi—ne," he repeated, but even those words were marred by a yawn.

"You're falling asleep on your feet."

"I don't—" Jacks yawned again, mouth stretching wide as his eyes fell all the way shut.

"Jacks!" She quickly shook him awake.

He blinked at her, fuzzy-eyed, as if he were intoxicated.

Nothing about him was sharp. He was all soft around the edges, with his tousled golden hair and his drowsy blue eyes. It might have been amusing under other circumstances—and it was a little comical now. She pictured it as a scandal sheet headline. THE PRINCE OF HEARTS SLAYED BY SLEEP! DISPATCHED BY A NAP! DESTROYED BY DREAMING!

But this fatigue did not seem natural. "Jacks, I think there's something wrong with you."

"That's not anything new." He gave her a slow, impish smile. "I just need to . . . find a bed."

He staggered from her to the closest cemetery plot, as if it would suffice.

"Oh no—" She grabbed his solid arm and tugged him back toward her. But she didn't know how long she could keep fighting him. If Jacks actually chose to lie down, she was not strong enough to pick him up. "You can't sleep here, Jacks."

"Just for a bit, Little Fox." His pale eyelids fluttered up and down. "This is probably just a side effect of the venom," he murmured. "There's always a cost to unearned power . . ."

He swayed toward the ground.

She grabbed his shoulders to steady him once again. Side effect or not, they couldn't stay here. "We need to get somewhere safe, remember? Tell me where you're living."

Instead of answering, Jacks pulled away and sagged against a nearby tree covered in posters with her likeness. They seemed to have multiplied overnight, growing like a paper plague. Only now they didn't simply say she was missing.

EVANGELINE FOX

WANTED

for MURDER

Princess Evangeline Fox, formerly known as Valenda's Savior Sweetheart, is wanted for the murder of her husband, Crown Prince Apollo Titus Acadian. Believed to be highly dangerous and possibly in possession of magical abilities. If you spot the princess, do not approach her. Contact the Royal Order of Soldiers immediately.

Evangeline didn't know if she wanted to scream or cry or just let Jacks curl up with her as if she were his blanket. It wasn't enough that her parents had died, that her first love had been cursed by her stepsister, that she'd been turned to stone, that she'd lost her father's curiosity shop, and that she'd married a prince who was cursed and then killed—now they were officially blaming her for his murder.

"Jacks, please come back to your senses! I'm no longer missing, I'm wanted for murder." She shook him until he opened his eyes. But if she'd expected a coherent reply, she would have been disappointed. Jacks's only response was to rip down the poster and shut his eyes again.

It was not easy to get Jacks out of the graveyard, and it was even more challenging to find out where he lived. Whenever Evangeline asked about his home, Jacks just kept shaking his golden head and saying, "LaLa's is closer."

Unfortunately, either LaLa's flat had moved during the night or Evangeline was too anxious to be any good with directions. She climbed back to the spires, but she couldn't find LaLa's home among the many shops and stacked cottages. It didn't help that as they scaled the endless steps, Jacks kept slumping against the nearest doors and walls and muttering about apples.

She risked buying a few pieces of fruit from a vendor, but after taking one bite, Jacks dropped it and leaned heavily against her shoulder.

Her heart fluttered at the contact, which was the absolute wrong response.

A woman carrying a load of wash stared at the two of them a little longer than would have been deemed polite, and Evangeline's panic increased. They needed to find somewhere to hide. They couldn't keep wandering around like this. Someone would figure out who they were and call the royal soldiers.

The world was waking up with each passing second. The cries of vendors selling papers and clams and morning sea tonics were filling the bustling streets below. She tried to shut out all the noise and concentrate on finding a safe place to hide. But Evangeline kept hearing the sound of a bell, merrily ring-ring-ringing an endless string of tinkling sounds as if to say, *Look at me! Look at me!*

Evangeline, of course, knew that bells could not speak. But her mother had told her bells had a sixth sense. She'd said to always polish them, always mind what you say in front of them, and always listen to the bells that ring when they shouldn't.

Evangeline cast about the spire until she saw the cheery iron bell wildly swinging back and forth above a closed black door with a sign that said *Go Away.*

Ding. Ding. Ding.

The bell didn't stop until Evangeline briefly left Jacks, approached the door, and knocked.

No one answered.

The bell kept ringing, more furiously.

Evangeline tried the knob.

It didn't budge. The door was locked, but no one seemed to be inside. Hoping the bell was doing her a favor and showing her a place to hide, Evangeline pulled out Jacks's dagger and pricked her finger with the tip. "Please, open."

The knob turned with a gentle click.

Evangeline quickly found Jacks curled up in front of the nearest door, clutching a scandal sheet to his chest like a blanket.

"Come on now." She crouched down to slip an arm under his shoulder, and for once, he didn't fight her or try to drag her with him to the ground. His head lolled against her as she walked him toward the black door, slouching under his weight.

"You're so lucky I'm here," she grunted.

"Luck had nothing to do with it," Jacks mumbled. "I wanted you here, Little Fox. Who do you think asked Poison to save you and suggest to his empress that she send you to Nocte Neverending?"

46

Evangeline and Jacks stumbled through the door to-gether. The room was cold, and she thought it held the scent of apples, but that might have just been Jacks.

A skylight provided just enough illumination for Evangeline to see walls of haphazard bookshelves broken up by a fireplace, a scuffed desk piled high with papers, a sofa of dark amber velvet, and a pair of mismatched armchairs. They'd stumbled into someone's private library. She just hoped the owner didn't return while they were hiding there.

As soon as the door shut behind them, Jacks pulled away and fell on top of the sofa, head resting against one of its velvet arms, long legs dangling off the end.

"Jacks!" She tried to shake him awake, hoping she could get him to answer at least one more question before he fully suc-cumbed to sleep. If he'd been more alert, he would have never admitted to asking Poison to cure her or to help lure her to the

North. Not that she was entirely shocked; she'd gathered from her first night there that Jacks had been expecting her.

"Tell me more." She softened her voice. Maybe she could get him to think she was only part of a dream. "Tell me what you want inside the Valory Arch."

Evangeline stopped shaking his shoulder and smoothed back a lock of golden hair that had fallen across his sleeping face. She wondered why he'd dyed it before. If he'd been in disguise, the blue was a terrible choice; it was far too bold and arresting. Not that the brilliant gold was easy to ignore. Even without the vampire allure, it tempted her to stare, and it felt incredibly soft against her thawing fingers as she ran them through—

Jacks's hand covered hers, cold and firm atop her fingers. "Bad . . . idea . . . ," he murmured.

She snatched her hand away. She hadn't meant to touch him like that. Jacks was not a thing to idly touch. He wasn't even a thing she liked. Although, as soon as she had the thought, she knew it wasn't true. Not anymore. Evangeline wasn't ready to say they were friends, but after last night, she no longer felt as if they were enemies.

An enemy wouldn't have spent the night with someone to make sure he didn't turn into a vampire. And an enemy wouldn't have held her quite so close or tasted her neck the way Jacks had. Evangeline knew he'd wanted to bite her, but his tongue on her neck hadn't been just about biting.

She didn't want to think too much about it—sort of like

the jeweled dagger she'd taken from the crypt and placed in the sheath at her hip. She was glad Jacks no longer felt like her enemy, but it would be dangerous to let it go further and consider him a friend.

Evangeline allowed herself one small smile as she felt the ruffled cape he'd placed across her shoulders. Then she stepped away from him.

A paper rustled under her foot—the newsprint Jacks had been holding.

She'd thought before that he'd clutched the crumpled black-and-white sheet like a blanket because he'd been so tired. It probably repeated the news she was wanted for murder. But one glance at the headline changed her mind.

The Daily Rumor

THE CURSED BRIDE AND THE NEW CROWN PRINCE

By Kristof Knightlinger

It's official: the new crown prince, Tiberius Peregrine Acadian, is engaged to Marisol Antoinette Tourmaline, also known as the Cursed Bride. I know many of you will find this difficult to believe, but I would not have printed these words without confirmation from Prince Tiberius himself. "It was love at first sight," he said. "The moment I laid eyes on Marisol Tourmaline, I knew that we were meant to be together."

I've heard whispers that many members of the royal court are upset that Prince Tiberius plans to wed before his brother's body is even in the grave. Of course, there are also rumors Prince Apollo's body has gone missing, but no one in Wolf Hall is talking about that.

The wedding will take place tomorrow morning, and one can't help but wonder why this event is happening so soon—

(continued on page 6)

Evangeline did not have page 6. But she didn't need to continue reading. She had been trying to give Marisol the benefit of the doubt. She didn't want her stepsister to be a murderer or a monster. But all Evangeline could think was that Marisol had used another love potion to put Tiberius under a spell.

And Evangeline feared that wasn't the only thing her stepsister had done.

Evangeline had suspected Marisol of Apollo's murder, but she hadn't been able to think of a reason her stepsister would want to murder Prince Apollo until now. With Apollo dead, Tiberius was the crown prince. Once he married Marisol, he would become king and Marisol would be queen.

It would have been easier to just put a spell on Apollo, but perhaps Marisol had tried and it hadn't worked because Apollo was already under Jacks's influence. Or Marisol just found Tiberius more attractive? It was hard for Evangeline to really comprehend any of it.

When Evangeline thought of Marisol, she remembered the way she'd hugged her before the wedding as if they were really sisters. But what if that hadn't been an I-love-you hug? Maybe it had been an I'm-sorry-I'm-going-to-kill-you hug.

It was still a little incomprehensible to think that her step-sister had tried to murder her. But Evangeline had also never imagined that it was Marisol who had cursed Luc, yet she'd done it.

Marisol had also acquired Northern books of magic so dangerous LaLa and Jacks acted as if Marisol was a villain just for owning them. Marisol could have easily been the witch who'd gone to Chaos's crypt for the malefic oil.

The motive was the only thing that didn't feel entirely right to Evangeline. She could understand her stepsister putting a love spell on someone. But she couldn't imagine Marisol killing multiple people for a crown. That didn't seem like something Marisol would do. But maybe Evangeline didn't really know what things Marisol would do.

Evangeline flashed back to the horrible words she'd over-heard Agnes say:

"Look at you. Your complexion. Your hair. Your posture is like a damp ribbon, and those circles beneath your eyes are hideous. A man might be able to overlook your little cursed reputation if you were something to look at, but I can barely tolerate the sight—"

Evangeline believed in love and fairytales and happy endings, because that was what her parents had taught her. But Agnes had told Marisol that she was unattractive and un-wanted. Was that why she had done all this?

It was all so ugly either way.

"Jacks, wake up!" Evangeline put a hand on his chest, hoping the touch might jolt him awake, but his sleep was so deep, she might have suspected him dead if not for the rise and fall of his chest and the steady beat of his heart.

His heart.

It really was beating. It might have felt a little slower than a human heartbeat, but Evangeline didn't let her hand linger. She would have liked his help for this, but if he didn't wake up soon, she couldn't spare the time to wait for him.

It wasn't just that Evangeline needed to prove her innocence or that she wanted to save Tiberius from the person who might have murdered his brother. Evangeline wasn't physically capable of merely sitting in this lost library and waiting. She needed to know if she was right about Marisol.

And she knew exactly how to do it. There was a way to prove if Marisol was either innocent or guilty. Evangeline needed to find a cure for a love spell. If it worked on Tiberius, it would reveal Marisol's guilt. The same for her innocence if the cure failed.

But Evangeline would have to work quickly to discover a cure and administer it before tomorrow morning's wedding.

According to Luc, vampire venom could break a love spell. But Evangeline didn't want to risk another visit to Chaos, and infecting Tiberius with vampire venom might cause more harm than good.

She'd have to find another way.

After lighting a fire in the hearth, Evangeline wandered closer to the bookshelves. It seemed a little too coincidental that she'd find a spell book with an antidote for a love potion, but at least it was a place to start.

Tall and scuffed, the **book**shelves covered nearly three-quarters of the library's walls, and their owner did not care much for organization.

For example, on the first wall of shelves, nearest to the front door, Evangeline found a number of different books about time travel, but none of them were grouped together. They were scattered haphazardly, placed next to volumes on topics like the color blue, how to write poetry, an encyclopedia for the letter *E*.

Having determined these shelves did not hold any spell books, or cookbooks disguised as spell books, she moved on. She was about to attack another set of shelves when she noticed the desk in the corner—or, more specifically, the pop of color that came from the bottles of Fortuna's Fantastically Flavored Water sitting on top of the desk. They came in four flavors—luck, curiosity, sunshine, and gratitude—and all were tied together with an elaborate purple bow that clashed with the rest of the room.

She shouldn't have touched the bottles; they were clearly a gift. But one look at their brilliant colors and she couldn't help herself from picking up a cerulean-blue bottle of curiosity.

Her throat went suddenly dry as she tried to remember the last time she'd had something to drink. She'd never tried Fortuna's Fantastically Flavored Water, but she'd seen it on several occasions, and like the bottle's label, she was curious.

The liquid bubbled on her tongue, and it tasted like cotton and—safety pins? It was far from a fantastic flavor, and yet she finished the entire drink.

She meant to put the bottle back and return to her task, but she was still thirsty. She grabbed a shiny bottle of luck, wondering if it might taste better. The liquid inside was a sensational shade of green, but it tasted of grass and old celery.

How were these drinks so popular?

Unless it was not the flavors that actually drew people to these waters? Evangeline studied the gleaming green bottle in her hands. Maybe the drinks inspired some sort of thirst compulsion? Despite her best efforts to put the drink down, Evangeline couldn't help but continue to guzzle the bottle of luck.

When she finished, she was tempted to grab yet another. And she might have done it if she hadn't noticed the pile of missives sitting next to the lovely bottles.

Evangeline didn't make it a habit of reading other people's correspondence. But she was giddy with physical fatigue and the strange rush provided by the drinks, and she noticed something familiar about the folded letter on the top of the pile.

The note was in her handwriting, and it was addressed to Lord Jacks. It was the letter she'd written him last week.

She picked through a few more notes. *All* of them were written to Jacks. No wonder the bell had been ringing so wildly—this place belonged to him.

47

Evangeline knew Jacks would be unhappy with her going through his mail, but he was asleep and she couldn't stop. It was like drinking from the bottles of flavored water, except the only magic at play was her curiosity about Jacks.

The letters, sadly, did not give her any indication as to what Jacks wanted from the Valory Arch, but they did confirm that this was Jacks's place of business. Most of the correspondents asked him for favors or meetings. So many people were far too eager to become indebted to him, just as she had once been.

She'd never really thought of Jacks as someone who *worked*, exactly. His office appeared that way as well, with its disorganized bookshelves and mismatched chairs. But after spending time with him, Evangeline knew Jacks was not as reckless or careless as he led people to believe. He was a calculated collector. She'd seen him cash in favors from two different Fates—Chaos and Poison—and the letters on this desk held promises of even more.

It would have been easy to get derailed from her search for a book containing a love potion cure to see what sorts of things Jacks took from people. And she may have briefly paused to rifle through his desk a little more—he would have undoubtedly had no compunction about looking through her things. But all she found were some ugly coins, a blue silk ribbon, some recent scandal sheets about her wedding, and, of course, apples. Then she was back to the bookshelves, hunting for a tome with a love spell antidote.

Most of Jacks's books were crookedly stacked and next to volumes without any apparent reason, except for a small collection of the last book she'd have expected to find here: *The Ballad of the Archer and the Fox.*

Something warmed inside of her at the sight of so many copies of her favorite storybook.

Jacks owned seven volumes, ranging from old to very old. Positioned more precisely than anything else in his den, they sat side by side, on the tip-top of the shelf, the sort of place where a person stored books they didn't want anyone else touching.

What was all this about?

She wished Jacks were awake so that she could ask him, but he hadn't moved from his position on the sofa, where his limbs were recklessly sprawled, making him look unmanageable even in his sleep.

Evangeline reached for the first volume—she knew she was being distracted. But all she wanted was to look at the last page and see what sort of ending the story had. She wanted to know if it had a happy ending—if the Archer kissed his Fox girl or if he killed her. And maybe seeing all these books felt like a sign. She was starting to think that sometimes she imagined things were signs when they weren't. But that didn't mean there were not actual signs.

She opened the first book, but the pages in the back were all ripped out. And unfortunately, she did not have better luck with any of the other volumes. Every copy fought her. One book kept falling from her hands every time she tried to open it. Another book only had blank pages at the end.

Finally, she reached the seventh copy. Her fingers tingled as she lifted the cover.

This book opened easily, and it was the perfect example of a person finding what they needed instead of what they wanted.

The Ballad of the Archer and the Fox was printed on the spine, but when Evangeline opened the book, the title page said: *Recipes of the Ancient North: Translated for the First Time in Five Hundred Years.*

It was the same title as Marisol's illicit spell book.

The table of contents only listed recipes. And the first few entries were all made with innocuous ingredients like turnips, potatoes, and celery. But about a dozen pages later, the recipes turned to spells and potions and magic, and some of it did sound just as horrible as LaLa and Jacks had claimed.

Evangeline furiously flipped past spells to summon hellfire and to drain a person's soul until she found one section on love.

For Finding Love
For Ending Love
For Turning Someone into Your One True Love
The first two spells weren't any help, but the third spell looked as if it might be useful.

For Turning Someone into Your One True Love

Warning: *Love spells and potions are among the most volatile and unpredictable. If you choose to proceed, please note all cautions below.*

You will need:
A vial of malefic oil*
Hair, tears, sweat, or blood—your own and that of the person you desire most†
A candle dyed the color of the love that you wish for‡
Spoonful of sugared rose
Pinch of cardamom
Sprinkle of orris root powder
Pure glass bowl

* The substitution of other oils is not recommended. Although difficult to procure, malefic oil is the best way to ensure that your love potion will work only on

the person you desire most. However, be very careful. In its raw form, malefic oil is extremely toxic.

† Hair is the easiest to obtain and therefore will produce the mildest results. For the most potent outcome, blood is recommended. However, when it comes to spells involving love, this book would encourage the use of milder ingredients. Extremely potent love potions can result in dangerous and highly volatile emotions.

‡ The purest red will result in a feeling closest to love. Pink will produce something more akin to mild affection. Dark purple will result in obsession and is not recommended.

Combine all ingredients in bowl, set above candle aflame, say the name of the object of your desire seven times, then let the flame burn through the night.

To use: Once the solution is complete, use your fingers to brush the mixture against the skin of the object of your desire. Just a touch is needed.

Warning! There is a cost to every spell. The intensity of the love will determine the intensity of the cost, which may range from rain on your wedding day to a deeply marred happily ever after.

To undo spell: Love spells and potions rarely reverse on their own, though the people who cast powerful ones often come to regret their choices. If you wish to undo a love spell, this book recommends Serum for Truths (recipe on page 186).

Evangeline could not flip to page 186 fast enough. Not only had the love potion mentioned malefic oil, it said one side effect was ruined wedding days. More evidence of Marisol's guilt.

Evangeline might have been to blame for Marisol's first failed wedding, but Jacks had sworn repeatedly the wolf attack that had prevented the second attempt had never been his doing, and Evangeline was finally inclined to believe him. Luc's attack must have been the cost of Marisol's love spell.

Evangeline looked once again at Jacks, negligently draped across the sofa as he slept, and she wondered if there were other things she'd been wrong about as well.

But there'd be time to ask him later. Right now, the only thing she needed to do was brew the cure mentioned in her book.

Serum for Truths

Truth is often bitter, particularly when a person has been tasting more enjoyable lies. To remedy, you will need to erase the sweet taste of falsehood.

Recommended ingredients:
Crushed bones of the dead or charred dragon skin
An honest pinch of earth
A handful of pure water
Seven drops of blood from a magical vein

Mix all ingredients over a fire made of young kindling for best results.

Warning! There is a cost to every spell. More truths than people want are often revealed. Additional effects of Serum for Truths are usually temporary, and they may include fatigue, impaired decision-making and judgment, dizziness, the inability to tell a lie, and the urge to reveal any unspoken truths.

48

It was dusk when the potion was done. Jacks was still sprawled across the sofa as if he hadn't slept in years.

"Jacks." She rocked his shoulder, but when he moved his golden head, it was only to burrow deeper into his pillow. She jostled him one more time. She thought he'd be awake by now. But maybe he needed the rest—she didn't think he'd slept at all the night that she'd been poisoned. He must have been exhausted even before the mausoleum.

And perhaps it was better for her that he took his rest. Evangeline doubted he would be enthusiastic about her plan.

She already knew he wouldn't want her to go back to Wolf Hall, and he probably wouldn't trust her potion either. Although she was quite proud of her work. For the earth, she'd scraped the dirt from her boots. For the water, she'd taken snow from outside and let it melt. The crushed bones of the dead had been a tricky. She hadn't discovered any skeletons inside Jacks's office, but she had found a dead spider. For the blood, she'd contemplated borrowing a few drops from Jacks, as he was clearly more magical. But Jacks was so far from honest Evangeline wondered if his magic blood might do more harm than good. She'd decided her blood would have to suffice. It worked well enough to undo locks; hopefully, it would help undo spells.

After that, she'd poured her concoction into one of the remaining bottles of Fortuna's Fantastically Flavored Water, hoping the drink would be as enticing to Tiberius as it had been to her. Then she wrapped the bottle up in paper.

All she needed to do now was write Jacks a note.

Dear Jacks,

If you wake up and I'm not here, do not fret. Unless it's well past dawn, then I may be in trouble. I think I know who the killer is! I fear it's Marisol after all. (For motive, look at the scandal sheet, which you've been using as a poor substitute for a blanket.) I've gone to Wolf Hall to save Tiberius from marrying her and to hopefully clear my own name.

—Little Fox

Evangeline didn't know why she signed her name that way. She felt a little silly as soon as it was done. But she didn't want to waste time rewriting it.

Maybe if she were very lucky, Jacks would never see the note. If everything went her way, she'd get in and out of Wolf Hall before Jacks even woke up. Evangeline almost laughed at the idea of *everything* going her way. But there was a chance that it would happen.

She kept her plan simple.

She would enter Wolf Hall via the same hidden passages she'd snuck out through to meet Jacks. Then she'd leave her love potion antidote in Tiberius's chambers, where he would be sure to find it and with any luck be compelled to drink.

If the antidote worked, Tiberius would be cured, and Marisol's duplicity would be revealed to him as it had been to Luc.

If the antidote didn't work, it would prove Marisol was innocent, but the killer would still be out there.

And if Evangeline got caught delivering the antidote, then the killer would never be found—because she'd be blamed for the murder.

49

Evangeline wasn't scared. She was terrified. A shuddering breath of broken white puffs escaped her lips as she reached the outskirts of Wolf Hall and took in its snow-white stones and pointed tower caps. For an icy moment, she couldn't move. Her entire body tightened with memories of Apollo. Of how he'd scaled these walls to climb into her chamber and then held her all through the night. She could still see his broad smile on the day of their wedding and his heartbreak on that night when he'd died.

With another burst of white breath, she forced her legs to move forward.

Step.

Breathe.

Duck.

Dart toward hidden door.

Prick finger.

Open door.

Enter passage.

She tried to take one step at a time and not to think about how the corridors of Wolf Hall were wider and brighter than she remembered, and how anyone who stepped inside would be sure to spot her immediately, scurrying about like a frightened mouse. Fortunately, most inhabitants of Wolf Hall were currently occupied with supper, and she just needed it to stay that way a while longer.

She was almost at her old bedchamber next to Tiberius's former room, and she desperately hoped it was the same suite he was using now.

Her hands grew damp with sweat, making it difficult to pull one glove off and bare her fingers as she reached the door that she needed to open.

Another drop of blood.

Another undone lock.

Another small surge of victory as she stepped inside the darkened room. The fire was out, the candles unlit, but she detected whiffs of smoke and musk and soap, telling her that someone had been living there.

Her eyes adjusted to the dim, allowing her to make out the hulking shape of the bed. She'd hoped to find a nightstand beside it, something that Tiberius would be sure to see before retiring. But there wasn't a bedside table.

She'd have to settle for either the low table in the sitting area, where there was a line of bottles of liquor, or the vanity.

If it had been Apollo, she would have chosen the vanity. But for Tiberius, the table where he kept his libations seemed best.

Her hands shook as she unwrapped the bottle of curiosity. Then she rapidly set it on the table and fled the room before she could be tempted to drink it.

It all took under a minute. She was terrified and she was quick, but she wasn't quick enough. She heard the footsteps as soon as she was in the too-bright hall.

And then she saw her—Marisol.

Evangeline felt an almost childlike fright, as if she were watching a monster rather than just another girl her age.

Marisol was looking at something in her hands as she turned a corner, cheeks flushing prettily and beribboned braids of light brown hair shining under the torchlight. Her dress was the color of spun gold. The overskirt had an impractical train, and gilded ribbons crisscrossed over the bodice, matching the bands in her braids and the cuffed bracelets decorating her arms in an intricate lattice pattern. She already looked like a princess.

Run.

Leave.

Get out.

A hundred variations of the same thought raced through Evangeline's head. If she ran, she might beat Marisol. Her stepsister's lovely gown with its princess train wasn't designed for running.

But Evangeline didn't move fast enough. In her split second

of indecision, in the moment when she looked Marisol over, taking in her happiness instead of choosing to flee, Marisol looked up. "Evangeline?"

It had felt like a long hall before, but clearly it was not. Within a heartbeat, Marisol was there, hugging Evangeline as if they shared blood rather than betrayal. She didn't seem to notice that Evangeline stiffened, every muscle tensing all the way to her clenched hands.

"I'm so relieved you're all right," Marisol gushed. "I've been terribly worried—but we can't talk here." Marisol let go of Evangeline to open the door to Evangeline's former bedchamber.

"Hurry! My guards are just around the corner." Marisol waved a slender arm, frantic, as a single lock of hair fell out of its coiffure. If she was acting, it was a flawless performance.

"Evangeline, hurry—if the guards catch you, even I won't be able to help you. Tiberius is convinced you murdered his brother."

Boot steps thundered closer. If the guards found Evangeline dressed like a stylish assassin and scowling at the queen-to-be just outside the prince's room, they would not only arrest her, they might suspect that Evangeline had done something nefarious. If they were smart, they'd search Tiberius's room, find the bottle with the antidote, and there was a chance they'd be compelled to drink it instead, ruining her plans.

Evangeline knew she couldn't trust Marisol, but she had no

choice except to follow her stepsister into the suite, warm from a hearth that appeared to have been recently lit with a fire.

The room was just as Evangeline remembered, with hand-painted paper on the walls, a fireplace made of crystal, and an enormous princess bed. The only difference was the scent of vanilla and sweet cream, which told her this was Marisol's room now.

At least she looked a little abashed.

"Tiberius wanted me close to him—his rooms are just next door." Marisol worried her lower lip between her teeth. "We'll have to get you out of here before he comes back. I can put you in one of my gowns. It will be a little small for you, but you'll blend in better."

Marisol pursed her lips as she looked over Evangeline's leather boots, her short, tiered skirt, and her lacy I'm-off-to-meet-a-vampire corset, and Evangeline would have sworn there was a flicker of jealousy, as if now Marisol wished to be a fugitive instead of a princess. It was the sort of look Evangeline would have disregarded before. Something there and then quickly hidden before it was found, as if Marisol didn't even wish to acknowledge it. But Evangeline couldn't ignore it.

She had been wrong to think she could just drop off the cure for Tiberius and then wait from a distance until she learned if it worked or not. That would never be answer enough. She needed to know why Marisol had done all of this.

"Why are you helping me?"

A tiny line formed between Marisol's thin brows, but Evangeline swore her skin went pale. "Did you think I would betray you?"

"I think you already did. I finally figured out that the cookbooks on your night table were really spell books."

"It's not what you think," Marisol cut in.

"Stop lying to me." It took everything Evangeline had to keep her voice low so that the guards outside wouldn't hear. "I saw your spell books. I know you gave Tiberius a love potion just like the one you gave to Luc."

Marisol's jaw went slack, her shoulders fell, and she stumbled back, spine hitting one of the bed's posters as she shook like a ribbon blown by the wind, undone by this single accusation.

50

It felt like all the confirmation that Evangeline needed, and yet there was no sense of triumph as she watched her stepsister struggle for words.

Marisol opened her mouth, and a sob ripped free. Dry and tearless.

But Evangeline knew she couldn't let herself be fooled again just because Marisol looked like a kicked baby lamb.

"I—I'm sorry about Luc. But I swear, I—I didn't put a spell on Tiberius." A flicker of hurt crossed her fragile features. "I learned my lesson after what happened to Luc and after all the names the papers called me, though I suppose I really did deserve that. But you have to believe me, Evangeline. I never meant to hurt you."

"You stole the boy I loved, then you framed me for murder. How was that not supposed to hurt?"

"I didn't frame you for murder! How could you even think

that? I was trying to hide you just now. I'm still hiding you—if I wanted you caught for murder, I would just have to yell for the soldiers outside my door. But I'm not doing that, and I'm not going to." Marisol clamped her mouth shut, more determined than Evangeline had ever seen her.

But just because Marisol wasn't completely heartless didn't mean she was innocent. She'd admitted to putting a spell on Luc. Evangeline couldn't be tricked into feeling sympathy for her stepsister because of her shaking chest or her pleading eyes or the way her voice cracked when she spoke.

"I know you don't trust me, and I don't blame you after what I did to Luc, but I really didn't mean to hurt you."

"Then why did you do it?" Evangeline asked. "Why did you pick him if it wasn't to hurt me?"

The fireplace crackled, filling the suite with a surge of fresh heat as Marisol breathed a ragged exhale.

"I'd never done a spell before, and I didn't even think it would work. But I suppose I was jealous of you," she admitted. "You had so much freedom and confidence in who you were and what you believed. You didn't even try to fit in the way my mother always told me I needed to—you kept your hair that strange color and talked about fairytales as if they were real and everyone else believed in them, too. You should have been a pariah, but people loved you and your odd little shop, and even though your father was gone, he'd been so proud of who you were. I just had a mother who wanted me to sit straight and look pretty. But I was never pretty enough because I couldn't catch the attention of any suitors, and my mother couldn't stop reminding me of it day after day after day."

Marisol swiped at a few errant tears. She'd looked so lovely in the hall, but now she appeared miserable. She was hugging her chest, curling further into herself as her body was racked by sobs. And Evangeline couldn't help but feel some sympathy.

Her words stung—no one liked to be called *strange* or a *pariah*—and Marisol's choices had been terrible. But Marisol's mother was awful, and she'd been feeding her daughter poisonous ideas for her entire life.

"One day, I couldn't take it anymore, so I decided I'd try to be a bit more like you. I looked into . . . magic," Marisol said it on a whisper as if it still made her nervous. "One of the cooking books you had gifted me was actually a spell book, and I suppose I picked Luc because he was so good to you. I knew you would sneak out to see him. One day, I followed you, I saw the way he looked at you, and I wanted that. I wanted someone kind and someone my mother would be impressed with. But I didn't think it would work, and I didn't think it would be so potent."

"Then why didn't you undo it?" Evangeline asked.

"I wanted to, but the book I had said the only methods of undoing the spell were vampire venom or killing the person. My only choice was to marry him or leave him miserable."

Evangeline felt her first stab of guilt, and it became a little harder to stay angry with Marisol. Evangeline wasn't sure her stepsister was being entirely honest, but she couldn't argue with this reasoning or judge her for this part of the story, as Evangeline had done something very similar with Apollo.

"A love spell doesn't feel like regular love," Marisol explained. "At first, it was exciting, but that quickly wore off. Then everything went sour. I lied to you about Luc avoiding me. I was the one who tried to break things off after the second failed wedding. I was petrified of what would happen if we tried to marry again, and I've felt miserable ever since. When you and I were traveling here, and you were telling me all your mother's weird stories, I decided to find another spell book with a cure for Luc in case he ever returned to Valenda. That's why someone spied me looking for spell books. It wasn't because I wanted to hurt you, it was because I wanted to mend things. I've felt so terrible, Evangeline. You turned to stone for me and then you brought me here so that I could get a fresh start, and all this time, I've walked around with the knowing that I don't deserve any of your kindness. I'm so sorry. I've felt so guilty and so ashamed, and for so long I've wanted to tell you. But I've been terrified you'd hate me."

"I don't hate you," Evangeline said. Her stepsister had made mistakes, but Evangeline was starting to believe that murder wasn't one of them.

As far as the love spell she'd used on Luc, Evangeline couldn't entirely fault her. If anything, she related to Marisol.

Evangeline had been living with the same guilt and fear for the secrets she'd been keeping. If only she hadn't been so afraid to be honest, both of them could have been spared some pain.

"I wouldn't blame you if you did hate me. I swear I didn't kill Apollo or enchant Tiberius, and I didn't frame you for murder. But I know I've done unforgivable things. I deserve to be the Cursed Bride."

"You're not the Cursed Bride," Evangeline said gently.

"You don't have to keep saying that. The spell that I used warned me there would be consequences. That's why the Fates attacked my wedding, and that's why a wolf attacked Luc. I know I shouldn't be engaged to Tiberius now," Marisol mumbled. "I keep fearing that something horrible will happen to him, too. But I also keep hoping that I've suffered enough."

Marisol closed her eyes, and a tear fell as she shook. The bedpost at her back seemed to be the only thing holding her up. Evangeline imagined that if she were to tug on one of the ribbons in Marisol's hair, her stepsister would unravel like a skein of yarn.

Evangeline might have wanted that earlier, but now she'd rather help hold her stepsister together. She reached out and gave Marisol a hug. Marisol had made mistakes, but she was not the only one. "I forgive you."

Wide, shocked eyes met Evangeline's. "How can you forgive me?"

"I've made some poor choices as well." Evangeline squeezed her stepsister a final time before letting her go. Now it was her turn to be nervous. But Marisol deserved to know the truth. It wasn't fair to let her carry all the guilt or believe that Evangeline was entirely innocent. Evangeline didn't know if they would ever be true sisters, but they would never mend all their wounds if some were still infected with lies.

"You're not the only one who was jealous," Evangeline confessed. "I was so upset and hurt that you were marrying Luc, I prayed to the Prince of Hearts to stop your wedding."

"You what?" Marisol's spine stiffened, and her shoulders straightened.

"I didn't think he'd turn you to stone—"

"What did you think would happen?" Marisol spat.

The words hit like a slap, stunning Evangeline.

"You're just as selfish as my mother always said. You ruined my wedding so that you could become a hero and I could become the Cursed Bride."

"That's not what I—"

"You let me believe I was cursed!" Marisol cried, but there weren't any tears this time. Her eyes were two pools of anger.

Evangeline thought Marisol would understand and then maybe they'd laugh about it. But clearly she'd made a great error in judgment.

"Marisol," Evangeline said, alarm slipping into her voice. If her stepsister kept raising her tone, the soldiers outside the door would surely hear. "Please, calm down—"

"Don't tell me to calm down," Marisol raged. "I felt so guilty, and all along, you'd done something just as bad, even worse. You made a deal with a Fate to curse me."

"That's not what I—"

"Guards!" Marisol screamed. "She's here! Evangeline Fox is in my room."

51

Evangeline had thought Marisol had betrayed her before, but she hadn't, not really. Bewitching Luc wasn't betrayal. There'd been nothing to betray. Evangeline and Marisol had lived in the same house, but they weren't really sisters. They'd never shared secrets, they'd never shared heartaches, and they had never been as honest as they'd been with each other tonight. But Evangeline should not have been so truthful.

"Marisol, don't do this," Evangeline pleaded.

Marisol's only reply was to sink to the ground and hug her knees, making herself look small and vulnerable as the door to her suite flung open.

Evangeline frantically searched for an escape, but there was only the balcony. She wouldn't survive a jump, and there wasn't enough time. Two guards, quickly followed by another pair, rushed into the room in a clatter of drawn swords all pointed at her.

"She just confessed to murdering Prince Apollo," Marisol lied.

"That's not true—" Evangeline was cut off as several soldiers converged, grabbing and restraining and cutting off her words.

"My heart! My heart! Are you all right?" Tiberius burst through the open doors. He sounded just like his brother, when he'd been cursed, as he rushed into Marisol's arms, and Evangeline felt utterly stupid once again for believing her stepsister had not bewitched him. Marisol might have confessed some things, but clearly she hadn't been honest about everything. She was really behind all of this.

"Put Evangeline in my chambers," Tiberius ordered.

"Darling, are you sure that's a good idea?" Marisol latched on to his arms, doing an excellent impression of a helpless maiden. "Shouldn't you take her down to the dungeon? Lock her up where she can't hurt anyone else?"

"Don't worry, my heart." Tiberius pressed a kiss to Marisol's forehead. "I just need to question her. Then I'll make sure she's put somewhere she can't hurt anyone else ever again."

The guards used little care as they dragged Evangeline into Tiberius's chambers and tied her to one of the chairs. After they relieved her of Jacks's dagger, her ankles were roughly secured to the legs, and her arms were stretched behind her. Her hands were bound at the wrists and then tied again with a rope that went all the way around her midsection, cutting into her ribs and making it uncomfortable to breathe.

Tiberius didn't spare her a glance as it was done. He didn't acknowledge it when she repeatedly cried, "I swear, I didn't kill your brother!"

Tiberius simply stared into a great black stone hearth and ran a hand through his long copper hair, watching as one of his guards started a fire.

He no longer looked like the impish rebel prince she'd met at her wedding. Lines that had not been there before bracketed his mouth, and his eyes were full of red. He didn't appear bewitched right now; he looked as if he were in mourning. Which was one good thing. If Tiberius were really mourning, if he really loved his brother as she believed, then he would want to know who the real killer was.

All Evangeline had to do was to stay alive long enough for Tiberius to see the blue bottle of Fortuna's Fantastically Flavored Water containing the antidote she'd made. It was sitting on the low center table across from her, next to his other bottles of liquor. If he just saw it and drank it, all would be right in the world.

Evangeline would have tried to bring the bottle to his attention, but she imagined mentioning it would only make them all suspicious.

She sensed how each of the soldiers in the room had felt

about Prince Apollo from the way they regarded her. Disgust. Anger. Loathing. There were no hints of pity. Although Havelock—his personal guard, who'd also been there the night that Apollo had died—looked regretful. He probably felt as if he'd failed his prince.

Tiberius continued staring into the fire. He picked up a fireplace iron shaped like a trident, placed its tip in the burgeoning flames, and watched as it turned red.

Evangeline started sweating, skin going slick against her bonds. She didn't know if Tiberius was planning on torturing her with the fire iron or killing her, but she feared either option.

"Your Highness," Havelock said softly, "now that we have Princess Evangeline in custody, we should delay tomorrow's wedding. This news may—"

"No!" Tiberius's voice was slightly unhinged.

The soldiers did a good job schooling their expressions, but Evangeline swore at least two went wide-eyed, and she wondered if they suspected something was amiss with the young prince's engagement.

"I can handle this from here." Tiberius tore the heated iron from the fire and blew on the tip until it went brighter. "You can leave us. All of you."

"But—" Havelock again. "Your Highness—"

"Careful," Tiberius seethed. "If you're about to imply that I can't handle one tied-up female, then I'm going to either be offended or think you're incompetent at tying knots."

The soldiers filed toward the door.

"Wait!" Evangeline begged. "Don't go! He's been bewitched by Marisol—"

"Do not besmirch my love!" Tiberius whirled around and brought the fire iron down on the low center table, shattering one of his liquor bottles.

Glass flew like arrows.

Liquid sizzled.

Evangeline sucked in a gasp as she watched the bottle of Fortuna's Fantastically Flavored Water totter back and forth.

It fell on its side.

Thankfully, it didn't break.

That had been close. Evangeline would have to be more careful. Mentioning Marisol was clearly out of the question unless she wanted to risk her only chance of surviving. There was also the hope that Jacks might make a perfectly timed appearance and come to her rescue once again, but she couldn't rely on that. For all she knew, he was still asleep on his sofa.

The soldiers all left the chamber.

Tiberius stalked closer, boots pounding on the broken glass—

He stopped abruptly and eyed the tipped-over bottle of antidote with a scowl. "How did this get in here? I hate these things." He picked up the bottle with two fingers and brought it toward the fire.

No! No! No! She wanted to scream.

But instead of throwing it in, the bottle worked its magic.

Tiberius stopped, took another look at the concoction, popped the cork with his mouth, and drank.

Evangeline felt her hope grow bright.

But after only a few seconds, Tiberius wrenched the bottle from his lips. He shuddered and gave the drink a foul look. "Once I'm king, these drinks will be the first thing I outlaw."

Tiberius weighed the fire iron in his hand as if deciding how he wanted to do this.

Evangeline could only take shallow breaths. She needed to buy more time for the antidote to work. She doubted begging would help, but maybe she could get him to talk without triggering a violent reaction. "The last time I saw you, you said that when we met again, you'd tell me why you had disappeared."

A bitter laugh.

Another drink.

Followed by another wince.

"I left after my brother and I fought about you," Tiberius said grimly. "I told him you weren't the savior everyone claimed. I told him you'd be the death of him."

"Why would you think that?"

"All that matters is, I was right." The prince pointed the fire iron directly at Evangeline's throat.

"No—I didn't do this." She rocked her chair, urgently hoping by some miracle it would fall hard enough to shatter the arms and legs and set her free. But the chair was too heavy. She couldn't even get the seat to budge. "I didn't kill your brother—"

"I know," Tiberius said. "I've known it the whole time."

"Wh—what—" Evangeline sputtered. He was telling her what she'd hoped to hear, but the young prince still looked as if he had no intention of letting her go. His freckled face was that of a stubborn soldier with an order he was determined to carry out.

"I don't understand," she said. "If you know I'm innocent, why are you doing this?"

"It's too dangerous to let you live." Tiberius shook his head, expression determined, and yet Evangeline sensed he didn't get any pleasure from this.

He took another drag from the antidote bottle and then pulled down the neck of his striped doublet, revealing a dark black tattoo of a broken skeleton key. "Do you know what this is?"

Evangeline shook her head.

"This is the symbol of the Protectorate."

The Protectorate. She had heard the name before. But where? Her heart quickened as she tried to think. Then her heart stopped altogether as she remembered.

Apollo had told her about the Protectorate the night he'd shared the stories of the Valory Arch. They'd been in the first version of the story, where the Valors had made something horrible. Apollo had said the Protectorate was some sort of secret society responsible for protecting the broken pieces of the Valory Arch and making sure it would never be opened again.

Evangeline looked again at Tiberius's broken key tattoo. The Fortuna matriarch had worn a chain with a similar key around her neck. She must have been a member of the Protectorate as well, and as soon as she'd suspected that Evangeline was the girl mentioned in the prophecy that kept the Valory Arch locked, the matriarch had tried to kill her.

Evangeline's hope crashed and died.

Tiberius took another swig from the bottle in his hands. Even if the antidote worked and cured him of his artificial love for Marisol, Evangeline knew that she was never getting out of this room alive. Not if Tiberius believed she was part of a prophecy that once fulfilled would allow the Valory Arch to open and release the Valors' terrible creation into the world.

"I'm sorry, Evangeline." Tiberius's voice hardened, and his hands gripped the fire iron tighter, knuckles turning white. "From the look on your face, I'm assuming you know what the Protectorate is, so you know what I have to do and why."

"No," Evangeline said. "I don't know how you can kill someone because of a story that's twisted by a curse. Your brother told me there are two different versions. In one, the Valory—"

"It doesn't matter which version of the story is true!" A muscle popped in his jaw. "The Valory Arch can never be opened, which is why you have to die. I knew it as soon as I saw your hair. You're the prophesized *key*. You were born to open it." Tiberius lifted the iron once again, bringing it dangerously close to her skin.

Evangeline's breathing hitched.

She was running out of chances to talk him out of this.

Sweat beaded at his brow and dropped onto the broken glass near his boots. But she was looking at the other glass—the almost-empty glass bottle in Tiberius's hand. He'd nearly finished the antidote. It didn't seem as if the truth serum was breaking Marisol's spell, but Evangeline wondered if the side effects of her potion were kicking in: *fatigue, impaired decision-making and judgment, dizziness, the inability to tell a lie, and the urge to reveal any unspoken truths.*

Tiberius was definitely experiencing the inability to tell a lie, or she doubted he would have told her he didn't believe she was guilty. Maybe if she pushed him enough, she could somehow lead him to confess the truth to his soldiers. Or she could finally get him to tell her what the entire prophecy was. Then maybe she could prove she wasn't the girl in it. Maybe it was just a coincidence that she sounded like this girl.

"At least tell me what the Valory Arch prophecy says. If you're going to kill me because you think it mentions me, don't I deserve to know the entire thing?"

Tiberius swished the blue remains of the bottle, appearing torn between drinking, talking, or ending all of this right now. But her theory about the antidote's side effects must have been correct—it appeared he couldn't stop himself from spilling secrets. After a moment, he began to recite:

"This arch may only be unlocked with a key that has not yet been forged.

"Conceived in the north, and born in the south, you will know this key, because she will be crowned in rose gold.

"She will be both peasant and princess, a fugitive wrongly accused, and only her willing blood will open the arch."

Evangeline sagged against her bonds. It was so short. And almost every piece of it fit her. She had heard the line about her being crowned in rose gold and being both peasant and princess from the Fortuna matriarch. It hadn't been true at the time, but now it was. She was also a fugitive wrongly accused, thanks to whoever had killed Apollo. She didn't know where she'd been conceived; her parents had always joked that they'd found her in a curiosity crate. Now she wondered if there was a reason why they had concealed the truth—if they had known about this prophecy. Had they seen her rose-gold hair and her origin as a sign that it could be true someday?

But there was one line of the prophecy that she could ensure never came to pass. She just had to convince Tiberius of this. "You just said only my willing blood will open the arch, which means I have to want it open, and I don't."

"Doesn't matter." Tiberius gave her a bleak look. "Magic things always want to do that which they were created to do."

"But I'm not a magic thing; I'm just a girl with pink hair!"

"I wish that were true." His voice was torn. "I don't want to kill you, Evangeline. But that arch must remain locked. The Valors had too much power. They weren't evil, but they did things they never should have done."

He finished off the remnants of his drink, and this time, he pointed the iron at her heart.

"Wait!" Evangeline cried. "Can I have a last request? I don't think Apollo would want you to murder me."

"I'm sorry, I really am, but you're not leaving this room alive."

"I'm not asking you to spare me." Her voice cracked. If this didn't work, these could be her last words. "I'm just asking you to call in your soldiers. Tell them my crimes, and then let one of them kill me. Your brother wouldn't want you to murder his wife."

Tiberius frowned. But she could see another bout of indecision ghosting across his face. He sensed this was a bad idea, but his judgment was impaired from the antidote; he wasn't certain.

"Please. It's my last request."

Slowly, Tiberius lowered the poker.

The soldiers were called back in, but Tiberius didn't waste time with pleasantries.

"I need you to kill her." He shoved the fire iron into the hand of the closest guard, a tall woman with a heavy braid and fury in her eyes.

"Wait," Evangeline breathed, hoping she hadn't just made a terrible miscalculation. "You need to tell them my crimes first."

"Evangeline Fox," Tiberius ground out, "you have been sentenced to death for the crime of . . ." His jaw seemed to stick. He opened and closed his mouth several times, but no words came out.

"You can't say it, can you?" she asked. Her antidote might not have worked as exactly as she'd hoped, but it was working. *Additional effects of serum for truths may include . . . the inability to tell a lie.*

Evangeline could have cried with joy. Although Tiberius looked as if he really wanted to kill her now.

"What have you done?" He glowered at the empty bottle in his hands. "Did you poison me?"

"I gave you a truth serum, which is why you can't honestly say that I killed your brother. Ask him," Evangeline begged the female guard with the iron. "Ask him who killed Apollo."

"End this," Tiberius ordered the guard. "She—she—"

The guard had lifted the iron, but she hesitated at the prince's stammering.

"Can't you see—she's fed me some sort of magic," Tiberius growled, sweat beading on his brow. "She's obviously—" But he couldn't call her anything untrue.

"He keeps breaking off because he can't lie," Evangeline said, "and he knows that I'm innocent. I had no reason or desire to kill Apollo—I was the person with nothing to gain and everything to lose, and Tiberius knows that."

"She's—she's—she's telling the truth—" The prince's face turned red. "Evangeline didn't kill my brother. I did."

52

Tiberius staggered on his feet.

If Evangeline had been standing, she would have undoubtedly lost her footing as well.

She expected him to try to take the confession back or grab the iron from the guard and run her through. Wasn't that what a murderer would do? But perhaps it wasn't just the antidote side effects that had torn Tiberius's confession free.

Instead of fighting back, Tiberius fell to his knees and brought his hands to his face. "I didn't mean to kill him. It was supposed to be you." Eyes rimmed in grief and anguish met hers. "I didn't want to hurt my brother. I found a poison—a Fate's tears that were only supposed to affect females. But it seems that story was a lie." Tears finally streamed down Tiberius's cheeks, long, endless rivers of them.

It was almost like when she'd cried from LaLa's tears, only his heartache was entirely real. Tiberius sobbed the way that only broken things could, and Evangeline couldn't help but start crying with him. She cried once more for Apollo, she cried with relief that she was still alive, and she cried for Tiberius. Not for the part of him that had tried to kill her but for the part of him that had killed his brother by mistake. She didn't know what it was like to have a sibling, and given all that had happened between her and Marisol, she doubted that she would ever understand. But Evangeline understood how it felt to lose family, and she could not fathom being responsible for that loss.

She didn't know how long they both sat there crying. It could have been half the night, a handful of hours, or minutes that merely stretched out to feel like forever.

The female guard who'd been poised to kill her had untied Evangeline right away, but it wasn't until after dawn that several of the other guards escorted Tiberius out to take him to a holding cell. He didn't try to fight them.

"What's going on?" Marisol chose that moment to come out of her room. "Tiberius—"

The defeated prince looked up, his anguish briefly departing, but this time, it wasn't replaced with love. "If I ever see you again, I will kill you, too."

It seemed the spell had finally broken, though Evangeline didn't know if it was because of her antidote or if Jacks had been right about real love being strong enough to break love spells, and it actually was Tiberius's love for his brother that had broken through when he had confessed the truth. He turned back to Evangeline. "For my last request, I never want to see her face again."

"No—my love!" Marisol started to cry, and she kept the performance up even as Evangeline had soldiers lock her inside of her room until further notice. Like Tiberius, she didn't want to see her stepsister anymore.

Evangeline couldn't blame everything that had happened on Marisol. Marisol hadn't been the one to poison her or Apollo. But Evangeline did wonder what would have happened if Marisol had not put a spell on Luc. Would fate have intervened in another way to turn Evangeline into the girl in the Valory Arch prophecy? Or would things have worked out differently for her and Luc and Apollo and Tiberius? Was she destined to end up here, or was it just one of many possible paths? She would never know, but she had a feeling this question would always haunt her.

It didn't take long for Evangeline to transform from fugitive back into princess. She was moved into another untainted royal suite, with a roaring fire and lots of thick cream carpets that felt wonderful beneath her tired feet. Everyone seemed to want to fuss over her, exclaim how glad they were that she was safe, and how they all knew she couldn't have killed Prince Apollo.

Evangeline wasn't sure if she believed any of them, but she accepted all the fussing.

At the urging of servants, she'd bathed and changed into

a much more comfortable gown of white satin with a striped black underskirt and a bodice decorated with pretty black embroidery. Northerners didn't wear full black for mourning, but it was customary to at least wear some.

Even more guards and servants and half-awake palace officials were called into the suite after that. For hours, it was a flurry of maids bringing Evangeline warm food, and officials making requests and suggestions that sounded a lot like orders. Jacks had yet to appear, and she tried not to worry too much about it. Maybe he just hadn't come because her name had been cleared?

Hours ago, a messenger had been sent to Kristof Knightlinger and *The Daily Rumor* so word could get out about Evangeline's innocence. Given how fast gossip spread, the entire kingdom probably knew by now.

But she still would have liked to have seen Jacks and told him the news herself. Ever since she'd proved her innocence, Evangeline had been eager to see Jacks's face when she shared that she'd confronted Marisol, discovered who had really killed Apollo, and cleared her name on her own.

Only now that it was nearing late afternoon, her eagerness had turned into tightness in her chest.

Why hadn't Jacks shown up at Wolf Hall? He should have seen her note. Unless he was still asleep? Yesterday, she'd been amused by the idea of Jacks being slayed by slumber, but now it unnerved her. What if his fatigue hadn't just been a side effect of the vampire venom?

"I need a coat," she said.

One of the many maids in the room stepped closer to the blazing fire. "Would you like me to put another log on?"

"No, I need to step out," Evangeline said. She knew no one wanted her to leave Wolf Hall. The Council of Great Houses, which now included Evangeline, was being called to assemble as soon as possible to discuss what was to be done now that one direct heir was dead and the other was in prison. Any minute and she'd be summoned to meet them, but she wasn't sure she could sit and wait any longer. She needed to make a quick trip back to the spires to check on Jacks.

She knew she shouldn't care so much, but she couldn't stop fearing that something was wrong.

"Your Highness." A soldier near the door cleared his throat. "There's a gentleman who's just arrived, and he's insisting upon seeing you. He—"

"Let him in." Evangeline didn't allow the soldier to finish. It seemed she'd been worrying about Jacks for nothing.

"I'm afraid he's not with me. We've put him in the receiving solarium."

"I'll take you to him, Your Highness." It was Havelock.

Evangeline would have rather gone alone. But earlier, Havelock had been the sole guard who hadn't looked at her with pure loathing. He'd also suggested that Tiberius postpone the wedding to Marisol, which showed bravery as well as good intuition on his part. If she were going to be safe with anyone, it would probably be Havelock.

There were more protests as they ventured out the door:

"The council members are on their way!"

"You can't leave now!"

"You're too tired—you're going to pass out if you walk all that way!"

And then there was a lower voice, inside her head, speaking only to her.

Little Fox. Where are you?

It's about time, she thought. *I'm heading to you right now.*

Don't—Jacks's voice turned worried. *I'll come to you.*

Evangeline found herself smiling just a little. She liked that he sounded concerned.

Just wait for me, she thought. She was already on her way. And she thought it wasn't very far.

Evangeline had only been to the brightly lit receiving solarium once, with Apollo. He'd taken her and Marisol on a tour of Wolf Hall when they had first moved into the castle. She'd been enchanted by the beautiful fortress that Wolfric Valor was rumored to have built as a gift for his wife, Honora. Evangeline had imagined there were secret passages behind every tapestry and trapdoors hidden beneath the carpets. But now, with fatigue clouding her vision, everything was a blur of stones and vaulted ceilings, fireplaces to battle the endless drafts, sconces full of unlit candles, the occasional bust, and the not-so-occasional portrait of Apollo.

When she passed one of Apollo and Tiberius, with arms around each other's shoulders, she had to pause. Apollo looked so happy and vibrant. It was the same way he'd often looked at her. She'd thought his expressions had been pure enchantment, but now it was painfully tempting to wonder if things had been realer than she'd believed, if she'd been right to hope they could have really fallen in love. But she would never know. *What would have been* was a question that no one ever knew the answer to.

Evangeline started walking again, following Havelock into a windowless hall void of tapestries and lit by crude torches that smelled of earth and smoke and secrets. She might have only been to the receiving solarium once, but this was utterly unfamiliar.

"Is this the right way?" she asked.

"We had to take a detour," said Havelock. His face was impassive, the perfect palace soldier.

If not for the creeping feeling of unease crawling over her skin jolting her back to alertness, Evangeline might have believed him.

Did you get lost, Little Fox? Jacks's voice again, but he sounded farther away than before.

Maybe you should meet me after all, she thought back.

Then to Havelock: "I think I'm going to turn around."

"That would be a mistake." The lilting voice came from behind her.

53

Evangeline spun around.

The girl was about her age. Her face was round and her long dark hair was tied back, giving a clear picture of a starburst mark the color of currant wine on her left cheek.

"Who are you?" Evangeline asked.

The girl was dressed as a palace servant in a little cap and a wool gown with a cream apron, although Evangeline wondered if the clothes were borrowed, for they were ill fitting and she'd never seen this girl before. Her birthmark was something Evangeline would have recognized.

"What's going on?" She reached for Jacks's dagger, tucked into the belt of her mourning dress. It had been seized from her during her arrest, but it was one of the first things she'd taken back.

The girl held up her hands in a peaceful gesture, revealing a tattoo on the underside of her wrist: a circle of skulls that reminded Evangeline of something that her overtaxed mind couldn't remember just then. "Havelock and I aren't here to hurt you. We have something we need to show you."

Evangeline gripped her knife tighter. "Forgive me for being a little dubious on that front."

"Prince Apollo is alive," announced Havelock.

Evangeline shook her head. She believed in a lot of things, but not people coming back from the dead. "I saw him die."

"You saw him poisoned, but it didn't kill him." The girl gave Evangeline a taunting smile. One part triumph, one part dare to argue back.

She was definitely not a servant, and Evangeline wanted to ask exactly who she was, but that didn't seem like the most vital question. "If Apollo is alive, then where is he?"

"We've hidden him to keep him safe." Havelock stepped forward several paces and threw back a carpet to reveal a trapdoor that opened up to a flight of stairs. "He's down there."

Evangeline gave him a skeptical look.

But when Havelock and the girl both took to the stairs, leaving her free to go, Evangeline's curiosity got the best of her. She decided to follow.

The flight of steps was mostly dark, and her heart beat faster with every one. If Apollo was truly alive, then she was still married. They had a chance at the future she'd just been wondering about. She tried to feel excited. But if Apollo cared about her at all, why had he hidden in the palace as she'd been running for her life?

She could understand if he were still upset from the undoing of Jacks's spell. But hours ago, his brother had almost killed her. And Evangeline would have definitely died the night of her wedding if it hadn't been for Jacks. Had Apollo not known these things, or did he think she deserved to die?

As Evangeline neared the lower steps, she still hoped Apollo was alive, but it was a complicated sort of hope. Before, when she'd believed everything was a sign and her trip to the North meant finding her happily ever after, she would have been sure that there was a second chance waiting for her just a few feet away. Now she didn't know what to expect or even what she wanted. If Apollo gave her another chance, would she take it? Did she want him, or just the happily ever after she'd thought that he could give her?

The last step creaked beneath Evangeline's slippers. The room beyond was small, with a low wooden ceiling and not nearly enough light. The air was stagnant and a little stale, and almost as soon as she entered, Evangeline wanted to leave.

This was a mistake. Just past Havelock and the girl, Apollo was lying down on his back, but he didn't look right. He didn't look alive.

Evangeline almost silently called for Jacks to tell him she was in danger.

But the girl quickly said, "Apollo is in a suspended state. I know he looks dead, but you can touch him."

"Please," Havelock added softly. "We've been trying to revive him, but we think that *you* might be the only person who can bring him back."

Evangeline wasn't even sure she believed Apollo was actually alive. He lay on the heavy wooden table, as unmoving as a corpse. His eyes were open, but even from the distance, they were flat as pieces of sea glass.

She still wanted to flee. But Havelock and the girl looked so expectant as they watched her—they weren't trying to hurt her or trap her. If she left, Evangeline would be running away from hope, not danger.

Carefully, she approached the table.

Apollo was still dressed as he'd been on their wedding night, in only a pair of pants. The oil had thankfully been wiped from his chest, leaving just his amber pendant and the tattoo with her name. Gingerly, she touched his arm.

His skin was cooler than a person's should have been. His body didn't stir. But when she moved her hand to his chest, after a minute she felt it. Just one barely there beat.

Her heart fluttered as well. He really was alive!

"How did the two of you discover this? And why does no one else know?" Evangeline took another look about the room, which was bare save for the table with Apollo and another small stand containing a water bin and some cloths.

"We didn't know who we could trust," Havelock said. "I was there the night Apollo was poisoned. I was in the room with you after, when you wouldn't stop crying. It haunted me, made me think you might not be guilty. I knew that you had nothing to gain, unlike his brother. I didn't want to think Prince Tiberius had tried to kill Apollo. But when Tiberius became engaged almost immediately, a few other soldiers became suspicious as well. We borrowed Apollo's body from the royal morgue and reached out to Phaedra."

"Phaedra of the Damned at your service." The girl flashed another smile that made Evangeline think she should have recognized the name.

"Have you not heard of me?" Phaedra pouted.

"Phaedra, get on with it," said Havelock. "Someone will notice the princess is gone soon."

"Fine, fine," Phaedra huffed. "I'm rather famous in some circles for having special talents. I can steal the secrets that people take to their graves. Havelock here thought that if I paid our prince's corpse a visit, I might learn some of his secrets, including who killed him. But Apollo didn't have any secrets. And everyone has secrets, even if it's just a secret fear of caterpillars or a tiny white lie they told to a neighbor. That's when we realized Apollo wasn't dead. Whatever toxin was used on him didn't kill him, it put him in this suspended state."

"What's a suspended state?" Evangeline asked.

"It pauses life," Phaedra said. "Unless he's revived, Prince Apollo could stay like this for centuries without aging. There aren't a lot of stories about it. It's believed Honora Valor used to use it as part of her healing—for people who she couldn't help immediately. Unfortunately, no one knows how she did it or how to wake someone up from it. The practice of it was believed to have been lost with her death. But we thought you might be able to help." Phaedra looked up at Evangeline the same way people had looked at her right after she'd returned from being stone, as if she were the hero the papers all claimed.

Evangeline felt more worn-out than heroic, but for the first time, she no longer felt the need to deny all the stories about her. What she'd done that day in Valenda had been courageous. Luc really had been under a spell, and she'd stopped him from marrying the girl who had cast it. Then Evangeline had turned herself to stone to save him and the rest of his wedding party. She might have mostly done it because she felt responsible for what had happened to them, but that didn't mean that what she'd done wasn't brave. Having faith was brave.

But Evangeline wasn't sure bravery was enough to save Apollo. What did they think she could do for him?

In some of her mother's stories, kisses could cure the same way that Jacks's kiss could kill. But those kisses were almost always ones involving true love.

Of course, those stories were also cursed. So, who knew what was really true?

"I could try to kiss him," she said.

Phaedra gave her a tentative smile. Havelock nodded soberly.

Evangeline moved her hand to Apollo's cheek and pressed her lips to his. He tasted like wax and hexes, and he didn't move or change.

Disappointment twisted inside her. But this was merely her first try. If she couldn't cure him with a kiss, perhaps she could find another way to heal him. Maybe she could go to Jacks. He had enchanted her kiss before; maybe he could—

Evangeline broke off. She'd forgotten that Jacks had told her that there had never been any magic in her kiss. But what if he knew something? Maybe he could help her.

She almost tried to ask him with her thoughts. But she stopped herself again. She couldn't repeat the mistakes she'd made with Luc. She couldn't compromise to save Apollo. If Jacks helped her, he wouldn't do it for free. Perhaps they weren't enemies anymore, but she couldn't forget what he was. At one point, she'd thought Jacks had used her to kill Apollo.

But he hadn't. Jacks had nothing to gain by killing Apollo, and Tiberius had confessed.

Of course, during his confession, Tiberius had also said that the poison he'd used—LaLa's tears—was only supposed to work on females. And although Jacks had nothing to gain by poisoning Apollo, he did have a great deal to gain by turning Evangeline into a fugitive and making another line of the Valory Arch prophecy come true.

She will be both peasant and princess, a fugitive wrongly accused, and only her willing blood will open the arch.

Evangeline tried again to push the thought away. She was being paranoid. Jacks hadn't done this to Apollo for the prophecy. Tiberius had confessed.

But what if Tiberius's poison really had only affected her? After Evangeline had kissed him, Apollo hadn't sobbed the uncontrollable way she had from drinking the tainted wine. What if Tiberius had poisoned Evangeline, but it was actually Jacks who had done *this* to Apollo to turn Evangeline into a fugitive wrongly accused?

Jacks had said there hadn't been magic in her kisses, but what if there had been magic in his blood? The first two times she'd tasted Jacks's blood, it had been sweet. But on the day of her wedding, right before she'd kissed Apollo, Jacks's blood had been bitter. It had scared away the ghost fox. What if it was Jacks's bitter blood that had done this to Apollo?

Again, she tried to bury the thought. The idea of it all turned her stomach, and yet Evangeline couldn't let it go. She wanted to hope that Jacks wouldn't have gone this far. But he was the Prince of Hearts. According to the stories, he'd left a trail of corpses as he'd searched for his one true love. He would definitely go this far if it gave him what he wanted. And he wanted to make that prophecy come true.

But this still didn't mean her suspicions were right.

Earlier, she'd been convinced Marisol was the killer. But looking back, Evangeline now wondered if Jacks might have been manipulating her about Marisol as well.

In LaLa's flat, Jacks had just happened to be reading the same spell book that Marisol owned, revealing that Marisol could be a witch. Jacks had then taken Evangeline to Chaos's underground kingdom, where Chaos made it sound as if a witch had poisoned Apollo. Then Luc had confirmed that Marisol was a witch.

Evangeline had almost been convinced of Marisol's guilt

after that. But it wasn't until she'd seen the scandal sheet that Jacks had been clutching—the one with Marisol's wedding announcement—that she'd been certain her stepsister was a killer.

Maybe it was a handful of coincidences, but Marisol made the perfect scapegoat. If Tiberius hadn't confessed, and instead it had been revealed that Marisol put a love spell on Tiberius, everyone would have been happy to believe that she'd also killed Apollo.

But suddenly Evangeline wasn't even sure that Marisol had been the one to put a spell on Tiberius. Jacks could have willed it to frame her.

Was anything as she'd originally thought, or was everything Jacks had done just to make the prophecy come true? But if Jacks had done all of this, why had he left Apollo alive?

Havelock cleared his throat, and Phaedra gave Evangeline a curious look, both no doubt wondering why she was staring at Apollo's unblinking brown eyes. But Evangeline couldn't look away. She felt too close to figuring everything out.

Phaedra had said Apollo could stay this way for centuries, not aging, not moving, not quite alive but not really dead. Just like Evangeline had been when she'd been turned to stone.

Her stomach dropped.

And in that moment, she knew.

Jacks would know that Evangeline could never leave Apollo in this state. This was why Jacks had left him alive—Apollo was Jacks's bargaining chip. If Jacks had done this to Apollo, then he could undo it. And Evangeline knew exactly what Jacks would want in exchange for his help. Jacks wanted her willing blood to open the Valory Arch, and she would have bet anything this was how he planned to get it.

He'd poisoned Apollo to manipulate her.

Evangeline didn't know if she wanted to laugh or cry.

She knew what Jacks was. She hadn't been foolish enough to believe that she was different or special and that he wouldn't destroy her. But maybe she'd believed it a little. She'd clearly believed it enough to spend a night with him inside a crypt. And just an hour ago, she'd been terrified at the thought that Jacks had been trapped in an enchanted sleep. She'd been ready to race to his rescue because she'd also been silly enough to think that something had changed between them that night in the crypt. When he'd told her the story of Donatella, she'd thought she'd understood him. She'd thought he was opening up, that he was just a little human. But she should have listened when he'd told her that he was a Fate and she was nothing but a tool to him.

Jacks no doubt knew that she'd want to save Apollo. But he was deeply mistaken if he thought she'd ever open the Valory Arch for him. Evangeline would find a way to cure Apollo on her own, then she'd make sure that Jacks never hurt anyone else ever again.

Jacks was not her friend, but he'd taught her that she could open any door she wanted, and Evangeline knew exactly which door she needed to open next.

54

In another part of Wolf Hall, a door that had not been opened for centuries began to stir. Its hinges creaked. Its wood groaned. And the wolf's head emblem carved upon its center curved its mouth into a smile.

Acknowledgments

The Magnificent North would not be the same without a number of wonderful people who shared bits of their magic with this book.

Thank you so much, Sarah Barley, for believing in this story from the very first messy moment that I pitched it. Thank you for seeing the magic when it wasn't really there and for helping me to get it there. I'm so grateful for you, for the way you love books, and that you are always able to spot the flaws in my books, so I can fix them before they are seen by others.

Thank you, Jenny Bent, my extraordinary agent. The longer we work together, the more grateful I am for you. Thank you for being the first person to love this story and for giving me confidence when mine began to fail. Thank you for your brilliant editorial advice and for your endless support in all things large and small.

I can't imagine what my writing would be without the encouragement, love, and support of my wonderful family. This last year, especially, I needed all of you. Thank you for always being there even if it's the five hundredth time I've asked you to help me figure out a new character name. Thank you, Mom, Dad, Matt Garber, Allison Moores, and Matt Moores. I love you all!

By the time this book is published, I'll have been with Macmillan for more than six years, and I am so thankful for everyone there. Thank you to my excellent publishers, Bob Miller and Megan Lynch, and associate publisher, Malati Chavali, of Flatiron Books. Thank you, Nancy Trypuc, Jordan Forney, Katherine Turro, Sam Zukergood, and Erin Gordon, for being the most fantastic marketing team and for working so hard to share your endless excitement with readers. Thank you, Cat Kenney, for your constant enthusiasm, and Marlena Bittner, for being there from the beginning. Thank you, Sydney Jeon, for all your work behind the scenes. Thank you, Donna Noetzel, for once again giving my books stunning interiors. Thanks to Chrisinda Lynch, Sara Ensey, and Brenna Franzitta, for your incredible attention to detail. And thank you, Vincent Stanley, for overseeing the production of such beautiful books.

Thank you to narrator Rebecca Soler, and to Mary Beth Roche, Steve Wagner, and everyone at Macmillan Audio, for truly bringing *Once Upon a Broken Heart* to life via audiobook. Thank you, Jennifer Edwards, Jasmine Key, Jennifer Golding, Jessica Brigman, Mark Von Bargen, Rebecca Schmidt, Sofrina Hinton, and everyone with Macmillan Sales, for making sure this book is on so many shelves. Thank you, Alexandra Quill and Peter Janssen at Macmillan Academic, for putting this story in the hands of teachers, and thank you, Talia Sherer and Emily Day at Macmillan Library, for working to ensure this book makes it into libraries.

Thank you, Erin Fitzsimmons and Keith Hayes, for all the work and imagination you've put into making the US cover absolutely extraordinary. Thank you, too, to Kelly Gatesman. Thank you, Virginia Allyn, for your marvelous and magical map of the Magnificent North.

Thank you so much to everyone at Hodder & Stoughton for giving all my books such a tremendous UK home. Thank you, Kate Howard, for being such a wonderful champion of this story and for your brilliant editorial advice. Thank you, Molly Powell, for stepping in while Kate has been away and for being such a fun and sensational person to work with. Thank you, Lisa Perrin, for creating a UK cover worthy of a fairytale.

Thank you, Molly Ker Hawn, for being a gem of a UK agent. Thank you, Amelia Hodgson, for working your foreign rights magic. Thank you, Victoria Lowes, for being on top of things that I would certainly let fall through the cracks. I'm so thankful to be a part of the Bent Agency.

To my marvelous and extraordinary friends! My heart bursts with love for you. Thank you, Stacey Lee, for hours of phone calls and years of remarkable friendship. My stories always have more heart because of you. Thank you, Kristin Dwyer, for never thinking my ideas are too ridiculous and for always reminding me of the importance of leaning into love. Thank you, Kerri Maniscalco, for the most inspirational of brainstorming sessions and for countless conversations about vampires. Thank you, Adrienne Young, for your authentic encouragement and for always bringing a fresh perspective. Thank you, Anissa de Gomery, for loving Jacks even more than I do. Thank you, Ava Lee, Melissa Albert, and Isabel Ibañez, for the early reads and insightful feedback. Thank you, Kristen Williams, for all the amazing book talks and story talks and for looking at every early cover. Thank you, Gita Trelease, for your words of wisdom. And thank you, Katie Nelson, Jenny Lundquist, Shannon Dittemore, and Valerie Tejeda, for being the best.

And finally, I thank God, always, that I get to do the thing that I feel I was made to do.

Not every love is meant to be.

Continue reading the story in

THE
BALLAD
OF NEVER
AFTER

Words of Warning

Dear Evangeline,

Eventually, you will see him again, and when you do, do not be fooled by him. Do not be tricked by his charming dimples, his unearthly blue eyes, or the way your stomach might tumble when he calls you Little Fox—it's not a term of endearment, it's another form of manipulation.

Jacks's heart might beat, but it does not feel. If you are tempted to trust him again, remember all that he's done.

Remember that he was the one to poison Apollo so that he could frame you for murder in order to make a long-lost prophecy come true—one that would turn you into a key capable of opening the Valory Arch. That is all that he wants, to open the Valory Arch. He will probably be kind to you at some point in the future, to try to influence you into unlocking the arch. Do not do it.

Remember what he told you that day in the carriage—that he is a Fate and you are nothing but a tool to him. Do not let yourself forget what Jacks is or feel sympathy for him again.

If you need to trust someone, trust Apollo when he wakes. Because he will awake. You will find a way to cure him, and when you do, trust that the two of you will find your happily ever after and that Jacks will get what he deserves.

Good luck,
Evangeline

She finished writing the letter to herself with a deep breath. Then she sealed the note with a thick dollop of golden wax and wrote the words *In case you forget what the Prince of Hearts has done and you're tempted to trust him again.*

It had only been a day since she'd learned of Jacks's most recent betrayal—poisoning her new husband, Apollo, on the night of their wedding. The duplicity of it all still felt so raw, it seemed impossible to Evangeline that she might ever trust Jacks again. But Evangeline knew that her heart longed to hope for the best. She believed that people could change; she believed that everyone's life was like a story with an ending that was not yet written, and therefore everyone's future held infinite possibilities.

But Evangeline could not allow herself to hope for Jacks or to forgive him for what he had done to her and Apollo.

And she could never help Jacks open the Valory Arch.

The Valors, the first royal family of the Magnificent North, had constructed the arch as a passageway to a place called the Valory. No one knew what the Valory contained, since the stories of the North couldn't be fully trusted, thanks to the story curse that had been placed on them. Some tales couldn't be written down without bursting into flames, others couldn't leave the North, and many changed every time they were told, becoming less reliable with every retelling.

In the case of the Valory, there were two conflicting accounts. One said the Valory was a treasure chest that held the Valors' greatest magical gifts. The other claimed the Valory was an enchanted prison that locked away all manner of magic beings, including an abomination that the Valors had created.

Evangeline didn't know which account she believed, but she had no plans to allow Jacks to get his cold hands on either magical gifts or magical monsters.

The Prince of Hearts was already dangerous enough. And she was furious with him. Yesterday, after suspecting Jacks had been the one to poison Apollo, Evangeline had thought five words: *I know what you've done.*

Guards had then removed him from Wolf Hall. To her surprise, he had left without a fight or a word. But she knew he would be back. He wasn't done with her yet, though she was done with him.

Evangeline took the letter she'd just written to herself, crossed the length of her royal suite, and placed the note atop the fireplace mantel, waxed side out—making sure she'd see the words of warning if they were ever needed again.

1

There is a door deep inside the royal library of Wolf Hall that no one has opened for centuries. People have tried to set it on fire, break it with axes, and pick its lock with magic keys. But no one has so much as left a scratch on this stubborn door. Some say it mocks them. There is a wolf's head wearing a crown emblazoned on the door's wooden center, and people have sworn the wolf smirks at their failed attempts, or bares its sharp teeth if a person even comes close to opening this unopenable door.

Evangeline Fox had once tried. She had pulled and tugged and twisted the iron knob, but the door would not budge. Not then. Not before. But she hoped it would be different now.

Evangeline was very good at hoping.

She was also rather good at opening doors. With one drop of her willing blood, she could undo any lock.

First, she needed to be sure she wasn't being watched or

followed or stalked by that deceitful, apple-eating scoundrel whose name she wouldn't even think.

Evangeline checked behind her shoulder. Her lantern's ocher glow chased the nearby shadows away, but the bulk of Wolf Hall's royal library stacks were nebulous with night.

She fidgeted nervously, and the lantern flickered. Evangeline had never been afraid of the dark before. Dark was for stars and dreams and the magic that took place in between days. Before losing her parents, she had constellation-watched with her father and listened to her mother tell stories by candlelight. And Evangeline had never been frightened.

But it wasn't actually the dark or the night that she feared. It was the spider-thin prickle crawling across her shoulder blades. It had been with her since the moment she'd stepped out of her royal suite on a mission to unlock this door, in the hopes it would lead her to a cure that would save her husband, Apollo.

The uncanny sensation was so subtle, at first she let herself think it was merely paranoia.

She wasn't being followed.

She'd heard no steps.

Until . . .

Evangeline peered into the library's dark, and a pair of inhuman eyes stared back. Silver blue and brilliant and broken-star bright. She imagined they shone just to taunt her. But Evangeline knew that even if they sparkled now, even if these eyes lit up the dark and tempted her to lower her light, she couldn't trust them. And she couldn't trust him.

Jacks.

STEPHANIE GARBER is the #1 *New York Times* best-selling author of *Once Upon a Broken Heart*, *The Ballad of Never After*, and the Caraval series. Her books have been published in thirty languages.

stephaniegarberauthor.com
◎ @stephanie_garber

WELCOME, WELCOME to CARAVAL

Stephanie Garber's sweeping tale of the unbreakable bond between two sisters

It's the closest you'll ever find to magic in this world...

FLATIRON
BOOKS

LISTEN TO
STEPHANIE GARBER
ON AUDIO

Read by Audie Award–winning narrator
REBECCA SOLER

"Soler embodies a fairytale world full of vibrant characters with unique voices. . . . This sultry fantasy will leave listeners guessing to the very end."
—*AudioFile* on *Once Upon a Broken Heart*

"Actor Soler's narration, by turns curious, afraid, frustrated, and exhilarated, immediately draws the listener into this world. **In a story full of colorful characters, she gives each one a distinct voice that is faithful to their descriptions in the text.**"
—*Publishers Weekly* (starred review) on *Caraval*, a Best Audiobook of the Year

Visit MacmillanAudio.com for audio samples and more!
Follow us on Facebook, Instagram, and Twitter.